Ravens and Lavender

by

Rachel DeFriez

Two Cents Publishing

For Curt, obviously
and
For Elizabeth and Ethan,
There's something about Elizabeth—

PROLOGUE
1980
—From the unfinished manuscript of Ethan McCarthy

I dropped my brush into a paint-smeared can of thinner. On the canvas in front of me, I had breathed life into the image of death. The brush of the angles was sharp. From writhing shades of grey, blue, and brown, the beauty of misery gazed back at me, cursing me for having created her. The painting provoked in me a pleasant revulsion mingled with morbid attraction. The genius of my work—slave though I was—mortified and thrilled me at once.

Overhead, the sunroom lights flickered. My shoulders stiffened. The appearance of the leanan sidhe, my muse and master, invariably troubled the current.

The mantel clock ticked relentlessly. A bronze peasant boy adorned the clock. Beneath his smiling gaze, a horse plodded under its burden. I felt more of an affinity with the beast than the boy. A relic from more than a century ago, the clock had been ticking since before the Civil War. How many times had it ticked since Elizabeth died? Seconds, such flimsy strands of time. But how they bind together to flog the mind of he who mourns!

A whistling breeze swept down the chimney. In its wake, an ebony cloud wound a crooked path from the flue to my shoulder. The fog slithered along my neck, through my hair and the paint-crusted stubble on my jaw, caressing and coaxing.

Fixing my eyes on the pendulum swinging below the clock's bronze foundation, I refused to respond to the muse's advances. Rebuffed, the mist spun itself into a vortex of tiny, black feathers. An evening gown appeared in the torrent. The raven muse, Brann Sidhe, appeared in the dress.

The birth on canvas of the seed she had sown in my dreams tantalized the fey. She licked her fingers and breathed the aroma of my sweat. Drawn to the nectar of life set free in the act of creation, her violet nail brushed the skin on my neck.

Brann's fingers shredded my locks, which would have been iron-gray by now, were it not for our hellish bargain. The muse snaked one hand through my arm and around my back. She could be quite humanly solid when she chose to be; with me, she chose to be often.

Her purple lips murmured at the base of my rigid neck. "Never has a lover of mine so perfectly fashioned the visions I sowed as I walked in his dreams. You are an exceptional artist, Ethan." The tip of her pink tongue wandered down my earlobe.

I flinched, but promise of a forthcoming end to my servitude emboldened me. "Are we finished here, then? You're satisfied?" My monthly offering would conclude at sunset—sooner if she were pleased. The end of this slavery was only a wedding vow away.

"Satisfied?" Brann scoffed. "A leanan sidhe is never satisfied." Her eyes focused on my chin. "Is that a gray hair?" A playful squeak pursed her lips. She reached a finger to my unshaven face. Tiny feathers of her sleeve scurried to keep up with her motion.

A violent riot of emotions rippled from her touch. Compelled and repelled at once, my breath hitched before I recoiled into the sickly sunlight shambling through the window panes.

Far from angry at the rejection, Brann giggled. "One hundred and seventeen years, and you look barely ten years older than when we first made our little bargain."

Decades of scalding experience had taught me the folly of rising to her flirtatious baiting. Any response only stoked her appetite. Turning my back on her, I strode to a wall of heavy purple drapes.

"Always in such a hurry these days." She pouted and then smiled seductively before disappearing altogether only to reappear so close to my face that the tip of her nose touched my chin. Her hair smelt of savory wine—thick, intoxicating, earthy. "Admit it, Ethan. The power of creative genius moves you. Ah, I could give you such pleasure in exchange for the three days a month I require."

Our wager gave me fifty years in which to win Elizabeth again— heart, soul, and child. If I succeeded, God help me, it would all be worth it. One hundred years of raging despair and bondage I would gladly trade for a few measly days more in her arms.

A demon of deceit, the leanan sidhe was ever true to her word. After I had served my century, Brann restored my Elizabeth's soul to the living vessel of a baby named Sara Elizabeth Vale, born in 1962.

The muse surveyed her feast on canvas. "It's worth a small fortune, you know, if you choose to sell it."

The walls of the renovated mansion were covered with tortured masterpieces. I had recently purchased the house surrounded with orange groves flourishing beneath the warmth of the Southern California sun. Tiny bits of soul and life that I sacrificed on the altar of this vile goddess purchased me a second chance to win my wife's love again. "The life of the eccentric, reclusive artist suits me. I can transform into the seventeen-year-old version of myself, pass him off as my son, and send him to school with Sara Elizabeth. My tastes and appetites are not as voracious as yours, mistress. The few paintings I sell provide well enough for me and my 'sons'."

At the mention of the younger selves in which I spent most of my time, a craving sparked in the muse's eyes. She threw her arms around my neck and pleaded, "Ethan, dearest, why do you not spend more of your days as the small boy? It slows the aging when you do." Her gaze penetrated so deeply that I imagined she could see, hidden between the folds of the clay I currently wore, the child I had been so long ago, yet so recently. "He is so soft and warm—and playful."

"He is only four. It doesn't matter that he has been four for over a century; he is still four. He can't be left unattended. The neighbors would notice."

"But it delights me so to attend to him. They think me the doting, devoted aunt. It's quite touching." She drifted closer, her raven dress fluttering about her. Her fingertips strummed the flesh beneath the unbuttoned plaid I had pulled over jeans. Time should have faded and stretched the lines across my chest, but I had thwarted time. Elizabeth was right. My crime was to hunger for more instead of contenting myself with the easy abundance of our lot. When Brann's nails found bare skin, she smiled. The beauty of her face, her weapon and her allure, distorted my rationality. "I would see to his every need."

The muse was irresistible. She compelled to the surface, into my muscles and all along my skin, the passion of anger, the brine of injustice, the ardor of violence. It washed over me like a flood that swept me into her arms.

I ravished the purple lips with the fervor of my disgust and then pushed her away. Craving and remorse, they are the steps to my unholy waltz with the leanan sidhe. "You have me; you will never have my youth." The coin that hung around my neck drew my hand. In its metal lay the ages of my youth, stored up to appear at my bidding, fortified against the siege of time.

Brann Sidhe retreated, gingerly wiping the corner of her mouth before she pouted. "This feast at the full moon fills me to the brim, and then I must languish for weeks, gnawing on the carcasses of the woeful creatures you lure to me."

I flinched at her calloused words, knowing well the cost of the carcasses. This evil dressed as beauty left in her wake emaciated youth, shriveled genius, and desperate insanity. I'd watched dozens of fragile artists wither in her web. Even after decades of failure, I still tried to free them from her silken bonds. But inevitably, their obsession to birth beauty consumed them, numbing all instincts for self-preservation. There was nothing to be done. The vibrant faces grown pale, the bright eyes gone opaque, racked my every waking thought. Anger, tainted with guilt, fueled the exquisite darkness of my art—just as the muse intended.

"But you are anxious." Brann Sidhe felt my thoughts and nourished herself with the pain she extracted from them; it is the way of the Leanan Sidhe. "You have waited already seventeen years. What difference can one day make?" She sighed and sank into the purple velvet of an armchair. "I suppose you must have your turn in our game. Go! Win her love—if you can." The wave of her hand released me.

The amethyst curtains hid a time-warped wooden table covered with the tools of my alchemy. With mortar and pestle, I ground dried herbs and smoking liquid into paste. Hope animated my fingers. I was so close to winning my wager with the demon muse, so close to redeeming the soul I had tossed recklessly into the pot. In my mind, burned the memories of the seventeen-year-old boy that the alchemical elixir would bring forward from the past. My wife reborn, Sara Elizabeth, the young woman she had become in this purchased new life, loved that boy. She'd said as much.

But even as the drops of mercury dripped into the wooden chalice etched with runes, doubt shook my hand. The tiny bottle of silver liquid tipped and stained the wood. Elizabeth's reincarnation, was so spritely and capricious. I could not tell if it was the influence of the new flesh her soul wore or simply the time and place that had shaped it. Of one thing I was certain, the leanan sidhe that gambled with my soul would not hesitate to conceal within her feathered bodice an ace to play against me. Her deceit lay, not in the words she spoke, but in those she left unsaid.

Unclasping the gold chain, I dipped the dangling coin into the cup and then refastened it. Never looking back, I downed the potion. My body shivered. The air around me shimmered translucent and then folded in on itself. Reaching out a hand, I took a step forward. The bones of my fingers uncurled, the skin smoothed and lost the freckles of age. My hair, reflected in the mirror above the table, thickened, and the stubble on my face disappeared into a smattering of light fuzz. The creased canvas around my eyes and mouth turned to pressed silk as I transformed into my seventeen-year-old self. The plaid shirt and jeans of the man hung limply on the sturdy but slight limbs of the youth I had once been. Only the old deck shoes still fit.

I had enrolled this boy in school as Elliot Fey. As my adult consciousness faded into a corner of the boy's future, Elliot turned to look at the muse but said nothing as he left. Instead, his first thought was to glance at the mantel clock. It was early. If he hurried, he could still make the Friday evening performance of Eurydice. Sara Elizabeth was playing the role of one of the three stones. Her rendition was to die for.

Dearest Elizabeth,

How did I find myself the slave of a creature such as Brann Sidhe? If only I could say that I was cheated, deceived, or ignorant of the consequences of my bargain. But the Leanan Sidhe do not take unwilling victims. The truth is, I made my choice—as did you. But I, unlike you, struck a bargain with full intent and understanding. And I fear that, even now, drowning in the river of ruthless tragedies that flow from her hands—although mine are in no way clean—I would make the same choice a thousand lives over, if only for the mere possibility of one life in which to entwine again the threads of our souls. This is the hope that drives me.

Listen to my story, Elizabeth, and tell me if there is redemption for such a man as I.

Forever,
Ethan

PART 1

Chapter 1
1860

—From the unfinished manuscript of Ethan McCarthy

Looming rumors of a southern rebellion lapped at the edges of the forest surrounding the home I shared with my new bride, but did nothing to disturb my slumber. Rather, the calm startled me awake. Pacing through my thoughts in the night, investigating sudden flashes of inspiration by candlelight—such was the normal routine of an alchemist. Reaching for the scent of lavender that hung about my wife, I found her pillow empty. My cat, too, had abandoned our bed in favor of her company. Sunlight hissed through the open crack in the green drapes. The gravel drive crackled beneath the trample of horses' hooves and carriage wheels delivering milk. The day was still new.

My feet in slippers, I padded down the stairs and through the house in search of my bride. Our plush, smoke and spice feline lounged in the window seat of the kitchen nook. Beyond the windows, the lush shades of Pennsylvania's green forests tickled the baby blue of the sleepy sky. Elizabeth's hair reflected gold in beams of sunlight. The rays stained the white marble floors a timid yellow and revealed the gentle curves of her body through a thin nightdress. The vision wrought from my lips an awed whisper of wonder, "My God! My wife is beautiful!"

From behind, I slipped my arms around her waist, wondering at such reversal of fortune that filled the void of parents and brother lost with thick, pasty love. Instead of turning, she leaned her head back to rest on my shoulder. My lips kissed her hair, and I breathed her in. She sighed, abandoning the brush in her fingers to the base of the easel. I abandoned every thought in my head to the warm, satin of her skin.

"I missed you in our bed." My lips brushed the slope of her neck.

Basking in a shiver, she closed her eyes. "I had a dream. I had to paint it."

"I had a dream, too. I think I would very much like to paint it." Sliding my hands down her body to the hem of her dress, I slipped it up her thighs, embracing the lily softness of bare skin. Every muscle in my body flickered to life. Elizabeth was the anchor my unmoored ship had been seeking since my parents died. She threw her arms back, around my neck, and turned to find my mouth. Our bodies pirouetted and dissolved into one.

When the sun was a bit higher, she slipped back into her nightdress and padded away, barefoot, in search of coffee. Wrapping my robe about me, I admired the canvas she'd painted. Boo yawned, meowed, and stretched in the sun-drenched luxury of her perch. Hopping down, she strolled over to rub against my legs.

For a very long while, I stood quite still, ensnared by the image on the canvas. The painting defied tradition and convention. I'd never seen the art interpreted in such a whimsical fashion. Rather than an accurate depiction of the subject, she'd captured, in shifting shades of light and color, a visual impression, the feeling of a dream. Such virgin frontiers of inspiration could have only one source.

Handing me a steaming cup of coffee in a yellow mug, Elizabeth smiled dreamily at the painting. There was much to smile at. My wife had breathed life into an angel garbed in a robe of white down—a serene seraph in a tangle of trees. Her nails, and hair, and the belt that hung carelessly at her waist, sparkled in gold. But the face drew my eye and troubled my serenity. The seductive tilt of the lips and eyes was so unbecoming in an angel.

I reminded myself to breathe while I gazed at it. "This is what you dreamt?"

"My dreams displease you?"

My face flushed with inner conflict. My love for Elizabeth, a naked desire to shower her with compliments, strangled before her divinely glamourized rendition of the fiend who had murdered my parents. But even worse, I knew now that the dove muse stalked my beloved in the forest of her dreams. "It's divine." Rage at my parents' untimely demise choked the words in my throat. I reached down to bury my fingers in Boo's smoky fur.

"Isn't she lovely? She was singing to me as she drew me through the trees with a little cord of silk. By the time I woke, I thought my head might explode if I kept her bound there much longer." Elizabeth's breaths swelled her chest.

My heart clenched. Vivified in paint, the sight of this demon unveiled the host of tragedies that I kept shrouded just beyond the reaches of my thoughts. "You cannot do this, my love."

She bristled. Of course, she did. What I loved about my bride was her defiant stance against the culture that bound her. Her "liberal education" had severed her from the society of the neighborhood drawing rooms. Her aberrant pursuit of painting fueled the gossips. "Whatever do you mean? I already have done it." She laughed at what she imagined were my conservative reservations. A cool breeze passed between us. The contrast made it bitter. A frozen draft on a midsummer afternoon unsettles so much more than an icy wind on a winter's day. "It pains me that you find nothing redeeming in the uniqueness of the artistry." Sipping her coffee, only thinly veiled her disappointment. "Perhaps others will."

Still warm from making love, and already wanting her again, I hastened to reassure. "No, love. You misunderstand. The portrait is stunning. You are, without doubt, deliciously talented." Her eyes softened, but still looked wary. "You are certainly gifted enough to paint her. That is exactly why she has come to you. But you must not paint her." Laying my hands on her thin shoulders, I spoke the words I knew she would not hear. "You must reject this muse and all she offers."

"I will not." Elizabeth set her chin briefly before she shrugged, and, ever generous, relented, reaching for my hand. Even wounded, she could never bring herself to wound another. This kindness that drenched her soul attracted mine, so steeped in loss, as if she were solid, warm earth, and I bits of snow, falling from the tree limbs in the grey sun of a winter's day. "I simply cannot, darling Ethan. She grows wild inside of me and threatens to burst my skin. Even if I could reject her, why would I ignore such inspiration?"

"Because of the cost."

Wriggling her shoulders out of my grasp, she giggled, sauntering away to the window. "Silly man, there is no cost!"

I grabbed her wrist, pulling her back, wanting desperately to wrest my bride from the spell of the muse. "There is a cost!"

The force of my grasp furrowed her brow. She yanked her wrist and rubbed the pinch of my fingers. Her feet slid away from my reach into the shadow that sat heavily on her creased brow. Her eyes moistened and glared. "I have my own purse. Your fist will not dole out the dues of my imagination."

Conflicted, mortified to have caused her pain, I sank into the yellow chair near the table, as astonished as she at my outburst. I looked away, past the cutting board and the yellow teapot, back into the lonely, orphaned years of my childhood. "Forgive me, love, it's—" How could I make her abandon this insanity without telling tales of fairies that inspire masterpieces in order to suck the life from the artist's hand? "—it's my mother."

Elizabeth's face melted into lines of pained sympathy. "Oh, Ethan. I'm so sorry. I—it's just that—" she knelt beside me, "—well, darling, you have no portraits. How could I know?" Her breath caught as her face blanched. She shivered as if the ghost of my mother hovered between us. "How is it that your mother's spirit walks in my dreams?"

"No, love. This is not my mother. It only reminds me of her."

She breathed again and the astonishment in her eyes faded into compassion. Hand on my cheek, she swept away the years of lonely misery. Her lips sought out the lines on my face and brushed them away. "Don't worry so. It was only a dream."

The naïveté of these words bristled my spine, and I leaned away from the sedating calm of her fingers. "Oh, but she is so much more than a dream. What was the price, Elizabeth? What did she offer you?"

"She was only a spirit in a dream, Ethan. She offered me nothing. She asked for nothing." She caressed the hair from my brow. It required all the self-discipline in my being to refrain from grabbing her shoulders and shaking her free of this delusion.

Tearing myself from the compelling warmth of her hand, I confronted the portrait. "Do you think me a fool? Do you think I do not know who this is?" I stabbed a finger at the creature smiling at us from the canvas. "She is more than a dream, Elizabeth, and she always has a price. What did Cailen Sidhe offer you?"

"Kaylin Shee? Yes! That was her name. How come you to name the spirit haunting my dreams?"

The witch's name on my wife's lips ignited the orphan's rage smoldering in my heart. No boy can watch the murder of his mother and not carry the coals of hell in his soul. Exasperated, I let the truth fall from my lips. "Of course, I know her. The dove muse murdered my parents."

Stepping away from the canvas, Elizabeth backed into the ray of sunshine that spilled from the window. The embrace of yellow light rendered her little more than a shadow draped in white. Her eyes searched the kitchen for answers. "But you said—a murderess in my dreams?—but, so lovely." She hugged her chest. The mark of the Leanan Sidhe—the total disorientation of tantalizing beauty wrapped around awful suffering—marred her face.

In two strides, I joined her at the window, wrapped my arms around her trembling body, and held her steady while the truth shook the ground beneath her feet. "This is the white witch who hummed in my parents' ears while they slept. Her raven twin has stalked me with a paintbrush in her hand for my entire life. The Leanan Sidhe have come for you, Elizabeth. Think! Remember! What was the price? There is always a price."

"Two years." Honesty pierced the distrust that billowed about us.

I scoffed. "Yes, she always starts small. A trifle. And then she has you because the visions run through your veins; they quicken your heart, furrow paths through your mind. You crave the euphoria of reaching beyond the bounds of human imagination. In the cloud of her wondrous world, you lose your grip on your own." I faded away into the terrified eyes of the young Ethan who watched his parents shrivel and die in their gloriously avaricious pursuit of art. "She feeds, Elizabeth. She feeds off the life that you give to your visions. She feeds until she has consumed you."

Tears welled up in her eyes. She shook her head. "I can't stop myself. You don't know what it's like."

"Oh, but I do know. She will murder you beautifully, my love—beautifully."

"But only two years, Ethan."

I looked to heaven but found only the ceiling. My wife was trapped. How to save from the huntress a poor creature that wants desperately to be eaten?

Elizabeth put her hands to my face, her fingers soft and smooth as orchids. "You didn't see what I saw. It's in me now, clawing to get out. If I don't paint it, it will rip me to shreds from the inside. It was beyond lovely. Only two years for such exquisiteness! I would rather live a short, beautiful life than a long, plain one."

"No!" I could not bear to witness the image of my parents' obsession creeping about the edges of my wife's face. She was so small, so delicate, so ephemeral. God, I loved her. Did I need any more of a reason? My mind raced in desperation. I could throw her over my shoulder and lock her in an upstairs bedroom. But, no! I could not hide my bride from the Leanan Sidhe. They would find her in the visions of her sleep. I could deprive her of paint and canvas, of every means of serving them. If I did, I would save her, but she would hate me. What was the use of saving her if she hated me for it?

No. Elizabeth had to choose for herself; she had to see the face of death hidden behind the mask of the visions. "My mother and father gave Cailen Sidhe two years. And then five. And then ten. I watched helplessly as they blossomed in blissful decay. And then they were gone." Pulling her close, I held her until I could feel her heart beating warm against my skin. "Please, Elizabeth, please. You are my life, my heart—my destiny. Without you, I am nothing but an empty shell." I wrapped my arms around her, enveloping her small frame in my full embrace. "Don't pursue this, Elizabeth. Please, don't."

Her face, so full of youthful optimism, beamed up at me, all wide-eyed and innocent. "I won't be like them. Only two years. I promise." Grinning coquettishly, she hugged me close. Death had not yet crossed the threshold of her mortal mansion. The Reaper played only a specter on a distant stage. "I'll have you there to keep me, darling. You won't let me die."

My whole body responded to the nearness of her. But when her palms embraced both my cheeks, her brow was set, her eyes taught with determination. "I want this; I need this, Ethan." Refusing to be refused, she stood on tiptoe, pushing the hair back from my eyes, all the better for me to see the independence that burned in her soul, forging her resolve.

Chapter 2

In the summer of 1862, while the country lay wounded and dying, life teemed around us. The garden, carved out of wetlands and forest, buzzed and chirped with the rushing traffic of nature's summer commerce. Hilltops beyond the house sported emerald coats. Hordes of winged tourists lounged in leafy treetop cottages.

The late afternoons were stifling, even in the shade. From the back veranda, I watched Elizabeth drop her paintbrush into turpentine and lean back, brushing beads of sweat from her brow.

The painting had started the day before as a sketch of the red columbine in full bloom before her chair but ended as a most mischievous looking creature. Elizabeth breathed deeply as if she'd been holding her breath in anticipation of this moment all morning. Her hand fell on the swell of her womb. Following her nights of ravishing dreams, I feared for the baby's health as much as for its mother's. While she contemplated her pale hand, a small tress of hair escaped the knot that confined it and dangled before her eyes. Grimacing, she plucked the strand from her head. Grey hairs at twenty!

Daily, I assured my wife that all would be fine once Cailen Sidhe stopped extracting her price for artistic genius. Perhaps I sought to reassure myself.

"We should rest," she whispered, lowering herself to the cool grass. "The two years are nearly over, baby, and then mama will be all yours."

"I certainly hope not." My voice from behind startled her and then brought a broad smile to her pink lips as she reclined onto the lawn. The wonder of such a striking creature bound to such an undeserving mortal as I had developed in me a propensity for watching her paint while she was unaware. "We'll boot the little beggar off to boarding school if it cannot learn to share." I grinned. The child was a work of art we shared between us.

"I would think it a much less formidable task to train this little one to share than her father." She caressed the mound in her lap.

"A girl is it, now? At least there will be no competition for your feminine affections." The lines on her face melted. That was the work I had undertaken: to banish those lines forever. If I had my way, at the end of two years, Elizabeth would never again taste even a crumb of time's bitter bread.

Kneeling beside her on the lawn, I produced a small box tied with a ribbon. Three holes aerated one side. Accustomed to the endless parade of gifts I laid at her feet, my wive ignored the box and surveyed the secluded grounds. "Have you seen Boo, love? I missed her company today."

Boo, a consummate serial killer, typically lurked in the shadows, camouflaged in her smoke and spice fur, preying on unwary birds. A full-grown Norwegian Forest Cat, she was much too large to misplace. I knew quite well where our cat had gone but chose not to divulge the secret. Not just yet. Bemoaning the loss of Boo's loyalty to Elizabeth's magnetic beauty and grace, I feigned the fear of losing my place in her heart to the tiny creature growing in the roundness of her womb. A smile on her face chased away the premature aging. I spoke directly into the tiny mound, "Lesson number one, dear child: your mother is mine, and I am only loaning her to you until you are old enough to fend for yourself."

Elizabeth rolled her eyes and smiled. Unable to resist the draw of her lips, I stooped and kissed them, my mouth taking possession of her and all that she was—or did she take possession of me? I couldn't be sure.

"Now I understand why the Leanan Sidhe most often take men as their consorts," she murmured, breathing deeply the rush of passion. She was so easily aroused when she'd been painting.

Seeking bare flesh, my hands wandered through the gaps of the dressing robe she'd thrown on after tying back her hair. When strange and lovely creatures walked her dreams, she could barely resist rising under the full moon to paint what the muse had conjured. For the sake of the child, I begged her to put off the hungry urge until the dawn.

The fruits of a morning spent feverishly creating were succulent. I tossed my silk robe onto the lawn. Elizabeth's fingers caressed the lines and curves of my chest as if I were her sculpture and sketch.

Intensity warmed her lips and she let herself be drawn as I slid my arms beneath her bare legs and shoulders, depositing her onto my robe.

The limp sides of her dressing gown slid away and I straddled her thighs, leaning over her, allowing my arms and chest to navigate the small obstacle of her abdomen. She closed her eyes and inhaled the breath-quickening rush of my hands exploring her roundness. They enveloped her shoulders and meandered down her neck onto the curve of her breasts. God! Touching my flesh to hers choked me with desire.

Elizabeth arched into the gentle circles my thumbs traced on her nipples. The echo of my caress rippled down below the unborn child. My mouth followed the trail of my fingers. She exhaled, sighing, setting free the verve of creation and passing to me the will of the artist. She was wet and warm with the heat of conception and I molded her with adoring hands.

The taste of fruit ravenously consumed still clinging to our fingers and tongues, we lay nestled together. The shade of trees separated the garden from the embattled world beyond our woods. Fading into dozing, I whispered my secrets in her ear. "I couldn't have lived a moment longer without you." My hand, thrown over her arm, rose and fell with the ebb and flow of her breast. "Before I touched my hand to yours, I was a dead man seeking life. Now I am alive because you are connected to me. You are the living part of my life. I want that forever." The visions in which I watched my hand slipping from the dead grasp of my father and then my mother, the bare hollow in the pillow of the large bed I shared with my elder brother, they drove my resolve to never loosen my grip on this life of the two of us knotted together.

She reached back and tangled her hand in my locks, pulling my face to hers, promising forever in her kiss. Then she entwined our fingers and led them to the roundness of the child. "*We* are the living part of your life." She breathed a deep, contented sigh, already half asleep.

When tree shadows tickled our toes, I touched her shoulder, willing her to wake.

"You distracted me." My lips brushed the fluttering of her lids. "I came bearing gifts."

Rubbing her eyes, she stretched her body along the silk of my robe. "What more could you possibly have to offer?"

Winking, I pinched her from behind. She squealed and sat up, pulling her crumpled dressing gown from underneath us and wrapping it loosely about her round nudity.

I retrieved the box with ribbon and air holes.

Her left eyebrow rose. "Darling, it's August already. My birthday was last month."

"This is a gift. But much too precious for any occasion. It is an occasion in and of itself."

Folding her hands, she leaned forward. I had adopted her every whim as my own and, in return, she lent all her attention to the opportunity of reciprocating. While the tide of her new talent swept her away, I had immersed myself in alchemy, my former obsession.

The box tilted and the contents squeaked. A little gasp escaped her lips. I cracked open the lid and a furry paw, adorned with tiny claws, tapped the edge of the box. Her nose crinkled. She removed the rest of the lid and drew from the box a ball of spice-smoked fur. "A kitten?" Her eyes twinkled with an atavistic lust for all things small and furry.

Elizabeth didn't understand the true worth of the gift she held in her hands. After half a lifetime of defeat, I had finally found the key to eternal youth. The tiny creature she cuddled was the proof. A decade of pent-up anticipation spilled out on my face. "Not just any kitten. Boo."

Her eyes popped wide open. Boo was an adult before she first made her feline acquaintance. The two of them had become fast friends. She turned the kitten to peer into its face. It meowed and wriggled. Indeed, there was an uncanny resemblance to Boo.

"You have managed it, then?" In her face, I found a subtle conflict.

"The two years are nearly gone. Cailen Sidhe visited my dreams, as she promised she would, a month since. But it was not so simple as I imagined. The process is somewhat more complicated."

"But how?"

"This coin." I pulled from the box a chain. A gold coin covered with markings dangled at the end. Elizabeth scrutinized the runes but could not decipher them. "An elixir, brewed with this coin and the proper elements and herbs, allows the one who partakes of it to transform into the body of a younger self. It is only when the subject assumes its true age that the natural aging process continues. By transforming to younger states, one can live indefinitely. The potency of the elements determines how far back one returns, and the dose, how long the change will last." The swinging of the coin in its arc of eternities fascinated me to the exclusion of all else.

"I feel quite transparent," she teased, setting the kitten beside her on the robe. The creature shimmied up close to her leg, curled its tail around its body, and purred lazily. "Should I be jealous of this nickel-sized piece of metal? I thought that you had given up this quest for immortality. Are you so dissatisfied with life in my arms?"

"Quite the contrary." From behind, I wrapped my arms about her shoulders, burying her in my embrace. "I find myself so complete that I would keep you forever."

Elizabeth toyed with the blades of grass poking up from the sides of my robe. The kitten stretched its paws and kneaded the silk of her dressing gown. "Life gushes from our cups, Ethan, overflowing the brim. With death lapping up the countryside, it seems greedy to grub in the mud for more minutes when we stand teetering drunk at the fountain." In the sweep of her hand, she took in the summer-kissed wooded estate, blue sky, and the baby rounding between us. "I would that a sip of the fine wine of my love were enough to quench this scorching thirst you have, but," her eyes fell upon the painting she had just finished, "I can hardly accuse you when I myself am so enamored of my own pursuits."

"You are my only pursuit." I brushed back the unruly tresses of her hair. The light reflected the gold hidden in the strands as they slipped through my grasp. "You see? The sun knows your true worth." My thumb caressed the full roundness of her mouth. "I would trade an entire lifetime of loneliness for one hour of sipping the honey from your lips. What do you suppose I would not give to have you forever, lying at my side, basking in the glow of summer?"

When she turned to look deep into the green of my eyes, I wondered if she knew something that could not be expressed in words.

"The summer will fade, Ethan, and my beauty and youth with it."

"It only seems that way." The swell of pride deafened me. I could not have heard my love, even if she'd spoken more plainly. "It's been at least three hours I would say. Watch the kitten closely."

The kitten mewed pathetically in the grass and crouched low. I watched intensely, with bated breath. A breeze and one hundred chirpings later, the tiny feline stood and yawned. The air around her thickened and folded. Boo stiffened, gurgled, and then convulsed. She took a step forward. Her face broadened, her body stretched. The fur thickened and darkened, and she assumed her former maturity.

Elizabeth's eyes and lips rounded to circles of confusion. Before staging my demonstration, I had watched Boo lick up the drops from the coin-tainted potion and transform into the kitten version of herself. The wonder of it had sent my heart racing and stopped the breath in my chest so that the blood raged in my head.

The second witness of this miracle left me jubilant. Binding my wife in my embrace, I exclaimed, "You see! It works." Of course, she was pleased—pleased to see me pleased. "It's for you, Elizabeth. As soon as the child arrives, we can use this. Death will never again cast her shadow on our doorstep. I will never leave you. We have eternity. You, my dearest, will be mine forever." I kissed her then—soundly and permanently.

Dearest Elizabeth,

There have always been—and always will be—beings who have stolen a key and unlocked the caverns of the infinite worlds. Brann Sidhe and her sister Cailen are two such beings. They are forever loitering on the fringe, enticing us with their magic, feeding upon our lives.

There are wispy parts of a human that may wander while the body sleeps. In such a form, in the blissful days before I lost you, I visited the Barrow—that deep cavern where the souls of those who have lived and died converge, seeking new horizons of existence. Brann Sidhe led me through the mouth of a vast tunnel under the hill. Her hand anchored me in the rush of wind that howled in torrents and sloshed about, untethered, a multitude of beings.

I felt as Dante traversing the underworld. No eternal torture or lamenting racked the souls of the dead here. Only a wave of voices roared in the wind storm. "What next? What lies beyond?" My leanan sidhe had surely escorted me to the realm of the after-life, and yet my life was not done.

With one glowing purple nail, my guide indicated a tangle of roots that glowed white, almost blue, on the earthen ceiling above us. These roots pulsed until one expanded, its mouth gaping wide as a passing soul felt its magnetic draw and whistled away from the tumbling horde. The hungry root swallowed up the wandering sliver of soul.

My astounded curiosity snared me. Knowledge, once sought, will not be forsaken. Brann Sidhe ushered me upwards to the web of roots swirling above us. The irresistible tug of one of the roots seized me. Propelled into the force, I flew, electrified. Relief engulfed me when, upon contact, the root did not swallow me up. How ironic! At the very moment when the oppressive burden of my entire, interminable existence fell upon my consciousness, I felt relief.

These roots were portals. Universes and time tangled inextricably together. A portion of my soul had already lived inside the universe that attracted me and I inhabited still a flesh in the world from which Brann had abducted me. So, although it did not consume me, the contact with my prior existence awoke forever that shard of my soul that had lived there.

I understood, in that moment, that the souls of all beings are shattered. At death, the winds whisk away to the Barrow the slivers inhabiting the spent body. The conglomerate spins in the vortex of lost souls until it finds a root, portal to a universe where other abandoned pieces of its whole have bonded together to rest. This newly deceased sliver sleeps quietly there with its fellows until that flesh, too, passes on and the convergence of slivers seeks itself in another existence. The fragments of the soul continue thus until, like drops of mercury, the shards have all reunited to form one perfect whole.

You must understand, Elizabeth, the dormant fragments of our souls were never meant to awaken, but only to dream, casting a vague shadow of influence upon the whole. This awakening was disaster.

At the touch of this root, my thinking faculties flooded with images of another life and with the scene of your death during that life. Brann Sidhe towed me past every port where the winds of history had swept you away from my grasp. The anguish of my resurrected losses clung like barnacles to our passing entourage until they fairly sank the flimsy craft of my being.

Hardly had I opened my eyes when the horde of mourners in the recesses of my consciousness began their howling. When my gaze fell upon your face, Elizabeth, a tangle of blonde tresses strewn across your cheek, did I know? Did I know, too late, I would lose you again—and again—and again?

Forever,
Ethan

Chapter 3

Elizabeth dredged up a heaving groan and pushed a small body into the rays of the drowning sun. Exhausted, she fell back into the pillows. Shadows shrouded her face. I knelt by her side. My wife of barely two years lay sweat-soaked and pale in the crimson sheets of our four-poster bed. The salty, iron aroma of blood bludgeoned the sweetly pungent lavender perfume that normally hung about her.

At the foot of the bed, the midwife stopped her work. Iron curls escaped the confines of the cap she wore tight against sharp cheeks. No pity seeped from her steel-grey eyes when she shook her head and produced a square of linen from her bag to wrap the still, bluish infant my wife had pushed into this world. The child never even took a breath of the life Elizabeth had broken herself to offer.

The midwife might easily have wrapped my heart in that cloth. It hung lifeless in its cage. My glance fell on Elizabeth as the old woman picked up her bundle. She shook her head again and turned to leave as if my whole life weren't disintegrating with every fading breath that rattled Elizabeth's chest. Strangling tears, I seized her arm. "Do something! She is only twenty! You can't just leave her like this!"

The matron unlatched my hand. Her trade, in this time of war, served up gluttonous feasts of bloodied soldiers and bedsheets. The sight had grown mundane. "I'll send for the doctor, but by the time he saddles his horse, it will be too late." As she left, the exposed nail that pierced the sole of her shoe clicked a death knoll against the wooden floor.

Passing the paintings on the wall, she paused to cross herself. The hag made no secret that she suspected I had brought with me, from Ireland to her Pennsylvania woods, the echoes that stalked her when she scavenged the roots and herbs of her trade. "I won't disturb the minister."

The veiled snub rang hollow in my loss-dulled ears. Elizabeth's dying fist was clenched about my heart. As she slipped away, the beating mass tore from my chest. But no! I would not stand powerless by her bed, as I had beside my parents' and brother's. I had devoted my life to eluding the cold grasp of the Reaper; I would not stand by while she dragged my wife away.

My hand fumbled at the coin hanging around my neck. "Stay with me, love—just a bit longer. The baby—there's nothing to stop you now from drinking the elixir. We have forever." For a brief moment, I glimpsed eternity. Drained of the woman that gave my existence meaning, it shriveled into the desert of hell. I shuddered.

Her eyelids flickered as I brushed the sweat from her brow. The corner of her mouth curved contentedly. "Ethan—" She could barely speak from loss of blood.

"Stay still, love." While the coin could halt the onslaught of age, it was powerless to heal a broken body. Clasping her hand, I whispered in her ear, "The doctor will come; he'll fix this."

"—no. I am done. But—sweet Ethan, this life—so lovely—" she gasped for more air, struggling to place a hand on my cheek "—spent together. I would not trade one moment—" her lungs stuttered, "—not for another fifty years without you." Exhausted from the effort of speaking her love, Elizabeth sank back into the pillows. Her hand fell limp beside her.

"Stay with me!" Pressing my chilled lips to her feverish mouth, I forced my passion for life into her. My tears mingled with her sweat. I wanted to give her life, but found, in her gaunt cheeks, that I had only succeeded in stealing a portion of what she had left.

"This cannot be!" Raging against the inevitable, tumbling current of existence, I pushed back my chair and took stock of the room. My eyes fell on the washbasin and towels. I seized one, doused it, and returned armed to the bed, my fingers soaked and dripping. "You're burning up."

Deep inside I knew the end was coming. Elizabeth could not survive this loss of blood. My world contracted to the space around us. Death, with her dull axe, hacked slowly at the tendrils that bound our souls, our lives, our destinies, but she had not yet severed them. I held my wife's fingers next to my lips as if I could breathe more life into her. In her face—no, I could not bring myself to look there. Exhaling in sobs, I buried my grief and tears in her matted hair.

Grasping the sticky crimson blotches that I could do nothing to erase, my fingers wandered down the length of her body—oh, they knew it so well. "Oh, God! No, please!"

On the mantel, the six-inch bronze farm boy that decorated the clock smiled obliviously down upon the tragedy ticking away below. Unlit candles on the mantels and nightstands faded into the dimming light. Shadows skimmed the faces of the jubilant beings that inhabited the paintings on the walls. They flaunted the life they had stolen from Elizabeth's brush. But I, too, had stolen. The tilt of her nose, the silk of her cheek, I had stolen them from another. Was this tearing apart the price I should pay for my theft? My head slumped forward onto her chest.

In the solitude, I whispered into the softness of her breast. "Elizabeth, darling Elizabeth, if only I had known—" Her fingers, barely animate, found the tips of my hair. The slight gesture of comfort in the face of this overbearing farewell strangled my apologies. Boo purred as my body convulsed in sobs. "Please, Elizabeth—"

Her chest rattled again. "Bring—" The one word was all she could manage.

"Stay still, love. Save your strength."

Gasping, she refused, "—baby!" This was what drew me to her—the indomitable drive to touch what she had created. Nearly lifeless, she summoned her final strands to reach for the magnum opus we had fashioned together. She did not know it had died in her womb. The single word she uttered stabbed at the hollow in my chest and I collapsed in sobs.

Nothing. I could do nothing for her.

And I would have done anything.

Chapter 4

An errant breeze swept in from the chimney and ruffled my hair. I squinted at the red glow of the coals. A ribbon of fine ash rained down from the flue. The ebony mist slithered along my neck, through my hair, brushing my cheek, insinuating itself between me and my dying wife. Hovering, the cloud caressed me until, in a rushing breeze, the tiny cinders spiraled.

They gathered themselves before the windows near the hearth. The lines of an evening gown appeared in the torrent of cinders. Each speck of ash blossomed into a downy, black feather until a dress of plumes fluttered empty at the foot of the bed. A woman appeared in the dress. The gown hovered about her as if her nude body were immersed in a fluid flock of birds. Raven hair reflected the sheen of the feathers. Skin, too pale to be human, glowed in the twilight. Purple eyes narrowed beneath long lashes. Her lips pursed in pity, the apparition reached a nail toward my shoulder. "Ah! My dear boy."

I knew, all too well, Brann, the raven muse of the Leanan Sidhe. I recoiled from her touch.

"My dove sister Cailen played you a naughty trick." The petal-smooth purple of Brann's lips brushed my earlobe. "Eternity entices only lovers; the lonely tremble before it."

The creature floated closer to the bed, observing its contents. "Now you have forever and no one with whom to share it." Her brow bent. Miniature crystals fell from the corners of her eyes. The charade did not fool me. The Leanan Sidhe feel no pain and never cry.

I blinked twice at the muse's profile. Her brightness in the dim room, the sheer beauty of her, stunned. Looking at her roused the pain of wanting in mere mortals like me. A film of pasty gluttony emanated from her as she fed on the misery about the bed. "Why do you torment us, Brann Sidhe? Elizabeth's bargain with your sister is done. She has nothing left to take."

Brann caught from her cheek the tear and admired it on the edge of her finger. "Perhaps I am here not to take but to give. I knew when my sister struck her bargain that Elizabeth's life thread was fragile, that the weight of the child she craved might sever it." The muse observed my wife's struggles. "See how strong she is? Yes, she might have survived, were it not for the two years she bargained away."

The words fell like stones on my conscience. My hands covered my face. Unbidden tears stung and welled up in my eyes. "God curse me! I am a fool! I wanted to tie her up, stop her." My gesture swept along the paintings. "I refused at first—" The excuses froze on the leanan sidhe's upraised brow. "—Cailen Sidhe came to Elizabeth in dreams, tempted her with such consuming visions that she deemed the price of two years as paltry in comparison."

The dark muse scoffed. "You knew only too well the price of trafficking with the Leanan Sidhe."

"I tried to stop her. I did."

"Did you?" Was that pity in her voice?

The gold piece that hung at my throat attracted my fingers to its magnetic metal. Damn the piece! Damn my insatiable thirst to drink from its elixir! Brann Sidhe's words had unlocked a heavy door.

The muse saw me wince and spoke my thoughts. "You allowed her to agree for the sake of the coin. Admit it, Ethan." Brann floated forward. Leaning down, she whispered the ugly truth in my ear, "My sister saw the desire that stalked your heart and offered to whisper the path to that coin in your ear—a gilded trap for a precious prey."

"It was for us!" Truth unveiled always engenders violence in the deluded. Throwing back my chair, I stalked to the hearth. From above the mantel, I ripped the canvas of a being much like the one that stood at the foot of the bed. Where her sister was black and purple as the raven, Cailen Sidhe's portrait shimmered gold and white as the dove.

I slammed the frame against the mantel. It cracked and splintered in my fist. A sliver tore my flesh as the painted canvas ripped. The gurgle of the fabric echoed the tearing in my soul. "I did not know I would lose her!" My voice rose up and then cracked in anger. Impossible to sort out the target of my fury, myself or the dove demon who had conceived the bargain. "I would never have agreed. I would have stopped her from having the child if I had known it would steal her from me." Mangling the painting of the leanan sidhe did not quell the sorrow and anger drowning me.

"Cailen Sidhe could not have told you. Life is the art of my sister; death is my realm." Brann Sidhe's next question was all earnestness. "Tell me, boy. Do you think you could have stopped her? If you had known?"

My temples throbbed. The shredded canvas still dangled from my hand. It was devastation to lose Elizabeth's love after so short a time immersed in it, to lose the child that might have filled the void left behind—to know that I could have saved her, this was the hell that broiled my sorrow. The gold piece seared my chest with the irony that the key to our immortality came at the cost of her life. "I would have stopped this if I had known. I would have refused Cailen Sidhe and died like everyone else."

"Would you have, indeed?" Her gaze passed from my wife's dwindling body to her paintings. "But just look at them! Delicious." She traced a purple fingernail along the curves of the painted creature nearest her and then breathed in deeply some ghost of flavor lingering at the tip. "Never have such beings graced the imagination. They breathe. They dance amid the light and shadows." The muse swayed gently to the melody of her own voice. Trailing her nail across the obscenely white flesh of her chest, she shivered, her eyes tasting the paintings. "They smile and are remembered as someone long since loved. These are shores never envisioned in the human mind, not even in dreams."

I could only lament that it was true. Elizabeth had painted the inner life of nature; the gritty man of mud, the perky sprites of the pines, the dancing water selkies. She had captured the life of their pristine habitats in stark realism that faded into abstraction in the portrayal of their spirit so that it was never sure she had truly painted them. As her life flowed out on bits and pieces of her imagination, Cailen Sidhe had feasted upon it.

The mangled painting, I tossed into the fire. Resurrected, the flames licked greedily at the canvas. The muse retreated, her dress fluttering to follow, as I stormed past her to Elizabeth's bedside.

"Those creatures only live because of my wife. Without the beauty that is her soul, they are dead, nothing but cold paint on canvas!" The words strangled in my throat. My finger caressed her fevered cheek. "This is beauty. The only beauty is love."

My shoulders shook for a few silent moments until I raised my head and croaked, "The only life is love. Do you understand me?" My eyes bored into Brann's. Anger and misery gleamed wet in the icy stare. "Of course, you don't. You have no soul with which to love. Have the decency to let me spend my final moments with my wife in peace."

Turning back, I took Elizabeth's hand. It hugged ever so faintly my fingers. "I would die for you, love. Over and over again."

An achingly beautiful smile illuminated the face of the muse. She pressed her lips to my ear. "You could, you know."

Chapter 5

Desperation fueled the train of my thoughts. They hurtled toward the abyss of Brann Sidhe's proposal. "You would save her?" The madness of the question rang hollow against the cold brick walls.

Elizabeth was not yet gone—not quite yet.

Joy rippled through the film of tragedy that hung upon the twilight when Brann Sidhe laughed. "My dear Ethan, my sister Cailen and I, we are Leanan Sidhe. We do not grant life; we feast upon it."

Her honesty was unsettling and appealing. I knew I should fear this creature, but I was grasping for a foothold on a crumbling cliff.

"You see? You prefer your traps set boldly in the open rather than cloaked in flowers and sunshine. Cailen Sidhe appears wrapped in light-drenched doves and sparkles in golden splendor. Her presence dispels the grisly truth of her nature." The dark muse grimaced. The room darkened a tinge. "But I, in my shadows, bear the burden of the age-old myths of men and gods that offer my sister such an advantage among humans. So, I must be much plainer, being less trusted." She shrugged off her misfortune before narrowing her eyes. "Make no mistake, Ethan McCarthy, shadow or light, my sister and I are, neither of us, benevolent and both voracious."

"Then why do you trouble us?" My palm caressed Elizabeth's pale cheek. She tried so hard to smile for me. The faint tilt of her lips cracked my heart. "My wife has no life left to feed on—" To speak the truth racked my chest with a sob, and I braced a hand against the blood-soaked mattress.

The creature waved away the loss that meant so little to her. "Because we are predators." Brann Sidhe drifted closer. She licked the tip of one purple nail and then touched it to the base of my ear. I flinched. "I come to wrest the prey from my sister's trap." Slowly, she dragged her purple claw across my jaw. Visions engulfed me—gods in the violent arcs of battle; lovers wrapped in the turbulent throes of illicit passion; the pathetic lines of hunger and suffering on the faces of the miserable masses; the ache and awe of beauty in darkness. An exquisite mixture of pain and pleasure shuddered my bones.

The gold talisman halted the progress of her nail. "Do you know why my sister would grant such a gift as the secrets of this coin?"

"You already told me. She wanted to feed on my wife's talent."

Brann Sidhe giggled. "Ah, so naïve, my sweet. These paintings are indeed lovely, but the inspiration for them can hardly be called a fair bargain. Two years nibbling at the crumbs that fall from the creations of a woman never destined to be immortal? I would say my sister suffered a calculated loss."

"Do not dare to disparage her!" Infuriated, I grasped at Brann's lily-white throat. My hands sank into a pillow of down and I fell forward, clutching only a wisp of ashes. My face hit the wood planks of the floor and I pounded it with a fist. The dress of feathers reemerged beyond my fingertips.

"You wear no iron, Ethan. Have you forgotten the old ways in this new land?" Her whisper bristled in my ear. Every child in Ireland knew well enough that only by iron or fire could the Leanan Sidhe perish. "Perhaps you might not be so eager to dispatch me when you hear what I can offer you." A sardonic smile cut the lines of my face as I rolled onto my back, pushing my elbows against the notches in the knotty, wooden floor. Brann stooped to place her hands lovingly on both my cheeks. "Your wife was mere gruel in the face of the feast that could flow from your hands."

Jerking my head from her touch, I buried my face in my knees.

"You are the artist, and yet you squander away your time and passion with your studies in alchemy, chasing life instead of the beauty you were born to bring to this world. My sister snared your wife, knowing it would kill her, hoping you would be easy prey to her consoling grasp. And did she offer the coin out of the largess of her murderous heart?" Brann's hand slithered back to graze my shoulder.

"You insinuate that she did not." I dared not spurn her, knowing full well I toyed with a trap. For Elizabeth, I would have walked into hell. "Please enlighten me as to her true motives."

An opium mist flowed from the downy folds of the muse's gown. "My sister agreed to whisper to your dreams the making of the coin because she knew your wife would die. The Leanan Sidhe is born to love. My sister saw in you a lover. She gave up the secret of endless life so that she could wrap up your broken heart in her bonds of gold and feed off the infinite flow of your genius."

"Why are you telling me this?"

"Because I do not think you will strike a bargain with my sister knowing she plotted to let your wife murder herself."

"If I see your sister again, she will find I have recently acquired a taste for iron accessories."

The smile on the muse's lips could have conjured a tinge of desire even in the most desolate of souls. "Or you might find greater satisfaction in robbing her of the prize she sought, the way she has robbed you of your love. What chagrin she would suffer if her sister were to pry the prey from the sprung trap!"

Brann Sidhe's designs began to come clear. "What do you want from me?" Every piece of my soul strained to warn me away from bargaining with this creature. I paid no heed.

"The endless flow of nectar from your fountain of youth."

"And what do you offer in exchange? You are powerless to save her. You said so yourself."

In response, her lips arched into a smile. "Did you know, boy," the feather dress fluttered about the muse as she stood and tip-toed toward the paintings, "that when humans create a piece of art, tiny bits of their life break free and animate the work? The greater the passion, the deeper and richer the life it extracts." The muse licked the tip of her purple fingernail, traced it down the length of the painting, and then savored the smell of it with eyes shut. "In each bit of life, flourishes a tiny mist of soul. The Leanan Sidhe feed upon the life, but the soul remains in the art and gives it life."

"Are you saying that these paintings hold Elizabeth's soul?"

The muse nodded.

"And you can extract it?"

She nodded again. "If we hurry before her soul has drifted into the caverns under the hill."

"And you can bring her back?"

She nodded again.

Raising myself from the floor, I stood to stare into the hollow purple eyes. Truth is such a fluid thing, so wide and ever-flowing, one drop into another, so difficult to dam it up and keep it whole. But I wanted to believe—more than I wanted to live.

I knew Brann said nothing because the Leanan Sidhe may only speak the truth and she was hiding truths she did not want to reveal. I didn't care. Availing myself of Elizabeth's hand, I fixed my eyes on hers so that nothing else in the room existed for me. I whispered to myself the truth I wanted to hear.

"Do it!"

"One hundred years."

"Anything. I care nothing for the price." Was it insane to want my love to live at all costs—even at hidden costs? Or was that the only sanity?

"Give me the diamond on her finger."

Elizabeth,

I had no choice. What price would be too dear for a piece of your soul, my love?

> *Forgive me,*
> *Ethan*

Chapter 6

The once sturdy logs, bereft of life and darkened in the flames, began to crack. I groped in a drawer for matches and lit the two candles on the mantle and one on the table by the bed. In the undulating shadows of the light, I bent and pressed my lips to Elizabeth's brow. Damp hair clinging to her cheek and the wilted pillow, she tilted her head toward my touch. She was not much more than an empty shell—delicate, fragile, broken.

"Why do you wait?" I demanded of the muse who watched, unmoved.

"You understand, Ethan, that during your 100 years of service as my protégé, you will grow old despite the power of your coin? Each time you return to your most mature form, the sands of your life will flow, and more freely because you serve me. It will be your life that nourishes mine. The coin will no longer protect you from the inexorable tide of age; it will only shelter you. You will grow old, slowly, ever so slowly, but surely. It is your immortality you have agreed to forfeit."

"I understand. Get on with it." For another stolen season with Elizabeth, I would have given a piece of my soul.

Brann Sidhe seized upon my wild desperation; her face pouted and the room dimmed just a tinge. "A century is so short a time for me. I feel the loss of my prize already. And you, once you have served your 100 years and I bring Elizabeth back, you will have love again. I must also have a fair price for the love."

Forebodings of hell sat in a lump in my chest. Were it not for the gaping and throbbing hole it filled there, I'd have spurned the muse's greed and her offer. But, I wanted Elizabeth. I wanted her. "You and your sister have robbed me of my child, my love, and now my very life. I have nothing left to offer."

The leanan sidhe circled me, her new toy, letting her fingertips stroll through my hair, down my neck, and around the broad curve of my shoulders. She paused at bare skin exposed through the crumpled folds of my shirt, torn open in the agonizing moments of my wife's travail. "I must have a game." The point of her nail stopped in the carved hollow above my heart, just below the coin that hung from its thick gold chain. She shivered in anticipation. "Are you sure of your Elizabeth's love?"

Confusion wrinkled my brow. I shook my head, unable to grasp the pertinence of the question, so random and irrelevant to the present urgency.

"Is her love as deep as yours? Will it endure time and circumstance?" Her touch enveloped me and drew my breath away.

Turning to Elizabeth, her breath shallow, her body limp, I ran a thumb lovingly around the dark, clammy circles that engulfed her eyes and brushed the matted hair back from her moist, pale brow.

The bare hint of a smile moved the corner of her lips. She opened them, and I had to bend to make words of the air that slipped out. "—always."

The muse paused to give me time to consider. "Ethan McCarthy, in exchange for your service, I will bring Elizabeth back in five score years, but if, in half that time again, you do not seal your love in the mixing of your blood with hers in the bonds of marriage, I will take your soul—and hers as well."

"After one hundred years of service, when you bring her back to me, I will have fifty years for her to fall in love and marry me?" The very generosity of her gift cast suspicion on it.

"And have a child."

"What do you want with a soul, leanan sidhe?" In the end, it didn't matter. I would have given my soul for the mere chance of Elizabeth.

The anger that deepened the purple in Brann's eyes belied the rigid smile that curved her lips. "A human soul is a powerful bauble to my kind and the souls of lovers even more so."

Spreading my arms wide, I bowed in mock allegiance. "I am yours for one hundred years. My soul is a tattered empty rag without her love; you may as well have it. If she is gone, I have no use for it."

"There will be no tricks and no scheming." Ever deceitful herself, the muse could not but doubt my integrity. "Your love alone must draw her covenant or the game is forfeit. You will never speak of our bargain." She touched her finger to my lips. Frost permeated them and spread through my tongue. This contract was not to be left to my honor. "She will not be coerced or manipulated. And you will serve me three days with every cycle of the moon until she is yours again." Her purple eyes narrowed.

On the bed beneath me, Elizabeth's breath began to rattle. My heart skipped. I wanted so desperately to do something where nothing could be done—except by this vampire creature—except on her terms.

"Enough of rules and terms. I agree: one hundred years as your consort, my immortality in exchange for her mortality, and our souls for our love. I serve you until she is mine again. The bargain is struck."

Brann Sidhe ripped the seam of my shirt at the right shoulder. Inches below, her nail scraped a purple scroll of runes and ravens in a band around the flesh. The ink burned and the muscles tightened, but my resolve remained stiff. "There! You are mine. Now, give me her wedding ring."

I hesitated before twisting the ornate gold band from my wife's finger. The ring, a family heirloom, cradled a modest round diamond. Turning to the canvas nearest her, Brann whispered, coaxing by word and song. A nearly imperceptible glowing yellow fog slid out of the painting and made its way to the diamond. The mist penetrated the stone and turned it pale yellow. The paint, bereft of life, turned to dust and spilled onto the frame and the floor. Brann Sidhe wandered about the room, enticing bits of yellow mist out of the canvas creatures until two years of Elizabeth's soul had floated into the diamond.

The canvases in the room wiped clean, the muse turned to Elizabeth's wilting flesh. "Say your goodbye's, Ethan, my love. I will feast upon my century, and then I will lick up the drops that fall from our half-century game. One hundred and fifty years will pass much more slowly for you than for me."

Chapter 7

"Wait!" I grabbed Brann Sidhe's hand. "She wanted to hold the child. She must not pass from our life together with empty arms."

The diamond of the wedding ring, pregnant with the mists of my wife's soul, glowed vaguely yellow. The raven muse glanced dubiously at her nearly vacant body. "We have very little time."

"I insist. Or I refuse your arrangement." Pulling the gold coin from my neck, I raced through the doorway into the adjoining room and accosted an apothecary cabinet. A Bunsen burner, elements and herbs, chalices of various shapes and sizes littered a large worktable. Dropping the golden coin into a cup of water, I began adding ingredients. The potency would determine how far back I would transform, and the dose how long the change would last. I made it strong and swallowed very little.

Brann Sidhe watched, annoyed, as I returned to my wife's bedside. "If she dies before you have finished, the soul will be lost and our bargain null." Her threats fell on deaf ears. Obviously, my taste was already on her lips—spicy, warm, and satisfying. She breathed it in, and the tip of her tongue sought me at the valley of her upper lip.

What was it like, to feel the man that I had become shrink into the baby I once was? Perhaps only the child knew. But hidden deep within the recesses of one corner of the babe's subconscious, I watched Elizabeth's last moments.

A cry broke the deathly silence of the room. The tiny boy that I had donned squirmed upon the blood-stained rug at the side of the bed, wailing for his mother. The muse smiled at me—a lovely plaything. As my consciousness receded into the cloudy mind of the infant, she gathered me up, tickled my chin, and cooed at me before carrying me to Elizabeth's arms.

She rattled a deep breath and exhaled, "—baby," then pressed her scorched lips to my temple.

"Perfect," the leanan sidhe whispered, almost giddy. "A kiss will bring her soul to her lips." Singing and cajoling, she placed the ring near Elizabeth's open mouth. When she exhaled her last breath, the diamond surged to luminescent yellow. The baby cooed, Elizabeth's face froze in utter serenity, and the muse giggled. Placing the ring on her finger, Brann danced from empty frame to empty frame along the walls, waving her prize and chanting. She continued her waltz into the adjoining room. Upon retrieving the golden coin and chain from the cup, she skipped back into the death chamber.

Shooing away the cat that had come to sniff at the body, the muse leaned over me nestled in my wife's arms. "We must not leave such a precious trinket lying about. We will need this, you and I, my sweet Ethan." She draped the necklace around my neck.

Elizabeth, my most cherished one,

This is my penance—to know and observe, powerless, all that passes in my absence whenever I retreat into the ignorant oblivion of my child selves' subconscious. When I reemerge, the memories of Brann Sidhe are there, licking up the drops of my youth.

> *Forever,*
> *Ethan*

Chapter 8

I n 1883, seeking fresh fountains to quench her insatiable thirsts, Brann Sidhe settled in a small art gallery with living quarters near the San Francisco Art Institute between Columbus and Hyde Street, not far from Fisherman's Wharf. It offered easy access to a smorgasbord of hidden talent. The muse masqueraded as an art dealer, benevolent patron to her resident, reclusive, often absent, but gifted artist and his "motherless nephews."

The window of the back studio was open and the sheer white curtain, training like a veil, ushered in a brine and smoke-shrouded breeze from the bay. Brush poised, I stood before a rendition of a man languishing in a lifeboat. The shore, barely visible upon the edges of the horizon—now a fog-drenched peninsula in a seething green sea—vaguely recalled Elizabeth's profile.

My monthly offering for February nearly finished, I was expecting Brann.

All the younger alter egos of myself—brought into consciousness through my repeated use of the coin that extended my years—fidgeted deep inside my subconscious, upsetting the flow of the vision sprouting from the seeds Brann had planted in my dreams. My youth ought to have dozed quietly in the corners of my past, sometimes watching and whispering. Youth is not meant to stir up ripples of awareness, clattering its cup unnaturally at the bars of age, demanding to be set free again.

The tiny boy that I had been only hours before lay curled up in my memories, wallowing in Brann's fluffy, maternal caresses. My stomach turned at my weakness in escaping into the innocence of the toddler. But by then, I had fed my muse so many innocents, I could hardly spare my own.

I turned back to the canvas to drown my conscience in its stirring seas. The waves before me were not angry enough; they needed more black. At the creak of hinges, I turned, scowling. "Leana" used the doors these days. It pleased my leanan sidhe mistress to pretend to be human.

In the doorway stood not a demon muse masquerading as a patron of young artists, but Antonio. Tousled black hair, mid-twenties, dark circles under his eyes. The desperate look that ran up his brow and through his hair, the paint stains embedded in the cracks of his skin marked him as one of her recent victims. Desperation swam in his eyes and in the lines of his face. Brann Sidhe had left him.

I had brought this aspiring young artist to Brann's studio and offered to take him on as a student. Antonio watched avidly, swallowing up the broad strokes of my misery, painting by my side until the day the muse slipped between us, caressed the boy's hand, and whispered into his ear. Antonio was indeed gifted. He could paint the face of death, a fearsome sight that longed for love. And then Leana sent me away. I retreated, relieved, into the small boy until she had worked her spells on this lad who was not much older than I on the night I lost Elizabeth. How she haunted my dreams and canvas. Everywhere her eyes and the curve of her lips shimmered, laughed, and cried in fleeting wisps along the brushstrokes.

"I'm sorry. Are you looking for Leana, Antonio?" I tossed my brush in the can. Brann always left her toys the night before I, in the eldest skin, reappeared at the full moon to hold up my end of our bargain.

"Where is she?" Antonio fixed his crazed stare on my unfinished work. Despair, followed by entrancement and then lust, invaded his features. "It's you! She's thrown me over for you, hasn't she?"

Brann had gone too far with this one; the madness was setting in. I could see why she was tempted to be careless. A Latin, olive skin highlighted the young man's tall, broad shoulders, square jaw, and deep green eyes. She was fond of green eyes—like mine. "It's not what you think." I wiped my hands. "Leana and I, we are colleagues, since many years."

Antonio wasn't listening. His arm went to his stomach, his face convulsing as if he might wretch. She had pulled the plug on the bath of inspiration in which she had immersed him, and now all his art was gushing out, leaving him dry inside his artist's shell.

"You're better off without her." I stretched out a hand to console Antonio, knowing all the while that, as much as I believed my own words, I would never convince a man writhing in the throes of withdrawal that he had no need of his opium.

Antonio's knees buckled, and he sank to the weathered planks of the floor, melting into sobs.

"It is not real what she gives you, you understand? The greater pleasure is to paint what springs from your soul—human, flawed, mundane—but your own. Why be a slave, boy? You have no chains."

"No chains! You must have no soul, to paint by her side and fail to feel the cold metal of her tepid love. The paintings be damned! The woman owns my heart. She has taken her property, ripped it from my breast, and carried it away, dripping with my blood and life."

"Then her skill in the crafting of such an illusion marks her as a true artist. Beware. She is neither woman nor lover. A lover gives in equal measure that which she takes, but she, she is a thief that offers up smoky visions to mask her thievery, a demon that pilfers men's lives."

My heart longed to believe that while I said these words, the poor man cringed inwardly to finally hear the truth spoken. Alas, I knew the symptoms that plagued Antonio. I had seen them in Elizabeth: the blind eye and the deaf ear. Antonio had traded his own sight for Brann's visions in the night and his hearing for the soft words whispered through her purple lips.

My blasphemy offended Antonio's soul. To his deranged mind, a word of evil spoken against his goddess was a sin—a mortal one.

Livid with indignation, Antonio wrenched a revolver from his pocket, pulled himself off his knees, and pointed it at my chest.

It was not the first time I had stared down the barrel of such a weapon as it trembled in the fist of a jilted lover. My old friend Fear had long since moved on in search of a more constant association. Of course, I knew one small bullet, well-placed, could render worthless the golden coin hanging on my chest. But my interminable days had become beggars, starving beneath the dripping spoon of hope.

At times, my soul craved an end to the incessant hunger. More precisely, the piece of my soul that had trudged through two decades without my beloved craved an end. My younger selves, their existences parched and crumbled as dust wiped clean by the winds of time, still clamored to quench their thirst in the coin's abysmal pools of life. It was their chorus that moved me to step lightly backward, never losing eye contact with our besotted foe.

For just such moments as these, which, in Brann's studio, were not uncommon, I kept upon a convenient shelf attached to the back of my easel, a knife. I had become quite adept at throwing—or rather, it should be said, the adolescent selves into which I retreated to maintain my youth had become quite adept at throwing. I simply remembered the skill they had mastered in the long, lonely hours they spent masquerading as the sons of the absent, eccentric artist. In my all too vast experience with them, I had surmised that artists—especially lovesick, shriveled, and desperate boys—were not, generally, good shots. Ever so casually, I reached for a towel.

Antonio, no doubt perturbed by my apparent calm in the face of the rage of violence that drove him, shook the revolver. "You don't deserve her." The young artist struggled to stop the flow of mortified tears that sprang to his deep-set eyes.

"How I wish that were true." Covering the blade with the cloth, I made as if to wipe my hands. For as long as I could, I would endeavor to heal the boy's wounded passions with words of reason. "And yet, I fear I do deserve her, whereas you, my friend—" The bell on the door jingled loudly, interrupting my logic and distracting Antonio.

The door flew open, admitting an angry cloud of black mist. Wind ravaged the room, papers flew, the easel toppled to the ground. The shadow engulfed Antonio, spewing a torrent of black feathers, binding him. Wantonly brandishing the pistol, he flailed his arms, protecting his eyes against the torrent of plumes. I dove behind the fallen easel as Antonio's finger bowed against the trigger. The shot shattered the dull roar of the windstorm.

As quickly as the gale had risen, it died. The feathers converged into black silk. The silk conjured within its folds the pale figure of Leana and her flowing raven hair. "Antonio." The muse cooed into his ear, imprisoning him from behind. "I set you free, my pet. Why have you wandered back into the cage?"

"I need—" He couldn't finish. The ecstasy of her touch slackened his face. He melted into her embrace. "He doesn't deserve an angel such as you." Closing his eyes, he tilted his head to her crimson lips. "I had to—I had to free you from him—so you would see—so you would come back to me."

"Free *me*?" Brann giggled. "What a quaint thought."

"He is unworthy." The tortured boy glared at me, raising the barrel of his weapon from beneath the muse's embrace. "He called you a thief." My fingertips reached for the handle of the knife that had clattered away in the fall.

"But he is right. I am a thief. I have stolen your heart, my dear, sweet Antonio. I only wanted to return it to you. But how sweet the scent of this jealous rage!" Through rounded lips, she sipped the bubbles of nectar fizzing off his neck. "Perhaps I was a tad hasty in setting you free." The point of her nail trailed from the tip of his ear to the base of his collar. Her tongue tasted the essence of his anger. She shuddered.

Poor Antonio staggered under the drenching tide of her favor. In the slow turn of his face and the narrowing of his eyes, I knew the boy would not let me live to tempt her again. In one sweep of my arm, I grasped the blade and let it fly. The knife pierced Antonio's shoulder as his finger tightened on the trigger. His scream bled into the crack of the pistol. The bullet flew wide and ripped a hole in Brann's purple armchair. Like a bolt of lightning, Brann's lily-white hand flattened against Antonio's chest.

For a brief moment, I assumed she was stopping the bleeding, cauterizing the knife wound. And then Antonio's eyes flew open wide. He moaned in tortured ecstasy. Brann grabbed his shoulder with her free hand, pressing her palm more deeply to his heart. He hung there in her grasp for full seconds, suspended in blissful agony. I suddenly became aware that she was not healing him—she was murdering him.

"No! He's just a boy!" I sprang from the floor as Antonio's knees buckled, and he collapsed in a heap at Brann's feet.

"What an exquisite exit to such an ordinary existence," Brann murmured, licking her fingertips.

Falling to my knees in front of the limp body, I grasped the face, distorted in a grotesque mixture of pain and pleasure. I listened at the boy's lips for the passage of air and heard only silence. His chest was still. The only thing I knew to do was to breathe for him. Opening his mouth, I struggled to force the air into his throat, guessing all the while that it was his heart she had stopped. Even as I breathed in and out, willing Antonio to take up the rhythm, my veins boiled with hatred for the calloused devil that was my mistress.

Antonio died. At Brann's hands. In my arms.

Ah, my dear angel,

I should have fought in the great war and died with the other hundreds of thousands of men who forsook their families to affirm in blood their ideals. But it was not my war to wage and I was a slave to another master.

Was I to blame, Elizabeth? Even now, at night, alone in my bed, when the wind billows the curtains, blows sleep from my eyes, and shivers into my veins, I fear I was to blame. My fevered mind retreats into the consciousness of the younger ones. They know no guilt—

Ethan

Chapter 9

I stared at Antonio's face, frozen and lifeless, still masked in exquisite ecstasy. My eyes cast daggers at Brann, but the blades had no iron, no fire to destroy.

Distraught, my insides writhing with rage, I stumbled into the narrow city streets. For hours, I wandered, mud splashing onto my shins, the smell of fish and salt invading my hair, sticking to my skin, invisible, yet oppressively pungent.

I wanted to find a way out, but I could not cut the cords that bound me to Brann without cutting the thin strands from which dangled a life reunited with Elizabeth. It hung there, tantalizing, just beyond my reach. Iron would kill the raven witch, but the ring—the smoky yellow mists of Elizabeth's soul that the muse's magic had conjured from the paintings—might dissolve with her.

The night was grey, and along the wharf, the wind howled the lament of what I had just witnessed. Waves crashed against the barnacle-encrusted posts, stirring up a frenzied turbulence, spitting the salty blood of the earth in my face.

I meant the boy no harm. The knife would have done nothing more than cool Antonio's anger. But I had encouraged his art, lured him into the muse's web, just like so many others. It had never gone this far, but it was Antonio's choice. They all had a choice. They accepted her bargain and paid the price for her inspiration. I coerced none of them, and when she finished with them, I buoyed them up against the abyss of loss that consumed them.

The ocean spray slapped my face. What would it be like to fall? The waves would cradle me, wrap me in their fluid shrouds, and I would be done with the witch. Obscured in gray clouds, no star in the grumbling sky whispered tinkling sparks of hope.

Inside my skin, the ghosts of my former selves clamored to the surface. They knew what I intended, my foot sliding toward the splintered edge of the boards. It was the Ethan who first loved

Elizabeth that stopped me. Hope still harbored a perfect picture of my wife silhouetted in the morning light of the breakfast room where she painted her life away. The younger man's zeal to grasp at the immortality of that image dilapidated my doubts. I closed my eyes to the foaming breath of the gale, closed my eyes to the madness that followed in Brann Sidhe's wake.

Turning, I followed my feet back to the purple door. With every step, I felt the desolation of guilt and the pain of impotence. A stew of saltwater and fever dripped from my brow.

The body was gone. Brann was gone.

My head pounding and burning, I fell into a chair. But sleep does not loiter in crowded corridors and my mind seethed with images of Antonio. Images of the boy's hand moving with broad strokes over a white canvas tortured me as the wind howled and rattled the windows of the small studio.

The door flew open. A flurry of smoke buzzed like a swarm of black wasps and targeted my chair. I hoped it was death come to fetch its due. I would have gone willingly.

The cloud engulfed me, spinning around the chair. Nausea churned in the depths of my belly. My head weighed heavy upon my shoulders. Inside the feathered vortex, the leanan sidhe whisked me away into a forest so fertile green as to be black. Deep undergrowth hid the ground in shadow. Vines wound up to grasp at my legs and arms as I stumbled, in her wake, to a craggy hill.

She smote the cliff wall with the flat of her palm and cracked it wide, spilling out light into the darkness. As a child, I had heard old women speak of the Barrow, the mythical kingdom beneath the earth where, among the roots, floated creatures, once inhabitants of a human existence somewhere, on other planes, in other worlds— copies upon copies, flawed and torn. A somber chorus of these souls chanted their united funeral dirge. A multitude of existences awakened inside of me, churning up tragedies, floating to the surface of my memories. And always, everywhere, each cherished their portion of Elizabeth, or whoever she had been to that shard of me—murdered, martyred, betrayed—so that I could capture on canvas the dross of that thread of my sorrow and feed my mistress.

At the touch of Brann's hand, an electrified tuber awoke itself and burst to life. From within, Elizabeth's voice called to me.

Lonely, she sought the ties that bind her to me across universes. The root expanded, breathed, and sucked me up.

Chapter 10

The root under the hill vomited me back into reality—into what reality, I could not tell. I found myself seated on trodden dust, gazing down upon a cobblestone conduit for runoff. Behind me, the chips in the stucco wall reeked of mold. My knees clasped in my arms, I raised my eyes to a signpost depicting a lively rabbit hopping from a pot, wine bottle in hand: *Au Lapin Agile,* The Agile Rabbit. Paris? Had the leanan sidhe simply transported me across the sea? It would not have surprised me. At what other copse in the late 19th century would the ravenous wolf sniff out her next quivering prey?

In the residual fog of my metaphysical journey, I had heard Elizabeth's voice, calling to me, below the murmur of all the other voices of myself that had awoken during my tour under the hill. I surmised that the root could not have returned me to my proper time and place because she was alive and living here in Paris in this world to which Brann had transported me. In the world from which Brann had ripped me, Elizabeth had been dead for two decades. I sensed that, until that moment, I had not existed in this universe and never would have, had it not been for the contrivances of Brann Sidhe.

Perhaps this world, in which I had landed, was one of the infinite copies to which the hill granted access. Perhaps they exist one on top of the other. Or, perhaps they nestle one within another like Russian dolls, exact replicas, varying by tiny inaccuracies, fault of the hand that paints them. Little matter.

Through the magical machinations of Brann Sidhe, the roots under the hill had transported me into a copy of Paris that flourished in another realm—a realm where I had never existed and where Elizabeth wandered untethered and seeking.

Tufts of pink and orange dabbed at the fading blue sky. A breeze of ribaldry seeped from the cracked stucco walls of *Au Lapin Agile* as the door opened and a young woman stepped into the street.

Elizabeth.

I had no doubt. Not the compact and agile body, nor the broad cheeks, not even the curve of the lips did I recognize. Something much deeper, something hidden in the coves of each small element of the flesh, recognized my love and the ties that bind us—always and everywhere.

The shards of my soul, that Brann had awakened on our midnight tour beneath the Barrow, called to Elizabeth with one voice. Like a man deprived of air for decades, I gulped at the sudden affluence of her presence. I could not avert my eyes when her assured stare returned my own.

I didn't even pause to wonder if Brann knew that, without knowing why, or perhaps intrigued by the vague stirrings of her inner selves, this shard of Elizabeth would stop and speak to the forlorn stranger on the street? Of course, she did.

"You are an artist, no? I have a gift, you know. For picking the talented ones. It is uncanny how I feel you—" Hearing her voice silenced and sated the starving hordes of past Ethans that had awakened within during my journey. "It is quite evident. This is why you wait for me with such hunger in your eyes. But it's not for me that you hunger, is it? It is for him." The French, tripping off her tongue, caused me no confusion. I was a well-bred young man with a proper continental education. "Come along, then. Follow me." This new version of Elizabeth exuded confidence, unleashed, perhaps, by a life of hardship evident in the coarseness of her hands and the nearly imperceptible hitch to her step.

Knowing the wiles of the mistress I served, I should have refused the hand this Elizabeth held out to me, let her wander on in her lonely existence. Did some deluded corner of my rationale imagine that, motivated by a tinge of mercy, Brann Sidhe had dropped me in her path to relieve the consumption of my longing? If it did, I was a fool. But then, I knew I was a fool.

Foot and hoof traffic streamed along both sides of the dirt road. Steering us along the *Avenue des Saules* with the fluency of a river that has long since cut its path, this young version of my deceased wife navigated the mud splashes. My wonder at finding myself again in her hypnotic presence translated easily into the awkward awe of an amateur confronting a master. Pausing, she dropped a hand on my shoulder and tilted her head. "I am only the model, Marie Clémentine, the bastard daughter of the washing woman whose name I bear. You must save your worship for Auguste."

Oh God! What vibrant stirrings rocked my core at her touch! "Is that where we are going?"

"You are English, no?"

I stumbled on a knobby cobblestone as she glanced once to her left and then, lifting her skirt, dashed to the other side of the street.

"Irish, actually." The response had already escaped my lips before I realized that, as far as I knew, I was nobody in this time and place and could be anybody. "I am—Ethan. Ethan McCarthy." In vain, I dared to hope the name would awaken a deep vein of her consciousness.

"And you have come to Paris to join our revolution? Ah, but you are too late, Ethan. Auguste has already broken from the rebellion. He wants more than light. He has fallen in love with form, and line, and Her Highness Black." The hunger in my eyes reflected in hers as we passed *Chez Maurice*. The subtle aromas of *herbes de Provence* and wine flooded the street.

Glancing back to hurry me along, she detected my dismay at her hunger. "It was the circus." Too late, I realized that, self-conscious, she had misread my grimace and attributed it to disdain for her infirmity. "I go to Auguste Renoir for the same reason you do, Ethan. A few strokes from the brush of the master and my body becomes light and graceful once again."

"No, no—you misunderstand. It wasn't—"

Marie Clémentine's—my thoughts stumbled upon this novel appellation because I had known her soul so intimately as Elizabeth—laughter sprinkled colorful prisms over the brown-smudged greys of the streets. "I've always had this need, you know. The same one I see in your eyes. When I was young, I fancied myself a painter. But then I found the tightrope in the Cirque Fernando. There is so much art in the curves of a body precariously balanced upon a single line. Madame Morisot painted me on the wire. Did you know? But it lasted only a year. After I fell, I could no longer perform." She paused, allowing me to match my step to hers.

"Even so, it was only natural that my body should still be my art. You'll see in the studio. It was Pierre that first showed me. Chavanne. You've seen his work also, *non*?"

"Ah—I fear, having arrived most recently from America, from San Francisco—" The lavender scent of her distracted my words. The swell of her white breasts exposed beneath a low-cut, peasant smock left me speechless with wanting. Her wide and frank stride seemed unfettered by any social compunction to grovel in modesty.

"San Francisco? We have seen many of your compatriots here, eager to join our revolution—our insurgence that we paint in the streets. I do my part for our cause. I give them my body like a good soldier, and they paint my soul."

I would not waste, to lap at the gruel of jealousy, one sip of the nectar from this cup of time that Brann Sidhe had pressed to my parched lips. Like the mob stirring within me, I wanted nothing more than to touch the skin and paint the unveiled form of the woman I had loved so briefly and lost for so long.

"And from time to time, Auguste lends me a bit of paint and canvas on which to play, like a good little girl, at painter, in my own little corner of his studio. Did you know, when he was young and unknown, he often had not the money to buy his paint? Tragedy. But I study the painter as he paints the study. And when the studio is dark and empty, I learn well the lessons embedded in the paint upon his canvas."

For the first time in decades, I felt an urgency to take up my brushes, commit to the muscle memory of my hand, impress upon my brain, the face and body of this piece of Elizabeth, so novel, so independent and free in her lack of social restraint. "Will he— Auguste—will he let me paint?"

"Oh, but this is why we are not going to the workshop. There he is bound by his commitments to Durand-Ruel or the demands of the Salon. No, what he paints now flows from a deeper, more primal source. A new mistress has claimed the slant of his brush." Her smile hid a secret knowledge and I knew that curve in her lips. I'd seen it in my bed and could only assume that this new mistress she spoke of was a leanan sidhe. "He will most certainly allow you to paint."

Did I seethe? Of course, I did. My arms throbbed with the impulse to enfold this version of Elizabeth in my arms and sweep her away from the rapacious grasp of Brann Sidhe. But how should one hide from one's nightmares?

"He is painting in seclusion at his *jardin sauvage*—how do you say—uh—wild garden. There the forms express themselves unfettered by studies and conventions." Pinching my shirtsleeve, she steered me into *Rue Cortot*. Tripping along the cobblestones of the narrow street, she swiveled in her skip. "The muse hangs about you."

"And does she not hang about you?" The new skin my wife wore exuded a bawdy frankness of artistic expression.

Far from pleased, distaste—no, fear and suspicion—flashed across the wanton lines of her mouth. "She will steal you away, you know? Body and soul. You should run home, boy."

Boy. My forty-some years hid in the elixir of life that Cailen Sidhe had sold me in exchange for Elizabeth's two years—for her life. The outer pup cached beneath its downy fur an alley-worn, mangled dog.

The scuffed toe of her brown shoe paused upon the path. Beyond the gate at which she stood, the gravel receded from the street toward a trim, but rustic dwelling. "I warn you, I've seen them come and go." Whimsical gardens, flanking the narrow walk, disappeared into trees and shrubbery along the outer sides. "With cheap talent, they leave quickly, return only slightly paler to their fathers and their fields or to their drawing rooms. But those with the gift, they flourish, and yet wither as the passion presses the juice from their brushes."

Was it possible Marie Clémentine knew of the Leanan Sidhe or had she only observed, unwittingly, the trail of glory and waste they left in their wake? Perhaps the demon muses stalked Elizabeth through her several existences as well as me.

The caution in her face turned almost to remorse. "You are one of the latter." Her hand wandered back to her breast. I hoped stirrings of our familiarity were awakening within her. Having walked beneath the Barrow, I knew that, in whatever skin we wore, our two souls sought each other out. "You mustn't follow me here. Go home. It's not safe." With a swish of her skirt, she turned her back on me and hurried up the gravel path to the house. The rusted handle grated. The door creaked open.

Emboldened by her hesitation upon the threshold, I hastened up the path. My fingers locked about her wrist. "Don't leave me!"

"This passion you have, it will ignite and consume you. Go home."

"I have this!" I lifted the coin around my neck. "It protects me!"

"A parting gift from your dear mother?" Marie's laugh sprinkled sugar on my bitter soul. Her bare flesh collided with mine when her free hand grasped the talisman. The Celtic markings flashed in the grizzled Paris sun.

On her fourth finger flashed the wedding band crowned with the round and yellowed diamond into which Brann Sidhe had bled my Elizabeth's soul from her paintings as she lay dying twenty years earlier. "Where—how did you get this!"

She snatched away the hand. "It was a gift from my godmother. She gave it to my mother when I was yet in the womb. It hung from my neck the day I was christened and has not left my finger since the day I was old enough to slide it on."

"And was it given to protect you?"

"Of course." The words melted into a sardonic laugh. "And yet, while I wore it, I fell from the tight rope."

"But you did not die in the fall. Neither will I."

Eyes narrowed, she tossed the curls from her face and abandoned her scruples. "Come then, armed with your old woman's trinket. Perhaps a mother's love will, in the end, save the soul of her errant son."

Had she known how right she was, she might have left me standing on that path in those haunted fairy gardens and slammed the door in my face.

Chapter 11

My footsteps echoed on the herringbone planks of 12 *Rue Cortot*. The entry gave way to a generous drawing room. Instead of furniture, easels and wooden chairs littered the space, sentinels among the stacks of frames and stretched canvas leaning against the walls. Shadow figures sprawled in charcoal lounged upon canvas, waiting for color to breathe into them the life of the serene faces that smiled down upon the scene from the rough-hewn walls. Paint smeared the floors.

Adjacent to the windows, hung at least a dozen landscapes, rolling grassy hills, tinged with orange and red, descending into bays of green and blue. The lightness at the soul of these paintings pierced the darkness fossilizing my heart and, at that moment, I desired nothing more than to paint Elizabeth once again, not in the somber hues of my nightmares, but in the warm, innocence of this studio.

"These are the landscapes of Guernsey," Marie Clémentine whispered as if we had entered a chapel. "In three months, these sprang from his brush. When she is with him, he cannot contain the creative flow."

I saw her then, perched upon the shoulder of the thin, angular profile of an artist who sat before a large canvas about three feet wide and five feet tall. His paint box, smeared and splattered in oils, offered a treasure of colors, lively and warm, into which he dipped generously. My own pallet offered no such illumination to the tormented creatures I imagined.

So engrossed in his work, the artist paid no heed to Marie and me or to the ravishing demon that lurked at his shoulder. The tip of her nose slid across his neck, harvesting the delectable drops of life set free as he worked. The aroma of him so tantalized her that she bent to lap directly from the lobe of his ear. Cailen Sidhe.

The sight of her awakened the boy in me. Hate? Fear? She was not designed to foster such emotions. Her platinum hair fell in cascades as dove white as Brann Sidhe's was raven black. The dress she wore clung to her curves and floated about her in feathery tufts. The whiteness of her skin radiated a golden glow, not quite tangible, that drew the eye to the ornate chain hanging loosely about her hips. At the bottom of this chain, swung a medallion. The carvings etched into the gold recalled the coin that hung round my neck.

Cailen's glittering beauty could not quell the erupting anger my acquaintance with her inspired. Fists tightened, my breath stopped. Had I iron, I would have driven the rod into her cold-hearted breast. She had robbed me of all that I loved beyond life—brother, mother and father, child—and Elizabeth. Her calculating manipulations had driven me to contract my hellish bargain with her sister.

Catching the scent of fury mingled with artistic passion, Cailen's nose twitched toward the prey lingering at her doorway. Nearly imperceptibly, her eyes and mouth curled up with the fire of victory. "Why look, Auguste! Our dear Marie Clémentine has brought us fresh talent. And where did you find this lovely specimen, my girl?" Gliding over, she never once glanced at Marie. Instead, her eyes cast hooks into mine. No matter what name or flesh Elizabeth wore, the muse had always overlooked her talent, dangling her as bait to lure me.

"Groveling in the street outside our little den of bohemian artists. He clearly knew where to find me. I had no need to even sniff him out." The deep, almost rude undertones of Marie's laugh roused the artist from his work. Leaning to the side of the canvas, he dropped his brush into a can and revealed his face. Pierre Auguste Renoir. At the time, I had only seen newspaper accounts, heard anecdotes in drawing rooms and galleries, of the upstart artists in Paris and their "impressionism." Apparently, this artist's life, like mine and Elizabeth's, repeated itself in myriad planes of existence and manifestations.

Pierre hastened across the room, threw his arm possessively about Marie's waist, and thrust her to his chest. His brow, no longer crimped in concentration, revealed the faintly receding line of his dark hair. The loosened and crevassed skin of his stained hands and the tiny lines etched along the corners of his eyes marked him. He was a good twenty years her senior—and her lover. I saw it in his eyes before they closed in ecstatic enjoyment of the full fruits of her lips.

As mine had Elizabeth's, Renoir's hands had wandered along the smooth curves of Marie's body, seeking the soft points of pleasure. He painted in the day the woman he adored in the night. "Come, Marie, *mon enfant sauvage*, we must subdue this fire and transform you into an angel on my dance floor." He waltzed her from the room, and she followed his lead with unabashed abandon. She loved him—or maybe just his art.

Without the overwhelming aura of Elizabeth's soul emanating through it, the room waxed bare. The new warmth in the cracks of my stone heart waned. I could not breathe. I could not move. My gaze fixed itself on the doorway through which my love had vanished in the arms of another man.

"Paint!" The gracious fiend beside me thrust a wooden box, well-smattered in the colors of joy, into my cold, black world.

Where was that wall of fury and vengeance that should have blocked her advances? The very being of Cailen Sidhe dissolved all that was not light and pleasing in my blood. While her sister ravenously instigated and devoured misery and pain, the dove muse nurtured and regaled upon all that was pleasant and peaceful. How I tried to rekindle the brimstone of my rage against her! But, from the dark coals of loss and obsession, Cailen Sidhe fashioned sparkling jewels in my imagination.

"Paint!" The tinkling bells of her voice rang in my head. The room was silent and void, but in my eyes danced the vision of Elizabeth dressed in the skin of Marie Clémentine, waltzing upon my arm. A vision of what might have been, in another time and sphere. The muse's gilded lips moved, and molten gold flowed into the cracks of my memories. "Like me, Marie loves the artist, not the man. It feeds her yearning. She does not know the flavor of your brush, Ethan, nor the tantalizing delicacies conjured by your hand. If she knew, she would be yours, wouldn't she?"

How was I to resist? The vision in the muse's eyes hypnotized me. I took the brush.

She led me to one of the three life-size canvases near the windows. Upon the blank white, I sprawled in bold black lines the figure of this new Elizabeth, this Marie, and of myself—the intruder—our forms locked in a dance that blurred and ignored the world in the background. Feverishly, I blended the colors that would breathe vivacity into the faces. The bodies, I left to chance and shifting times.

I fashioned a red bonnet against the gold-tinged white of a dress. The bonnet garnished in fruit would draw Marie's eye. I wanted her to see, to look into the painting and recognize us, remember our tumbling waltz—the intensity of my longing for her, the interminable movements of the dance of fate that turned her face demurely from mine, drew her into its undulations, and refused to quench the thirst of my languishing.

I painted as in a dream, waking for only a moment when the flurry of satin ushered Marie, primping and giggling, back into the light-drenched studio. Auguste had adorned her in tufted white satin and gloves. But I needed no living, breathing model to guide my lines. The vision of Elizabeth refashioned in flesh had rekindled the light behind my own darkening memories.

I remembered only too well another dress, sweeping and flounced, trimmed in red that tinted the rosy glow of Elizabeth's skin. Elizabeth belonged to Jackson Richards when she wore it, and I had stolen her from him, if only for the fleeting moment of a summer flower bloomed too late in the fall to withstand the first snap of winter. Relieved of the hoops of decades past, draped back to free her movement, the dress danced interminably through the fading corridors of my memories. While Marie stood for Renoir, a cool, sculpted goddess, my hand breathed into our forms the vivacity of our interminable dance.

Behind a straw hat and faded beard, I hid the deceptive youth of my face. I painted the man I should have been. Marie Clémentine would not know, but maybe would sense, the gossamer ties that bound her to the image of this man that held her waist, turning her body to his steps, her fingers draped along his neck.

The yellow of my hat, I blended with the swirling motion of the trees and the sun-stained dirt beneath our feet. This stolen moment of mine would not last, but while the light of my love's presence broke through the slatted shutters of my caged life, I committed to oil and canvas the yearning that groveled in the dark cell of my existence.

Sweat beaded along my forehead and neck as I resurrected our love and my longing. And all the while, Cailen Sidhe hovered at my shoulder, sipping at the nectar of my life set free in the release of my soul onto the canvas. I did not care. She could have sucked me dry in that moment and I would have skipped into oblivion—I could feel again.

Chapter 12

The rays of the sun forsook the windows and dim shadows fell about the studio before Auguste sighed and his brush clanked onto his pallet. "*Mais*, Colombe, you have abandoned me. And for what?" On a smudged towel, he wiped the paint from his hands, releasing the pungent smell of turpentine into the cramped room. He strode, somewhat annoyed, toward the canvas that had come to life before me. "For a mongrel street pup?" Gathering her skirts, Marie Clémentine followed, curious.

In a barely perceptible rush of feathers, the muse stepped back, releasing me from her spell. It was not for the master painter that I had begun this half-finished expression of my tragedy; it was for my love masquerading as Marie. Auguste's head started back slightly upon his shoulders. He had not anticipated such skill from the untrained hand of a starry-eyed street boy. But then I was no boy. And my hand was not untrained. The master's gaze shifted from the painting to the painter's face. A thin film of resentment crusted Auguste's professionally frank admiration.

A small "o" curved Marie's lips. Wide-eyed astonishment flushed her cheek as she peeked around the master's shoulder and encountered the naked expression of my pent-up adoration. Her gaze pivoted from painting to painter. She saw, for the first time, the man behind the tortured eyes. Her lids fell, and she recoiled, just slightly, hand upon the bare skin exposed by the plunging neckline of the gown she wore. She knew.

I turned toward Auguste's guttural curse in time for the master's fist to slam into my jaw. My head jarred back. Throbbing pain coursed along the bone. My brush clattered to the floor as I lost my balance. "You know this boy?" Renoir whirled on Marie, catching her shoulders. Who could say whether it was the art or the sentiment immortalized within it that engendered the sneer, the lip trembling with rage, and the accusing finger he thrust at me?

A narrow stream of blood trickled from the corner of my throbbing mouth as I raised my bones from the floor. Years of torture, anger, and guilt churned to the surface and clenched my fist. Once upon my feet, it flew of its own accord.

Only in the harsh and violent strokes of my brush, had I allowed my anger to seep to the surface, wreaking their havoc on the worlds I painted. When I had usurped Elizabeth's affections before, Jackson had been so kind as to capitulate without a fight, exiting the stage to wage his patriotic war.

In the face of Auguste, I saw no such valiant surrender. My fist slammed into the master's gut, doubling him over. Renoir's wheezing gasp sated my hunger for violence. In almost vengeful euphoria, mingled with the slightest tinge of gratitude for this cleansing opportunity, the moment the master struggled to right himself, I repaid with interest his earlier blow to my face. The crack of my fist against the bone of his nose sent him sprawling to the floor. Small droplets of blood, like paint flicked from a brush, mingled with the chaos of color on the wooden floor.

In the space of a breath, Cailen Sidhe fluttered to Renoir's side, ripping him from my hands.

Humiliation brimmed in his red eyes. Through gritted teeth, he rasped, "Do you know this whelp?"

"No." Marie's word rang hollow in the nearly empty studio. Stepping back, she searched my face, unsure of her memory, grappling with the dormant whisperings of lives already lived. "I only just met him. He was so anxious to come and learn from your hand."

"Come, my sweet Auguste." Cailen's gold-tipped fingers raised Renoir's shoulders, turning him from the scene on the canvas. "The boy has talent. Did we not charge our petite Marie to bring us blooming talent? She has the gift." She managed to unbend Renoir's form and console the lines from his face. "'Tis a lovely spring night. Let us dine at the Moulin-Galette and leave her to groom your new pup. She will make of him an adequate schoolboy."

Cailen swept Pierre away in a daze. I doubted he would even remember this night when she had finished walking in his dreams. Not sure how to proceed, uncertain of Brann's purpose in transporting me here to stand before this incarnation of one piece of my love's infinite soul, I bent to retrieve my brush.

"Well," hand on hip, Marie surveyed the painting, "evidently, it is not the master you seek but the model."

If only she knew.

"Will you stay? Will you pose for me?" I was indeed a dog, desperate for the hand of the master.

Why did she not question the origins of this stranger's passion for her? Why would she release so brashly the floodgates that inundated my unquenched thirst? Because she was a product of the Bohemian world of Montmartre that, in the night, indulged in the mind-numbing elixirs of absinthe, opium, and sex and, in the morning, ripped pungent reality from the wilted and ragged vines of Bacchus to fashion art. I could only hope.

"So much devotion to your chains." Marie's head tilted to align with the face of the dancer in the painting. Sloughing off her studied insolence, she donned a thoughtful, professionalism that perhaps her absent master had never cared to see. "One should never put suffering into drawings. This is what Mistress Colombe tells me when she surveys my work."

"But one has nothing without suffering." Taking her hand, I admired the work I had fashioned for her. *Oh, sweet life! To touch the skin of love once more.* Her fingers snuggled into mine. Our footsteps rang in the twilight-shrouded emptiness of the room. This was my perpetual existence, nothing but the two of us, surrounded by paint in the shadows. "You see how she looks away? She looks beyond him to something more substantial than his adoration. His face is lost in her distraction. This is the story told in the splashes of the paint. Suffering is our lot."

"Is that what art does for you, Ethan? Eternalize this life we hate?"

"You hate this life?" My hand dropped hers.

She searched the darkening floorboards for the answer. "Something is missing. I can't seem to find it, and I don't know where to look. But I am drawn here—" the flutter of her hand encompassed the studio "—and yet, I don't find it here either."

She led me out of the main hall into a smaller room. Through the window, a waning stream of light illuminated an easel. Pastels drenched the small canvas balanced upon the wooden frame. A young girl, with the eyes of a woman, stared searchingly from the canvas. Tints of yellow fading into blue shrouded the girl in an aura of dim realism that bled into the smooth, sneering lines of her profile and cast shadows of frank suffering upon her skin.

The self-portrait exuded the promise of a talent unschooled and a vision unfettered by convention. "Here, in this tiny room, the pastel in my hand, I feel whole—almost."

No sign of the leanan sidhe marred the bold, defiant stare of the girl in this image. The profound independence provoked in me a sigh of relief. For the first time, I gazed at Elizabeth's soul on canvas. I had never seen this before. My wife's work under the hand of Cailen Sidhe, though breathtakingly incomparable, held no trace of this blunt freedom of expression. Would to God the stirrings of her own imagination had satisfied her when she was mine and I was hers! But this was the trap of Cailen Sidhe, to cheapen in the artist's eyes the sublime expression of humanity and imagination so that she might usurp its realm with her dreams of immortality.

My admiration needed no words. The silence between us resounded with glowing approbation. The straight line of her lips curved in a secret thrill of victory. I wanted to warn her. "Has the painter seen this?"

"I invited him once—when Mistress Colombe was not hovering at his side—to guide my hand and instruct my brush."

"And did he?" Fervently, I willed this painting to be her own, untainted work.

"He looked down at me, over the top of his canvas, brimming with the pride of the master. I had stumbled from the lowly life of mere men and women into the kingdom of his professional reign."

Marie's finger stroked the deep lines of the haughty brow that crowned the portrait's defiance. Traces of color lingered beneath her squared nails. "Shall I tell you what our revolutionary master said? 'I think of women who are writers, lawyers and politicians as monsters, mere freaks. The woman artist is just ridiculous.' You see, he will never teach me. This is why the dancer looks away from the face of her lover. He desires the wild, independent fervor that burns within me. But he wants only to cage and domesticate it. It would die on his hearth."

The image of Elizabeth dying upon the hearth pierced my memories; her blood trickled into my consciousness. "So why do you stay?"

She pointed at the painting as if the answer were evident there. "Because he instructs my hand without a word. One can watch and gaze for hours, and the paintings themselves reveal the craft."

Stepping closer, I whispered into her ear, "You should leave them, you know."

Her fingertips lightly repulsed me. "Do *you* know?"

I gave no ground. "Yes. I know."

An eyebrow arched, she squinted in doubt. "Hmm." In a whirl of satin, she flounced toward the door. "Come, pup! I will change from my adornments and, in the streets of Montmartre, we will strengthen our resolve to set ourselves free."

While Marie changed, I found a bit of coffee-brown pastel. The lowly window cast only a teaspoon of light upon the doorway when she returned. "I suppose I should feed you."

"Wait. You haven't signed your portrait."

"Ah, yes, of course!" She giggled—a warbling that could turn a hunter from his target to pursue the soothing balm the tones injected into his blood-thirsty soul. "Did you wish to purchase this masterpiece, good sir?" Sauntering over, she snatched the chalk from my hand.

I caught her wrist, drawing her to look me in the eye. "You are destined for so much more than to wear a dress and sit for them. Leave them. She appears to give so generously, but she will suck you dry, make you mad. Leave her. You do not need her; your gift is a seed buried within. Nurture it yourself or she will harvest the fruit and blight the roots."

Unwrapping my fingers, she offered no promise. Instead, she dropped her eyes to the canvas and gracefully scrawled the inscription: *Suzanne Valadon 1883.*

"Valadon?"

"It is my mother's name; the only name I have."

"And Suzanne?"

"Did you know it means 'lily'? Such a versatile flower—symbol of death or devotion." Brazenly, she insinuated her body into the space surrounding me. She smelled of herbs, sweat, and olive oil. A hint of lavender clung to her hair. I had thought myself a dead man walking, but not even a dead man could resist wrapping his arms around a vision so fleshy. "Such diversity for such a delicate bloom, *non*?" Her fingers waded through the unkempt locks at the back of my neck.

For only a brief second, I weighed the consequences of stepping foot into what was surely a trap carefully laid by Brann Sidhe. "And will your master painter object to a vagrant pup plucking the lily from his garden?"

A defiantly delighted smile crossed Marie's lips. I had never seen this before. The dirty streets of Montmartre had engendered, in this realm's version of my wife, substances unknown to the polite society of 1860's Pennsylvania. Absinthe and opium, bohemian love and art, swirling in the streets and wafting through the air, had shaped the flesh and mind. How could I possibly resist the spicy tang of such an offering? "He most certainly will object. But do not worry yourself. He will take solace in his empty-headed Aline. She wants nothing more than to grace the mantel of his hearth. He will settle for her adoring tranquility because he finds that the fires of his *petit sauvage* burn too fervently." Her toes flexed. Her chest rose, brushing mine. The soft curve of her pink lips parted. Without looking at it, her finger dallied lightly with the coin bound around my neck. "Will your old woman's charm protect you from my burn?"

"Most likely not. But my lips are already parched, my soul in ashes with longing for you. I would burn in hell for one sip of the nectar from your lips."

I carried her away, our lips locked in an eternity of knowing, to the small boudoir down the hall.

Like tracing the lines of distant clouds, my hands followed the curves of her naked image. A true model, she instinctively curled into the forms most desirable and I painted them all with my fingers, brushing my lips through the roundness of her breasts and descending to the valley of her thighs. The rapture of our present oneness engulfed me, and yet, could not block from my mind the fervent hope of a future. Every contact of my moist flesh on hers shivered, not with lust, but with love's languishing to awake the morning after, still entwined.

I woke in the morning alone, sprawled on the crisp white sheets of the bed behind the purple door of Leana's San Francisco studio.

Dearest soul of my deepest desires,

After that night, my art sank to its knees at the daunting task of unveiling the eroticism locked in such a kiss as reunited our lips. The muse's magic only gave me power to paint the tragic lines of loss.

Such an exquisite trap! My sweat still tingled with the traces of you. God, Elizabeth, I would have trudged another thousand years through the murk of Brann's glorious swamp for one other such night!

Faithfully yours,
Ethan

Chapter 13

Cailen Sidhe, the muse of light, had traded a few months in the company of her current pet Vincent to her sister Brann, the muse of darkness, in exchange for one night of my presence unbound in another universe where I had not previously set foot. But why?

I still questioned Brann's motives, nearly a year later, as I stood before an incomplete painting—my offering of the full moon. I twisted the ring on my wedding finger. No gold had rested there since I had made my bargain with Brann Sidhe. Not long after she had again ripped me from my wife's embrace, this time in the body of the blossoming artist Suzanne Valadon (né Marie Clémentine), I had taken advantage of her prolonged absence to secure a new, plain wedding band—a band of iron.

The setting sun cast purple rays through the western windows, tainting the dappled brown of the wooden floors at my feet. The door clicked open, admitting the familiar breeze of San Francisco sea salt and the rustling of feathers.

Brann breathed deeply and then sighed her disappointment. "Still it lingers, this sweetness of light my sister has instilled into your artist's sweat. Does she truly hold such sway upon your being that you should continue in this flavor for so many months? How I long to savor the exquisite perfumes of bitter agony once again. Why do you deny me, ungrateful slave?"

Only the self-indulged vanity of the leanan sidhe could allow her to believe that those she bound and devoured ought to worship her for her condescension in destroying them.

"It was you, yourself, who led me to the one blissful night." Rarely did I gaze into the vapid pools of Brann's irises where life groveled in picturesque agony. It pleased her to catch my eye. She seized the moment to lay her hand upon my breast and puncture my heart with a searing lance from her arsenal of misery. "Come back to me, my bitter love."

The picture she drove into my chest was one of a tiny baby, a boy pulled from the belly of the model Marie Clémentine, a boy whose seed I had planted in her womb on that one night. I stumbled back, my foot catching upon the easel, my hand planted squarely in the wet paint of the unfinished work. The brush clattered to the floor, splattering its dark hues across the worn wood.

"He is mine?" The picture of the demon Cailen in possession of such innocence choked me. "You sold my son to your sister? Elizabeth's—Marie's son?" I backed away, horrified as the full scale of the sisters' plot began to flesh itself over in the bodies and lives of warm-blooded humans. I could accept my own lot. This slave's existence bound me not only to Brann Sidhe but to Elizabeth as well. There was a point of light in the darkness. But to have condemned my son to such squalor of life with no hope of redemption—unspeakable!

What could I do? I had no access to the Barrow and no transport to the universe where this boy was enslaved. Once more, I could only stand helplessly by as Cailen Sidhe ripped from my power both the woman I loved and the fruits of our love.

Brann Sidhe ignored the horror that sank me into her chair. This was what she had gambled for—the means of mingling the depths of my despair with fury. She would wring from this new blow a profundity of suffering only a true demon could relish. "It was but a small sacrifice in exchange for a few days in the company of the young Vincent. Our dear Madame Colombe has garnered quite a select collection of delicacies in that realm. Vincent is a rare prize. But suffering is buried inextricably within his fibers. She tries so hard with him—the burning yellows and oranges, the vibrant blues and purples—and yet, always the darkness lingers below, oozing to the surface. He paints so well this all-consuming misery in his soul—a delightful feast, but not to my sister's taste. She was so willing to bargain, at first I feared I had overpaid the price; but one small drop from the tip of Vincent's ear—" She quivered with delight at the mere suggestion of the memory.

"A son? You have stolen a son from me?" The stone front that masked my servitude cracked.

Too long had the sidhe wrapped herself in the cloak of security afforded her by my love for Elizabeth. She had grown careless and unwary. Somber greys and deep purples from the wet canvas still stained my hands as I grasped her throat. The stunned fear in the eyes of the hunter stoked my fury. Her wager had not foreseen my willingness to end the possibility of my reunion with my wife to protect my son. The iron upon my finger sizzled in her downy skin. The band leeched the magic that would have allowed her to dissolve the human form in which she had locked herself and flee my grasp. "You stole my son! You had no right."

Struggling against my grip, she rasped, "We are not thieves. We pay the price of every drop we drink."

"And a newborn child? What bargain can he have possibly struck in his innocence? You will take me back now, or, by God, I will destroy you, all else be damned!"

Throttled in my fingers, her laugh gurgled. "You can never go back—a piece of your soul is there now. It found a new home in the child you fathered. That door is now closed to you."

Confusion subdued my rage. Brann Sidhe melted from my grasp and reappeared, shimmering, behind me. She clamped her palm upon my chest and planted there the end of my story.

That realm had attracted a wandering shard of my infinite soul into the body of Marie Clémentine's son. Maurice, she called the child and gave him the name of another painter—Utrillo.

"I have seen this story. As the boy, you will wander, lost, from alcohol to asylum, from the stability of your mother's hearth in the country to the studios of Paris. The images of sorrow and serenity that clash in the mind of this child will torture your life until your mother, in desperation, places the brush in your hand, to paint, for a bargained few years, in white, the images of life and home unattainable."

My fingers, bereft of Brann Sidhe's neck, sought refuge in the locks of my hair. "What do you want? What is the price to free him?"

"You must not love Elizabeth well enough, Ethan, to risk the iron." Rarely did I witness an emotion other than satiation in the face of the muse. For a brief flash, no longer than a mere blink, her petal features cracked and revealed the hissing anger of a snake. "Do you not fear that if I cease to exist, the power that gives her this second life vanishes with me? Would you lose her after so few years? I thought you fashioned of more sturdy sentiment."

"I would sacrifice us both here, to save our child there."

"Then you love yourself more than you love her." The muse fluttered to my ear. A rare sentiment of jealousy tinged her serenity. She played the jilted lover well. My attempt to snuff her out had shaken her deeply. "Think beyond your puny existence here, boy. Have I not instructed you in the layers of life? The baby is you. You passed through the tubers under the hill into that realm because your dust had not yet entered its gates. But now a shard of you is there in the flesh of the boy. You will be, in that plane, her son—as you are in others her teacher, her slave, her brother. She will love you as a son with the same devotion she loved you as a husband. And she will put the brush in your hand."

"I am her son? But how is that possible if I fathered this child?"

"You never truly inhabited the realm you visited that night. Once you left, after fashioning with Marie such a lovely clay refuge, a splinter of your fractured soul, wandering upon the winds under the hill, found refuge there. My chattel, you are mine—everywhere, in all your infinite fragments, to sell, if I choose—until our bargain is fulfilled."

There was no chair. My knees buckled as the implications of what I had sold to this muse wrapped their thorny limbs about my mind. The wooden floor, washed into the grey of twilight, offered a cold seat for my infinite tragedy.

"Do not fret, boy." I braced for the blow to come. "She will not be alone, seeking without finding love. He is late, but he will be there."

Bewildered, I stepped foot into her trap. "Who?"

"Jackson. He is always there." The iron jaws of her snare snapped shut. "And you, my dear Ethan, will bring him to her." Her tongue, inhuman, shimmering, and smoky, brushed my ear as she spoke. "André, they will call him, and he will give her what you cannot."

Hunched over my knees, I felt the transformation behind my back. Warily, Brann Sidhe allowed the solidity of her feigned humanity to reemerge, the better to taste the acrid fruits of her sowing. "Perhaps you will hate again now—for the sake of your love." Her lips brushed the bowed stem of my neck.

Shadows encrusted the room. Groping, I found the brush. Weighted with the throngs of my enslaved existences, I painted in blackness.

Chapter 14

Jackson Richards was a fool. An apt name for a man who would trade Elizabeth's love for the rush of a battle and a medal of valor. In 1860, the talk of a southern rebellion and the preservation of the Union blinded him, or perhaps it was the easy familiarity between the two of them. The whole town had always assumed that Elizabeth would go with Jackson wherever he went. When their paths diverged, the gossips in quiet drawing-room corners blamed her liberal education at the Young Ladies' Academy of Philadelphia.

As the socialites watched the bond between Elizabeth and her childhood sweetheart sag, I slipped in to pick up the slack, showering her with lavish gifts and remarkable attention. Within months the drawing rooms changed the tune they hummed. But I would not say that the notes were altogether harmonious. Bath's elite looked with suspicion upon me, an Irish recluse that had invaded their well-ordered society and stolen a gem from the heart of one of their own sons.

From the lengthening shadows along the edges of the veranda of the Richards' Pennsylvania estate, I waited for Elizabeth to arrive. A small boy scampered about the lawn lighting torches. The musical notes of violins and flutes twittered from the gazebo, through the trees, and onto the veranda. White satins and shiny buttons glowed buttery beige in the lowering sun as guests filed past to congratulate Jackson on his commission in the army and to wish him farewell before he reported to his first post at Fort Sumter.

Beneath the columned porch, Elizabeth hugged Jackson's mother and then moved down the receiving line to the boy who had so muddled things between the two of them by growing up. His eyes smiled when she presented her hand, and he dutifully brushed his lips across her fingers, lingering a bit too long for my taste. Together they mourned the swirling winds of political turmoil that had ruptured their love. The evening breeze carried Elizabeth's voice into the shadow of the leaves where I waited. "What words must I utter to convince you to stay, Lieutenant Richards?"

My eyes narrowed, even though I knew that she only lamented Jackson's departure the way a young woman would drop a sentimental tear for an old ragdoll sent out with the trash. It isn't the doll, but the substance of the memories sewn into the fibers that she grieves.

Jackson smiled down at her, hardly bothering to hide the rumblings of desire that passed between them. From his vantage point, a foot or more above her head, his eyes fell past her turned-up nose and dropped, momentarily, straight into the gentle slope of her cleavage. The low-cut, lacey bodice barely served its purpose.

"I fear, Elizabeth, mere words have no power over the call of duty, God, and country. Are there words with such power to compel you to accompany me?"

Her eyes crinkled. "If I follow you, who will care for the hungry and poor of Bath? God fashioned my hands for sturdier work than hanging from your arm at military balls." Dropping her head against the young officer's chest, she reached from tiptoes and threw her arms about his neck.

I smiled. I had plucked her from the turbulence that had unmoored and carried her away from Jackson's affections.

More guests in stiff blue uniforms poured onto the porch, curled and laced wives bouncing on their arms. The greeting line pressed Elizabeth to tear herself away. Jackson relinquished her waist, but his hand caught hers as she stepped aside. Her palm lingered in his while his smile met the oncoming guests.

Stepping into the fading light, I slipped my fingers into her free hand and drew it through my arm. She turned her gaze to the smile in my green eyes. A being trapped somewhere in my middle danced to life as she followed my lead into the twilight of the garden. Could she feel it, the silent chemistry that bubbled between us?

Torches quivered in their glass cages. "I love to watch the flames at night—so alive, light shrouded in shadows." Her fingers reached to touch the magic but stopped just short of the burn.

The flaming undulations mirrored the raging in my chest. "The rising passion of discovery and the descent into the despair of failure." My breath caressed her naked shoulder, and she shivered in the warm night air, turning so that the sprigs of lavender woven into her honey-blond ringlets tempted my nose.

She spoke to my profile. "You should be an artist."

Laughing ruefully, I stepped back, weighing my response. The warm gentleness of her fingers found mine and coaxed to my tongue secrets I had never shared. "My parents were artists. My mother painted as you do. My father was a poet." Perhaps, having denied my soul the art it craved, I found in the creative flair oozing about Elizabeth an elixir to quench my thirst.

"Ah, to bring beauty into the world. This is life." The moonlight reflected in the pale skin of her face when she turned to confront me. "Mr. McCarthy, to find a gentleman of your culture, science, and wealth engrossed in the vulgar magic of alchemy, I must confess, leaves me somewhat astonished and dismayed. I imagined you engaged in a more philanthropic pursuit—medicine, electricity—something more beneficial to the common good of mankind than the fashioning of gold from lead."

"That is only a side effect, Elizabeth. What I seek is something of much greater value. Life, the quintessence of being. I seek the perfection of elemental matter."

"So, you desire not to be rich, but to live forever? I find that hardly more noble a cause. Of what use is immortality in a world of pain, sorrow, and conflict? Better, it would seem, to live briefly and beautifully and be done with it, than extensively and beggarly."

Silence hung between us. My eyes tightened as I struggled against the lines of mourning that her words had conjured. Her smile faded into bewilderment.

"Forgive my reticence. I do not often speak of the misfortunes that led to my choice of occupation—indeed, one might call it an obsession. A heart such as yours, so full of compassion, will surely find its way to the path of sympathy." I wasn't sure I could voice the words, but pushed forward against the swarm of emotions pricking at my heart. "When I was nine, I watched my brother die of smallpox. By the time I was seventeen, I had seen both my parents waste away from…natural causes." I turned my face toward the shadows in the garden orchard. "I have had quite enough of watching the souls I love slip through my fingers."

Moved by my burdens of sorrow, Elizabeth lent a consoling hand to my shoulder. The featherweight of her touch brought my face back to hers. Her fingers drifted to my neck, her thumb caressed my cheek, drawing from me the sense of loss. My pain wrung from the depths of her compassion a balm that I needed to heal the wounds of loss and live again.

Pinpricks of light, liberated from the dampening rays of the sun, began to pierce the blackening sky. The scent of pine dust mingled with her lavender. The path was deserted. The guests had all found their way back to the lighted lawn and their assigned dinner seats.

My hands found the bare skin below the curve of her neck. She inhaled the rush of our touch. My body rippled with it as I folded her naked shoulders in my arms.

With no ring, no flowers, no offering in my hands, I wanted something from her. The space between us was full of the wanting. It seemed the air was not quite thick enough, and I struggled to find enough of it to sate the pounding demands of my heart.

A ruby bracelet, one of my many gifts, slipped down her wrist. Her hand trailed away from my neck onto the silver buttons of my vest. Her forehead creased as she bit her lip. Indecision flitted across her face.

The voice of eternity whispered through the breeze. To me, the message was clear. Why couldn't Elizabeth hear it? I eased her shoulders forward so that she either had to turn her cheek to rest on my chest or lift her chin to answer the unspoken question lingering on my lips. Her gaze rose to the full, selfishly generous offerings of my mouth.

Our lips found each other, and in the taking of my rush of ardor, hers flowed back to me. Sliding my fingers softly across her back, I drew her into the crush of my arms. The demand of my mouth moved on hers, soft and open, and I breathed her in before setting her free.

Through open lips, she gasped at the night air. Resting my chin on her hair, I felt our oneness resonate. The rise and fall of my chest cradled her cheek.

I gazed up at eternity in the skies and felt it secured in the embrace of my arms. "From the moment a fistful of dirt left my hand and sprayed the coffin of my father, my every breath and desire I have devoted to finding the key to immortality—the weapon with which to strike a blow at the Grim Reaper herself. But, Elizabeth, now I know that to live is to love you." Bending my head,

I took her face in my hands, lifting her chin. "To live forever means nothing unless it is to be with you."

Her lashes fluttered. "Ethan McCarthy, I am at a loss to tell if I love you or if I only love being loved by you." Standing on tiptoes, she sealed herself to me with a kiss, deep and giving.

"Let me love you forever, Elizabeth."

Forever? I was a fool and I did not know it.

She took my hand and led me back down the path to dinner.

Dearest Elizabeth,

This dream of two halves joined, these poignant deep colors Brann Sidhe paints across the dark canvas of my sleep in the night, every night, as endlessly as we creep from one existence to the next.
Why?
So that in the morning, the gripping, searing darkness of its absence stabs my soul, bleeding out the stark poison of lament through the strokes of my brush.
And then she feeds.

Save me, Elizabeth,
Ethan

PART 2

Most Cherished Elizabeth,

In September of 1962, Brann Sidhe, through the machinations of her kind, skirted the laws of time and defied the decrees of the Barrow to return your soul to the living in this realm where you had previously walked. The moment the body of flesh you wore cried out, I felt your return ripple through the affluence of beings caged within me. Your parents bestowed the name Sara Elizabeth on you. Seventeen years later, I freed the boy within me and called him Elliot. To him, fell the momentous task of winning again the heart of the woman, now a girl of his own age, for whom we had groveled for a century in the service of the muse.

What was it like to throw back the contents of the elixir and step into the boy I had once been? I wish that I could tell you, Elizabeth. When I stepped into the body of my seventeen-year-old self, I became nothing more than an inkling of a future to come. This young version of me shared none of the memories of what I had experienced beyond his age.

When I walked back into being, Elliot's memories, laden with the tiny twitches of Sara Elizabeth's face—your new face— whispered the meaning of his memories, memories of what the boy had lived but would never be able to decipher.

Forever Yours,
Ethan

Chapter 15
—Excerpts from the unfinished manuscript of Ethan McCarthy

Elliot scraped the point of a pocket knife through damp mud, glancing back and forth from Sara Elizabeth's profile to his sketch. Sara tossed a crumb of bread to a thin female duck floating forlornly in the pond. A mob of competitors converged on the soggy chunk. Snatching up the prize earned the lonely hen a frenzied thrashing. Elliot shooed away her attackers with a willow stick and then bent his head back to his primitive art.

With dryer dirt, he highlighted the streak of vibrant red in the dyed black of Sara's asymmetrical haircut. Three diamond earrings glimmered in her right lobe. The diamond on her finger was a lonely spark of light that glimmered beyond her black painted nails. Elliot knew the stone well. Sara had "inherited" it from a distant relative in Ireland. But Elliot knew from my journal that this was the diamond Brann Sidhe had used to harvest my wife's soul over one hundred years ago. Elliot was too young to have ever met Elizabeth, the woman for whom I, 'his father,' had fractured our soul into so many pieces. But if her soul was the same that animated Sara, he could definitely relate. This girl gushed through his veins and flooded his dreams like the art that he could only dam up by stopping his heart.

"Sorry I was so late. I would have called, but—'Sara Elizabeth, nice girls don't call boys'. Sara was a thespian of blossoming talent. The fairly accurate impression of her mother's chastising voice pierced Elliot's concentration and curved the corner of his lip. It was all the encouragement the aspiring actress needed. Her left eyebrow arched above the gleam of conquest in her eye and smile of the vanquisher on her lips. He'd captured that image on more than one canvas.

Sara's mother was more of a prude than a Victorian spinster. To Elliot, it seemed her child-rearing philosophy consisted of only one prime directive: whatever the cost, Sara must reach the altar worthy of the spotless, white dress she wore. Perhaps the fate of Sara's older sister had spawned their mother's vigilance. The promising and talented young vocalist had succumbed to a handsome face and a fast car, become pregnant, abandoned scholarship, degree, and career, married, and given birth to two children before she was twenty. With no money or time to pursue her dreams, they had wilted on the dead vine. Regardless of its origins, Sara's mother's profile perfectly matched the maternal vigilance required to suit Brann Sidhe's designs and thwart my own. The witch would grant me no quarter.

Twisting the ring on her finger, Sara grinned wickedly, "I'm not such a nice girl." In a mischievous pout, she offered him her lips. He dropped the knife and cradled the nape of her neck so that his mouth could taste the silky curves that he craved in his sleep. He could draw those lips from memory. Sara allowed the indulgence— a subtle, rebellious strike against the rigid puritanism of her parents that both sheltered and suffocated her at once.

The exotic make-up and the seductive darkness of her role as one of the three stones in the matinee performance of *Eurydice* bled from her lips into his. As quickly as she had offered them, she took them back and frowned at the smudges his passion left on her portrait. Elliot could not help but feel that he was nothing more than a supporting actor in the scenes of subtle, adolescent rebellion that Sara staged against her throttled upbringing. When they were together, she played her role well—the adoring, affectionate girlfriend. But when they kissed, his lips whispered eternity while hers only hinted at a prelude.

"I got my gown."

Ever unsated, Elliot picked up the knife again, scratching at the damp, trodden soil that he'd mangled with his hand. "For the prom? I'm sure it's gorgeous, but it will probably wilt off your shoulders because it pales next to your beauty."

Sara giggled at his prose. Deep inside the recesses of his mind, where his memories lingered when the boy disappeared, Elliot wondered if she loved him or just his art. He didn't really care.

"Not the prom. Graduation. Class of 1980? You're such a space cadet sometimes." She leaned closer to distract his eyes to hers. "Cap and gown? Who wears a 'gown' to the prom?"

"I can't help it. My dad's from an old aristocratic Irish family. Sometimes he uses old words. It's contagious."

Sara tossed a stone into the pond. The ripples bobbed the ducks floating in their path. "I don't want to be gorgeous for the prom. I want to be otherworldly—and just a bit threatening."

Snorting, he sculpted out the line of hair that bounced around her face. "That won't be hard. Sometimes I think you're not human. You're a demon that's put a spell on me so that you can use me for your pleasure and then rip my heart out and eat it."

"I'm sure I will." She pursed her lips insolently and brushed an imperious finger through her hair. "At least, your short life will have been exotic." She favored him with one more brush of her lips. Like Marie Clémentine, this reincarnation of Elizabeth possessed a brazen streak, buried and suppressed by her society and religious molding, that boiled within and, from time to time, bubbled to the surface. Had it not wandered the veins of the Elizabeth I knew and wooed? Had it been so suppressed by her nurturing and milieu that I had failed to even sense it? Without doubt, the leanan sidhe that stalked me had sniffed it out and, as is the way of her kind, had gloated and exploited my ignorance.

Tossing the knife, Elliot caged Sara in his arms, determined to savor every moment of his death sentence. "I wish you weren't going away to school." Sara said nothing, but wriggled from his grasp. "I could come with you."

Leaning over, she admired her portrait. Even at seventeen, the scent of the artist hung heavily on Elliot. He wondered if it wore off onto Sara because she hung around him, or if she hung around him because it attracted her the way it drew the Leanan Sidhe. "It looks just like me, only a little wilder."

"Listen, Sara," Elliot laced his fingers into hers. "I could come with you. We'll hardly see each other for a couple of years." To this boy, two years without Sara Elizabeth stretched on, in his innocent imagination, like an interminable desert.

Sara turned her shoulders and stared distantly past the pond, towards the mountains on the horizon. Reaching for his hand, she let her fingers slide up his wrist to the silver bracelet she'd bestowed on him along with her first kiss. "It says FOREVER. College is only a few years. You'll hardly even miss me. Besides, you'd be miserable at a religious school. You won't even come to church with me."

He shrugged. He couldn't enter churches. His "father's" journals made that clear. The mark of bondage Brann Sidhe had imprinted upon my shoulder forbade it. My younger versions bore no testimony of my oath, but they lived by its terms.

"Just promise me you won't waste all those brains of yours running off and getting married in your freshman year."

Sara's mouth dropped open. She huffed indignantly, one fist on her hip. "What are you trying to say, Elliot? That I'm going to turn out like my sister? Real nice." She stood up and pointed a finger at her chest to punctuate. "I'm studying three languages because I want to see the world. And I want a career. I don't know what yet, but I feel it in me, and I'm not going to stop until I get there." Turning her back on him, she stomped her lace-up boots down the narrow path that led to the lower park. Man-high Oleanders stained with pink blooms fenced in the dirt trail.

Elliot pocketed the knife and hustled to follow her footprints until she was close enough to hear him. "We could do Europe together."

"Oh, yeah, brilliant. 'Hey, dad, my boyfriend and I are going backpacking around Europe for the summer.' Maybe I should just announce it in Sunday School."

Elliot had nothing to say to that. Sara's dad was having trouble condoning his daughter's choice of companion to the Senior Prom, in a hotel. He would have much preferred she'd chosen to accompany a young man from their congregation. Sara was not alone in choosing a university that would separate their paths. She turned her shoulders and stared distantly up the dirt trail to the disappearing edges of the pond.

Tangling her fingers in Elliot's, she sculpted her lips into something between a pout and secret grin. "I'm the one that should be worried. You're gorgeous and smart; girls love you. They'll hunt you down and, before your first semester ends, I'll just be some girl you used to know in high school. You'll be able to have whatever girl you want." Her words released the latches on the flimsy hooks she'd woven into his heart without breaking and ripping them out.

But he would not be freed. "There's only one girl I want."

The intensity in his eyes caught her breath. She laughed it off. "Yeah, for now!" She wandered toward the playground. "That's what I love about you, Elliott. You know what you want and go get it." Sara trailed her hand along the sharp, thin blades of the hedge. "I don't know what I want. I think, maybe, to go to France, take a backpack, sleep on the train—"

"*I* want you." In two long strides, he'd caught up with her and wrapped his arms around her waist. She squirmed, giggling, and he swept her up over his shoulder and carried her down the stone steps as she squealed. Clearly, it pleased her to be the object of such soul-consuming passion.

In the clearing below, he set her on the grass. She left her arms around his neck, and he lay next to her, two lines askew, their lips the point of intersection. This season of her kisses was for him the torrential storm—lightning, thunder, driving winds—that broke the lulling monotony of blue, summer skies drenched in sun. He would not see that the darkness of the skies brought the deluge of separation that would drown his love and leave him bobbing helplessly in a hollow craft.

Dearest Elizabeth,

As Elliot, I could feel what was happening but refused to see it. Of course, I refused. I was seventeen and in love. Locked forever in immaturity, I would never understand that you couldn't breathe. You loved my adolescent arms around you, but they were part of a bubble you were outgrowing.

In the twilight of the full moon, when I reemerged as my adult self to fulfill the terms of the bargain with my mistress, I knew. Elliot's memories told me that the boy I had been had lost you— again.

And so, I sent Elliot away. As far as you knew he went to a university across the continent. The winds of distance blew away the memories that had only cluttered the surface of your young heart, like leaves fallen from a tree with no roots. You called once, in the early days, but never wrote. I did not expect you to. With Elliot, you had only played at love. Your restricted globe had dwarfed everything in it, including the murmurs of destiny. You wanted the wide, wild world. Only there would you hear the full-throated tenor of fate.

Undaunted, I gave you the space you craved and then called upon a part of me that knew you well. Having forged the way once before, he was sure to know the path to your heart. But, my dear, marred and jaded by my hundred years of servitude, I wondered if I could woo a soul as light and whimsical as yours.

Forever,
Ethan

Chapter 16

A tiny gasp of pleasure escaped Brann's lips. "It's you! How I've missed you, my sweet."

Of course, she missed the twenty-two-year-old version of me. The young man had watched Elizabeth die and agreed to the muse's bargain. She missed him the way a cat misses the raw meat of a fresh kill.

While I played the role of "father" in Brann Sidhe's century-long charade, truly the obsessions of this version of me had fathered the man I had become. It was nearly a decade after my wife died before my 22-year-old self, after contracting our bargain, had aged enough to become one of my younger versions and disappeared into our subconscious. After that, he lay dormant, wallowing in the pain of loss, while our younger versions swirled about him, clamoring for another shot at their dreams.

I speak of myself as *we* and *our* because age fractured and broke inside of me. No more whole, the ages within vied for hours of life, man against boy and child against adult. A century later, the first sight to greet the eyes of my 22-year-old self, after so many years of hibernation, was our elegant tormentor, lounging in her purple chair.

Springing from her perch, fairly twitching with delight, Brann's fingers caressed the unblemished flesh of the man she had pried from the iron-jawed latches of her sister's trap. The flood of a century of memories from all my younger versions rocked him on solid ground. As he teetered, the sidhe, overcome with lust, breathed in deeply the thick scent of sorrow that hung about him, sank to her knees, and buried the tip of her lily-white nose in the flesh below his navel. Her pink tongue tickled the hairs peeking from the rim of his jeans, slung low on the body that was, evidently, a bit trimmer than my present day's. He shivered and stiffened at the same time. Brann's presence revolted him, but his skin answered the magic in hers.

She trailed her lips up his torso until his senses emerged and he shoved her back. Brann fluttered away to devour the sight of him from a safe distance. The charm of her siren voice wrung the ire from the despair in which he had marinated for so long.

"My dearest, I shall call you Easton, for you have returned to me from the dawn of our love affair."

"Love affair? Is that what you call this demented captivity? Slaves do not love their masters, benevolent or malevolent, it makes no difference."

"But I am no master. I am love itself. Is not art the most sublime expression of love? And do I not inspire yours?"

"Elizabeth inspires my art. That is love."

"As you say, love." She smiled seductively and wiped the corner of her purple mouth.

"Where are we? Why has he brought me here?" Easton demanded, surveying the Victorian opulence of the room. Wherever they were, Brann had sold one of our paintings to furnish the house to suit her taste for somber colors and heavy, ornate wood. Carved grapes and leaves shimmered down at them from the moldings on the ceiling.

"We have followed Sara Elizabeth to Utah. She fancied a university education at a good Christian school."

"She's back? You kept your bargain?"

"Easton, my pet, you offend me. The Leanan Sidhe always keep their word. You know this."

A quick flash of memory from the boy Elliot told him that Brann Sidhe had played her cards well. She had reincarnated Elizabeth's soul into the body of a baby born to a stanchly religious family. Clever fiend. Brann Sidhe would wring dry every second of her 50-years wager.

"When are we, then? How old is she now?"

The muse floated to the desk on the far side of the sun-drenched studio where Easton had appeared. She moaned. "Ah, your questions bore me. Look inside the memories. It's the young Ethan, your 18-year-old self, who seems to quite enjoy this university life of fast vehicles and beautiful girls. Of course, he never knew Elizabeth, so he has none of the bitter taste of tragedy I so crave.

But he has such a zest for living—." She breathed deeply at the memory of Easton's younger self. Touching a finger to her throat, she sighed.

Easton didn't have to search far to know that the year was 1981, this was January, and Sara Elizabeth was 18-years-old. From deep inside, he felt the irritated annoyance of the ambitious, life-guzzling 18-year-old he had supplanted. The whelp wanted out again.

The long mirror across the room caught his eye. "She'll recognize me, you know. I am not that much different than the boy we called Elliot."

She waved away the obvious flaw in her scheme. "Cut your hair. Wear glasses. Grow a bit of stubble." The idea pleased her. She ran a finger across Easton's jaw and above his lips. He felt the prickle of whiskers bloom.

"Still—"

"Is it sheer stubbornness, my love—"

"I'm not your love."

"—that you dwell in ignorance? The leanan sidhe's first power is glamour. I wield it like a child brandishes a toy. Glamour created and nurtures this beauty you see before you. Once learned, it becomes second nature. We paint reality in glamour as easily as you paint a white canvas. She will not know you." She tapped her lips and then raised a finger in clarification. "Perhaps she will shiver with a rumbling of familiarity. Like paint, glamour molds only the surface. A love like yours burrows deep into the fibers of your being. But not to worry. I would not jeopardize our game. She will not know you."

"It's been so long. Why did he bring me back?" Easton sank into Brann's purple chair.

She sighed. "Your questions bore me, my sweet." From the desk, Brann lifted a heavy, leather journal and placed it in his hands. The writing on the pages he recognized as his own, the words not at all:

> *I am splintered. My younger selves grow ungovernable, each seeking his pleasure and losing sight of the prize. Perhaps though, I have always been thus. It is this singleness of purpose that won me Elizabeth—and lost her as well. But, the voices.*

How they clamor so loudly within my consciousness. This is surely madness—

The witch watched with such gluttonous anticipation as Easton perused the pages that he could hardly doubt we had played once more into her trap. But how could we hope to thwart an immortal beast who knew so well the intricate workings of our soul? In the final written entry, I left him a message:

You know what it is to lose her. For you, it is not a distant, faded memory. The crusted crimson of her blood stains your nails, the sweet, saltiness of her sweat, you taste on your lips. Your cheek remembers the imprint of her fingers. You will not lose her again. You won't allow it, having paid the price of her loss from your own wallet.

Chapter 17

The lowering sun sulked red on the horizon when Easton drove his yellow Porsche into the parking lot of the Centennial Arms apartments. Half-melted snow mounds hovered over the mud-splattered grass squares between the concrete walks. A nipping breeze ushered out the day.

The door to his new apartment swung open without a key. He stepped into a spartan living space furnished with boxy wooden couches, chairs, and tables. A scrawny red-head on the sofa watched a Flock of Seagulls music video on MTV. He nodded. "Hey, bro', you the new roomie?"

"Yeah. Easton." He settled on the name Brann Sidhe had uttered when she saw him.

"Nick."

I had chosen Nick as his roommate because no scent of the artist plagued him. Brann Sidhe posed no threat here. Trash overflowed the container, dishes spilled over the brim of the sink, multi-textured crumbs littered the counters. The faucet dripped. Nick nodded toward the hallway. "First room on the left. Your dad left your stuff in there."

The windows of his quarters looked over the courtyard that encompassed a pool, sloppy gardens, and crisscrossed, cement paths. His view gave directly into the stairwell of the opposite building. Although my thoughts were a mystery to him, my intentions were clear. Sara lived in the building directly opposite.

His elbows on the window sill, he stood for quite a long moment as the knowledge of his younger selves, stored up as memories, sculpted the new world in which he found himself. The changes staggered his world views. The industrial revolution had been well underway the last time he had walked in the flesh. Now, it was fully grown and had moved on to a technical revolution. On the modest, pox-scared desk, next to a streamlined telephone, sat a plastic box and keyboard that the memories of young Ethan informed him were a personal computer, a cutting-edge development.

A young woman in tall black boots and a black leather jacket appeared on the stairway opposite him and froze all the musing in its tracks. Although the styles of the period sat heavily on her so that Easton might not have recognized the honey-color of her hair and the well-proportioned features, he knew her immediately. The soul speaks on hidden wavelengths heard only by the heart. This was his Elizabeth in new skin. The soul of the woman he'd loved, over and over again, had shaped the face. Every fractured, sleeping fragment of him woke with longing to the resonance of her voice emanating from a flesh called Sara Elizabeth Vale. His palms gripped the window sill to steady his knees. They seemed to have vanished at the vibrating of long-dormant threads.

Sara Elizabeth, too, stopped abruptly on the last step and grabbed the railing. She scanned the courtyard. The moment her eyes settled upon the window behind which Easton stood, another tenant, a guitar slung over his shoulder, bounded down the steps and wrapped his free arm around her waist, carrying her down to the bottom. The spider threads that bound Easton and Sara snapped. She giggled and threw her arms back around the musician's neck. Their bodies melded, dancing to music that eluded Easton behind the window pane.

Elizabeth had bled to death in Easton's arms. That moment consumed and defined the rest of his existence. To see her living and breathing, wrapped in the embrace of another, choked the ragged lump of his heart. The boyfriend's mouth guzzled the nectar of Sara's, for which Easton had so long languished for but a single drop. He couldn't breathe, he couldn't move. All thought abandoned him. A vortex of loss and wanting engulfed him.

What was I thinking? he wondered. *Could I not predict that the mere sight of the woman with whom he had lived in utter bliss for two years of his life, the woman for whom he had gambled his soul and sold his brush and canvas to a demon of darkness, would not paralyze him from soul to fingertips?* In that moment, he knew he could never approach her, never let one word fall from his tongue without risking an unchecked gush of the passion he had known. Even now, his hands trembled from the memory of his fingers tracing the curve from her breast to her waist, across the slope of her hip. Having devoured Elizabeth's intimate delicacies when she was his wife, how could he now content himself with the crumbs of a casual acquaintance? Impossible.

When the couple disappeared from the courtyard, Easton opened the fist clenched around his car keys. A drop of blood swelled, trickled, and fell to the ratty gray carpet. Without a word, he left the apartment, slamming the door shut behind him.

Chapter 18

The witch was waiting for Easton, languid in her plush armchair. Ignoring her, he beat a path to the carved sideboard stocked with a generous assortment of bottles. What he wanted was whiskey to numb the senses throbbing with memories of Elizabeth.

When he had thrown back a glass of something called Jack Daniels, he felt the presence of Brann Sidhe behind him. Her skin emanated hunger and passion for tragedy. The raw meat of his imagination dripped with blood. Of course, she couldn't resist. The cold tip of her nail scraped the nape of his neck. She inhaled and sighed. A film of contentment fell about the room but could not penetrate the hardened scales of his skin.

"You saw her, then?" The finger on her tongue lent her voice a slight lilt. A hint of gloating invaded her pity.

"—and her guitarist." Sinking into the wooden chair beside the bar, Easton dropped his face into his hands. He felt like one who had seen a ghost, and yet, feared that he was the ghost.

From behind his chair, the muse presented him with a paint-smeared brush. "Paint for me, Easton, my sweet. It's the only way to release the sting."

"Never again." He slapped the hand away from his face but felt only the wooden handle strike his skin. The brush clattered against the windows.

Brann sauntered to the glass and sighed. "You weren't astonished, love, were you? It's only natural. Sara is quite as lovely now as when she was your Elizabeth. And, that young musician, the guitarist—he shows promise." From her lips, she trailed her nail down her neck and into the delicate lavender tip of her exposed nipple.

Easton's ears pricked. If Brann's whim had settled on the guitarist, the boy would never be able to refuse her bargain. What man could love a mere mortal woman when offered the affections of the eternal muse? The field would be clear. Sara would be heart-broken and free falling. Easton would be there to catch her.

He recoiled abruptly. What had he become to even consider benefiting from the devastation that his mistress wreaked upon her victims? He was not naïve. He knew that his presence in her studio camouflaged the razor-sharp claws of the plush beast he served. But those she preyed on sought her out. They made their choice. To stalk the guitarist, with the intent of removing him from the field of Easton's struggle, that was different. He would be complicit in her deviltry.

The sidhe roamed the forest of his thoughts, her shadow hovered behind every sapling. "You don't even know the boy, Easton. He stands between you and your love." Her arms wrapped around his shoulders from behind, her lips nipping at his ear. "Sara is your destiny." The brush in her fist lay across his chest. "Paint for me. Paint for me and he will disappear from her arms, his image will fade from her thoughts. Paint for me."

The raven chains that encircled his arm burned, shuddering his soul. He had only to take the brush. Paint. It was in his blood. All obstacles between him and Sara would disintegrate under the touch of the sidhe. Sara Elizabeth was our right. We had earned her love with a century of servitude.

But no. We had not earned Sara Elizabeth's love. We had only redeemed the life we allowed Elizabeth to pawn—the collateral of her breaths had purchased this life of tumbling leaves we led. Easton could not—would not—deceive himself. That was the realm of the Leanan Sidhe.

Easton had been retired to the catalogue of younger versions. Elizabeth's soul had its life back. WE owed only one weekend a month to the witch until our wager should be won. The burden of that monthly offering rested with me. Easton resolved to never again lift a hand to serve the muse. He would not condone and profit from her thievery. In the decade he had painted for her, every stroke, every drop of paint, he'd abhorred. His hand had nurtured the demon and abetted her in the seduction of the young talent he brought to her door. It was after him that I must have grown weary of loathing and settled into inurement.

Breaking the muse's embrace, Easton stood, fleeing the oozing cajolery. "I will not. I will never again take up the brush in your service. And I will never become like you, sucking the life off of others to nourish myself."

She stepped forward as if to be certain she'd heard him properly. "What? You surprise me, my chattel. Is this honor? Integrity? I thought you were made of more passionate stuff. You would forfeit your love to shelter Sara's nameless, paltry musician from the muse? His contribution to the arts will not even merit a footnote; his music is barely palatable."

"Liar. You told me the boy had promise."

"All artists have promise in my hands."

"I am out of your hands. My time is done. Your wager is with the man I have become. You'll collect your monthly dues from him."

Brann's lily hands folded gently across her waist. Her irises flashed green in a face hardened to stone. Murder narrowed her eyes and lips. A chill rippled through the room.

As soon as her wrath sprouted, however, it died. The façade of fragile beauty reemerged and, with it, an errant flicker of diamond light. She smiled softly, tilting her head. The pointed toe of her feathered heels peeked out from the edge of her fluttering gown as she turned away.

"Yes. Yes. Of course, my pet. Perhaps you are right. It is too much to ask that you paint for me again. Your youth has not yet developed the pragmatism of your elder. You still suffer from your convictions."

Had Brann been angry, Easton might have felt more confident in thwarting her.

She settled herself into the armchair, sighed, and lolled one finger toward him. "Of course, I do have to nourish myself. That is the way of nature. Everything feeds on something less divine than itself. If you insist on starving me until Ethan returns, I'm afraid I may not be able to restrain my appetite. The young guitarist offers such a meager sip of tasteless gruel. One would hardly blame me if, famished beyond reason, I were to lick his bones dry."

Easton's stomach lurched. The revulsion rippled through his consciousness to the crowd huddled within. Possibly there is no greater abomination than to turn a man's altruism against him. Easton was trapped and the witch knew it. The blood boiled in his clenched fists. Brann was petty enough to suck the young guitarist dry just to spite him if he refused her. With a flick of her wrist, a pen appeared in her hand. "I have a craving for letters, Easton. Perhaps you could see your way to writing your unrequited love."

His feet would not move. To touch the pen was to sign a contract of servitude. For as long as Sara loved her musician, Brann would stalk him, unless Easton sated her ravenous hunger, scribbling the words she craved. There was really no choice. In three strides, he had crossed the wooden planks, snatched the pen from her hand, and secured his tattered honor with his bondage.

Dear Elizabeth,

 The moment Easton took up the pen, his nights became a gluttony of visions of Sara Elizabeth. Brann Sidhe walked his dreams, flooding them with vignettes—Sara's lost loves, her academic triumphs, her insecurities and secret desires. In the morning, drowning in images, he grasped at the pen, a floating oar in a turbulent ocean of wanting and needing. The poor boy had not the callouses that time and torture had granted me over the decades. He still felt deeply and bled his words onto the page. To his clenched fist, I now confide the telling of our tale in our roles as Sara Vale and Easton Ravenscroft.

   Yours,
   Ethan

Chapter 19

—Excerpts from the unpublished writings of Easton Ravenscroft

Sara Elizabeth and her roommate Margaret spread mayonnaise over rows of bread slices laid out on the massive chrome counter and then slapped a slice of cheese onto every other one. The kitchen of the Food and Care Coalition rattled and clanged halfway through the lunch hour. The babble beyond the double metal doors confirmed that the clientele today was larger than projected. The donated sack lunches were gone and some of the volunteers had been pressed into service to raid the storage room and refrigerators for tuna and cheese.

"Can you take these out to the tables?" Sara's roommate pushed a large serving platter stacked with tuna sandwiches into her arms. Margaret's dark, curly locks bobbed in her face when she leaned close to Sara's ear. "And while you're out there, check out the total fox serving in the soup line."

Sara rolled her eyes. Margaret was determined to repair the jagged rent the guitarist had left in her love life, but Sara was tired of the roller coaster, the ups and downs of falling in and out of love. And yet, there was this lonely meadow tucked deep inside in which she longed to stroll. She watched Margaret and her boyfriend Joe frolic there with a distant sense of envy.

Backing into the swinging door, she pivoted through. The line was still long and the faces longer. They followed her progress as she deposited the new tray on the crumbs of the empty one.

Sara glanced at the clock, hoping she'd be able to finish her volunteer hour in time to merge into the stream of traffic headed toward the humanities building and her 18th Century French Lit class. A large lock of her long wavy perm flopped languidly over her padded shoulder and dangled above the tray.

She had no intention of checking out the row of boys making small talk with the patrons as they served up ladles of canned soup to go with the sandwiches. But the sparkle of the gold coin, hanging on the chest of one of them, lured her. Her glance collided with the green-eyed gaze of a cliché dark stranger. It was a catch and release kind of stare. His eyes had, obviously, been hooked to her face with that starving look for a second or two until an empty bowl in front of his ladle yanked them away. She met his desperate regard for a fraction of a second before catching her breath and heading back to the kitchen.

"Have you ever seen anything like that?" Margaret demanded when she returned. "Totally addictive. Serious eye heroine."

"I have to admit, he was exceptionally good-looking."

"Gorgeous. Where has he been all semester?"

The door opened and the man in question walked in with an empty soup pot. Margaret gasped as he strolled over to the sink, set down the empty container, and then lifted a full one from the burners on the stove.

Sara's heart did a disturbing little dance, like butterflies in a hot jar. Reflexively, she primped her hair, but needn't have troubled herself. He walked by without a glance. She followed the silhouette of his receding form, mouth open, just a tad, wishing her mother had raised her to be one of those girls that chased boys and wondering what kind of girl got a boy like that.

The human masterpiece pivoted and leaned back to open the kitchen door. His eyes found Sara's again. He winked. A hairsbreadth later and she never would have seen it.

The door flapped closed behind him. Margaret and Sara stared wide-eyed at each other for a full two seconds before breaking into uproarious laughter.

He wasn't at the serving table when Sara carried in the last batch of cheese sandwiches. He probably had a class. She and Marg pulled off their aprons, excused themselves, and hopped into Sara's brown Toyota.

"You know, Margaret, all through high school I always wondered if any other boys would have liked me if I hadn't been so attached to Elliot."

Margaret snorted. "Oh, please!" She rolled down the window and waved her hand in the spring breeze. "Boys line up to date you."

"Yeah, and then they dump me." The guitarist affair was still a bit raw.

"Only one dumped you. It gnaws at you because it's your first time. And he didn't dump you. You just didn't want to put up with his douchebag crap." Glancing at her watch as Sara pulled into a parking spot, Margaret hauled her backpack from the back seat.

A car pulled into the space that crossed their path to the stairs. Three boys jumped out, laughing.

"Sara, look! Aren't those the guys from the soup kitchen? Too bad Mr. Gorgeous isn't with them."

Sara rummaged through the costume box in her brain for some brazen inhibition. "I'm going over there. How do I look?"

Margaret frowned. "You look better in my pants than I do. You have hips."

Before she had time to lose her nerve, she sauntered over to the group as they took the first stair up to campus. The air was still nippy even though they should have been well into spring. In California, they'd be breaking out the shorts and sandals about now. She pulled flirty, confident Sara from her bag of stage personalities.

"Hi! I saw you at the soup kitchen." Tipping her head, she flashed the redhead a smile. "I'm Sara."

"Nick."

"And—what's your friend's name, the one that isn't here?"

"Easton." The one word was clearly all the kid could manage in the face of her assault.

"I've never seen you before. Where do you all live, Nick?"

"In your apartment complex, across from the pool." He sounded a bit offended.

"Are you serious?"

"Yeah, I recognize you."

"Really? I know I've never seen your friend before. Is he your roommate?"

"Yeah. But he doesn't go out, much. He's a writer. I mean, he goes to school here. He started in January. But he doesn't go out, not with girls—not once this semester."

"Well," Sara leaned seductively close to his ear, her silver chain tapped the alligator logo on his polo shirt, "tell him I said 'hi' and not to be such a stranger."

The boy nodded and stumbled up the stairs.

It only took an afternoon for Nick to show up at their door wanting to know if Sara would go out with Easton. Mirth twinkled in her eyes. "Is he that shy?"

"I don't know. He doesn't talk to girls much. Can he pick you up at 6:00 for pizza next Saturday?"

"Yeah—wait—no. Darn! I have a sorority thing. Does he want to go with me?"

"Yeah!" The kid said it like maybe he wanted to go with her. She grinned. Her insides hadn't bubbled like this since she first met guitar boy. She hadn't been on a date since he stood her up to catch a concert with a buddy. The douche never even apologized. She kept seeing him at church and, every time, the scrape cracked open. But deep inside, she wondered if her ego was more broken than her heart. The boy had played her like she was just another guitar.

Chapter 20

Sara Elizabeth coughed, then sniffed. Tissue wads mined the floor around her bed. Her Friday due dates wouldn't wait while this spring cold torched her insides, but as soon as she looked down at her textbook, snot dribbled onto the page. She was running low on tissue. The ridges of her nose flamed pink and swallowing was torture. She was completely out of groceries and if she wanted to get some, she'd have to brave the snowstorm.

The doorbell rang. Wincing, she hauled herself out of bed to open it. A guy stood there with a vase of half a dozen roses and lavender in his hand. Her snot-congested brain struggled to figure out what he was doing on her porch.

"These are for Sara."

"Wow! Thanks!" She took them with the first smile on her face since the virus had infiltrated her bloodstream. For a moment, she didn't feel so grungy. She almost hugged the guy—which would have been a grave mistake considering she was infected.

Her first thought as she set the vase on the counter was the guitarist. He'd finally grown some sensitivity and sent flowers to apologize.

When she pulled the card from the envelop and read the note, her mouth dropped open, and even though she was standing alone in the room, embarrassment flushed her cheeks.

Feel better soon, Easton

Sara hadn't even properly met him. How did he know she had a weakness for all things lavender? An hour later, the doorbell rang again. The man himself stood on the porch with orange juice, chicken soup, and a box of tissues.

"Hope this isn't too forward, but I was stopping by to thank you for the invite and ran into Margaret. She said you were deathly ill. Thought I'd drop off a few essentials." He winked and her congested head swooned.

"That's so nice." Sara seriously wanted to cry. She hadn't felt all warm and fuzzy like slippers on the inside since she left her mom back home in California. And then she remembered the deplorable state of her hygiene. "I'd invite you in, but then you'd be sick, too. And—God, I'm so embarrassed that I look so bad."

He shrugged. "Your bad is everyone else's great. See you Saturday."

Oh, this was trouble—how she was longing for a little trouble.

Chapter 21

At precisely 6:00 pm, Sara's doorbell rang. Easton wore a black crewneck t-shirt under a grey cotton blazer with sunglasses propped on his head. His cologne had to be pheromone laced because the raw attraction made her want to ditch all her Sunday School training, drag him into her apartment, and rip the Ralph Lauren t-shirt right off of those chiseled abs. She wanted him so badly that she was afraid she would say the wrong thing, or he'd turn out to be some kind of crazy conspiracy theorist. Her whole body tingled with apprehension.

Even worse, Easton ushered Sara over to his yellow Porsche. Her dad was an English teacher with six kids. If she didn't have a scholarship and work three jobs in the summer, she couldn't afford the university. There was no way this guy was going to give her a second look after he found out who she was. She shook herself. The whole guitar boy affair had trashed her confidence.

"Have you been up to Sundance before?" Her finger twisted up a lock of hair as the blood buzzed her brain.

Easton turned the key and revved the engine. "Once or twice."

"Do you ski?" *Of course, he skis. Geez, Sara! He's loaded. What else would he do with all that money in Utah?*

"Some. I'm from California. I prefer the beach."

Thank you, God! The common thread wound between them. "Oh, yeah! Me too. I don't get the whole *drive up to the canyon with all this gear just to freeze your butt off riding a chair up the mountain and race back down* thing. I must not have the gene. Give me warm sand, sunshine, and a good book any day."

"I miss it," he paused to glance at her profile as the car zipped out of the parking lot, "everything about it." Sara needed that glance. Essentially, love is some mysterious formula of chemistry plus time wasted on a person. Between the chemistry that bubbled her blood and the flowers and chicken soup, she was falling fast.

The problem was, she didn't know Easton well enough to know if it was only happening to her. She hadn't put in the time yet. His glance filled in all the blanks.

They drove past the brick storefronts of old Main street to the freeway. The sultry notes of Sade's "Smooth Operator" seeped into the silence.

"Is that you? The Smooth Operator?"

"I wish." The sun was setting in orange taffy out his window. He pushed his glasses up. "Maybe when I was younger."

"So, Easton, what are you doing here? My parents and a scholarship sent *me* here, but you don't go to church—at least I never see you—so why would you come here to our good Christian school?"

"Uh," he bought a little time exiting onto the canyon road to Sundance. "My dad. After his, uh, wife, left him, he had to get out of California. Too many memories."

"Oh, I'm sorry." *Foot straight into mouth.* Reaching her hand to the console, Sara placed it sympathetically on his. She didn't expect the jolt that rattled her senses when their skin touched.

"You remind me of her." Once the words were out, he looked like he wished he hadn't said them. "You know, at the soup kitchen wasn't the first time I've seen you."

"Uh, oh. Should I be worried? Are you going to tell me you've been stalking me all year?" He took her seriously. "I'm joking." Sara pushed his shoulder with one hand and couldn't resist the temptation to let her fingers skim the thick dark curls at the nape of his neck. They both shivered and she mentally scolded herself for being so forward. But then, his hand captured hers as it fell. Their palms met like two planets falling into a dance of gravity. She wove her fingers into his. He brought them down to rest on the black console between them.

When she walked into the party with Easton—full-curved lips, thick, dark hair, and green eyes—she could practically see the other girls salivating.

They danced, and he looked at her as if he'd just returned to the mainland after a harrowing decade as a castaway on a remote, lost island. When little beads of sweat dampened their foreheads, Easton nodded toward the refreshment table. Breathless, Sara nodded back.

The room was full now. She waved at Margaret dancing with Joe as they passed. Marg mouthed "Oh, my God!" behind Easton's back. Her mouth hung open just a bit and Joe looked a little offended. "I know!" Sara mouthed back as they pushed through the crowd of dancers getting physical to Olivia Newton-John.

Easton and Sara found some reddish thing in a punch bowl. He sipped it and shrugged. "Punch."

"—alcohol got the Greeks banned at our good Christian school."

"Good Christian school." He chuckled, nodding. "You want to go outside?"

"Yeah." A few round tables surrounded the dance floor, but on the patio, little metal chairs and tables offered some privacy drenched in outdoor fire-pit flames and moonlight. "Let's go stand by the fire."

He grabbed her hand. *Serious déjà vu.* Whenever Elliot held Sara's hand, it felt like two halves of a circuit had just been completed. Maybe that was why she'd ripped through a fast string of boyfriends her freshman year. She hadn't found that mystic connection. What she felt with the guitarist was a cheap, dollar store knock-off in comparison.

They wandered onto the lodge balcony, into the crisp air. The moonlight streamed through the gap in the pines and illuminated the last patches of spring snow twinkling like small galaxies fallen to earth. Sara took his other hand in hers. "So, Easton, what is it you do all day long, hiding away in your apartment? I haven't seen you all semester."

He grinned, weighing his response. Whatever he was going to tell her was, obviously, not going to be the whole truth.

"I write. It's an illness. Don't worry, it's not contagious."

"You're a writer?" Sara's fingers twitched. Another artist. Figures. It was what she missed most about Elliot. The beginning painting class she had this semester had fulfilled her fine arts credits and released a caged part of her soul. "What do you write? Poetry? Short stories?"

He shrugged. That's what she found so attractive about him. He wasn't as impressed with himself as she was. Even though he was the hottest guy at the party, this odd sense of insecurity floated around him, like he was treading around rattlesnakes and she might leave him standing alone in the fray. Sara could only hope he was as smitten as she was. This kind of love was always a mixed drink of fear and wanting. "I'm working on my second novel. It's sort of a romance, but dark. My agent has a deal pending with some publishing house in New York."

"You have an agent? How old are you?"

"Twenty-two."

"Geez, I feel like a baby. I'm still eighteen—September baby." Sara leaned her elbow on the crisp wood railing and cradled her chin in her palm. She didn't know what she wanted from life. Easton was on his way to professional already. "So, who inspires you more, St. Exupéry or Camus?" Most of her dates stared back blankly when she mentioned names.

"I prefer the hint of romance in St. Exupéry. But why would you choose a couple of existentialists? I thought you were a good Christian at your good Christian school."

The silence in the darkness inspired confidence. The spring had not quite sprung and woken the gossips in the mountains. "Don't tell anyone," she stood on her tiptoes so that her lips touched his earlobe. "I think I might be an existentialist…and maybe even an atheist—although I like the romance of God."

He stepped back to look in her face and see if she was serious.

Sara's eyes narrowed in firm frankness. "I kind of agree that the only pursuit not absurd in life is creating connections—friendship, love. We're all lonely little vines, winding around each other, looking for something to cling to. There might be life after death, but I'm not banking on it."

"Sara Vale, you surprise me." The hint of a smile reassured her. He wasn't mentally flipping through his little address book for someone more worthy to date.

"Why? Are you a heaven and hell kind of guy?"

He sniffed and looked into the shadows beyond the balcony. "We all make our own hell. You don't have to die to get there."

"That's dark. Is that what creeps into your romance?"

"Probably."

"So, you think there's a soul?"

He nodded. "When I look at you, I do."

The full moon broke through the pines in ragged beams. Sara's heart pounded out a fight-or-flight beat. So strange how falling in love and deadly pursuit triggered the same physical responses.

Instead of crying out for help, her eyes fairly shouted, "Kiss me!" An icy spring breeze shivered along the tree branches. She snuggled up to his shoulder.

When he wrapped an arm around hers, his chest shuddered—or was that a shiver? Tilting his face away from the intensity locking their eyes, he seemed to be asking for permission in the stars. Tiny points of light peppered the dark canvas peeking through the pines. She could feel the strain of him holding back and the random thought occurred to her that he had a girlfriend back home.

The heavens must have answered his question. Looking down into her face turned up against his chest, he ran a finger along the edge of her hair. Taking a deep breath, he turned away. "What about you? What are you going to be when you grow up?"

"Ugh. I'm not sure." Unsettled, she stepped away from the moment and leaned on the railing. "I like the idea of teaching. I thought I would teach elementary school, but the classes they offer here are remedial. I switched to secondary French and English— and I want to go to Europe. I guess I want to see more of the world before I decide what to do in it."

"It's more fun *with* someone. Believe me."

"Oh? And with whom did you see the world?"

He choked a little on a sip of his punch. When he blanched, Sara wondered if she'd hit an exposed, raw nerve.

"I see! Now the recluse's secret past comes out." She was teasing, but just a little nervous. This was the first time, in a long time, she'd felt an attraction that could give birth to a life of its own. She didn't want it to die in the womb. The connection was so deep, it scared and intoxicated her, made her feel alive.

"No one—uh—I was by myself most of the time and wished I could share the landscape and the food with someone."

"Uh-huh."

"God, you are way too gorgeous."

So then, why aren't your lips on mine?

He pulled his arm away and tugged her back toward the open hall. "Come on, you're freezing. Let's get our coats."

They wound their way home. The euphoria of the *best date ever* lulled Sara into dozing on Easton's shoulder as he navigated the curves of the canyon road. Snuggled up with the oneness of a perfect fit, Sara floated away into the oblivion of love unchained.

The car slowed. The tires crackled on the gravel along the shoulder. The emergency brake crunched.

She sat up, startled. "What's the matter, Easton? Tired?"

"No. I can't stand it anymore. You're so beautiful. I can't sit this close to you and not have you."

He leaned across the seat and Sara wrapped her arms around his neck. His eyes asked and hers answered. Their heads tilted and eased forward until his lips barely sipped at the curve of hers. His whole body relaxed beneath her like he'd been waiting stretched on a rack for ages and the touch of her mouth sprang the locks. His hand wandered to her neck and their lips slow-danced in the dark. His fingers explored the curves of her back and tangled themselves in her hair. Their bodies synced in rounded rhythms of desire. Sighing, Sara immersed herself in the flood of his wanting. His hand slid beneath her shirt.

Reluctantly, drawing his lip after her, she pulled away. "Too fast," she whispered. "I'm already fudging on my *no kissing until the third date* rule." With the sting of the failed guitarist affair still a little raw, she wasn't ready to jump in. Sara occupied Easton's lips again. "I want to savor every second," she murmured at the tip of his ear.

"I want to savor you."

The cold leather of the seat cushion creaked as she unlatched her body from his arms and sank back into it, a coquettish grin on her face. "Just drive, boy."

Chapter 22

The Red Pine Lake Trail in Little Cottonwood Canyon put on an undulating fall showcase. From the trail overlooking the Salt Lake Valley, aspen leaves shivered in coats of burning red, orange, and yellow. The pines, more daring than the fragile aspens, stood firm and regal in their deep green hues, stretching up toward the craggy stone summits. The clean air perfumed with fresh pine and wet earth and the wide-open blue sky vented the claustrophobia of a small university bubble in the middle of a valley inversion. Sara could breathe again.

Easton wrapped his arms around her waist, and she leaned against his chest, taking in the view that opened up the world. Her foot itched to get out there, to see more. "Looking down on the kingdoms below, I'm torn between feeling omnipotent and microscopic. It's grounding and exhilarating all at the same time. Thanks for bringing me here." Her lips brushed his.

"Happy Birthday. In honor of your 19th year, I offer you the wonders of nature. But, wait! There's more. Wait 'til you see the lake." He tugged on her hand. Exuberant Easton was something of an oxymoron. A wariness and hovering somberness stalked him in the valley bubble below. On the mountain, surrounded by plump, squabbling squirrels, deep green underbrush, towering pines, and sparkling views of the city below, Sara loved him more.

The trail meandered through shades of tan and green. The winter lurked in the high altitudes, waiting to pounce in all its fury on the unsuspecting Indian summer below. The trees thinned and the beaten path leveled into a wide-open meadow where the black-eyed Susans still bloomed. The slope of the mountain descended into a V-shaped glimpse of the valley. A broken log, notched and greying, sat in a heap, contemplating the view.

"Oh, I need a photo," Sara said. "This is breathtaking."

Easton dug in his pack and pulled out a Nikon. "Go sit on that log over there."

"But I want you in it with me."

"Hmm. I have a timer, but it'll be tricky because I don't have a tripod." He glanced around for something to set the camera on. "That boulder over there might work." While he positioned the camera, Sara settled herself on the log.

Glancing at her cozy sweater—brown wool with a masculine beige trim—she chuckled. Easton hustled over and she scooched down the log to make room for him. Smiling coyly at the camera, Sara cuddled up under his shoulder. "Oh, Margaret's going to be stoked. This photo will forever immortalize Joe's old sweater and all the heartbreak woven into it. It was her favorite. I refused to let her donate it—except to me."

"What do you mean?" The Nikon clicked as he looked over at her, forever capturing the bewildered astonishment on his face.

"Didn't I tell you? Marg broke up with Joe. Tragedy. I thought they'd get married for sure."

"But…" confusion crimped the skin between his brows, "how is that possible? They were so in love. What happened? Did she meet someone else?" Sara knew Easton was romantic, she had no idea he was so sentimental. She dragged her fingers through his hair and kissed his forehead.

"No. She wants to, though. She just thought they both wanted different things. Joe's an engineer, Marg's a dancer. She wanted someone she didn't have to drag to a play. She doesn't want to marry someone who tolerates what she loves. Dance is part of who she is. He has to love the whole package. And then, Joe got all annoyed when she told him the dance team was going on an Eastern European tour this summer."

Easton's eyes wandered, lost on the horizon. "But it's so sudden. Do women just change their mind like that—for no reason?"

"No reason? The timing is just bad. No girl wants to fence herself in before she's had a chance to expand her borders. I totally agree with Marg. A girl's gotta see the world before she's stuck in a house with two kids and a dog and doesn't get to go anywhere more exotic than Chucky Cheese." Sara teased him with a cheeky grin.

She suspected Easton was hiding a gnarly breakup. He never said anything, but it was random flashes of profound, nostalgic sorrow like these that made her wonder. This wasn't the first time she'd noticed.

"Geez, baby. I had no idea you'd be so upset." Standing, she tugged on the sleeve of his Argyle sweater. "Don't worry. You're everything a girl could want." She leaned over and treated him to a seductive, pouty kiss.

Breathing deeply, like he was about to take a plunge off a craggy cliff, he dug in his pocket and pulled out a folded square of crumpled notebook paper that looked like it might have been in his pocket for a while. "I have—uh, I wrote—something for you, for your birthday. I was going to wait until we got to the lake, but I think I should read it now. Do you mind?"

"Mind? Are you serious? I've been dying to read something you wrote."

"It's not…well, I usually stick to prose. You inspire me."

Her fingers wiggled expectantly as she snuggled next to him on the log. "Me? Ooh. Romance. Read! Read!"

His lips seemed to have gone dry. He licked them once and glanced at her sideways. She thought he was going to change his mind. But then his salted caramel voice quenched her craving:

See how the trees embrace the ground
Their roots and the soil lovingly wound?
And how the grand mountain forever tries
To stretch up and kiss its blue sky?

How the rivers caress the land
Leaving traces of their touch on the sand?
And how the wind whispers sweet things
Beneath the sparrow's soft wings?

Look how the sea and the moon
Dance in the horizon's amber spoon,
And how the peaceful night sky
Sleeps soundly with the stars by its side.

You are my mountain,

My wind and my sea,
And like the mountain, with tears of mist,
Sorrow would shroud me without your kiss.

You are my land,
My rivers, my wind,
And like the desert, alone with its dust,
The sand and I yearn for our lover's soft touch.

So, like the moon and the sea,
The earth and the trees,
Let us never be
Me without you, nor you without me.

His words floated on the twilight air, caressed Sara's skin, and wandered into unknown crevasses in her heart. Her chest swelled warm, her hands shook, her breath caught.

When the echo of the last word died, Easton turned to look at Sara. She couldn't meet his eyes. She felt like he was inside of her wandering through her veins. Standing, she backed away.

He followed her off the log. "Sara, I—you… Oh, God, I'm an idiot. I'm so sorry. I shouldn't have—sometimes I'm a little much. I get carried away while I'm writing—"

On tiptoe, she threw her arms around his neck. With her mouth, she stopped the fountain of his apologies. Her lips poured balm on the dried and cracked residue of his heartache. Ravenously, he soaked up every drop she offered. Her fingers wove themselves through the strands of his hair. His wandered along the lines of her curves. When they reached the rounding mounds of her breasts, his chest shuddered against her. She inhaled the flush. The tip of her tongue brushed his lip. He breathed in the craving and pushed his mouth against hers. Their tongues tangoed in the silent music of the mountain. Yearning welled up between them.

Their lips locked, he reached down and wrapped an arm beneath her legs, swept her off her feet, and lay her on a soft tuft of tall grass. Straddling her waist, breathing heavily in time with her heaving chest, his eyes devoured her face—or was it her soul—before he lifted the hem of her sweater and made love to the ivory line between her navel and the lace trim of her bra. Sara's blood blushed.

She moaned when his mouth reached the valley below the mounds of her breasts. They were all alone on the mountain, two creatures of nature locked in her palm, tiny specs moving to the gravity of the universe and destiny. God, she wanted him so badly, all of him. She felt like they were pieces broken off from each other and tossed into the sea. The tide had brought him back to her. Her hands slid beneath his sweater and explored the smooth contours of his abs and chest. He groaned and squeezed her flesh in his hands.

Overhead, a deep-throated croak cracked the stillness and Sara's eyes shot open wide. Above their heads a raven soared, floating on the autumn breeze, wings spread wide, wedge tail fanned out. Suddenly, it folded its wings and dove straight for them. Gasping and breathless, she pulled her hands from Easton's sweater and crossed them over both their heads. "Oh, my gosh! Look out!"

Easton twisted in time to see the bird diving at them. Leaning over, he sheltered Sara's face with his body and his head with his hands. The bird swooped within inches and then arced upwards, wings thrashing the air.

Perhaps, the bird awakened the voices of Sara's upbringing, or more likely the yawning emptiness in the center of her being that longed to sample distant tastes and breathe a broader air. Logic flooded her senses. Breathless, she wrapped a leg around Easton's hips. With both palms, she shoved his chest from hers and rolled him off so that she was straddling him. He was half her bulk again, but in that moment, he'd have followed her lead into hell.

"I can't—"

"Can't?" First bewilderment and then mortification scrambled across his features. His body deflated into the grass, palm slapping his forehead. No words filled the open mouth of his apology.

Sara stood, tugged on her hiked-up sweater, not sure what to say. Turning, she faced the lonely trail back up the mountain. She couldn't look him in the eye, so she trotted up and retrieved the camera. Trailing her hand behind, she invited him to walk with her, "Hey, babe, show me that lake."

Chapter 23
—Excerpt from the personal journals of Easton Ravenscroft

Sara's lavender perfume still mingled with the scent of pine in the fibers of my Argyle sweater. I ripped it off and tossed it onto the rug as I stalked down the hall of Brann's mansion.

Reaching the bedroom, I sank into a chair. This was the elder Ethan's private sanctuary. Not surprisingly, he chose to live in shades of black and grey. Modern lines and angles defined the metal and leather furnishings. My hands covered my face and swept into my hair. I had lost Sara for sure. I couldn't do this. My elder self was a misguided simpleton to believe that I could spend two years making love to Elizabeth, two years consumed in a passion aroused in the service of a leanan sidhe, and then reappear, one hundred years later and, just like that, touch the flame without burning in it.

If only I'd stopped at the poem. But, God help me—Sara's lips! When she threw her arms around me and pressed them to mine, she sparked an inferno of memories that smoldered across decades. She woke the slumbering shards who clamored to bask just once more in the warmth of her touch. The cascading rush of love, lust, and loss overwhelmed and carried me away. And not just the memories, those lips expressed the compassion that sensed my inner pain and soothed it, the independent determination that drove her to seek knowledge and find her voice, the desire to create from invisible intimations of inspiration something tangible and breathtakingly exquisite. Her lips were irresistible one hundred years ago and even more so now. Far easier to resist the draw of gravity than to tear this flesh I wear from the magnetism buried forever and always in her soul.

Across from my chair, a single portrait illuminated the somber walls. In shades of golden yellow, white, and green hung the image of Elizabeth. She stood silhouetted in the flood of morning sun that broke through the windows of our Pennsylvania estate. Her hair, tousled and voluminous, cascaded over her bare shoulders. The curves of her lithe body peeked through the sheer fabric of her nightdress. The painting was a memory stolen from my past, a moment forever burned into my brain—the day I woke to find my wife had bargained with a leanan sidhe, the morning I agreed to let her sell her life force in exchange for some paltry beans of inspiration. I pulled off a shoe and hurled it at the portrait. The first boot struck the wooden frame and knocked the picture askew. The second struck with such force that the portrait jumped and clattered to the floor, wood cracking on wood.

In the lines of the ceiling, I contemplated my failure. A familiar breeze wafted through the open crack in the doorway and stirred around my feet until Brann Sidhe knelt at my knees, a pen in her hand.

"Are you here to gloat at my loss?"

"Loss?" She giggled and the aura around her shimmered.

"It's over." I spilled my guts to the demon. It was a lonely life I led, a single piece of Ethan, with no one to share the realities of my misery but this muse that licked it off my skin. "I can't stop myself. Elizabeth oozes through Sara's pores. I look at her eyes and I'm talking to my wife again, kissing my wife, making love to my wife."

Brann slivered up my body, her hand soaking in the misery as she went. "Ah, Easton, you understand nothing of the women of this time." She petted my hair and the musky smell of wine in hers penetrated my blood. I felt a bit drunk. "They believe they must break free from the oppressive yoke of men, and yet the unheard pieces inside of them find the protective, ungovernable lust oddly attractive. They can't help themselves. A little trick of nature to ensure the propagation of the species. But they try so hard to subdue their instincts in their quest for social equality. Quite admirable, in a way. Don't you think?"

My head throbbed. All I could think of was that moment. The look of fear in Sara's eyes. I'd ruined our chances. "I think I have lost her—again."

"Nonsense." She tapped my nose with her nail as if I were five. "You'll see. You walked away unsated as a good lover should."

"How do you know I walked away?"

She smiled seductively. "You didn't think I would miss such a show as the poetry reading, did you? These mountains are foreign and yet I feel so at home in them."

"You're nothing more than a sick voyeur."

She shrugged, "If you like. But you'll see. The next time you see her, her eyes will be different."

Chapter 24
—Excerpts from the unpublished writings of Easton Ravenscroft

"I don't think I can do three weeks without you, Easton. I'm addicted." Sara leaned across the table and brushed her lips to his. "We've spent every free moment together for months now."

Easton grinned and chuckled. "Too much of a good thing—" At a study table on the third floor of the library, he declined Sara's invitation to drive home and stay with her family for the Christmas break. "They tell me absence makes the heart grow fonder."

"Or starves it into a shriveled lump." Sara closed the cover on her copy of *History of the French Revolution*. "Seriously, babe, I'm stepping into the shadows of the Dark Ages without you."

"You're the one that's leaving to chase the sun." Easton picked up her hand and kissed her fingers. "It'll go by fast—for you. I'll be wallowing in grey skies and muddy snow banks. At least you'll be warm on the outside."

Sara was torn about whether to feel abandoned or liberated. The moment she walked in the door and hugged her mother, the subtle pressure descended—to find the right guy, settle down, and disappear. Become someone's wife, someone's mom—no one. No one cared that she had a 4.0, that she spoke three languages now, or even asked what career she'd decided to pursue once she graduated. They only wanted to know if she was dating someone. She gloated stubbornly in the perverse pleasure of letting them think she was hell-bent toward spinsterhood.

But, at night, when the wind rattled the leaves of the maple tree across her windows, the empty corner of her heart, the torn away half her soulmate was meant to fill, throbbed and echoed loneliness. Not that she was lonely. Her three younger brothers and her baby sister were still at home. The house rattled and stomped from 6:00 a.m. to midnight curfew.

The morning after Christmas, Sara wandered into the living room where her father had started a crackling fire to read his newspaper. She curled up on the flowered sofa and dove into her copy of *The Thorn Birds*. If she couldn't touch love, at least she could read about it.

The doorbell rang at 7:30, while the rest of the house still slumbered. Sighing, Sara wrapped her robe about her and opened the door. Dawn stood on her porch after the long, cold night. Easton. She caught her breath.

"Against my better judgment, I couldn't last three weeks. Do you want to go to Disneyland?"

"Yes! Who doesn't want to go to Disneyland?"

Keeping the family in the dark was no longer an option. Easton was a prize to be sure, but Sara was inexplicably mortified that her mother, siblings, and even her father were so enthusiastic. She couldn't escape reality and immerse herself in fantasy fast enough.

"The Pirates of the Caribbean was much more impressive when I was ten." Sara grabbed Easton's proffered hand. He tugged her out of the boat. Fake fireflies twinkled in the roof painted a deep, night-sky blue. A faint hint of chlorine in the man-made river broke the charming spell.

They wound their way through the streets of Old New Orleans. Magic crystals and dangly earrings glittered from a sidewalk stand. A lavender beam flowed out the doorway of a tiny shop and flooded the strip of sidewalk in front of them. Sara followed the light to the window full of crystal balls, Victorian dolls, elegant tarot cards, and intricate glass vials: the fortune teller. Sara grinned at Easton. "Let's get our fortune told. I've always wanted to, but you know," her eyebrow arched wickedly, "cards are the devil's toys."

Easton shrugged and she pushed the door open to the tinkle of a silver bell. Scarves and silks in purple and black shrouded the walls and the shelves. A living tree, complete with a blinking raven—so real in this land of fantasies and façades—cast crooked-fingered shadows about the displays.

A tall elegant woman, clad in purple and black scarves, emerged from the curtain that separated the shop from a small chamber behind. The rich amethyst stone at her throat caught the light fueling the tree shadows and reflected a prism of color into Sara's eyes. Her dark, straight hair, so purple it appeared black in the shadows, cascaded down her back and over her shoulders. She chimed, like the door, when she walked.

His eyes fixed to her perfect face, Easton lost all words, almost as if he were fuming on the inside. He never failed to surprise Sara with his sudden mood shifts. "What's the matter, baby? Is fortune telling an abomination?" Mirth twinkled in her eyes.

"No. I don't think strangers should meddle in the future."

Sara giggled at his gravity. "It's just a game." She kissed the tip of his nose. "We make our own future."

"It's so much more than a game." Easton locked her eyes up in one of those stares that bared his heart to her so that she felt she reigned supreme over his universe. That power intoxicated her, made her chest swell, and her fingers long to touch the flesh of it. Love like his fashioned empresses and queens.

Shrugging imperially, Sara turned to the gypsy, "We'd like to do a reading."

"Of course. The energy of the universe is available to all. I am only a humble mouthpiece. I'm afraid, though, that I may only read one client at a time. Better not to confuse the energies."

"I'm good, Sara." Easton's eyes narrowed at the gypsy, who smiled back serenely. "You go ahead." He took a seat on the plush purple chaise lounge.

A small round table with two chairs stood in the middle of the heavily Victorian chamber behind the velvet curtain. On the black lace tablecloth lay a stack of tarot cards the size of Sara's hand. On the table, a three-lily brass lamp pierced the shadows with smoky yellow light.

Sara took a seat opposite the fortune teller. The gypsy folded her strikingly pale hands in front of her on the table. One long purple nail tapped delicately the shiny coated stack of cards. Her eyes, deep green like a forest lost in its shade, delved into Sara's own. No, the breathless gasp wasn't the revival of a memory or a familiar place, it was a feeling, a feeling Sara had lived this before—déjà vu, but not just a visual glimpse, a deep, visceral wave from a corner buried within.

Breaking the spell, the gypsy smiled. Sara's heart faltered a half-beat at the serene beauty emanating from the tilt of her purple lips. Fortune was this woman's slave, that was clear. The ambiance in this little chamber would convert even the most cynical. And Sara wasn't cynical, she was an aspiring romantic who just couldn't silence logic and intellect long enough to immerse herself in the delusion.

"So, Elizabeth—"

A little thrill chipped away at Sara's skepticism. "That's my middle name. I'm Sara." She held out her hand, but the gypsy looked down her nose at it. Sara reeled it politely back.

"Yes, the name hangs about you. Perhaps from someone close to you—or another life."

Great response. Elizabeth was such a common name. The whole world was bound to be related to an Elizabeth.

"Sara, then. What question do you have for the cards?"

"Question? None. I just wanted to know what's in my future."

"Well, then, let us see what is in your past and your present. The sketches of the past and present design the future, don't they?" The woman spread the cards into a delicate horseshoe arch. With a graceful wave of her hand, she invited Sara to choose one.

Sara slipped a card from the arc. The gypsy slid it in front of her, careful not to alter the orientation and then motioned for Sara to choose two more to adorn either side of the first.

In the center, the Lover's upside-down surprised Sara very little. Of course! She'd shown up in the shop with a boyfriend. Clever.

"You must choose Sara. And your choice is blocked. Shall we see what energy of the past holds you back?" The next card she turned over was Death. This one was right side up, a skeleton knight on a white horse. "You see, the ends of old relationships, they hold you back. You cannot move forward, you cannot let go. Shall we see where you might go if you choose to?" The last card revealed eight chalices and a pilgrim with a walking stick moving away. "Ah, the choice is there, Sara. Old love or new horizons of power and self-confidence. You will have to choose."

Easton must have been standing at the curtain, listening. Suddenly, he was at Sara's side, gazing down at the cards and casting dagger looks at the soothsayer who held her captive. Grabbing Sara's hand, he hauled her, sputtering and stumbling, out of the lair as if he had braved certain death to rescue her from the smoke and flames of a burning building. Irrepressibly, a tiny inexplicable voice trickled up from deep streams of her subconscious and whispered thanks. Throwing her arms around

Easton's neck, she sealed her lips to the love that would walk through hell to bring her back.

Dearest Elizabeth,

Easton couldn't speak. Our oath forbade it. And even if he could, what words would he have said? To expose the leanan sidhe was to expose himself.

Brann Sidhe knew the craving that stalks your soul, Elizabeth, the hunger you pursue across lifetimes. I had no choice. Like you, who, as Marie Clémentine, placed the brush in our son's hand— more precisely, in my hand—to save him from the mad pursuit, I had to place the brush in yours, to unlock the force that binds us across universes—the very force that stole you from me more than a century ago. It was either that or lose you to your wandering hunger.

Perhaps, I did not fear the Leanan Sidhe enough. I imagined they only sought you as a means to ensnare me. I was wrong. Forgive the arrogance that blinded me.

Forever,
Ethan

Chapter 25

A billboard drenched in blue flew by. "Did you see that?" Sara sat bolt upright. "The Laguna Museum has an exhibition of Picasso's Blue Period! That was *The Old Guitarist*. I totally love the way the old man makes love to his instrument. The bend of his wizened head and his wrist, his fingers stroking the strings along her neck and across the curve of her breast. And then the lean pallor of his legs wrapped around the base. His love drives him so deeply that she's absorbed his whole life."

"Hmm." Easton's face grew tight and a bit pale. "The guitar is maybe not the lover he imagined her." His glance was morbid. "He dwindles to skin and bone pursuing her because she gives nothing back but the music."

Deep down and darkly, Sara yearned to be loved like that. But more recently, she'd yearned to strum the strings herself. She walked a tight rope suspended between the disparity of her aspirations.

"Let's go!"

"We can do whatever you want, but I have something planned. I think you'll like it better." The wind garbled the words and music of the radio. Morning sun glared through the rear window. Flaxen hills flowed out to the ocean in undulating waves. Sara's fingers wandered absently through the curls at the back of Easton's neck.

Easton's Laguna Beach home sat on a rock outcropping isolated by ocean on three sides. Two cliff faces carved out a private beach, accessible only from wooden stairs on the south side of the veranda. Tufts of red blossoms and spiky greenery softened the jagged rocks. Sara knew Easton's family was comfortable—he drove a Porsche— but she hardly expected this from a boy who lived in her bargain-basement apartment complex.

Inside the house, a spacious gathering room with a fireplace and open bar sprawled against the backdrop of an entire wall of windows. The patio commanded a spectacular ocean view. Spritely sunbeams skittered across ocean eddies playing tag with seagulls.

Sara's bag dropped to the floor. Everything about the place was shiny: shiny black stairs, shiny marble floors, shiny lights, shiny leather sofas, shiny glass, shiny wood, shiny metal. "So, your dad lives here? What does he do again?"

"He's an artist. Doesn't spend much time here anymore. He has a stuffy, renovated Victorian mansion near the university."

"Your dad lives right next to us and you've never introduced me?"

"You never introduced me to your parents."

"They live in California. I thought your dad did, too. I love old mansions. Why haven't you ever taken me there?"

"I prefer the modern openness here—and the privacy. My dad bought this house when I was little, hoping to give me something to do besides throw knives and paint in the long, lonely hours while he was gone."

"Throw knives? You're, like, the second boy I've dated that threw knives as a child. I had no idea that was a thing. Are you good? Should I be worried?"

"Decent." He strode over to pick up her bag. "You should definitely be worried—but not about knives." He winked.

Sara's heart fluttered. "Where was your mom? Did she let you run with scissors, too?"

"Actually, my mom—died when I was very young."

"Oh, I'm sorry." Sara stepped forward, reaching for his arm. "When you told me your dad's wife left him. I assumed that was your mom." The image of Easton as a motherless boy pricked a needle into Sara's heart and wove another tiny thread in and out of the fibers.

Easton held out a hand to stop her sympathy. "No, don't feel sorry for me. I lost her a long time ago." He sniffed and shrugged. "My dad's agent tries to fill in, but she doesn't have a nurturing bone in her body."

"So, she's your stepmom, now?"

"Oh, God, no!"

"I'm sorry, I thought—"

"Well, she handles all his business affairs, like buying houses. And she's there—often."

Sara didn't miss the hesitation and the rise of his tone. She suspected there was more to the relationship between Easton's dad and his agent than Easton was willing to admit to himself. "Well, this is better than Disneyland. It's real. So, where are we going today?"

"Nowhere, actually. I can take you all over the world, Sara—"

"—yes, please."

"—but you won't find what you're looking for. What's driving you is trapped inside. I'm going to open the door and set it free."

Her bag in one hand and her fingers in the other, Easton led Sara down the hall to the south side of the house. He threw open the door to another room, less immaculate, more rugged, his father's studio. The exterior walls were all windows—natural light 24/7. Paint blotches smeared the wooden floors. Easels littered the interior walls.

Oh, the walls! Sara hadn't seen many art museums, but she'd taken Art History. For a second, the air around her hung still in reverence. "Your father painted these?"

"Well, some of them are mine."

"You paint, too?"

"More when I was, uh, younger. Now, only when I feel compelled—when I'm not writing."

Sara inspected some of the paintings and then wandered to a whole collage that featured her face. "Well, you must have been doing SOME painting recently."

Easton grinned. "You compel me."

Another string wove itself around Sara's heart and drew her to him. There was an atavistic pleasure that no woman can resist to lighting the passion of creation. The intoxication compelled her to taste with her lips the fruits of her power.

Easton needed a full thirty seconds to recover. Breathing deeply, he handed her one of the smocks hanging from coat hooks on the wall. "Put this on."

Her eyebrows arched, but she grinned and pulled on the dress shirt smattered with paint. It dropped below the shorts and cami she wore over her bathing suit. "So, how do I look in your shirt?"

"So good I want to take it off again."

"Cool it, boy. We're already breaking the strict *no sleepovers with boys* rule."

"My house; my rules."

"Sorry, but rules are like car insurance. They follow the driver. Nice try, though."

Easton handed her a wooden case from the table. "We're going to start you on your painting career. You have a gift for it."

"So, you're the fortune teller now? I've never painted in my life. How could you possibly know that?"

"I have a gift for knowing. And I peeked at some of your class projects."

"I see. And what am I going to paint?" Sara wielded the brush like a child with a toy sword.

"Something written on your imagination. Think of your childhood. What's the first image that comes to your mind?"

Sara stared out the window, into the blank canvas of sapphire ocean bleeding into azure sky. "Dancing. Dancing like a savage in the living room to 'Man of La Mancha'."

"Then that's what we'll paint."

"And you're going to be my personal tutor?"

"I'm expensive, but I'm worth it."

"I have no doubt. But can I afford you? I'm a starving college student."

"We'll work something out."

Chapter 26

The California sun bent low to kiss the ocean horizon and the sky blushed pink and red. Sara dabbed a hint of white into the complexion of the five-year-old girl she'd breathed to life on the canvas. Easton strode into the studio, toweling his wet hair, the skin of his abs still glimmering with saltwater. Around his arm, Sara noticed, for the first time, a tattooed ring of ravens.

"You see," he motioned to her work, "you have a natural gift. Look at the face, so alive and full of ecstasy. And the motion, it's— it rivals Renoir."

Sara giggled at the absurd comparison. Between the rush of unleashing the churning waters of her pent-up voice and the magnificent sculpture of Easton's bare chest, she could barely breathe. Since he'd begun teaching her to paint, everything else in life had faded to greyscale. "Well, that's debatable, but this," she motioned to the room and the whole spring break extravaganza it held, "was truly a gift. Thank you."

The brush still clutched in her fist, she dabbed tiny kisses across the open canvas of his chest. He stood for a moment, breathing her in, and then ran his fingers through the honey-flax of her hair and lifted her face to his. He smelled of aloe and salt. She felt all the blossoming of a daylily flowering for the sun that had awoken its petals.

"Usually I hate winter semester, but these last four months—I can't even put it into words."

"Relax! I've got you covered for the words." He treated her to a cheeky wink. "But, Sara," he grasped her shoulders firmly in his hands, "you have to promise me something."

"Anything. I feel like I've finally found myself."

"You have talent, Sara, rare talent. Promise me you'll never, never, paint the whispers in your dreams."

"What?"

"Just promise me. Bring the inspiration up from inside. If voices ever slip into your sleep, ignore them. Art like that comes with a cost and the only currency it accepts is love and life."

Bewildered, she giggled. "Okay. Whatever. I have no idea what you're talking about." She shrugged and kissed the tip of his nose. "But, I promise."

Easton exhaled loudly like he'd been holding his breath all day. "Aren't you starving?"

"Yes. Feed me!"

"Oh, I will. But not here. We're going to the yacht."

"You never told me you had a yacht."

"I told you I grew up in California."

"So did I, but my dad didn't have a yacht—or a mansion with a private beach. He said I got braces instead."

Easton showered and reemerged looking the part of the millionaire's son.

On the edge of the private dock, the yacht gleamed white under the spotlights. In the middle of the upper deck, sat a table covered with a white cloth and candles. Out on the water, the moon and stars lit the sky, more romantic than the flicker of a million candles.

Sara grimaced at the shorts, camisole, and flip-flops she'd worn for a beach day. "I am *so* not dressed for this."

"Relax. You can change downstairs." The engines rumbled to life below at the hands of an invisible crew.

"You brought me clothes?"

"I had my dad's shopper do it. You're a small, right?"

"Your dad has a personal shopper? Who is your dad, again? You told me he was an artist, but you never mentioned any of this."

"He goes by Ethan. Black. You wouldn't have heard of him, but he's a big name in art circles."

"Obviously. You'll thank him for me, won't you? For this amazing day, for opening my eyes and letting me sip—"

"Don't worry, I'll tell him."

Easton turned away from the edge as the boat began to pull out of the marina. "If you want to freshen up, there's a head and a stateroom at the bottom of the stairs over there."

Dazed, Sara wandered down below the deck. Through open double doors, lavender accented the white elegance of the stateroom. Her heart skipped and pattered at the size of the bed. She trusted Easton—mostly. A gorgeous lavender halter dress hung in the closet. Matching shoes in her size seven waited on the floor. The vanity displayed an assortment of expensive bottles she'd only ever tried as samples in the department store. She felt like Cinderella and wondered if everything would magically disappear at midnight.

When she stepped onto the deck, she felt more than freshened up. She felt reborn.

Easton was setting salads on the table. He caught his breath as she strode over and pressed her lips, warm and wet, hard against his. Their bodies rocked to the music of the ocean tapping at the sides of the yacht. "I have never even dreamed of anything so amazing."

"Neither have I. You shame the night sky." He hugged her with his glance. Heat, pleasure, anticipation, and awe all bubbled up in her chest so that she thought her head might explode.

"What's up, Easton? You have this excitement thing going on." Sara adopted her best poet voice, "...a glint in your eye, a hidden smile on your lips... I've never seen you like this before. Your signature 'composed chill' is cracking."

Winking, he handed her a cut crystal cup filled with shrimp cocktail and pulled out her chair. The tomato and vegetable flavors burst in her mouth in a harmony of textures.

Red, orange, and yellow beets decorated the plate of field greens in front of her. She pushed them around while she thought. "Easton? I might be wrong...I mean, I hope I'm not...but it seems to me we're getting 'serious' here."

Easton stopped chewing and leaned back in his chair, folding his arms across his chest, a mixture of worry and anticipation on his face.

She took a couple of bites, waiting for him.

Finally, he took a sip of ice water and gulped. "Too fast?"

"No! Oh, God, no. I'm in heaven. I feel like a fairy tale princess."

"Is that a good thing?"

"Yes. Due to a heavy diet of Disney, the four-year-old in every girl wants to be a fairy tale princess." They'd both finished their salads and he stood to pick up the plates. Sara thought he wanted to stall the conversation and waited until he came back with crab-crusted halibut.

"How do I eat this?" She poked at the crab leg on the side.

"Dipped in lots of drawn butter."

"Oh, butter! I adore butter. Bread and baked potatoes are only vehicles for butter."

He handed her a cup and then the tongs. Expertly, he gripped his crab leg, inserted the tongs, and extracted a long, thin strand. She followed suit but with slightly less finesse. Hers ripped and she was consigned to cracking and digging like a desperate cavewoman. When she'd finally extracted a piece, she soaked it. Leaning underneath the morsel dangling precariously from her fork, she caught the butter on her tongue before it dripped onto her lip— Nirvana. Easton was entertained. He didn't laugh often, sadness resided behind his eyes. But when he did, Sara's love ticked up a notch.

"You distracted me with butter. But I haven't forgotten." She leaned her elbows on the table and folded her fingers. "If this is getting 'serious', you're going to have to tell me the secret you've been hiding."

Easton gulped. "What do you mean?"

"C'mon, Easton. It's obvious. You know that, right?"

He tapped his knife on the table.

She nudged him with her toe. "That distant look you get sometimes when you stare at me? The moments of sadness? Inexplicable bouts of insecurity? Tell me truthfully, when you're kissing me, are you thinking of someone else?"

Astonishingly, he laughed, rubbing his neck, as if he couldn't believe some mysterious irony that Sara couldn't see—which was why she was asking. She wasn't about to take this relationship to the next level until she knew what was going on. His mouth opened, but her brilliant writer couldn't find the words.

"Who was she? Who broke your heart, babe? Is she still out there? If she comes to her senses and comes running back, am I just the girl that was standing in?"

The waves planted little smacking kisses against the hull. A gentle breeze flickered the flames in their glass cups. Easton avoided Sara's eyes. Reaching over the table, she covered the hand worrying the knife with hers. She lifted her brows expectantly when he glanced up, his eyes filled with a question.

"It's not a distant look, Sara. It's deep. The soul inside of you steals my breath. It's like I've known you for as long as the seed of my consciousness has been in existence—like I was connected to you before I ever met you. If you think I'm insecure, it's because I am. I can't tell if you feel what I'm feeling and it scares me because, yes, I did lose someone." He paused as if the tragedy of heartbreak had frozen the words on his lips.

"I'm sorry. I didn't mean to spoil our perfect evening. Sometimes, I feel like you want something from me that I don't have."

"She died." The confession brought moisture to his eyes. "I was with someone for two years and she died." He got up, picked up the spent plates, and carried them away to the kitchen.

Oh, God! So much worse than she'd feared. Sara wasn't just competing with another woman out there, she was competing with a ghost. She didn't know how to feel about that, knowing that time etches the best in misty gold and erases the worst. She didn't think she could live up to the virtues of a dead girl.

Quietly, her favorite love song of all time, Roberta Flack's "The First Time Ever I Saw Your Face" trickled through the night. The music pierced her skin and melted into her heart the way words alone just couldn't. Easton wandered up from the kitchen, hands in his pockets, head bowed. That was the moment that she made her choice.

Pushing back her chair, she strode over to him. Standing on tiptoes, she brushed his lips with hers. "It's okay. I don't care. I love you." They danced, clinging to each other, one small dot in a universe littered with stars, until the song died.

Easton dug into his pocket and produced an oyster shell.

"What is that? Dessert?"

"Sort of. Open it."

Prying with her fingertips, she split the two halves of the shell apart. She was expecting pearls maybe. Definitely not the huge diamond that caught the glint of the moon and winked back at her.

"Marry me, Sara?"

Her mouth parted, but the air abandoned her lungs. All around them, the wide rolling ocean stared back at her, no answers, an infinite expanse of undulating possibility, limited only by the sparkling lights of the sturdy shore. What else could she say? "Of course, I will."

For the first time, light sparkled behind the deep sadness in Easton's eyes. His lips met hers and, together, their mouths slow danced to the rhythm of the waves. His hands wandered down her back and his lips swept the curve of her neck down to the point between her collar bones. Her breasts shivered and her nipples perked as she ran her hands through his dark curls.

A moan of pleasure rose from her chest to her throat. Her head fell back. The rush of wanting, the appeal of luxury she'd never had, the poetry of the man wrapped around her overwhelmed her senses. Their lips greedily consumed the moments as he carried her down the steps to the stateroom.

A flurry of lavender enveloped them when her head hit the pillow. He sank into the cushion beside her. Reaching down to her ankle, he studied the pale bronze of her skin as his finger trailed its way across the curve of her calf, along the rise of her thigh, beneath the hem of her dress.

Their eyes met again. "You have no idea—" he couldn't finish. Instead, his hands found her face and he kissed her solidly like he was sealing a contract. She signed her name with every flourish of their tongues. His hands slid to her shoulders and down the slope of her breasts. She gulped as the flesh engorged and, in a flash, the whole night played itself out in her head. She sat up abruptly.

"Sara?" He was as breathless as she was.

She dropped her head into her palm. "Oh, my God." She turned to look him in the face. "You know I love you, Easton. I have from the first glance. But that doesn't change who I am." Her eyes drifted away toward the ocean lapping at the porthole windows. The lights created shadows that morphed into images of her older sister—the lost opportunities, experiences, potential.

Sara still had two years left of school. She was not going to throw away her education. She was not going to slam shut the short window of life when she could satiate her cravings to taste the wide world, unfettered with adult responsibility, when she could explore this new self that Easton had compelled to the surface before she had to choose what she would be. And she wanted to be free to choose. She would not give that up. She wanted more and she would not let her world shrink too small to hold her aspirations.

"Baby, I'm not ready for this yet." Could she explain? Would he even understand? Probably not. But, there was more to it. Something the romantic in him could embrace. "Deep down inside of me, I want to find 'the one'. I want that intimacy to be part of the bond between him and me that I don't have with anyone else. I want to be sure. Maybe I'm just an incurable romantic, but I'm still a 'save it for the wedding night' girl." Her eyes met his again. "I'll sleep with you, but I won't have sex with you."

"Done." He enveloped her in his arms, his body curved around hers. "I want to feel what it's like to wake up next to you in the morning."

Relief, maybe a touch of disappointment, relaxed her muscles. Her body fit perfectly into the shape of his. She slipped the ring clutched in her fist onto her finger. It fit perfectly, like everything else between her and Easton. Under the weight of the diamond, something inside of her died and something else was born. She had this insane urge to paint and knew what her next project would be: Easton at sunset on the beach.

She woke alone to the gentle rocking of the boat just beyond Laguna and the sun streaming through the porthole window. Slipping from the sheets, she climbed the stairs. The ocean air cleansed her lungs. Seagulls screamed on the shore and fled the deck in a rustle of wings. In her groggy thoughts, she remembered something about Easton making a run for fresh croissants onshore.

She headed to the kitchen for coffee. On the counter, she found the crème brûlée that was supposed to be dessert—but made a decadent breakfast—and a poem:

Some names I taste,
like a smoky dry cloud.
Some names I hear,
just a voice in a crowd.
Some names I feel
how I feel my own age.
Some names I see,
just words on a page.

But I taste your name,
like a breath of fresh air,

and I hear it,
like a whisper brushed by my ear.
I feel your name
kiss me on the mouth
and from my chest, I feel it
burn its way out.

I see it when it is dark,
like fireworks burning bright,
because it's your name
that holds me in the night.
What's in a name
that it renders me so?
A slave to the word
that won't let me go.

These things that I feel,
when I hear your name,
are things that you gave me,
when I met you that day.

Chapter 27

The door of the library swung closed behind Sara. The entire courtyard shivered under greying piles of salted, soiled snow. Not even the fast approaching Christmas break could lighten the end of semester stress that hung over the university. She hefted the pile of books in her arms and twisted her wrist around to see her watch. She was late. She wouldn't have time to go home and change before meeting Easton. The huge diamond on her finger flashed yellow in the lowering sun. It overpowered her delicate fingers. She tucked it under her books. The modest diamond on the other hand, that she'd inherited from a distant relative, suited her small fingers better.

The end of the semester was closing in on her. Life was closing in on her. She inhaled like the air around her had suddenly gone thin and then replaced the doubts in her head with images of Easton's smile. She couldn't possibly be any luckier. He was to die for; but she didn't want to die, not just yet.

In the reflection of the windows of the humanities building, her home on campus, the load of books she was carrying dwarfed her. The poster on the entrance door was new, drab, colorless, written in a nondescript font. In her eyes, it seemed to be highlighted with neon lights and silver bells. ENROLL NOW FOR SUMMER SESSION STUDY ABROAD IN PARIS. SEE THE HUMANITIES OFFICE FOR DETAILS.

Her feet moved past the sign, through the door, and into the office. Marion Ravenwood sat neatly behind her desk. The most mesmerizing purple crystal hung at her throat. Lips parted, Sara stared at it until Marion looked up from her papers. A little silver chain attached to her glasses dangled from her ears. She pulled the glasses off and let them fall onto her chest.

"Can I help you?" The secretary's church-lady smile overwhelmed Sara with an aura of nurturing femininity. She felt sure Marion would hand her a Band-Aid and ask her to stay for milk and fresh-baked cookies. "I was interested in your Study Abroad Program? Is it too late to sign up?"

"No! Not at all. I think we still have a couple of spots open if you hurry. The first deposit is due next month."

Sara asked a few questions, found she was eligible, and slid an enrollment form off the pile. Bubbles of excitement gurgled up from the dreams that had been fading into the practicality of higher education. She still had a few months to go home and work. It wasn't as expensive as she'd expected and they offered classes she needed to graduate. She was sure she could convince her mother. No doubt about it. She was strict, but she would do anything for one of her children. It was her way of saying "I love you."

Sara hesitated at the door and Marion looked up again from her papers, her glasses perched on the edge of her nose.

"The thing is—" she shifted the books in her arms, exposing the ostentatious diamond, "—I'm engaged."

Marion tilted her head thoughtfully, tapping her lips with a deep purple nail. After a moment, she crossed her arms on the desk in front of her and leaned forward. "But you came in anyway?"

Sara nodded.

"Sweetie," the woman sounded like she was talking to a puppy tangled in a leash, "you can get married anytime. You can only do Study Abroad while you're in college."

The wrinkles on Sara's brow relaxed. The tethers snapped. She breathed the air like it was new, nodded, and skipped out the door.

She was late. Easton was pacing.

"Sorry, I got distracted." Not planning to stay, she had left the stack of books in the car. Clicking the door quietly shut, she turned resolutely to face her fiancé.

"You look a little worried. Are you all right? What happened?" He stooped a bit to see into her downcast eyes.

Twisting the bulky ring back and forth around her finger, she walked toward the kitchen, trailing Easton in her wake. "You remind me of my first boyfriend." The response seemed random but wasn't. "Everything is so intense, so serious, like life has to happen right this minute and everything is fixed into some plan I've never seen."

"What do you mean?" His face looked cool, studied cool, but his eyes were scared. He put his arms through hers and wrapped them around her waist. "We don't have to do this so fast, Sara."

The floor beside them suddenly became vastly engrossing to her. Kissing him, just looking at him, would talk her out of going. She'd be crazy to walk away from this man, this love. But the sole of her foot itched. Her mind was already floating in lands beyond. "I'm going to France."

His arms went stiff and then slid away. Sara took a step back to look him in the face. "I'll have to go home at the end of the term and earn some money. I probably won't come back to school until next fall—until you've already gone."

His mouth opened like he was going to say something. He shook his head in bewilderment and then looked away. His eyes found hers again, searching, and his hands sought words in the thin air between them. "What can I say? I love you. I want to marry you."

"You're graduating. You'll be gone before I get back."

"So?" He still wasn't catching the end game.

"I want to finish school."

"No problem. We can live here until you're done." Desperation cracked his voice.

"I don't want to get married yet, Easton. I mean, you're gorgeous; you're brilliant; geez, you treat me like a princess. But you're older than I am." She hesitated, looking out the window for the reasons. Half the girls she'd known as a freshman were married and expecting their first baby. "Any girl would be crazy not to marry you, but I'm just not old enough yet—I'm old enough—I—I just haven't done anything; you've done so much more than I have. You've written a novel! I don't want to get married and have kids and wonder what else is out there. I want to know and make a choice. I want to have already been there and done it."

"Whatever you want." He spread his arms wide, exposing his chest. "I'll be here when you get back. I'm yours, whatever it takes. I can write anywhere."

"No, you don't understand. I don't want you to be mine, and me to be yours. I want to be me." Wondering whether or not there was enough air in the room to fill up her courage, Sara took a deep breath. "Look, baby, the thing is...you're a dream. And, if your dreams come true so soon, what's left to reach for? It's a recipe for boredom—yours or mine." She twisted the ring off her finger. She handed it to him.

Instead of reaching for it, his hand found the gold coin that dangled perpetually at his throat. His face was blank, but his eyes were vivid. Jaw tight, he folded his arms across his chest and closed his eyes. Sara watched him swallow his pain in silence.

"I'm so sorry." Not enough air crossed her vocal cords for the words to be truly audible. Her breath caught and she put her hand to her chest to stop the throbbing. The stitches that joined her to him ripped, one by one. Each tugged and tore a tiny hole in the fabric of her heart. She hadn't imagined the pulling apart of the two of them would be such a violent affair.

Easton dropped his eyes into the visor of his hand. Sara bit her lower lip, hugged herself, and rubbed her arms. It seemed suddenly very cold. Water dripped from the faucet, splatting against the stainless steel. Walking past the table and counters, she cinched the knob.

When she stood in front of Easton again, he held out his hand. Sara put the ring in it. He closed it in his fist. She lifted her face to see his eyes. In one fluid, forward motion, he gathered her up in his arms and kissed her like she was dying and he'd never see her again. He kissed her so that, six thousand miles away and months later, she still felt the tragedy of his lips on hers.

Easton let her go, turned, and walked down the hall to his room. Sara let herself out.

She never spoke to him again.

Dearest Elizabeth,

Easton wrote her story. Every moment of his fragmented existence, he sketched her in words. And as he did, Brann Sidhe gulped voraciously at the bitter cup of his prose. You understand now the desperation in our soul and the ravenous, insatiable hunger that stalks us.

Forever,
Ethan

Chapter 28

(O)f course, Sara fell in love. She was nineteen and in Paris for the summer. She fell in love with fresh baguettes dipped in bowls of decadent hot chocolate, with gothic arches and stained-glass windows that adorned the churches so magnificent they had eaten up the lives of the men who had aspired to build them. She fell in love with chateaus, gardens, and palaces, with freedom and independence. She fell in love with art.

With her tiny bit of lead, she traced the curves and angles of a red columbine, filled its shades and shadows. In the Paris museums, the oil, dried and cracked, had whispered to her and seduced her fingers.

Parc Monceau stirred within her, something primeval, she supposed—no, perhaps an inkling that ignored time and place and just was. Tilting her head, she shrugged. The angles and shading were not quite what they should be to create the depth she envisioned.

The sun cast a yellow hue on the landscape. The tip of her nose tingled, signaling the burning phase of her sunbathing. She tucked the book and pencil into her backpack. Crossing the grass to the *Monceau* Metro Station, she tugged on the bottom of her shorts; none of the information packets had mentioned that only tourists wore shorts in Paris. Her French was good, but she would never blend in.

Sara caught the Nation line to the Gambetta line which would take her to Opéra, a fairly busy interchange where she could catch *Marne-la-Vallée* to *Les Halles* and then jump on *Saint Rémy* which would deposit her back in the Latin Quarter where her group was staying. After two weeks, she was navigating the metro like a seasoned sailor.

The train screeched to a halt at *Opéra*. Sara spilled out onto the quay with the human tide. The current carried her toward the exit.

She waded through the sea of people toward the long tributary that connected this line with the one she'd just flowed out of.

The musty, cement labyrinth beneath the elaborate green-domed theater on the surface spanned multiple city blocks. One of the more intrepid students, Sara ventured out alone into the exotic metropolis. The blondes traveled in packs, and her roommates, after being flashed in the metro during their first week, didn't leave the hotel without the supervising professors.

The crowds trickled away to branching streams, leaving her to walk alone in a pale-yellow corridor that disappeared to the right several yards ahead. Her flip-flops echoed on the cement floor. She missed the comfort of the churning crowds.

Halfway down the hall, the thump of brisk footsteps began to stalk her. Turning, she matched them with a face—male, olive skin, thick black brows and hair, medium build. Her step quickened of its own accord. Her skin crawled at the idea that the hall was virtually empty except for the two of them. No one in the group knew where she was. She glanced back. He was closer. Her heart and steps accelerated to the adrenaline pumping in her blood.

Determined to keep her cool, she chastised herself for being racist. He was probably some banker on his way home for lunch. Harmless.

It was only natural to feel threatened, she explained to herself. She'd heard stories of the New York metro. And everything here was foreign. If she were back home in Utah, she wouldn't even notice there was some guy behind her. It was just the sense of unknown sending the chill through her veins. Besides, it was the lunch hour. People were bound to show up soon. She held her breath, hoping it was just the pounding of her heart and the rasping of her lungs that was cutting out the echo of the advancing masses. The air was void of vibration other than the padding of her pursuer's soles.

It occurred to her to slow down a bit, let him pass, let the eeriness of being followed, of not being able to see what was coming for her, slip by. She slowed her steps. Her ears strained to hear other feet or voices floating around the corner. The rapidly approaching stride behind her sent a shiver of anticipation down her spine. She was so silly. She'd feel a whole lot better once he'd gone by. The distant rumble of a small crowd penetrated the hallway. Sara honed in on it. But—nothing.

The stranger still hadn't passed her. *What the hell is he doing?* was the last thought that flitted across her mind before he assaulted her from behind. The flat of his palm slapped against her butt. She whirled around, all her fight and flight reflexes firing. Adrenaline pumped, and her face flushed. A sense of violation choked her. Her eyes confronted him. What right did he have to touch her? It wasn't accidental, in passing. He stood there, leering at her. She should have been afraid, but she was too angry. Ages of genetic indignation rose up and screamed in her chest. Her eyes flashed disgust, her fist flew into the air, and she hurled French obscenities at the offending caveman.

Grinning, he grabbed her arm and reached for her shirt.

His touch kindled her fury to volcanic proportions. Twisting and yanking her wrist, she channeled generations of gender repression and resentment and buried her knee in his groin, the spot that made him think he had some innate right to touch her.

Groaning, her assailant doubled over as chatter and footsteps reverberated down the hall. "Hey!" a very American accent ricocheted off the gleaming tiles, cracking the solitude. Sara glimpsed a tall blonde, jeans, and purple t-shirt before she shoved the wounded brute away from her. Still fuming, her muscles shaking with surplus chemistry, she stalked around the corner and onto the quay. Her chest heaved, her jaw grated. The other waiting passengers stepped cautiously away from the indignation churning about her.

The train arrived. She stomped on. No one sat near her. She glared at the windows across the aisle. *How dare he? What if those kids hadn't shown up.* Her shoulders shivered.

The train signaled departure. A conspicuously American trio jumped through the narrowing gap in the doors. The tall, blond from the corridor glanced around the car while his two buddies laughed and took up positions near the doors. The cushion next to Sara exhaled as he sank into it.

"Is it safe to sit here?" His green eyes smiled. She could tell he was younger than she was—he had high school senior trip written all over him.

She glared and turned away. Although she would have gotten up and moved had some other man sat by her, the kid's immaturity exuded non-threatening, protective almost. Exhaling deeply the abandoned rush wandering in her blood, Sara found some tranquility in gratitude. "Thanks. He probably backed off because you came around the corner and yelled."

"Yeah, right! He backed off because you nailed him in the nuts." She couldn't dampen the smile that curled the corners of her mouth. "You're pretty small." He sized her up objectively. "He definitely wasn't expecting that."

"I was mad."

"I could tell. I'd have helped you out, but it looked like you had it under control. What was that you called him? My French sucks. Two years in high school and I can't even count to ten."

"I don't know any good stuff. I think I just called him some sort of cockroach. Seriously, though, what kind of complete moron would make a dick move like that in public?" The sudden grin on the kid's face rekindled her ire. "What? You think it's funny? That was assault. If I weren't so mad and freaked out, I'd have followed him until I found a policeman to arrest his pervert ass."

"No! It's just that you said 'in public.' I'm not sure I'd have the guts to make that kind of 'dick move' on you in private." She rolled her eyes, but the corner of her mouth arched up. "Absolutely no excuse for what he did. I can hunt him down and beat him up for you if you want. It would be the red-neck thing to do."

Sara laughed. Her shoulders and neck relaxed as she studied her semi-gallant knight's profile. He was therapeutic. He sported a pair of Vuarnet sunglasses propped on wavy blond curls. His forehead sloped to what should have been a small straight nose. The slight kink in the bone halfway down brimmed with a vague story of a rough encounter with a very solid object. Her glance brushed his very red, full lips. His store of one-liners failed him and his buddies began heckling his style. The train rocked on a sharp turn and they grabbed for a handhold.

Sara took pity on the kid and broke the awkward silence. "Are you a red-neck?"

"I'm from a small mining town called Castle Dale and I'm the first kid in, like, four generations to go to college. What do *you* think?"

"I think you're supposed to be a red-neck, but you're too much trouble for one small town to handle, so they're shipping you off to the city." Light flooded the car. The train pulled into her station, slowed and ground to a stop. Sara stood up without looking back at him and walked toward the doors.

"Hey!" The kid jumped up and followed her. In her flat sandals, she didn't quite reach his shoulders.

"I'll be fine." She only half turned around. "You don't have to walk me back. My dorm is close to the station."

"Actually, I was gonna ask if *you*'d walk *me* home. We're in a pretty sketchy neighborhood."

Sara rolled her eyes and smirked away the bullshit. "Whatever. C'mon. Do you know where you live?"

"I have no idea where the hell I am. I was following you. But you definitely look like you know where you're going."

She grabbed the metal bar as the warning bell sounded and the doors opened. "Do you at least know the street or the address?"

"Oh, yeah, something like, uh…If I saw it, I'd recognize it. I'm kind of visual like that."

"How about your name?"

"That one's easy. Jake—short for Jackson; Jackson Dawson."

"Let's go, Jake. I have a map in my room."

He winked at his buddies as he stepped onto the quay with Sara.

"You guys are on your own," she tossed over her shoulder. The warning bell whined and the doors shut behind them.

Chapter 29

Monday evening all the weekend sinners were atoning in the library. Sara's purgatory involved math problems.

By the time she looked up from her calculator and notebook, the windows had gone dark and she'd exhausted her supply of chocolate-covered raisins. In late September, the days were still long. Her stomach rumbled and her brain demanded carbs. Stuffing her books in her backpack, she headed for the stairs.

On the main floor, at one of the group study tables, Sara spotted a familiar face she hadn't seen for over a year, and frankly, never expected to see again. Curly blond hair, quick smile, broad shoulders, crooked nose. Young Jake Dawson was in college now.

She grinned and checked her outfit. Black knit maxi-skirt, knee-high leather boots, big black belt hanging loose on an over-sized red plaid shirt, Italian leather jacket with pleats and shoulder pads that she'd picked up in her European travels. It was a good day to bump into old friends. "Hey, stranger! Bet a red-neck like you had to do some pretty fast talking to convince them to let you in here." She came up behind him and winked when he turned. Jake's emotions played freely on his face. He was very pleased to see her.

"Yeah, I guess they're trying to redeem all the sinners. But, I had to work a year to afford the tuition. They're not giving red-necks like me scholarships." He stood up and drowned her in an enormous, small-town bear hug that adopted her as family. He'd grown a couple of inches and bulked up. This wasn't the lanky high school grad that had bummed around Paris with her for a summer. "Sara Vale. My partner in crime."

When he finally let her go, she stood on tip-toe and kissed him on both cheeks. "Speak for yourself, *M. Le Criminel*. You're the one the metro cops picked up for hopping the gates. And no one tried to escort *me* out of the Rodin museum for inappropriate behaviors around 'Le Baiser'."

No remorse. Cheeky grin. Life was a game to Jake. "Good times." He backed up and looked her over. "Wow, you look good, Sara. Those Frenchies have nothing on you." His eyes lit up. "Hey, you want to go to dinner?"

"I'm starving! I'd love to! Oh, but—ah, no, I better not. I have an essay due. But, hey, are you taking French?"

"Yeah. I've got that advanced grammar class. It's kicking my butt. I don't even know my English grammar. I been out working on the farm too long. Don't know much 'bout verbs, and conjeegations, and all that shit."

"You're such a poser. You speak English as well as I do."

"No one speaks English as well as you do."

"Well, not all of us had an English teacher for a father. You know, if you have a French class, you have to go to two cultural events. Have you seen *Les Misérables*? It's playing at the International Cinema. It counts for credit and I want to see it. I read the three volumes in French for my language study during my semester abroad."

"Of course, you did. I, on the other hand, became a refined connoisseur of *Astérix* comic books."

The thing Sara loved about Jake was his utter frankness. He was secure with himself, didn't have to hide his faults. In fact, he brought them all out in the open to laugh about. His depth of self-assurance and integrity charmed the hell out of her—well that and his candid admiration.

"We should get some of the old Paris crew together and see *Les Misérables*. Those books molded my soul. Better than Jane Eyre."

"Obviously, much—"

"Philistine. You don't even know what I'm talking about, do you? Well, I'd love to see if a two-hour movie can do justice to the books."

"Yeah, I'm up for a little culture. I'll call some people. What's your number?"

Digging a pencil out of the front pocket of her bag, Sara scratched her number on his homework and waved good-bye. Just before she merged with the foot traffic heading out the door, she turned around and caught him appreciating her receding form with a look she'd never seen on his face while strolling past paintings in the *Musée d'Orsay*.

Chapter 30

Sara was just nodding off with a copy of Trystan and Isolde when the phone rang on Wednesday night.

"Hey, Sara, it's Jake."

"Oh, hi! What's up? Did you talk to some people about *Les Misérables*?"

"Well, that's the thing. I couldn't get a hold of anyone, but I'm only free tomorrow. Do you want to go anyway?"

"Yeah, sure."

"I'll bring snacks. Pick you up at 6:30."

Jake picked her up at 6:25. They were in the ticket line at the International Cinema by 6:45. "You didn't call anybody, did you?"

He grinned and patted his pocket. "I brought chocolate."

"Not fair. One month in Paris and you know all my weaknesses. So, is this a date?" Even though they'd spent about a month solid laughing their way through Paris, she'd never considered Jake a date. He was a couple of years younger and a great friend, a security blanket in a dangerously exotic world.

"If you want it to be."

"Depends on what kind of chocolate."

He shrugged and wagged his eyebrows. Sara always thought Jake had puppy dog eyebrows—irresistibly cute. "The good stuff, of course. *Crème brûlée* and *noisette* truffles."

"You are the devil."

"At your service." He tipped his head. Jake liked to think of himself as a bad boy. Sara knew better. He was an accounting major. But then again, he was also a high school basketball star— at least he said so. She'd watched him play once or twice in Paris with his high school buddies. Pretty aggressive.

"You know, I don't usually date athletes."

"Uh, oh. Somebody screwed up."

"Maybe. I usually go for the creative types. But after Paris, I want to *be* an artist, not just date one."

The girl at the booth handed them two tickets and they settled into a couple of seats in the center of the nearly empty theater.

Somewhere between chocolate truffles melting on her tongue and Cosette meeting Marius for the first time, Sara wondered why Jake hadn't made a move on holding her hand. Assuming he was too intimidated—older woman, city girl, she didn't know—she took pity on him and let her fingers brush his thigh. He didn't need more than a hint. His hand slid easily into hers. It had a solid, elegant feel like it could work heavy farm equipment or massage her shoulders into heaven.

While Enjolaras incited the masses to revolt, Jake's knee bounced nervously and his thumb worried in nervous circles around her knuckle. When a soldier's bullet ripped Gavroche's chest, Sara's eyes welled up and she sniffed. Jake wrapped an arm around her shoulders and squeezed her closer. Heat ricocheted between them.

The lights came up and he held her coat while she slipped it on, but he wasn't giving up her hand. "Well," he asked on the way home, "did it live up to the books?"

"Nothing ever does. But, it came close. I miss the story of Éponine. It's so tragically and ironically romantic. What did you think?"

"First art film ever. You converted me. I'll watch another." He squeezed her fingers.

Back at her apartment, he hung about at the door, the puppy hoping for a bone.

"Three date rule." Sara winked and turned the knob.

"Surprising. When you asked me out and dropped your hand on my thigh, I thought you were one of those forward California girls with no rules. Wondered if I'd gotten in over my head."

"What? I thought you were a small-town boy, too shy to make a move."

"Hardly. Pick you up at 7:00 tomorrow?"

"Wasn't this the only night you were free this week?"

He grinned and jangled his keys as he walked to the car.

Chapter 31

Summer dangled her feet on Fall's porch swing. Ragged autumn coats cloaked the trees above the park while forest green grass and left-over petunias littered the valley.

"I still say the Rodin museum is far better than the Louvre. The sculptures are practically alive and you can focus on each one. The Louvre is so overwhelming that I couldn't remember anything after the da Vinci room." Third date tension rattled like a snake in the grass. Propped up on her elbows, Sara faced Jake, propped up on his. He had eyes that wavered between blue and green depending on his mood. They held no secrets. He watched her lips as she rattled on about their adventures in Paris. They had enough material to talk for hours.

"The museum shuffle, I do it well."

"I know. Right? You have to break the Louvre down into a whole bunch of Wednesdays and only visit, like, three rooms at a time or your eyes will O.D."

"Definitely. Although, it's all a blur to me. I only remember a bunch of dying saints, naked ladies, and this really hot girl trying to make up for my lifetime of cultural neglect in one afternoon. I have no idea how you remember all those names, periods, and history."

"I was taking a class." Sara's eyes dropped to the grass. Her fingers brushed along the prickly blades. Jake reached a hand over and fondled them.

"You amaze me. Sometimes, I can't believe I'm lucky enough to be with a girl like you. I wanted out of the small town and you're the girl I wanted to get out with." They simmered in the gentle chemical marinade of skin on skin. Jake stared off at a couple with a toddler and a new puppy. "Do you ever think about getting married?"

"Not on the third date."

He snorted. "No, I mean, like, what kind of person?"

"If that were a test question, I'd fail. I have no idea what I want."
She sighed. "I'm running out of time, too. I graduate next year.
After that, the options are slim. My mom keeps calling and asking
if I have a boyfriend."

"So, no prospects yet? And you still don't know what you're
looking for?"

"No, but I think you just know. Don't you? Like, I could never
marry you."

He shifted to his side, the sting of her words tensing his eyes and
jaw. "Why not?"

Sara chuckled, unnerved that he was offended. "I don't know.
We're best friends."

"Don't you think you should be married to your best friend?"

"Well, yeah. But there's gotta be, I don't know, passion. Like
when your hands shake, and you can't stop thinking about him, and
it feels like you're dying, but you're actually waking up."

"So, fear and death. That's passion to you?" He extracted a blade
of grass and chewed on the root. A couple of dogs ran by chasing a
Frisbee. A giggling, screaming bunch of kids chased the dogs. The
smell of hamburgers on the barbeque wafted over on the breeze.
"You're a strange one, Sara. I'm looking for someone I can grow
old with and never be bored. Someone I'll still be holding hands
with at sixty." He stood up and held out a hand to pull her up. "Let's
go get some dinner. I'm starving."

"You're always starving."

A little less than twice her weight, he popped her easily off the
ground. She landed facing his chest squarely. The intensity in his
eyes didn't scare her. She dropped hers to the grass, took his other
hand like she was apologizing for ruling him out, and then looked
back toward those full soft lips.

"So, this is the third date." His eyebrow arched in a question.

"Yeah, the third date in three days. I hardly know you." She
smiled and bit her lip. She could taste his already, she was just
hoping to add a little spice. She couldn't remember even wanting to
kiss someone since before Paris.

"You know me. Time has nothing to do with it. This is deep. It
feels like you and I have known each other for centuries."

It did. She tilted up her nose and stood on her toes. Jake didn't
need to be told twice.

His red lips pressed against hers. Centuries of knowing zinged across her skin and soaked into her blood. There were four children, a house in the suburbs, and solid, forever love in his kiss.

Chapter 32

The university ballroom crawled with couples dancing in the new year. Christmas trees still twinkled in all the corners and between the pillars. One more hour and 1986 would make its appearance.

Despite the ever-present dance police at their good Christian school, Jake draped his body around Sara's and they swayed to Journey's "Faithfully." He hunched over to whisper in her ear. Sara couldn't hear him. The crowd distracted her.

Across the room, she'd spotted a familiar face. The dark, unruly hair, sharp jawline, and flash of green eyes as he passed in front of a spotlight riveted her attention. Easton. Her heart bent in her chest, molding itself into a rapid series of poses: passion, love, heart-ache, regret.

The song ended and the room was quiet for a few seconds. "Hey, where'd you go?"

Jake's nudge brought her eyes back to his. "I'm sorry, did you say something?"

"Yeah, you want to go get a drink or something? The heat is stifling."

Standing on her tiptoes, she surveyed the room, trying to spot Easton again. "No, uh, no—I'm fine." The opening notes of Police's "Every Breath You Take" trickled out of the speakers. Turning, she smiled and took Jake's hand. "I love this song."

He shrugged and they danced, but she couldn't stop herself from searching the dance floor.

Then she saw the ghost in the flesh. But it wasn't Easton. This guy could have played his double except he wasn't any older than Jake. Easton never mentioned a younger brother. Besides, he danced like it was an art, not a social obligation. Easton never had that *joie de vivre*. He always seemed like he was just doing his time, waiting for real life to happen. Sara only saw life brighten his eyes once, that moment she pulled the ring from the oyster shell and said "yes."

Easton's doppelganger wasn't alone. His hands molded the subtle curves of the girl inches from his chest—tall, blonde, Victoria's Secret model type. Like two strands of kelp, they swayed in harmony to the tides of music. Even in her best little black dress and strappy heels, Sara couldn't compete with sophistication like that. Suddenly, she felt a fool. She'd held a pearl in her hand and tossed it back into the ocean to go looking for sand. And yet, her world was twice as big as it was before she left. But, for as much as she'd found, she couldn't help feeling she'd lost something on the way.

"Do you want to wait for midnight or do you want to leave now?" The irritation in Jake's voice wrenched her back to her senses. *Oh God, Jake.* What was she doing? "I'm so sorry. I'm just not…" What? What wasn't she? "Yeah, let's go."

Silence sat like a blindfold between them. Jake pulled up to the parking lot outside her apartment.

"What's up, Sara? I thought…" He was mad and guarded, but not enough. The tightness around the edges of his eyes gave him away. Sara knew he had a temper. She'd seen him get ejected from a ball game for punching a referee. Granted, the little weasel had made a string of bull-shit calls.

"I'm sorry. I—" What was she sorry for? When she was with Easton, she felt like she would die without him. Fear, love, and lust chanted and screamed in a thunderstorm that raged from her chest to her head. With Jake, it was something else. Quiet meadows, holding hands, reading the same book in the park—a little conversation about Tolstoy. This wasn't love, not the love she knew. This was—best friends. "I just think there's no future to this relationship."

Jake's face fell and his forehead crinkled. The angry tightness around his eyes crumpled into confusion. It would not have surprised her to know Jake had no concept of rejection. "What do you mean?"

"I mean, there's no passion here." His head tipped back like her words had physically hit his forehead. He turned to look out his window.

"No passion?" Apparently, she was the only one feeling that. Sara wasn't exactly teasing him when she abandoned her whole body to his kisses. He was just so comfortable—and those lips. God! She'd never kissed anyone with lips like those. And he had those basketball legs with the sculpted calves. But having dredged up all the feelings she'd had for Easton, so violent, how could she call what she felt for Jake "love"? "Look. I'm sorry. I mean, I love hanging out with you. But, there's just something missing."

"Right." He turned away and put both hands on the wheel. Jake never had to be told twice.

Sara opened the door, but stopped and leaned over to touch his arm. He flinched. "You're a good friend, Jake. Let's stay friends."

"Sure." He turned the key as she stepped out into the chill of the New Year's Eve night.

Chapter 33

(O)nly the shady spots that never saw the light still hid tiny drifts of brown, pox-marked snow. The tourist sun played in the *Côte d'Azur* blue of the skies. Students had abandoned their winter study cubicles and dotted the grassy squares of the commons in front of the library. French Lit 405 started in ten minutes. Sara had bought into the February thaw enough to dig out her little red Italian pumps. It was wishful thinking to imagine the winter was finished flogging them all, but the California girl in her couldn't get enough of the sun and was willing to pretend.

Glancing up from her watch, she smiled to see a familiar form that, like the sun, had been absent for the past couple of weeks. Purple t-shirt, well-cut 501's and Vuarnet glasses—the pair he bought with her in Paris—Jake lounged on the lawn behind a thick Economics book. Her heart pattered for a second, the way it did when the radio announcer predicted record-breaking temperatures for the week that would probably reach the seventies by today. Sara missed Jake the way she missed the sun.

Her leather heels clicked on the sidewalk and then sank a trail of holes into the damp soil beneath the warmed grass. Jake glanced up and smiled to see her. At least he wasn't bitter.

"You know," she pushed her sunglasses up on her head, "I was serious when I said we should still be friends."

"I've been busy. Economics."

"Yeah, I had that my Freshman year. Stopped going to the lectures like 98% of the other students and just read the text. Only got a B- on the final, though."

His eyebrow raised. "Sara Vale got a B?"

"That's what I thought. The curve made it an A." She grinned smugly.

"Of course, it did." He tipped his glasses up. "Nice weather for reading."

God, they were talking about the weather. The old Jake would have asked her out right now. She couldn't blame him for not lighting matches after he'd been burned. "Yeah. Beautiful. I missed the sun." She lit the match for him. "I'm serious, Jake." She knelt lower so she could look him in the eye. He had that rough country charm and blond curls she couldn't resist dragging her fingers through whenever she saw him. "Don't be a stranger."

He nodded, unwilling to pet the cat that scratched.

"Hey, my roommate picked up a video. *Lady Hawk*, I think. Have you heard of it? She said I had to see it. Do you want to come over? We could do a video night."

He shrugged. "Sure, why not?"

"Okay." She glanced at her watch. Class started in three minutes. "I gotta run. 7:00?"

"7:00."

Chapter 34

The living room window of Sara's basement apartment looked out onto the sidewalk that led to the front door. A familiar pair of well-sculpted legs strolled past. Some Man and Superman selective chemistry buzzed her brain whenever Jake walked by the window. Nature wanted those legs for her offspring.

Closing *La Chanson de Roland*, she hustled to answer the doorbell. Jake stood outside with flowers and chocolates in his hand.

"You shouldn't have." She was pleased that he did.

"I didn't. This girl in my complex, she's got this thing for me. She sent me flowers for Valentine's. What am I going to do with these?"

"Heartbreaker." She took them off his hands and dug a vase out from the cupboard.

"No, seriously. I don't encourage her at all. She's always coming over, making me dinner—"

Alarms went off in Sara's head—Jake loved food. Or maybe what he was saying slapped her upside. She stopped arranging the flowers. For three solid seconds, she stared. "What?"

"Nothing."

Like hell, nothing. For three seconds, she saw the Jake that other girls saw. The tall, rugged blonde, with the farm boy, basket-ball player build, the mysterious blue-green eyes, the raucous curls and the cheeky grin that never strayed far from his lips—oh, those lips. In that second, she realized she could lose him forever. He could decide to marry some love-sick co-ed in his apartment complex and suddenly, instead of his best friend, she'd be demoted to just some girl he used to know. The thought tilted her brain. Shaking herself, she finished arranging the flowers.

When the movie started, they were cozied up cross-legged on the couch with a fistful of chocolate bars each. By the time the credits started rolling, they were lying in each other's arms. Tears still wet Sara's eyes and her heart had swelled to twice its normal size.

The vision of Navarre holding up Isabeau in the center of the cathedral under the light of the receding eclipse still warmed her brain. Romance boiled in her blood. Her lips found Jake's like they were balm for the severely chapped. The soft imprint of his mouth on hers rippled down her neck, pinged into her fingers, and curled her toes. God, she'd missed him! Life flourished and flashed between them. Her fingers shredded those blond curls and his caressed the line of her waist. The credits ended and the violin and synth music that everyone hated played on repeat to the main menu.

Gasping, she crawled off the couch. "I—" she ran her fingers through her hair. "What a great movie! So glad you came."

Jake hauled himself off the couch. "You're killing me, Sara. Sometimes I think you're just using me, but I'm not sure for what."

"It's not that. It's…" She had no clue what it was. She just didn't know what she wanted, but she did know she didn't want to lose her best friend and it seemed like she was racing down that road.

"Forget it." He started walking to the door.

"Call me, okay?"

"I've got a big Accounting test. Then I'm out of town for the weekend."

"Oh." Now, Sara was dying.

He hesitated with his hand on the doorknob. "Why don't you come home with me for the weekend? It's a tiny mining town in south-central Utah, but we'll get out of the bubble for a while.

"Yeah! Let's do that!"

Chapter 35

The setting sun pricked at Sara's pink legs. The sun bouncing off the reservoir was stronger than the more distant California beach rays.

She and Jake walked into the valley of the creek bed. Green grass, cows, quivering leaves on white tree trunks, and willows rolled toward the mountains on the horizon. The setting sun blushed in pinks and purples behind the red rock castles. They stopped on the bridge and watched the water trickle by.

"Now I know why the girls line up to cook you dinner." Wet, on a pair of skis, Jake had glimmered with the free and fluid motion of a big fish in a small country pond. He jumped the wake, sent up rooster tails, did flips, and didn't give up until his arms gave out. "You have skills—and those adorable, unruly curls." She reached up and fluffed them with her fingertips. "You drive the boat, fix flat tires, back the trailer up to the dock like an expert. Is there anything you can't do?"

He shrugged and squeezed her hand. "We farm boys spent a lot of time on the reservoir. You weren't so bad yourself—for an amateur." Jake was a patient, funny coach, and had Sara scooting along over the waves by her third try. The looming threat of a watery crash exhilarated her. Her heart pumped until she rocked precariously, let go of the rope, and gently sank.

"The creek used to be bigger."

"Or maybe you were just smaller."

"Maybe. We used to ride our bikes along the edge of the road, and when a car came, we'd hop off. You can't see under there from the street and they'd think we crashed and drowned. We'd hang out underneath the bank laughing."

"Were you completely unsupervised?"

He chuckled and wagged his eyebrows. "On youth nights, we'd slip out of church and throw rocks at the bank alarm to set it off.

The cops could never catch us. Gave 'em somethin' to do, though."
He slipped into his accent a bit as he talked. "See those dunes over
there?" He pointed off into the distance where white, sandy hills
backed the boxy houses and trailers. "I used to ride my motorcycle
over there. That's how I got most of my scars." He lifted his sleeve
and the hem of his shorts to show her the faded pink gashes. Sara
inspected each scar with the tip of her finger. He shivered when she
brushed the inside of his bronzed thigh.

Below them, the creek babbled. The trees whispered in hushed
murmurs.

"Got this one when I broke my ulna." Glancing into his eyes,
she bent and brushed her lips on his forearm. He closed his eyes and
inhaled deeply as Sara trailed her lips to his shoulder. Wrapping his
arms underneath hers, he lifted her onto the railing of the bridge.
The sun was nearly gone. They were nothing but shadows on a
broad, dim horizon. His lips met hers and he devoured her with the
hunger begat of this life of open spaces and wide, uncharted roads.

Sara was gasping for air when he finally released her lips and
hugged his arms around her.

Pushing his shoulders away, she hopped down. They walked
silently back to the house, hand in hand, until she turned to face him
and the sunset. "Jake, I think I'm falling in love with you."

"You just now figuring that out?"

Chapter 36

The musical notes of the doorbell floated over the rush of the running water. Wearing nothing but one of Jake's oversized dress shirts, Sara rinsed and spit. Jake showed up early for dates—accounting major. She leaned around the wall of the bathroom door and shouted, "Come in." When the door opened, she called, "I'm not quite ready yet. I still have to blow dry my hair."

She shivered a little at the sight of Jake. He was so novel for her, such a drastic variation from the mold of boys she always seemed to attract. He was a universe foreign and unexplored, an unfamiliar terrain to attract the intrepid.

Striding to the kitchenette, he pulled up a chair and tossed a box of chicken strips onto the table. "Take your time. I just got out of class and grabbed something to eat." The hairdryer whirred to life. "Hey, I got an A- on that philosophy paper you wrote for me on the way home last weekend." Jake's voice floated just audible above the rush of the hot air whipping her hair.

"What?" She switched off the blow dryer.

"I got an A- on that paper you wrote." The words came out scrunchy, squished between mouthfuls of chicken nuggets smothered in dipping sauce.

Leaning around the wall that gave into the hallway, Sara had a direct line of sight to the kitchen table. "Oh, sorry. If I'd read the material you could have had an A. It's harder when someone is just telling you what they remember from the text."

"Sorry? For an A-?" Jake shook his head and rolled his eyes as the hairdryer spun back to life.

He was bent over his chicken strips when she snapped it off and stepped out from behind the bathroom wall. He turned and actually gasped, dropping the chicken strip and standing up.

The large, extra-long shirt that fit the stature of his chest covered her petite form like a dress just long enough to conceal the pertinent parts. With a wicked glint of pleasure, Sara watched Jake scan her bronzed bare legs and the shimmering sun bleach of her hair. She knew she should disappear into her room and come back in something more—well, just more. But the way Jake looked at her— as if he couldn't quite believe his good fortune—brought out a brazen streak. Jake made her feel like she was the only woman on the planet worth having.

Halfway down the hall, she met him and threw her arms around his neck. She wouldn't have done it with any other boy; it was too risky. She was totally bare underneath his shirt. But that was the allure of Jake. He could be teased mercilessly and counted on to do the honorable thing.

Her hair and lips, her whole body, were warm and humid from the shower and blow-dry. They melted into the unabashed desire that lingered candidly in Jake's demeanor when she was around him. She marveled that when she said they were just "best friends," he had still hung about hopefully, even though he knew she was dating other guys. His lips were warm and generous, soft and full. From his photo albums, she knew she wasn't the first girl he'd kissed, but she could tell she was the only one that counted. And when she pushed him away because the thick atmosphere of desire engulfed them and stole her breath away, he let her go.

Things had changed for Sara. Her world was broader, she'd found a vocation for teaching, all she needed was another road warrior to forge a path with her through the roaming fields ahead. It wasn't the exotic unknown that spoke love to her anymore. It was the broad arms of being home and the equality of mutual admiration. She and Jake completed each other and the oneness fueled a passion she'd never known, profound and timeless, something buried in the very essence of who she was beyond her flesh. Her voice was still husky when she reappeared in jeans and a t-shirt. "I don't usually go for blond, athletic guys. I've always been a sucker for tall, dark, artistic types with green eyes."

"Well, I've got green eyes."

"Today. Tomorrow they might be blue."

"Good enough."

He grabbed her hand and pulled her into another mind-altering kiss. "I thought you said there wasn't any passion between us." His voice was huskily full of it.

"That was last month. Actually, I think you'd better ask me to marry you before we get ourselves in trouble."

Chapter 37
—From the unfinished manuscript of Ethan McCarthy

Whitewashed spires and stained glass behind trimmed hedges barricaded me from witnessing the wedding of Sara Elizabeth Vale to Jake Dawson on August 16, 1986. The sacred halls would blister and boil the runes tattooed around my arm. The bankrupt organ in my chest beat out the minutes. A giant maple shaded the grass on which I stood in the park opposite the church. The hushed rush of wings rustled at my shoulder and the hot breath of Brann Sidhe slithered into my ear. "Dearest Ethan, will you give up the game so easily?"

My shoulders stiffened at her gloating. Fervently, I desired to hide from the muse the searing pain that burned the fibers of every shard of my being as if destiny had taken a blade to my skin and flayed it inch by inch. As well I should stuff bacon in my pocket to conceal it from a dog as bury the suffering she sniffed out voraciously.

"What is marriage? The bond meant nothing one hundred years ago when death broke it so easily. But you managed to cheat death. Is this man stronger than such a formidable foe that you cannot defeat him again?"

"Again?"

Chimes tittered in the leaves of the tree as she giggled. "Do you not recognize him? An old and faithful friend."

"You brought him back?" Rage gave me vision into the secrets behind her purple irises. Ah, the fiend! This was the card she concealed in the bodice near her cold, pale breast. She had not only fanned to life the embers of Elizabeth's dying soul, but she had also lit the wick of the man that inevitably challenged our love— existence upon existence. "Jackson Richards died. He died on the battlefield at Antietam, the same night Elizabeth died. He dragged a wad of her life threads away with him. He has already spent his sojourn here."

Brann Sidhe clucked as if the laws of the universes and the Barrow were such boring trifles. "He was so forlorn when I found him near the bridge, bleeding and broken. About his neck, on a gold chain, he still wore the ring, you know—the diamond she pulled from her finger when he left to fight his war, and she chose to marry you instead." With her pale white pinky finger, she feigned the wiping of a tear from the corner of her eye. "He's giving it to her now—a family heirloom bequeathed at the death of a distant cousin."

"Deceitful whore." The invisible chains tattooed across my forearm burned. The muse waged her game from a pinnacle overlooking ages and epics. How could I, confined to my narrow slice of time, hope to defeat her?

"Do not rant against me, dear Ethan. The playing field had to be restored, each piece returned to its square. But do not despair, of all these wispy beings that float under the hill, you know how fleeting are their vows and promises. They are so easily despised and broken. Be patient, my love. You need only uncover the flaw in the fabric and pull at the threads until the veil is rent."

God help me. Hope sprang from the muse's words. Not the hope of warbling bluebirds and spring buds, but the hope of black and bloody tendrils spawned from vengeance.

There was only one way to draw the pain out of my skin, away from my insides where it ripped and tore. In my studio, I slashed the lines onto the canvas, stopping to double over, muscles clenched. My colors were blacks and browns, reds besmirched in gray. With rage and vengeance, I fought against sorrow and loss. By the time the sun had set, I had fashioned the horror of the dead-man-living that I had become. Sinking to my knees, I strangled the sobs, lamenting years of torturous labor delivered to a still and lifeless love. When the storm had passed, I sank into the numbing folds of an armchair and stared blankly out the windows at the end of the day.

My mourning deluded me. I imagined the monster would leave me to suffer alone the agony of defeat. But when the flurry of ash danced before the windowpane, I knew that this was what Brann Sidhe craved, this was what she had hoped to draw from my depths—hope shattered and torn. Where a century of her demented love had failed to bring her the flavor of my soul she so desired, one word from Sara's mouth, spoken to another man, had succeeded.

The smile already graced her face before she even fully materialized. She let her head tilt back and breathed deeply the aroma of agony in the room. "For so long I have waited for this rare and exotic spice."

She savored the smell before she brought her eyes to rest on my broken form, sprawled in the chair. Raking four fingers across my cheek, she sucked each dry between amethyst lips. For a full minute, she stood still, absorbing the delicacy. "Cailen Sidhe's flavor is gone! You are mine."

Her victory kindled the rage of the defeated again. "I still have more than twenty years before you have won."

"Yes! Yes!" The purple muse gazed lovingly at the tasty morsel I had just created for her. "You must seethe against this perverse turn of fate and destiny."

"Witch! This is what you have craved all along. It is for the bitter that you lust."

"I have never denied it." She shrugged. Although it tore my soul and cast it to the dogs, I could not resist the power of her smile. A thrill of desire rippled from my spine to my toes.

Disgusted with the weakness of the flesh, I turned away from the sight of her. Anger was useless. It would only feed her gluttony. "Did you know that Elizabeth would spurn me in the end? How did you know? I was so sure of her love and loyalty—so sure that it would flow beyond lifetimes."

"I knew because you were so sure of her—and she was so fiercely independent." She chuckled at her cleverness and the room shivered with a tremor of wind chimes. "The very strength of love and loyalty that bound her to you will bind her to him."

Despair creased my brow and moved Brann Sidhe to boldness. "Unfortunately, the terms of our bargain strictly forbid you from seducing her from her husband. Perhaps you should murder him." She clapped her hands and licked her lips at the sumptuousness of such a scene.

One hundred years earlier, I would have recoiled from the source of such degeneracy. Knowing the depth and breadth of life, the Leanan Sidhe have no respect for its minutiae. Mere mortals, in the thick of ignorance, cradle each tiny speck of it. But my nose had grown accustomed to the stench of her calloused inhumanity, having so long wallowed in it. "You don't yet own my soul."

"No, of course not! Not yet." Her giggling tainted the air, infectious and tempting. "Oh, I am drunk on the flower of your wine." Unable to resist, she seized my hand and licked the icing of creation from my fingers. "Food of the gods!" Her tongue tickled the imagination and engendered images of such inspiration that I could barely restrain myself from picking up a brush to murder them on canvas.

Her eyes narrowed as if the soup lacked a tiny pinch of some seasoning which only she knew how to procure.

"Perhaps there will be moments of weakness or discord in Elizabeth's union. Marriage these days is such a fragile thread. If you are there, she might turn to you of her own will and choice when it snaps." The light of brilliance on Brann's face illuminated the room. "Shall I feed you visions of her and her happy home in the night? Would you like to know her every thought and movement, joy and pain, so that you might strategically position yourself at precisely the right moment?"

The glare in my eyes spoke the answer and confirmed to her the great benefit of not respecting my wishes. Her eyes gleamed. As long as Sara haunted my dreams, happy in the arms of another, Brann Sidhe would feast upon the tortured morsels of my gall. "They say that time heals all wounds, Ethan, my pet; how convenient that you have so much of it."

Chapter 38

—Excerpts from the unpublished writings of Easton Ravenscroft

The giggling of toddler girls woke Sara. Following the warbling into the bathroom, she found three-year-old Elizabeth pampering her nearly nude, eighteen-month-old sister Grace with a Vaseline facial and scalp massage.

Grace smiled broadly, wiped a glob of jelly from her tummy, and held it up. "Geeew!" Her little turned-up nose crinkled.

Sara taught English and spoke fluent French, yet she had no words for this situation. Standing in the doorway, her mouth open, and her eyes darting back and forth from masseuse to client, she wondered how one went about cleaning up the mess.

Face to face with an authority figure, Elizabeth became sensible to the possible inappropriateness of her morning's activities. She jumped up and stood behind her mother, hastening to cover her butt—literally and figuratively. "Gracy wanted to put it on. I helped her." Her little chest puffed proudly.

"Elizabeth Dawson! Look at this mess! You're a big girl; you know better than to do this! Mommy is *not* happy." Snatching Elizabeth's hand, Sara commanded Grace to stay put and hauled Elizabeth away to serve time-out for contributing to the delinquency of a minor.

Bathing Grace while Elizabeth railed against the injustice of justice, Sara felt like an environmentalist cleaning up small animals trapped in an oil spill. Grace would be slippery for a week.

When she was done, Sara carted Grace off and sentenced her to serve time with Elizabeth in the new living room chair, the only seat large enough to contain the two of them but small enough to discourage gymnastics. While Sara mopped up the floor, Grace whined in harmony with her sister.

Muttering to herself, Sara scrubbed and wiped. One more squirt of dish soap...she stopped abruptly, hearing all too clearly the "puff" of the dispenser and the "swish" of the cloth. The silence screamed sirens. She raced down the stairs. A mischievous chuckle trickled from behind the stripes of the empty prison cell.

In two strides she crossed the room and leaned around the backside. Grace grinned; Elizabeth cowered at the maternal monstrosity looming above. Slowly, the child handed her mother the butter knife she had used to saw away the threads along the stripes on the back of the chair. As Sara's fist closed around the prickly spikes of the metal, she wanted to cry. That chair was only two days old—and expensive.

Elizabeth broke into a sobbing frenzy. Sara carried her away into her room and plopped her into one of her plastic tea table chairs. "See your pretty chairs you just got for your birthday? How would you like it if mommy broke one?" Enough adrenaline was charging through her veins to crack the little chair with one good kick. The effort to hold back taxed the remaining thread of her patience.

"I don't care!" Elizabeth sniffed obstinately.

Sara didn't dare respond; she was afraid flames would spew from her mouth. Among the ample collection of toys, she found ammunition. She seized the baby doll from the cradle and shook her in front of Elizabeth's nose. "What about Baby Lucy? What if mommy broke her?"

A flash of panic invaded her daughter's face.

"You see? It makes people sad when you ruin their things. You just sit here and hold Baby Lucy and think about how mommy feels 'cause you ruined her new chair."

Clicking the door shut on her daughter's defiant sniffling, Sara headed back to the mess in the bathroom. For the second time that morning, words abandoned her. Grace had returned to the scene of her original sin, climbed up the drawers, stolen the fingernail polish, and painted a mural on her bare belly. And, of course, she'd spilled the remainder of the fingernail polish remover on the counter. Heaving an enormous sigh, Sara glanced at the clock. 9:15. It was going to be a long day. Mornings like these, she missed her professional days as a French teacher.

The girls were listening to stories in their matching Lion King pajamas by the time Jake got home at 8:30. The mood was generally sullen with a dash of exhaustion. Sara informed "their dad" about the girls' morning antics.

"Cutting up the living room chairs with knives!" he exclaimed in mock horror. "Maybe that means she has a future as a surgeon. Do you want to be a doctor, Elizabeth?" The imp nodded, eyes twinkling. Jake assumed his most sinister voice. "But you have destroyed the sacred living room chair! You must be punished severely." The little girls squealed and jumped out of the covers. Jake turned to Sara.

She couldn't help but smile. It was, after all, only a chair and no one ever saw the back of it anyway. "We will cut them up in little pieces and throw them in the soup!" she proclaimed ominously.

The little girls ran, screaming and giggling, for their lives. Jake and Sara caught them up, gnawed on their tummies, and hauled them into the bathtub to make "witch stew." Thirty minutes later, Elizabeth and Grace tumbled into the covers and cuddled up to good night kisses.

On the stairs outside their bedroom, Jake and Sara sat exhausted.

Jake ran his fingers through her hair. His touch still drew a contented sigh. "Our children are beautiful and smart—like their mother."

"Smart little shits!" she countered. He chuckled at the sound of his farm dialect rolling off her educated lips. Sara leaned her head on his shoulder. "They're intrepid and confident—like their dad."

"We have a pretty good recipe, you and I." He squeezed her shoulders.

"Oh, I see where this is going. You'd like to do a little baking." She checked her watch. "I'm afraid the kitchen is closed for the night."

"What if I make it worth your while?"

"What have you got?" She tilted her head up so that the breath from her lips touched his. He took the offer, pressing his against hers softly.

He reached into his pocket and produced a plastic bottle of massage oil. The expensive kind.

"Lavender. Unfair. You know I can't resist."

"I can offer back rubs, foot rubs—full-body massages."

"Done. Neck and shoulders." Sara scooted down to the lower step and ripped away her shirt. Spreading an ample pool of oil on his palms, Jake kneaded the frustrations and pressures from her muscles. His fingers and the lavender eased the tension and, in its place, trickled in desire and the warmth of two making one.

Leaning back, Sara looked in the face of family—friendship and love all molded into one—a recipe for endurance. A roguish grin curled her lips. "I'm tired of the usual spots. Let's spice it up a bit."

"I have the perfect spot for a little late-night snack." Gathering her up in his arms, he carried her down the steps and set her on the kitchen island.

"We haven't been here for a while." Nearly every room in the house dripped with remnants of stolen romance.

Sara pressed her body into the warmth of his arms. Their lips found each other in the dark. She marveled at the power of this man to transform all her life's dramas into comedies. The wonder bled into the passion of their kiss, sank beneath their skin, and bonded the two of them with secret strands that linked their souls.

Dearest Elizabeth,

Images of another man's lips on your bare skin tortured our dreams and added to our work the spice of torment that so sated Brann's hunger. Every scene drove the dagger to new depths. The conjugal bliss in which you bathed chiseled out the words with which Easton sculpted your story on the page. Oh, how we felt you as if we were nothing more than a puppet moved and manipulated with every tiny impulse of your joy and sorrow, lust and love, with every curve of your lip and frown of your brow. From the inside, these visions devoured our sanity and maybe our humanity.

Forever,
Ethan

Chapter 39

Grace sat on the edge of the bathroom sink while Sara brushed and braided her honey-blonde hair. Elizabeth, waiting her turn, sorted through the bows looking for pink to match their Disney Princess shirts. Jake showed up at the bathroom door toting Danny and carrying the baby, Annie, looking at his watch.

Twenty minutes later, they were all seat belted into the minivan on the way to Disneyland. After about three hours, stuffed in the car with an ample supply of M&M's, coloring books, and TY babies, Jake pulled off the highway into the Gas and Grocery. A minor exodus followed as the wild band, freed at last, invaded the candy aisle and overflowed ICEE onto the counters.

"For hell's sake!" Jake stood open-mouthed at the havoc his children wreaked, utterly astonished to find himself, a successful accounting executive, at the head of such an ungovernable crew. He gathered up their purchases and shooed them toward the door as they tumbled about like marbles dumped from the bag. After the siege, an amused smile brushing her lips, Sara brought up the rear of the retreat.

It was from that vantage point that, for a brief moment, she saw, really saw, her husband—saw him the way a tourist would: the tall, blonde executive with the sculpted calves, herding their four children under six.

Jake buckled the troops into their white mini-van. He drank diet Coke and chewed sunflower seeds to stay awake while his family slept.

Seven hours later, all of them plodded through the lobby of the hotel booked on Jake's points. After the last baby was breathing deeply and rhythmically, dreaming of princesses, castles, and roller coasters, Sara crawled in the sheets and quietly drenched Jake's road-weary body with a shower of kisses.

He was exhausted, but it wasn't every day Sara did the wooing, and he'd downed enough caffeine to give a zombie a buzz. She wooed her husband with her hands and lips, with her legs and arms wrapped around his like ivy on brick.

His fingers found her shoulders and neck. Following the curves around to her bare back, he wrapped his arms beneath hers and pulled her up until her breasts rested on his chest and his lips moved on hers. She knew well his look of complete mystification at the random nature of his wife that sparked such outbursts of passion. Sara didn't enlighten him; instead, she submerged her reasons in the silent pool of women's secrets from where they would bubble up when she stirred the still waters.

The endless black ribbon of road, the battles with small soldiers of chaos, the cell phone that wouldn't stop buzzing, everything disappeared. It was just the two of them—together.

Afterward, standing in front of the bathroom mirror with his arms draped around her naked body, Sara turned her back to the glass, took his face in her hands, and whispered, like an oath, "I love you."

He brought his lips down to hers, kissed them softly, and pressed deeper and firmer, imprinting her lips and body into his like memory foam.

Dearest Elizabeth,

Grasping at every flimsy opportunity that presented itself, prying at every chink, I turned to the twenty-seven-year-old version of myself and dubbed him Elliot Shee. I thought perhaps, overwhelmed with the daily drudgery of motherhood and household chores, a liberating dalliance with a younger man, the name of the boy you had first loved, might entice you. Elliot knew nothing but you lost and the one night spent in the arms of Marie Clémentine.

> *Forever,*
> *Ethan*

Chapter 40

"I think it's an excellent opportunity." Jake stuffed his keys in his trouser pocket. By the time she was ten, Elizabeth had bounced with them to four "great opportunities" and six homes.

It was a great opportunity, though, so Jake bought a house in the Boston suburbs. Sara didn't even see it first, but he knew what she liked, and she knew she could make whatever he picked look like home.

In September, their youngest, Annie, went to kindergarten. The fates smiled upon them. There was one charter school in the town that offered French courses instead of Spanish. By some stroke of magic, the school pulled Annie's name from the lottery hat first. That moved all their other children up on the waiting list so that they all started at the charter school that year.

Just when Sara was contemplating dusting off her brushes and easels to take advantage of her upcoming six hours of solitude a day, the French specialist's husband was transferred to Ohio and she stepped right out of mommydom and back into teacherdom. It was ideal; she got to work where her kids were going to school. Since it was part-time, she also got to paint.

To get serious about painting, she took a class. The brush in her hand filled one small corner of her being that longed to create, to bring to life something of beauty. In her quiet moments, in front of the canvas in the sunny room over the garage, trying out techniques she found on the Internet, she blossomed.

Thursday afternoon after her first week on the job, she breezed into the faculty lunchroom and sat down to a sprinkle of comments about her new chin-length haircut. "Thanks! It's so much easier." Sara dug into her lunch bag. She couldn't believe they were actually paying her to teach French in her children's school. She would have volunteered. Renewed professionalism exhilarated her.

"Did you see the new art teacher?" asked Mrs. B, Grace's fourth-grade teacher.

"No. I heard he was coming today, though. That was so sad about Ms. Cherry. I guess she just had some kind of a breakdown?"

"That's a nice way of putting it." Mrs. Sanderson, the second-grade teacher, snorted and popped the top off a plastic container of fruit. The other second-grade teacher, Karen, was Danny's teacher. She was more of an optimist and less strict than Mrs. Sanderson.

"He's absolutely gorgeous." Karen handed her a napkin from the container at the other end of the table.

"Oh, wait a minute! He's not that tall, dark-haired guy with the amazing green eyes I saw coming down the stairs?" Sara traveled from classroom to classroom. The charter school was a small, converted Catholic school with not a classroom to spare.

"Oh, yes he is!" Mrs. Sanderson folded her arms across the table and nodded ominously.

"Man! I was wondering whose dad he was. He looked so familiar. I thought one of his kids must be at the school."

"He's single." Karen shrugged her brows.

"There's a reason to stay." Sara nudged her. "I want you to be Annie's teacher." Karen was finishing up her Masters and thinking of taking an administrative job in a public school. "What's his name again, Karen? I think I remember reading the email, but my brain is overflowing."

"Elliot."

"You'd think I'd remember that. I dated an Elliot when I was growing up. Come to think of it, maybe that's why I thought I recognized him. He looks a little like the Elliot I dated. God! I hope they aren't related." Sara bit into her sandwich. "I'm only forty. I realize I'm old enough to be teaching the kids of my high school classmates, but please, tell me I'm not old enough to be teaching WITH their kids!" She plucked a cherry tomato from her salad and popped it in her mouth. "Looked about in his late twenties, like you, Karen."

Karen rolled her eyes, pleased.

"That would be so freaky if they were related." Sara chewed thoughtfully. "I'm not sure what happened to him. He went away to school in New York."

One random Tuesday, near the end of the school year, the art teacher bumped into her at the copy machine. "Hey, Mrs. Dawson."

"Oh, hey, uh, Elliot, right? How are you? My kids loved the Christmas snow creatures. You do the most wonderful projects." She dropped an original in the machine. Rifling through the stack in her hands, she smiled at the art teacher. Their paths rarely crossed. *He is truly gorgeous. Why hasn't Karen been all over him?* "I meant to come up and tell you, but I don't get up to the third floor much. With four kids, teaching part time, and my 'secret hobby' I just…well, you know…"

"That's why I came down—to find you."

"Oh?" She loaded the next original.

"I was going to do a French Impressionism unit and I wondered if we could collaborate?"

The copy machine ground to a halt. *Was that a shock from the copier or did I just shiver?* "Of course, I'm always up for a group project. Do you know Karen?" She scanned his face for some sign of reaction and found it blank. "Ms. Gregory? The second-grade teacher?"

"Oh, yes. Very nice."

"Karen spent some time in France. I bet she'd be happy to work with us, too."

He took a step back. "I wasn't thinking of a big production. Just a little cross-curricular project. Could we maybe get together and chat about it?"

This was a very reasonable request, so why did she feel like a sixth-grader being asked out for the first time? "Sure. How about lunch on Wednesday?" Pulling a stuck page from the copier's innards, Sara restarted the machine, then leaned in confidentially. "I'm a closet artist myself. It's so enriching! Art transforms existence into life."

"—or hell." After the words were out, the wrinkles that pinched his eyes spoke regret. "I mean art can be draining when you get too caught up in it."

Awkward. Maybe he'd spent too much time teaching art to kids. Maybe he wanted to be an artist more than a teacher. "I wouldn't know. I'm pretty much an amateur. There's a part of me, etched somewhere deep, that craves it." Sara hefted her stacks of copies.

Elliot dragged the hair back out of his face. "See you Wednesday?"

"Right!"

Wednesday, at 11:27, she wandered into his empty room. Sara ate rice leftovers and Elliot worked on a deli sandwich. They settled on the artists they wanted to highlight and exchanged reminiscences of their trips to Paris.

"I actually met my husband there." She nibbled off the end of a carrot.

"Hmmm." He took a large bite of his sandwich.

"How can you not fall in love in Paris?" She sipped her fruit punch from a juice box.

"Yes, how can you not?"

Sara suggested some fun art history games and activities. Elliot sketched out his end of the unit project. He clearly liked teaching the kids, but there was a vague deadness behind his eyes. It lingered there until she glanced up from the schedule they were writing and caught him looking at her like she was cheesecake and he was on a low-carb diet. When she felt a twinge of hunger rise up from some unexplored chasm within, a certain sense of creepiness washed over her. *I could have been his babysitter.* Abruptly, she finished her list, organized the papers, and stood up. "This should be fun. The kids are going to love it." Smiling encouragingly, she bolted for the door.

Sara sucked at the nectar of professional competence, domestic adventure and marital bliss. She wasn't about to throw over the sheer power of that nurturing to lick at the crumbs of some tantalizing cupcake.

Dearest Elizabeth,

Steeped for so long in the stew of Brann Sidhe's guile, Elizabeth, I had forgotten with what sturdy integrity you bound your heart to those you love.

Forgive me,
Ethan

Chapter 41

—Excerpts from the journals of Elliot Shee

The door slammed shut behind me. I found the raven muse lounging on the armchair in my studio, languidly stroking Boo, only a kitten now. Brann Sidhe was drawn to the aroma of this room like a child to bread baking in the kitchen.

"Such tantrums, my love. Did the children treat you poorly?" She nuzzled Boo's downy chest.

"I'm not your love." I sank into a chair.

"So delightful—children. There is one boy who shows such talent in your classes—if only he had the proper inspiration—"

"Fiend! They're children!" My revulsion lacked fire, having cooled and hardened over a century, but I could not dismiss from my mind the crime she had committed in stealing away the child I had never met. Perhaps knowing that this child was only another manifestation of myself in her chains resigned me to his fate. I had not, at least, jeopardized the soul of an innocent.

"Oh, I see. Another plan to lure Sara to you has gone awry."

Standing, I removed the kitten from her lap. Boo stretched and settled into my arms. I spoke to her rather than the creature in the chair.

"I thought maybe she'd go for a younger man."

"But you don't understand, Elliot, my dear. I'm trying to help you. Why do you pay no attention to the dreams?"

"The dreams are not for me. You only send them because they torture me with images of my love laughing in another man's arms, loving and nurturing another's children, sharing the rubies of life with a stranger. And because they feed you well. You're a glutton."

Brann Sidhe wrinkled her nose. "You are each so different, and yet all the same to me. You still do not understand me."

"We understand you well enough. You are death in a black diamond."

She paused; the image pleased her. Mincing across the floor, she stroked the cat and then knelt so that she looked me in the eye. "The Leanan Sidhe do not take without giving. We are not beggars. The dreams may feed me, but they are of great value to you. You must wait and watch. Just now, Sara's road is broad, paved, and straight; all her life is harmony and forward motion. Wait until the path narrows, curves, and becomes rocky. She will stumble and you, one of you, must be there to catch her."

PART 3

Chapter 42
—Excerpts from the unpublished writings of Easton Ravenscroft

Sara Elizabeth's arms shook with the turbulence of the plane. The obscenely good-looking man in the seat next to her glanced sideways at what she was reading. Reclining, she feigned fatigue—well, maybe not feigned. Her insides were at war. She remembered that somewhere they called moving a "life event."

The book she was reading didn't calm the situation any. The story drawn in its pages evoked a whole different torrent of emotions antithetical to exhaustion—but likely to lead there. Sometimes she glanced at the faces around her because she was sure that the heat billowing into her head and the images of bodies writhing in passion were visible to anyone sitting too close.

Her hand slid over the novel's title. She had avidly consumed regency romance in high school, but nothing like this. Even at forty-something, she didn't feel mature enough to be reading this book. She kept her eyes focused on the rounded ceiling, warding off any attempt at polite conversation. She didn't want to talk to the stranger in the seat next to her because the book had conjured up this absurd urge, an insane impulse, to lean over and taste with her lips the curves of his luxurious mouth.

Breathing in reality, she returned resolutely to the story of dysfunctional, unfettered twenty-somethings making wanton and blissful love. As she read, memories of youth lost licked at her toes and tickled her lips.

Through the cyan canvas framed by the eight-inch porthole to her left, clouds floated oblivious and plump. She glanced past her thirty-something neighbor—maybe late thirty-something, it was hard to tell—into the cabin. The flight offered a modest selection of assorted businessmen—bald with glasses hunched over a computer screen; polished executive with a splash of gray for credibility; slightly chubby, wide-eyed salesman. A grimace crinkled her face and she shivered involuntarily. Other than Jake and their son Danny, who seemed to take largely after her, she could only tolerate a handful of men. She wore a man like she wore a shoe. Once she found one that fit comfortably and looked great on, she wore it until it fell off her foot.

Either her foot had shrunk a bit, or Jake had stretched; the snug fit of him was feeling loose. The tingling, that seemed to be emanating from the man blocking her free access to the aisle, was either the odd needling effect of blood rushing into an extremity suddenly freed after a snug confinement or a side-effect of over-dosing on the romance novel. Either way, she couldn't slough off the odd impression that she knew him from somewhere.

Squirming, Sara Elizabeth devoured the next chapter. The pages of the TIMES rattled and shifted in her direction. An errant ray of morning sunshine streaming in the porthole caught the gold medallion that lay on the chest of the man behind the newspaper.

He tilted his head to see the cover of the book hidden by the flat of her palm. In the moment before his eyes met hers, she perused again his face and shivered to find him so familiar. Then again, his features were classic, like those that floated in her imagination and found their way into her paintings. In the flash of an eye, she absorbed the tousled hair that matched the stubble-fringed jaw. Normally, she was opposed to earrings on men, but the small diamond that pierced this guy's ear suited him. He had the requisite pirate look like he could steal her heart and ransom it back to her.

Their eyes met in a glance. She dropped hers, abashed by the frankly appraising gaze of deep green fortified by lashes that only men should have because they'd be such an unfair advantage to any woman. In that split second, a spark of recognition flared somewhere in her subconscious. He was so familiar. Still, she just couldn't place him. Someone she'd dated in college?—too young.

A former colleague? In the wake of Jake's professional wanderings, she couldn't keep track of all the faces that had come and gone.

"You going home or leaving it?" The familiar stranger folded the paper.

It was a bizarre way to put it. "Uh, leaving. I'm just going for a visit. House hunting. We're moving to the Dallas area. Do you live there?" It was only polite to ask.

"My son is transferring to UT Dallas."

"Oh, my daughter Elizabeth will be a freshman there this year. Maybe they'll run into each other."

"Lucky for him if he does—if your daughter takes after you." His smile triggered alarms in Sara's head.

"Ha! She might be safer if she doesn't—if your son takes after you." A shock of recognition unsettled her when they exchanged grins. She rambled through the discomfiture. "She does look like me. A little blonder, blue eyes, fewer wrinkles, about twenty years lighter." Sara could hardly believe she was in her mid-forties. She felt so much younger inside.

"I'll tell my son to keep his eyes open." He stuffed the paper in the compartment behind the seat in front. "You planning to teach after the move?"

The question shocked her. Perhaps she *was* talking to a former colleague—or a stalker! After three years of teaching elementary French at her children's charter school, the family had bounced to another "great job opportunity" for Jake and another home in another city where she had adapted, unboxed her files, and become a French teacher at Elizabeth's high school. Maybe she was sitting next to the parent of a former student. "What gave me away?"

He nodded at her carry-on. "The red pen sticking out of your purse. Only teachers have red pens in their purses."

She smirked and paused to think about whether or not she would jump back into teaching. "No, actually, I think I might paint for a bit." She offered him a hand. "I'm Sara. Dawson."

"Ethan McCarthy." He took the hand.

The touch of his flesh on hers sent effervescent chills tingling up her arm. She cringed at the utterly adolescent response and pulled her hand away abruptly. Shifting in the seat, she clutched the book. "Nice to meet you."

Chapter 43

The taxi from the airport dropped Sara at Jake's hotel in Plano, a large suburb just outside of Dallas. She could hardly put the book down to gather her carry-on and navigate the revolving door.

"I'd like a key to Jake Dawson's room, please." The pasty-faced desk clerk glanced at her license, looked up the number, and swiped her a key.

The card clicked in the lock and she opened the door to vanilla walls, a standard plaid pullout, and soulless sceneries hanging askew. A puffy queen bed labored under mounds of pillows in white cotton slips. Sick inside, thinking of the months and miles that lay between them, Sara wondered how Jake could stand this sterile life four days a week, month after month. At least, at home in Boston, she had the children and their extravagant lifestyles to paint color into her life.

Parking her suitcase, she pulled out her phone. Texting took longer, but Jake was in meetings and would answer a text but not a call.

S: *Your hotel room just got homier.*
J: *Did you get a key?*
S: *Yeah. Don't worry. I only found socks strewn on the floor. No panties… I could fix that.*
J: *What kind?*
S: *Purple lace thong.*
J: *Edible?*
S: *Did you want to do lunch in?*
J: *My meeting is nearly over. Strawberries in fridge.*

The idea came from the book. Sara slipped out of white capris and dug in the suitcase for the matching purple push-up bra and thong handed down from a girlfriend that got a boob job. She hadn't pulled them on for months and, truth be told, may have rounded out a bit since then. The last time she ventured down this road was probably two years earlier when Jake's company sent them to the Bahamas as a bonus.

Sara rarely did the seducing and never had even contemplated anything so brazen as showing up in his hotel room wearing so little. But with the months of living apart, they didn't have time together anymore; the bond between them was wilting under the heat of upheaval. It was time for something groundbreaking.

She stood in front of the sliding closet mirror, her head tilted to one side, her nose wrinkled. Fifteen years ago, this might have been a better idea.

Rolling her eyes, she stripped off the lacey underwear and slipped into a negligee. She just wasn't that comfortable with her body anymore. With four kids and a job, she relied on Jake's healthy sex drive to hunt her down, whisk her away, and unplug the world. For the first time in their married life, she was feeling lonely.

She fiddled with her hair and ran lipstick around the full curves of her mouth. Her nose crinkled as she took in the wrinkles in all the wrong places. Jake had always been a legs man, maybe some high heels would draw his eye away from the flaws. She slid her strappy red heels back on. Four extra inches of leg altered the landscape enough that she risked a second look at the lingerie.

Pulling off the nightie, Sara wriggled back into the bra and thong and turned a critical eye back to the mirror. The good news was she still had nice shoulders and she'd never had much of a bust line so there wasn't any sagging going on. A *Maison Lejaby* bra could work serious optical illusions.

Standing mostly naked in the kitchenette, she cut the green tops from strawberries. The impulse to run and slip into one of Jake's shirts haunted her. The adventure of seduction was a bit intoxicating and just a tad scary.

Strolling to the couch, she displayed herself and picked up her book and a strawberry. She needed more light to read, but at the moment, shadows were her friends. The awful thought crossed her mind that she knew most of the people that Jake was working with now. They were old friends and his office was just across the street. What if he brought some of them back to the room to say "hi"?

The scene played out in her head in all its awkward splendor. *Nice to see you again. You're looking well.*

It occurred to her that this hadn't worked out so well for the woman in the book. But then, *she* went to her husband's office. This was a hotel room. But, just to be safe, Sara opted for the bed, strategically positioned out of the direct line of sight from the door. She had just arranged herself languidly and bitten off the round end of a strawberry when she heard the key card click in the lock. Her heart pattered like a hummingbird trapped behind bars.

Jake walked in, paused at the kitchen table, and then rounded the wall. His eyes widened at the sight of her. She couldn't quite decide if he was pleased or—*God, is he annoyed?* "Look at you!" He smiled and kissed her lightly.

"You want a strawberry?" She handed him the bowl.

He plucked out the darkest one and popped it in his mouth. "A little too sour for me."

"Come here." She wagged a finger seductively, setting aside the book.

Jake glanced at his watch. "We're supposed to be at the house at 12:30."

"We can be a little late. It's a house inspection. They'll start without us and tell us the bad news at the end." Her eyelashes danced lazily over her eyes.

Jake's jaw set. She hadn't shown up at his office in all her seductive splendor, but he'd plainly brought the office back to the room with him. Still in full-on executive mode, his face tightened sternly. "Let's do this right, Sara, tonight, when I'm off work." Leaning back, he held out a smooth, masculine, sexy hand to help her off the bed.

From that hand, the severed head of her sexual revolution dripped bloody. Buried somewhere deep within her psyche, a metal link in the chain that bound her to Jake exploded and dissolved in the acid of rejection.

She gripped his palm, laughing off the humiliation, as he snapped her off the bed. She'd only been flirting anyway. It was more of a joke than anything. She tripped toward the bathroom, the floor reeling a bit beneath her—or was that her whole universe tipping?

Seriously? No kissing? No groping? Nothing? The shock waves amplified as she stared at her image in the mirror. How was that even possible? For as long as they'd been together, Sara had wielded a subtle seductive power over her husband. Any time, any place, Jake was in the mood. It was a constant between them.

Refusing to be refused, she turned on her heel and followed her husband to the miniature kitchen table. An open bag of assorted nuts sat on the counter. She cuddled up under his shoulder as he dropped a handful into his mouth.

"Your thirty-year-old self wouldn't have passed up that invitation." Standing on tiptoe, she teased him with puckered lips.

He raised an eyebrow, nodded with a grin, and kissed her. His lips were warm and reassuring, but the passion of reckless abandon was gone. Checking his watch, he gave her backside a little push toward the bathroom. "Later."

Unhinged, she slipped away and dressed behind closed doors. Desperate, her psyche recycled the tinge of pleasure she'd felt when the rakish stranger on the plane had unabashedly flirted with her. At least someone still found her desirable. Just thinking about it felt like a betrayal, and she pushed the scene away, but she needed something to bolster her dignity. It was sinking like an unexploded mine into the pit of her stomach.

She wanted to rage, but she hadn't seen Jake for weeks. She hadn't come to Dallas to fight. They were so close to putting an end to the distance between them. Anyway, it was a stupid, impulsive idea. If she hadn't been reading that book or sitting by that criminally good-looking man, she'd never have imagined pulling a stunt like that. Burying the devastating bomb in a foam of levity, she called from the bathroom. "I can't wear a purple thong under white capris."

"Why not? Impress the neighbors."

"Scare the neighbors."

Chapter 44

Sara did not wear the violet thong under her white capris to the house inspection.

Burnt orange. Who would choose orange stucco for a house caricatured as a small castle complete with a round turret? No wonder the house hadn't been snatched up already in a neighborhood where houses were sold before the signs went up. What drew her, though, was the cozy feeling of thick ivy tangled over the stucco. A mature forest of trees shaded the vines from the scorching Dallas sun.

Ivy wound along the hard masonry of their Boston home, breathing life into the mortar. Alone, the stark brick was "shelter." The ivy, climbing into the cracks and crevices, made the brick "home."

The inspector, Allen, frowned. "You have to be careful with stucco. Ivy can damage it. The vine creeps into the cracks. And don't even think about removing it. Even if you manage to rip it out without tearing the stucco off, you get stains. It's a mess."

Liz, the realtor, pointed out that if they were planning on changing the stucco color anyway, the ivy might just be part of that cost.

Jake frowned.

"I suppose we could just pull it up." Sara grimaced at the thought.

"Good luck with that. Ivy is incredibly resistant. You can pull it up by the roots, and two will grow in its place."

Sara glanced at Jake to gauge how he felt about it. He looked at her.

Allen pointed to the rafters. "You have some damage going on up there already. And over there, by the stairs. You can see how it's discolored. The flashing wasn't done properly. You have water seeping in. You're looking at a few thousand dollars of repairs here. More if you want to change the color."

At the kitchen counter, Sara's structural concerns churned with the leftover stew of rejection. The whole purchase felt forced. This house would strap their budget to its limits. They hadn't even sold their house in Boston yet. It was risky. But, Jake wanted it done. She didn't blame him, not with the bifurcated life he was living. On the other hand, the kids wanted to start school in Boston with their friends and move when the house sold. In their price range, the market was dead. Sara's gut just wouldn't let her sacrifice what was best for the kids and their future for a house that whispered medieval disaster.

She scrambled for concrete flaws to heap onto the ivy problem and kill the deal. The kitchen desk didn't seem to have any jacks and the couple that owned the house was a bit older. "Where does the internet come into the house?" She wanted to know what kind of cost and work would be required to set up a network.

"Why do you need to know that?" Jake had trouble shifting out of his project-manager face and shredded her worries with not a glance at the writing on the page.

Moisture seeped through the pores along her neck. *Don't say anything. Just don't say anything.* "Am I not allowed to ask a question?" *Too late.* Her eyes challenged Jake's. His mouth hung open as if the spicy retort surprised him. But to Sara, it was the inevitable radiation wave that followed the mortification imploding in her psyche. "I think you're confusing me with one of your secretaries."

"Don't be like that." The look on his face, she'd seen before. He was embarrassed like her bra strap was slipping and everyone could see that she wore underwear. "That's something we can work out later. It's immaterial."

Liz gasped, her hands springing off the counter as if to retrieve the million-dollar sale that the winds of discord were whipping beyond her grasp.

Silence.

Sara wanted to kick her husband in the shins. Instead, she lassoed the anger into a controlled sweet tone. "I'm just going to leave the checkbook here. You can fill in the amounts. Right, honey? I'll be outside."

"Oh, no. Don't go, Sara. I'm sure I can get you the information—" Liz fumbled for her phone. Jake made no move to stop his wife.

"No, no. I'm fine. I just need a walk." She escaped to the door before the tears welled up. It occurred to her that maybe her new birth control laced with testosterone might be overloading her circuits.

Half an hour later, she and Jake drove off. They were nearly downtown before he bridged the gap of silence. "Did you have lunch yet?" He scanned the road for fast food as if a bag of French fries would fix what was hanging in the air between them. To be fair, it often did.

Sara stared out the window. "I'm not hungry."

Jake whipped through the congested streets. She clung to the door handle. "Is that how this is going to be? I don't have time for this, Sara. I have to get back for a meeting. What's this all about?"

"It's about that what *I* want is 'immaterial'."

"It is. You always do this. You get hung up on the little things. That's just how you are. I squeezed the inspection into my lunch hour. I don't have time for every little thing."

The words punched at her gut. She inhaled deep to absorb the blow. A red light stopped Jake at the crosswalk in front of the hotel. "You mean every little thing like our four children? This is the third time you've uprooted all of our lives to suit the whims of your ambition. We all have to suck it up, fall in step, and adapt." She threw the door open, fuming. "It wouldn't kill you to stare down the barrel of that smoking gun for once in your life and show a little empathy—maybe even a 'thank you' would be nice." Door slammed. She stalked across the street and out to the mall. She needed leggings for the dress she'd packed. It was too short.

After work, Jake found her reading on the couch. "Where'd you go?"

"To the mall." Sara hated shopping.

"Look, I don't know what you want me to say. We handle things differently. We both acted badly."

She rolled her eyes. Jake had no idea what "badly" could look like. He flitted off to his antiseptic hotel and left Sara at home to deal with the messy, sobbing teen smudging tear-drenched mascara on her white down comforter as she begged to stay in Boston for one more year. Sara wanted to shake her husband so that he could feel the foundations rocking beneath his feet the way she did 24/7.

"Do you imagine I came all the way out here for an inspection?" She pondered the dark shadows of the curtains. "God, Jake! I came mostly to say 'thank you' for living on the road like this so the kids could finish the school year, to show you how much I appreciate it, and then..." She couldn't even speak the words that would force her to relive the gesture that had failed so epically.

"That?" He pointed at nothing, at the ghost of her ten-minute drama. "What am I supposed to do? I'm in the middle of my workday! We had an appointment. You show up like that and I feel like I'm being manipulated."

"I didn't mean it like that." Down to the last electrical impulse that mapped her consciousness, Sara could not find even an iota of understanding for what had happened. In over two decades of marriage, Jake had never missed a cue from even the hint of a side-long, smoky glance. Unwanted tears welled up. Frustration, doubt, loneliness—all of the above. Her hormones were in overdrive. In a flash, she wondered if this was what it was like to be a teenage boy swimming in testosterone. "I just feel so rejected—and old."

"Geez, Sara, I've got a lot of stress at work." He searched the ceiling for the explanation. "The implementation project is getting a lot of resistance. And now, if we're not buying that house, I'll be dealing with the fallout of canceling our plans to move into the apartment next week."

Sara squeezed her forehead, crushed between a sense of wanting to be supportive and feeling dumped. "I'm so sorry. I didn't come here to argue. I appreciated your agreeing to put off the move until we have a house. I know it's another worry for you, but we can't move the kids into an apartment and then have to change schools again when we buy a house in another district. I know how hard this is for you, but it's hard for me too."

Drops dribbled down her cheeks. *How could this possibly have turned out worse?* The humiliation of rejection was too novel. She had no idea how to cope with that kind of trauma. "God, I'm like a chain around your neck and you don't even like me anymore." A sob convulsed its way to the surface. "I'm old." The specter of a thirty-year-old Sara, who moved careers and entire households of four children, a dog, and a cat, cross-country, without skipping a beat in her stride, rose up and haunted her. "We've changed and I'm messing everything up."

"Why do you say things like that? Don't you get it? Everything I do, it's you. The kids, they're going to leave one day. The houses, the cars, the jobs—I don't care. If I lose you, Sara, I might as well just put a gun to my head. You're more beautiful now than you've ever been." His words reached for her, but his hand didn't.

Sara believed him in that quiet place where every human wants to be loved. But the comfort of the words was like a decaying cloth of tattered threads thrown on a freezing corpse. She shook her head. "That's only half true, Jake. Your job is as much about you as it is about us. You say I'm beautiful, but you're not even attracted to me now. Do you have any idea what it took to put myself out there like that? I keep having this crazy impulse to run into the hall half-naked just to see if someone, anyone out there, thinks I'm attractive enough to want to have sex with me."

"It has nothing to do with that." He stepped closer, but not quite close enough. "I'm older. I'm away all the time. I don't have the sex drive I used to." He paced the floor and then turned to look her in the eye. "I just don't anymore. It's going to dry up eventually."

The confession shifted the gravity of the ground between them. She wasn't sure where to find steady footing again. "So, what's left?" she asked, wiping the smeared mascara from her eyes.

"I was hoping something deeper than sex."

So was Sara—and yet, it still stung that he didn't want her the way he always had. She dried her eyes and tucked the scene away in the closet where she kept forgotten anniversaries, unfortunate birthday presents, and missed dates. They hugged. They dined in a trendy restaurant, smiling and chatting, but every so often, when she looked at him and remembered he didn't find her attractive anymore, she mourned the death of the passion she'd always identified as an essential ingredient of the glue that bound them. Tears invaded her eyes. The waiter looked self-conscious and she pulled sunglasses out of her bag and put them on.

"Don't cry. It hurts me when you cry." Jake set his fork down and reached across the table to fondle her fingers.

Untethered, floating in an existence without gravity and too little air, Sara smiled and took the glasses off. She didn't doubt the strength of the vines that entwined their lives. It would be nearly impossible to separate one of them without severing parts from the other. She stirred the spinach leaves of her salad into the cranberry dressing and then dropped her fork and escaped to the restroom. Convincing herself she wasn't falling apart, she stood at the mirror until the red rims faded and the watery film dried. This wasn't her. She needed different birth control.

They drove Jake's 135i around the block looking at houses. Now that they had done the inspection, neither one of them was sure they wanted the faux castle. Jake reached over the console and tangled her fingers up in his. His arms were perpetually tan and the blonde hairs that curled along the sculpted muscles flaunted the allure of arms that were meant to encircle a woman's waist and hold her in the dark.

In the hotel, Sara slipped into the lingerie he'd bought for her birthday last year and crawled into bed with her book, waiting. He slid in beside her and watched TV. She held the book at arm's length toward the lamp to see the words without glasses. Squirming, she couldn't concentrate and wondered if she should start something. She wanted him to start something. It was so obvious she was waiting for him. A book had never stopped him before. The remote clicked, and he was asleep before she could close the cover and turn out the light.

Lying next to him, untouched, her chest burned, and her throat swelled. She knew it was ridiculous. It was just sex. But was it? Was it just sex? That's what people said when they wanted to downgrade an affair from a felony to a misdemeanor. But it was so much more than biology and chemistry. It resonated beyond the physical into the emotional and the spiritual. It was a sacred ritual that bound them. And the bonds were breaking.

She moved to the couch. Maybe it was the house hunting, maybe the leather of their marriage had aged and stretched.

In the dim lamplight, Sara read about how other people loved each other and wondered how her own story would end. All she wanted was simply to touch the flesh of love. The ghost of a man with green eyes, dark, disheveled hair, and an earring whispered in her ear as her eyes fell shut and the book dropped to the floor.

Dear Elizabeth,

The upheaval of your move to Dallas, you, as Sara, saw as a jagged rent in the fabric of your marriage. I saw it as a flash of brilliant light behind the shroud of despair that had engulfed me for the past two decades as your reincarnated soul and Jake Dawson danced contentedly through marital bliss. It pains me, Elizabeth, that I found sustenance, hope, and the will to live in the loosening of the ties between you and your Jackson when that unraveling infused sadness into your reincarnated soul. Perhaps it was a symptom of what I had become and the company I kept—or perhaps it is always my destiny.

Forever,
Ethan

Chapter 45

The day after she got home from the inspection, Sara called their realtor and broke the news that they wouldn't be moving into an apartment that week. "Grace, my junior prom queen, is threatening emancipation. I'm not going to move her twice, Liz. We need to wait. It all feels so forced. Nothing is falling into place."

"That's perfectly normal. I mean you're far away and these things take time for all the kinks to work out, but…" The faux castle was a big sale in a soft market.

"I don't believe in fighting against the mysterious swaying of the universe. We're not getting any traffic on our house in Boston. The stucco problem in Dallas is discouraging. And then, I'm just not that comfortable with the schools. I know Jake wants to live in the city, but I think we should try some of the suburbs; the schools are better. Let's pull out of the contract. I can't explain it, but I'm convinced if we wait, everything will sort itself out the way it's supposed to."

Two days later, the Dawson's got an offer and then lost it the next day on the counteroffer. Sara's optimism was deflated but not popped. She had faith in her instincts. It would all work out well if she waited. In the meantime, she was going to make damn sure she didn't lose her husband in the process.

Friday evening, she pulled on her little black dress, red heels, and game face. She left the teenagers to fend for themselves. Planning to empty her arsenal of feminine wiles, she picked Jake up from Providence airport.

That weekend, they dated like teenagers courting Prometheus. At dusk, they biked through the trees along the creek to the town square where they listened to folk music and licked six flavors of Italian ices off tiny pink spoons. They shopped for a big screen TV and sun-bathed, holding hands by the pool, sipping lemonade, and reading Tolstoy. The vine still bound them, but the leaves had withered a bit, and the sun had singed their edges brown. All they needed were hydrating moments of oneness to bring them back.

She'd forgotten that passion happens randomly in nature, nothing but chemicals aligning. But friendship takes nurturing. In the end, it was the inner beings, inextricably wound together, that she had to awaken. The teenage drama, the shelter, the upheaval, the losses, the anxiety—they receded like sand beneath the wave of the time she and Jake wasted together.

Saturday night, she jumped in the shower. The water washed away the world for a moment. Stress melted off and swirled down the drain. Raking her hair back, she wiped the sheets of rain from her face and gasped at the form of a man shrouded in steam outside the glass doors. A little shriek escaped her throat. Covering her naked breasts with her arms, she jerked back.

Jake smiled through the water droplets streaking the door.

"Just admiring the scenery. You look good, Sara."

She smiled disapprovingly. "We'll just let that simmer for a bit. Hand me a towel."

He looked at the rack and found nothing.

"Oh, the dryer just buzzed. Would you get a warm one for me?"

Jake trotted off to the laundry room.

Sara was winning this game that neither one of them wanted to lose and knew how to score the victory point. When he handed her the towel, she took her shot. "I'm in the mood for some great salsa, *chile verde,* and a tall glass of root beer." The new towel was still warm from the dryer and fluffy on her skin.

Jake pulled her robe off the hook. "I'm always up for good Mexican."

Sara wiped the towel across her shoulder and down her arm, savoring the steamy warmth, winking seductively at Jake watching her. He admired the dance and then dropped the robe in a heap on the tile. "Forget this." Cutting in, he reached for the towel himself. In the steam, the Jake that Sara made love to at will emerged through the accounting executive frost-bitten by cold reality. The ground beneath her feet leveled out into familiar terrain.

Jake caressed the other shoulder, pausing to mold the cloth to the roundness of her breast. The warm towel cuddled every cell of skin it brushed. Her fingertips immersed themselves in the thickness of the curls along his neckline as he sank to a knee, draped the trailing cotton around her hips, and flattened his palms inside her thigh and across the small of her back. The touch of his fingers against the skin rippled shivers down to her toes. His lips caressed the descending line from her navel to the curls along her pelvis. Her free hand braced on the steamed glass door as she moaned and Jake turned his cheek into the softness of her bare skin. Drops of water from her wet tresses trickled down her back. All she wanted was for the two of them to meld into one misty form, close the gap between them, and come home.

But not just yet.

Inhaling the lust hanging heavy on the steam, Sara bent to kiss the top of Jake's head, tilted his face up, and mingled their lips in a promise of passion. "Hand me that robe, baby. I'm starving."

By the time they got back, filled to the brim with rice, beans, and salsa, the kids were home and clamoring for their absent dad's attention They made brownies and played "Oh, Hell."

"You know, mom," Grace bit into a chewy center-cut brownie and then pointed it at Sara, "you should paint romantic horror. Everybody's into *Twilight*. They'd love it."

Giggling with sleep deprivation at 10:00 p.m., Sara dealt the last card around the table. "Yeah, but if that's what they're into now, by the time I'm done, the fad will have moved onto 'the next big thing'."

"Zombies," Elizabeth plastered her card to her forehead.

Jake turned the top card over. "Hearts are trump."

"Perfect!" Sara stuck her card on her forehead and glanced around the table. No one had a heart. "I'll paint zombie romance."

"Have you heard of Ethan McCarthy?" Elizabeth set her fist out for the bid. "He paints dark themes. I saw one of his paintings at the museum with Seth and Jared. They're super creepy, but you can't stop looking."

"I saw that on our field trip last year," Annie peeked out from an ace of spades. "It was horrible and violent, but it felt weirdly erotic."

"Erotic?" Jake raised his eyebrows at their 12-year-old.

She shrugged. "I watch a lot of Grey's Anatomy."

"McCarthy, hmmm?" The name sounded familiar to Sara. "I've seen his work somewhere. A shop on the Cape, maybe? Recluse. Doesn't sell many." They pounded out three. Dany was the lead suit with a diamond and bet none. Sara assumed she must be the only heart in the bunch and bet one. They all laid out their cards and she grinned to find she'd won the last hand with a trump Jack of hearts.

Jake scooped up the cards and tossed them on the table. "The old people are going to bed."

Sunday night, Sara dug the purple thong out of the drawer. Twisting the lock on the master suite door, she sauntered into the sitting area that separated the bedroom from the sunroom where she painted the pieces she sold in a North Shore tourist shop. Easels displaying works in progress and stacks of experimental watercolors littered the room. Jake sat on the couch watching the sports highlights. Sara draped herself across his lap. He clicked off the television.

"It might just be the testosterone in my new IUD, but I'm thinking I'd love a good fuck right now…" Her lips found his and impressed images of passion into the fleshy canvas, "…if you're still up for it." A sarcastic grin spiked the corner of her mouth. "I feel like a teenage boy. Can't get a thought to the end without wandering into a sex fantasy."

Jake's hand traced the curve of her hip to the dip of her thigh. "I don't know. It's nice to be wanted."

"Oh, I want you. C'mon, boy." She grabbed a fistful of shirt and dragged him into their bedroom.

The sex was just a flowering on the living vine. And then everything fell into place just like Sara knew it would, like magic. Because, in the end, it wasn't passion that bound them. It was the magic of hands holding each other in the night, of Jake and her together, of the universe in balance, and of people and places where they should be.

Two weeks into the new school year, an astonishingly attractive, raven-haired, slightly eccentric real-estate agent named Leana Raventhorn brought a couple from London to look at the house. She was dressed all in purple and wore a very unique lavender crystal about her ethereally pale white skin—

Sara talked art with the husband in the lovely little upstairs sunroom off the master suite. A forest of wetlands isolated it from the world. The agent, who probably could have sold a muzzle to a dog, ushered the wife through the home, plying her with enchanting little narratives about its virtues.

At parent-teacher conferences, Sara's cell phone rang. She stepped into an open classroom between visits. The whole parenting ritual seemed futile given they were hoping to move soon, but she was trying to maintain a façade of continuity, knowing she was going to uproot the whole show. Her real estate agent presented the terms of an offer from the London couple. They took it.

She flew out to Dallas over Labor Day weekend and hunted frantically for houses in a better school district than the faux castle. The perfect McMansion had just come on the market in Allen, a suburb not far from UT Dallas where Elizabeth was enrolled and close to Jake's new office in Plano. They were moved in by mid-October.

Chapter 46
—From the unfinished manuscript of Ethan McCarthy

At my easel, I fumed beneath stark beams of sunlight that the Dallas September shot through the windows. Brann had purchased for us her signature Victorian home nestled in a neighborhood of pretentious mansions close to the university that Sara's daughter Elizabeth was attending.

Between my fingers, I rolled a bullet. At times, a bullet to the head presented escape—so many lives are worse than death. I could still die; I just didn't age. Knowing what I knew of the cave under the hill, I imagined I could terminate this strung out, hopeless existence, connect this pathetic shard of my soul with another less warped, and have a chance at reaching Elizabeth elsewhere.

Here, as Sara, she had again slipped from my grasp. She was so clearly floating unmoored on a sea of upheaval when I met her on the plane that I had foolishly allowed myself a flicker of hope. And now everything had fallen neatly into place for her. Brann Sidhe made no secret of the fact that her purple-tipped nails had stirred that pot to suit her taste. She'd ironed out all the wrinkles and restored the impregnable fortress of Sara's bond with Jake—or did Sara do that?

Dull, faded black, a murky void of color that I had smeared on the canvas reflected my utter despair. My voracious mistress gloated in the high-backed, amethyst armchair behind me. Disappointment whetted her appetite. The bullet in my fingers was no ordinary bullet. It was iron. It had only one purpose.

"Don't pout, Ethan, my love." Brann inhaled the aroma of the art. "It makes your work so tasteless."

"It's your own doing. You've left me nothing, not even the hope of vengeance—no anger, no grief, nothing but this bland mush of despair."

Her tinkling laugh, popping in bubbles of brilliant inspiration that normally brought men to their knees, drove bile into my throat. She rose and sauntered carelessly to my side. The iron encircling my ring finger burned. I closed my fist around the bullet. Should I try again? She'd left me no choice. Either she or I must cease to exist. But the muse was right. As long as a glimmer of hope, no matter how dull, flickered in the distance, I did not love Elizabeth well enough if I did not persevere.

Brann's petal-soft lip grazed the lobe of my ear. "I did this for you, my sweet."

The wicked irony choked me. Sometimes, I suspected that, although I escaped the physical erosion of Brann Sidhe's tide, the mental deterioration might be taking a toll. Rounding on her, I flung the canvas against the wall. The dim acrylic splattered and tumbled to the floor. I shoved the demon from my face, and she took flight within her dress. At that moment, I sensed the madness.

I had seen it in so many of her young protégés but had yet to feel it furrowing paths through my brain. "You have won! Let us put an end to this game. I've seen you rip a heart from its breast and stop its woeful beating. To what purpose does mine persist?"

Reappearing near the windows, Brann cooed coaxingly. "Ah, Ethan, still you do not understand me. Do you not at least understand your dear Elizabeth?"

"I understand that her name should never pass your lips." The rage died as easily as it sparked. Surely this was insanity.

"For one who worships her so well, you know her so little. Do you not see that the curse of women stalks her? I have done you a service and given the affliction an open field in which to pounce."

"Your riddles sicken me. I know only that she was lost and alone and I could have filled a space in her heart. But now you have closed up the gap."

"No, I have widened it." She stepped forward and, with one gentle finger, approached me as if I were a skittish animal who distrusted her advances. "Have you not witnessed the two-headed enigma that stalks the women of this time? She straddles the demands of a culture split between halves that cannot coexist. All her life she has struggled to assert the independence and self-fulfillment of a modern woman, and yet, she is irrepressibly drawn to a culturally engrained, but diametrically opposed, drive to pursue the romantic ideal. In seeing her so happily uprooted, I have cut all her ties. She is drifting, my dear Ethan. Will you send her a line and draw her in?"

The words sank into my psyche as they always did, laced with deception. But they held such promise that I walked slowly to the easel, picked up a new canvas, and returned wordlessly to my labors. From a small tube, I daubed into the murky dim of the palette a touch of vibrant red.

The purple lips at my shoulder parted and smiled. "And now we shall have our game in earnest. For this shall be the final round."

Dearest Elizabeth,

Perhaps love at all costs is nothing more than narcissism.

Forever,
Ethan

Chapter 47

—Excerpts from the unpublished writings of Easton Ravenscroft

A Thursday morning in October, sunrays ripped through the shutters barricading Sara's new bedroom from the dawn. The sick feeling of knowing she had nothing better to do than wash dishes, vacuum, and make the beds paralyzed her. Housekeeping was a time-consuming but soulless pursuit. She hauled herself out of the covers so she could haul the three children still at home out of their beds. Jake left without a word while she was coaxing her body away from the mattress.

"I hate school," Grace moaned when Sara woke her. "I don't have any friends." That wasn't exactly true. Grace attracted friends like barbeque attracts bees.

Sara pushed her toward the bathroom. "You have Ally and that nice boy that asked you to the football game. It's the rest of us that don't have any friends." Danny hunkered down in front of his PS3 connected by Bluetooth to his virtual buddies and Annie felled the long lonely day playing with their shih tzu Flash and watching Animal Planet. "At least we have each other."

Sara wished that were true. Stretched between two jobs, Jake hardly had two minutes to spare. She was isolated from all adult society. She'd always been a bit of a homebody, but it was a choice, not a sentence.

In search of adult stimulation, she opened her email, only to find a polite rejection from a small shop that had shown some promising interest in her paintings. It was depressing. She couldn't seem to rebuild her life.

She drowned her frustration in some vigorous vacuuming, the whole time wanting to call Jake and tell him what had happened. She knew that was a recipe for disaster. The last time she'd gone looking for sympathy and comfort after a rejection, the whole scene had taken a nasty detour into, "We all gave up everything for your job—you could at least acknowledge the sacrifice," and ended up down the road of, "Your art is poison between us. I don't want anything to do with it."

Her art was her soul on canvas. She wondered if he could love her and not her creations.

Feeling trapped, she pulled up her email:

To: jcdawson
Re: No subject
When you sleep with someone and then sneak out without saying good-bye, I believe it's customary to leave money on the nightstand.

It was mean and she knew it, but it eased the biting sting. Everything about her life was upside down and inside out. The college fund was losing money in the stock market; Sara was gaining weight at the gym—she was contemplating the possibility of taking her body to the market and her money to the gym. Even worse, she'd moved half a continent away to be with Jake, and Jake never bothered to come home. *No, that's unfair. He's working two jobs at once—which is WHY we have money in the stock market.*

By the time she'd finished the housework and showered, it was nearly noon. Her cell buzzed with a message from Grace:

G: *Can you pick me up and take me to Subway for lunch?*
S: *Are you out of lunch money?*
G: *No. I don't have lunch with anyone I know today and I don't want to eat alone.*

She knew the feeling.

S: *Be there in five.*

Sara got the same text from Annie about a half-hour later. The one friend that she'd gleaned out of the picked-over fields of junior high had succumbed to the appeal of eating with a larger in-crowd.

If she had to eat two lunches a day, Sara would blow up like a balloon. The inflation was well on its way. She couldn't believe her eyes when she stepped, dripping, out of the shower after her second lunch and the digital numbers just kept ticking up.

Her whole life was off-kilter, out of balance, askew.

Chapter 48

Blood pounded against the artery in Sara's neck. She glanced at her watch and broke into a mom run. Having four children had given her Chronic Late Disorder—very hard to treat.

She could feel her blood pressure rising as she passed the library's wall of windows. The glass reflected a forty-seven-year-old woman—attractive? It would depend on the beholder. She hustled to keep pace with the tattered, stretched-out leash she had on life. *Why don't I just let go?*

In desperation, she'd decided some art classes might fill the gaps left by the thinning of love and the hole that moving had left in her sense of self. Glancing down at the portfolio clutched in her fist, she wondered what they were missing. Her confidence was shot.

There were only a dozen other students in the basement classroom. Fifty-something Phil had long greasy iron-streaked hair. His stare followed her like a haunted-house portrait for the first ten minutes. She avoided making eye contact with the beady eyes protruding from pasty skin spread thin over pudding.

Joan, the brunette with glasses, sat next to Stephanie. They chatted as if they'd had a few classes together before. A quiet blonde woman with a butch cut sat across from Sara. Next to her, sat a timid-looking older gentleman named, oddly enough, Tim. Several other newcomers fidgeted farther down the rows, aspiring amateurs like Sara.

And then there was the guy Sara was sure she knew from somewhere. She summed the others up in a glance, but he took three or four carefully camouflaged perusals. The thick, unruly dark hair, the green eyes, and the full red lips accounted for the odd sense of acquaintance. Practically every guy she'd ever dated—other than Jake—looked like that. There was something in his face, though, something she would have remembered if she'd known him before. Pain? Sorrow? He couldn't be much older than thirty-five. *How much grief can one guy store up in so short a time?* He looked drained. No ring. Divorced?

The teacher swept into the room and interrupted Sara's musings. She wasn't a professor—this was continuing education. The tight knot that held captive her raven hair, thick-rimmed glasses, and a loose-fitting purple shift couldn't quite camouflage the bare fact that she was a work of art herself. Apparently accustomed to the mesmerizing effect she had on people, she gazed benevolently at the open jaws in the room.

What disturbed Sara was that pudding guy kept staring at her, even after the instructor began her introduction to the course. Sara angled her body away from Phil's gaze.

The teacher posed behind the lectern as if she were posing for a painting. "Good evening! I am Leana Brann and this is 'Educating the Visual Imagination.' Art is 97% inspiration and 3% talent. I hope to assist my students in developing their unique vision of the world and, in the process, improve their talent." She honored them all with a smile.

Sara's breath caught. That smile was…so compelling. A vision of Ms. Brann brushing her lips down Sara's neck rippled through her mind. She shook herself. A quick survey of the room told her she wasn't the only one hypnotized. Alice, the butch blonde, was practically drooling.

"You have all brought samples of your work. Let's gain an appreciation for the style and vision of our classmates. In the following months, you will bring pieces to class and we will offer our comments and suggestions. Feel free to scan and share your pieces digitally with the other artists between classes so that you can present to us your very best work in person. Look for an email with this week's suggested assignment and everyone's email address. Remember! The assignment is only a suggestion should your inspiration fail you. But if the muses favor us," she locked her eyes on Sara, "that will be a thing of the past."

Leana gestured to the tortured artist. He was the only student that seemed resistant to her spell—well, he and Phil. The wood grain of the table in front of him occupied his attention. No materials or art samples cluttered his desk.

"Before we begin. I have the most wonderful announcement. I have prevailed upon my dear friend and client, Mr. Ethan

McCarthy, to lend his unique talent and insight to our little gathering of artists." General gasps punctuated her words. Everyone in the class, anyone who had even a very shallow glimpse into the art world, knew the name McCarthy. He was legendary—a recluse whose paintings stunned the world when he deigned to relinquish one.

Mr. McCarthy nodded to acknowledge the introduction. No wonder he looked familiar. Sara was surprised she hadn't made the connection sooner. She was sure she'd seen his picture somewhere—in an art gallery, a magazine. This was the same Ethan McCarthy she sat next to on the plane to Dallas. She just never imagined she would be sitting next to THE Ethan McCarthy. There were never any pictures of the artist behind the art.

"Well, then. Shall we begin with you, Philip?" Leana leaned over his shoulder and commented on his work. His attention snapped away from Sara. Ms. Brann's touch summoned him like a slave on a leash. He spluttered and rambled, intoxicated by her proximity. "I had this dream—"

Sneering, Ms. Brann flicked the tips of Phil's greasy curls. She resembled a starving socialite resigned to eating bugs to survive. Finding the familiar intimacy unsettling, Sara wondered how many classes Phil had taken from this intimidating, and yet so compelling, woman. No one else seemed to notice. Maybe they were used to her style. The possibility occurred to Sara that she was struggling because she wasn't quite odd enough to be an artist.

"—the screaming and the blood swirled in my head, shifting and contorting. I made him." Phil sought approbation from his classmates and then gazed pleadingly at Leana.

"You demonstrate remarkable passion, Philip. Your inspiration is undeniably beyond compare." She pursed her lips. "But you fail in the realization of it." Leana continued unperturbed by the panic in Philip's face. "Look here." She bent until her lips nearly kissed his ear and pointed. "The face looks almost happy."

The teacher in Sara moved to pad the blow of Ms. Brann's blunt critique. "Don't you think that adds to the whole macabre ambiance? Almost like he finds pleasure in the degeneracy surrounding him."

Awkward silence. Puzzled faces. The other students exchanged raised eyebrows. Phil, grateful, rambled manically in defense of his art. Backing away, Sara looked about the room in confusion.

Her eyes met the steady gaze of Mr. McCarthy. In the first sign of life from him, she imagined for a fleeting moment that she was somehow the root of all his suffering. Maybe it was amateur artists like her, with their uninformed opinions, that troubled him so. She back-pedaled. No confidence. "Or, maybe not. It's just dark and I thought, well, you know, smiling in the middle of all that depravity—" The tortured eyes holding Sara's seemed to be siphoning all reasonable thought out of her head.

The instructor screwed her up in a steady gaze. "Well, 'Elizabeth,' is it?"

"Uh, Sara. Elizabeth is my middle name—and my daughter."

"Hmmm." Leana turned abruptly to Mr. McCarthy, drawing the spotlight from Sara's blunder. "Come, offer us your humble opinion, dear Ethan."

Sighing, he shuffled to Philip's display. Looking directly at Leana rather than the deflated and breathless artist, he pronounced his verdict. "Your work is truly *inspired,* Phil."

Philip, overwhelmed, babbled about the shading and the brush strokes. The exchange of looks between the instructor and her guest expert raised Sara's eyebrows. *Are they having an affair?*

"But I agree with Sara." His eyes met hers briefly, ever so briefly, and she caught her breath. She only ever met such warmth in the eyes of her husband—well not lately. And his voice—he might as well have reached out and brushed her cheek with the tips of his fingers; she felt the shiver. "The smile in the face of the pain is…diabolic." The last word he directed at their instructor.

"I see," she responded drily. "Let's take a peek at what you've brought us, Sara." Lowering her glasses, she peered at Sara over the purple rims.

Sara squirmed as the class moved toward her display of paintings.

"Very," the instructor twirled her hand in the air, "perky." Sara's teeth clenched, but she smiled pleasantly. Now that she was standing in front of another living, breathing human being, she wasn't sure if she could take the critique she'd come seeking. The other students gathered around. "Give us your thoughts, Ethan."

He waded through the crowd. With a gentle smile that gave Sara the impression she could trust her soul to this man, he reassured her. He stepped past Joan and Stephanie.

"It's not my genre—" Sara cringed. That was a polite way of saying he didn't have anything nice to say. "—but," he gestured at several points of the painting and commented on her use of shadow and light, the subtlety of the hues, and the technique of the brush strokes. When he had finished speaking, Sara was brimming with confident potential.

Expecting a shy nod in return for her grateful smile, she found herself unnerved by a wink that echoed down the corridors of her youth.

"As I said, this isn't my area of expertise, but I find the body of work compelling, and I hope to see more."

Sara fancied, in a brief second of insanity, that he wasn't referring to her artwork.

Chapter 49

L ight rippled and splashed in the pastel jade of the swimming pool reflecting the morning sun. Year-round sunshine was one of the perks of the move to Dallas. The garden always hummed— bees, birds, crickets, the dull snoring of the filter. Sara didn't hear the miniature slaps of paddling until she sat down in a chair. A rat! Her face convulsed.

She rushed into the house. "Jake!"

Her husband crawled out of the covers and slid into a pair of shorts he found crumpled at his feet. He looked mildly concerned.

"There's a rat in the pool!"

He nodded and took his time getting up.

"It's alive! It's going to drown."

"Probably." He shuffled out to the patio.

"Can you save it?" She gnawed at her fingertip.

Looking at her like she'd gone mad, he grunted and grabbed the long-handled skimmer.

"Oh, good. Maybe we can let it go in the vacant lots across the fields—"

A farm boy, Jake was better versed in the fleeting rhythms of life and death. "It's a rat." The net of the skimmer fell on the fatigued and ill-fated swimmer. "It'll just come back."

Jake pushed the lump of wet fur to the bottom of the pool. Cognitive dissonance paralyzed Sara. The rat was, without doubt, the source of the nasty gash on little Flash's nose. Her dog and the rodent couldn't live in harmony in the same yard. She turned, shoulders shivering, and fled to the bills that would distract her from the queasiness inside. Besides the payment notices, her email only had two new messages in it—a travel ad and a note with photo attachments from Philip.

She opened Philip's mail tentatively. *Please don't be love letters.* He'd sent her some pieces and wanted her opinion. She breathed a sigh of relief. This was easy—from the safe distance of a computer. She was a teacher. She knew how to make a C paper sound like a masterpiece in embryo.

He'd sent a scan of a hauntingly pathetic charcoal: a man watching his wife die in childbirth. Phil's sketches never failed to produce something to admire, so the critiques were easy enough. He might be a bit creepy, but everyone deserved to be encouraged by someone.

Sara downloaded the photo to a Word doc and typed all her positive remarks first: the lines in the face and the angles of the bodies reflected poignantly the tragedy of the scene; the shading to look like dusk enhanced the sense of loss; she loved the sparseness of the background that gave the impression that nothing beyond this scene existed for the man in anguish. She finished it off, highlighting a few spots where the shadows seemed heavy around the edges and noting the disproportionately large hands of the man that distracted the eye from the focal point of the piece.

Sara smiled as she attached the critique to an encouraging return email. It was rejuvenating to be helpful again.

Thirty minutes later, she got a response.

To: sdawson
Re: Critique
Dear Sara,
You've given me lots of help, thank you. I see that almost every line I drew has something wrong with it. I'm quite discouraged. I don't want to draw anymore. I don't even want to attend class. I'll try to do what you say, but I feel like such a failure as an artist now.
Thank you for your critique,
Phil

Her mouth dropped open. Apparently, the ability to graciously critique a student's French composition did not translate into the ability to critique an adult's artwork. There were maybe two suggestions! Everything else was a compliment. Why would someone take a critique class and then whine about being critiqued? Sara was dying for constructive feedback.

She exited her email and stalked away to do some vigorous vacuuming, ruing the half-hour she'd spent making a very thoughtful critique. She was very familiar with his pain, but she resented the emotional blackmail.

Fifteen minutes later, she crafted her response.

To: phildon
Re: Critique
Hey Phil,
You must not have been going to class for very long. You don't have the thick skin yet. :) Actually, you need to note the positive comments. You only had one or two things to fix—the hands and maybe some shading. Your paintings are full of life and I just didn't want to be distracted from the emotion by the size of the hands.

You can find lots of people to tell you your painting is beautiful and perfect; the real treasures are the ones who are willing to tell you how to make it better. Was that your purpose in coming to class? Or were you just looking for us to point out what we liked about your pieces and not say anything about how you could make them exceptional art? This sketch has that possibility. But I'd be happy to just tell you what I like next time and ignore the things I think could be improved. It's all up to you and what you want. But you'll have to let me know.

Anyway, you don't have to believe anything I say, not with an expert like Mr. McCarthy in the class. :) Honestly, I'd give a full year of my life for someone to frankly tell me what I need to fix in my pieces. Hope to see you tonight!
Best,
Sara

Feeling quite pleased with her self-restraint, she finished the vacuuming and washed the dishes before she looked at her email again.

To: sdawson
Re: Critique
I've been going to class for a long time. I've been working on this series of sketches since last summer. I've been involved in three classes simultaneously, getting criticism from all sorts of people.

I've never been discouraged until I started reading your comments. I'd rather you not give me any more critiques, over the Internet or in class. I'm sorry. Thank you anyway.

I taught for 16 years. I was taught not to put "chicken scratch" all over a student's paper because it just discouraged them. After reading your critiques, I now feel what it's like first hand to be that student who received nothing but marks all over their paper.

I can take criticism from other people but not from you.

I've changed what I could from what you said. I can make the other changes later. But I can't have someone taking away my inspiration or enthusiasm. That's what you've done.

Please, no more critiques from you. I know that you are at a level much higher than me…

She couldn't even begin to know how to respond to this madness and figured a gentle apology before class might be the ticket. She was paying a few bills online twenty minutes later when the next email came through with her receipts.

To: sdawson
Re: Critique
I am very sorry for what I just sent. I don't even think it's the critique I'm upset about. I think I have overreacted. I brought a lady friend to our class last week. She suddenly died this week. She and I painted together. I hope you will forgive me. I think I've taken some mixed-up emotions out on you.

Yes, I can have a tough skin. When I redo that piece, I will send a copy of it to you. I'm so incredibly sorry about everything. I don't know how to feel anymore.

Sara felt like a toad. How was she supposed to know? At least, she was a good cushion for the pain pins. She could take the prick without hard feelings. She perused the obituary and gathered that the girlfriend had a history with pills. Sad.

Phil stuffed a hand-written apology in her palm before class on Thursday. She put a hand on his shoulder. "I'm very sorry for your loss." She truly meant it. She couldn't imagine losing Jake. Phil dropped his head and nodded. During class, she made only a few positive comments about his work, mostly because he was staring at her the way Flash did at dinner.

It wasn't until the next week's class that she noticed the faded pink slits across his wrists. Shortly after she walked into the room, he raised his pudding arms above his matted, steel-gray hair and exclaimed, "I'm so glad you're here. You're the only one who sees what I'm trying to do."

Sara smiled politely—it wouldn't help him to be aware that he kind of freaked her out, but he spent the rest of the class bringing attention to the samples she brought and gushing over them. It was disconcerting. He followed her to her car. She listened graciously to his woes about his ex-wife and how disturbed he'd been by accidentally kissing his daughter on the lips when she turned the wrong direction unexpectedly.

Eeewww! Sara ducked into her car, locking the doors as she waved good-bye.

The next week, she opted to park in the expensive underground lot across from the college and engaged Stephanie and Joan in a conversation about proper lighting after class until Phil had left the building.

Dear Elizabeth,

Although I seemed to be making progress with you in your art class, I feared that a century of slavery had left me jaded, silencing the wild song in the soul of my 18-year-old self. 18 had been the age of my obsession, of my will to realize my alchemical dream.

"Ethan Jr." had enrolled in a Psych class. I hoped he might find another route to you through your daughter Elizabeth. I reasoned that if I expanded the field to two players, my chances of winning doubled.

How could I possibly conceive the consequences of my miscalculation? Perhaps this was what fate had intended for us all along—or perhaps there is no fate, only the mess we make.

Forever,
Ethan

Chapter 50
—Excerpts from the journals of Ethan McCarthy, Jr.

A student in thick glasses behind me scoffed. "So, you're saying there is no free will. What if I wake up and decide to go to the pool instead of class? Hey! I just exercised my free will."

Dr. Reber smiled. "But how did you come to make that choice? Would you have made it in the middle of winter? If your parents were counting on you to graduate and break out of poverty? All choices are traceable to determining factors, often a combination of multiple factors—thus determinism."

A pale red-head in the front raised her hand. "But what about a guy who visits his grandma over Christmas instead of going to Florida? He obviously wants to spend the week with his girlfriend at the beach more than he wants to visit his grandma in Utah. So, there you go—free will."

The guy behind the red-head leaned forward, "Nah, man, he's just not that into you."

"Or," Dr. Reber countered above the snickering, "even more than going with you, he doesn't want to regret blowing off grandma before she's gone."

"That's what we mean," the guy from the back pointed his index finger, "free will. He had opposing determining factors and he chose between them."

Rolling my eyes, I shook my head. The students in this theater looked my age but were a bunch of infants. They were so sure that they had a choice in their destiny.

"It's not so much what he wants that we're discussing here." The professor set down his dry erase. "What we're investigating is what are the factors that determined his wants at that time. Free will demands no constraining factors."

I didn't need to turn around to match a face to the next voice. Elizabeth Dawson was the pretty blonde—not the gorgeous kind of pretty, but the smart kind. There's a difference. Somewhere in the eyes. After so many years of hanging out in college courses—with college women—I could spot it. And there was something in her voice, this compelling call, almost as if it resonated and echoed across centuries and startled awake a million beings locked inside of me.

I hadn't introduced myself yet because she always showed up with some curly, brunette dude. Today, she was sitting alone.

"But if your choices are completely random, uninfluenced by your values or beliefs, your culture and conscience, they're meaningless. I'd rather make choices based on some conviction of what is right. Absolute free will negates meaning and our humanity."

My lip curled at the incisive logic that cut through the noise in the classroom and struck at the core of the question. The words that came from her mouth had infatuated me even before the pink curve of her lips had awakened a primal, exotic drumbeat in my blood.

I didn't bother to raise my hand. "And even if you believe we're all just puppets on the strings of our environment or destiny, or whatever, people act in totally random ways. Isn't that what moves us forward? A Darwinian act of random free will that changes the future?" Even though the question was addressed to the professor, I glanced back at Elizabeth. She was impressed. She was the kind of girl that had no time for stupid people. She'd make time for me.

"Exactly!" Dr. Reber responded, visibly relieved that someone had caught on. "Thus, the argument for Contextual Free Will." He went on to explain, but the words jumbled into white noise. My brain was rifling through the possible scenarios where I introduced myself to Elizabeth.

Before the last minute of class ticked away, she packed up her MacBook, pulled on her white peacoat, and headed for the door.

Students chatted in the aisles, blocking my path. I was going to have to chase her down and still manage to look cool. The weather was unusually cold for Dallas. A frigid January breeze fought me back. Refusing to veer from the path, I followed her as inconspicuously as possible past the rows of towering magnolias soldiering the long, rectangular pools in front of the library.

At the corner, she turned with a small crowd headed to the parking lots. She was twenty paces ahead of me when I turned the corner. Five strides more and she stopped abruptly. Eyes looking hunted, she pivoted, trapped between the library and the O'Donnell arts building. The only way out was back. I followed her glance back to the source of her worry. Dark grey hoodie with the sleeves cut out, gym rat caliber biceps, curly, brunette hair. The boyfriend.

Gloves still in my coat, my fingertips were pink with cold. I stuffed them in my pockets as Elizabeth's desperate gaze fell on mine. Recognition sparked and rippled through her features. Whirling about, she swam straight for me through the crowd like I was a life vest floating on a turbulent lake.

A convincing façade of surprise and pleasure masked her voice and face. The boyfriend was close enough to overhear our conversation. "Hey, I thought I missed you. Where'd you go after class?" Thinking for sure she must be talking to someone behind me, I glanced back but only caught a professor, a janitor, and a small group of girls that bumped my shoulder as they passed. Elizabeth skipped up and stopped in front of me, her turned-up nose barely reached my shoulder. "Help me!" she hissed. The urgency in her voice mingled sincere distress with a hint of the comical. "Hug me like you know me."

I didn't miss a beat. For months, from the next row down and across the room, I'd envied the curly, brunette who draped his arm carelessly around her shoulders. A mysterious revolt raged inside me when the guy let his fingers wander through the blond tresses while hers clicked the keys on her laptop. For months, the object of my propensity for obsessively pursuing what eluded me had been Elizabeth.

A little too enthusiastically, I wrapped my arm around her shoulder and hugged her to my chest. She was tiny but muscular and fit in my arms like they were home.

"Pretend we've been dating. There's this guy—" she looked up at my eyes, asking if I was down with the charade. I winked, all in.

The dude with the biceps stopped in front of us. I wondered how she'd handle the encounter, expecting something catty and gloating. The leanan sidhe that stalked my days had warped my perspectives on women.

"Hey, Mitch." Elizabeth opted for kind, but firm, apparently going to extreme lengths to avoid resorting to cruelty, but still end a relationship that wouldn't die.

Mitch glared. "Hey."

Elizabeth wriggled out of my embrace but caught my hand.

Her ex wore his melancholy like a medal.

Squeezing my fingers, she turned to introduce us. "This is—" Panic warped her face.

I extended a hand, jumping into the awkward gap. "Ethan. Ethan McCarthy."

Mitch shook hands, nodding. "Hey." He turned to Elizabeth, yearning in his eyes. "See ya 'round?"

"Yeah, maybe." She leaned in, clutching my arm.

Sighing, Mitch strutted away.

Elizabeth pulled me the other direction, glancing behind until her ex had disappeared around the corner. "Oh, my God! Thank you!" She dropped my hand abruptly like the rental period had expired and shifted her backpack to the other shoulder, wedging a gap between us. The explanation gushed out of her lips, punctuated with relieved giggles. "We just broke up—again. Dude, I couldn't take the gaslighting and emotional blackmail anymore."

"Hazards of being a Psych major."

"Yeah, right? He won't leave me alone. I was tempted to dye my hair raven and—"

"No!"

Elizabeth's brows raised.

"I have a personal aversion to raven." Of all my "father's" younger versions, I was the one who had never quite succumbed to Brann Sidhe's charms. Perhaps that was why the elder spent so many of his days retreating into my subconscious. And though I had picked up the brush from time to time, to pass the long and lonely decades, I had never painted the whisperings of the muse, preferring to experiment with my own voice. Stuttering, I back-pedaled. "I have baggage."

"Who doesn't?"

"Besides, blond suits you."

"So, you think I'm a dumb blond?" Defiantly, she hitched her bulging backpack.

Across generations of women, I had never met much feminine resistance to my charms. Deprived of my driving obsession with alchemy and possessing limitless funds, I had bounced from one all-consuming passion to the next: fast cars, sailing the world, planes, education, women. Having neglected the normal roar of my hormones in pursuit of eternal youth, I made up for the loss during my windfall years. "Anything but. It suits you—perfect camouflage. Blond on the outside; brilliant on the inside."

"I hope you don't mind. I was desperate and I recognized you from Psych." I liked that she skipped over the compliment but didn't demure.

"I'm the guy in front of you. The angles are different. I was looking up; you were looking down."

She studied my face. "You still look the same from down here."

"Ouch! I go on and on about how gorgeous and smart you are, and I only get 'the same' out of you?"

"Oh, were you looking for a compliment? I love your green eyes. And I'd kill for those eyelashes." She cocked an eyebrow and continued walking. "Thanks for going along with me. I owe you big time."

Grinning inside, I doubled my stride. The pursuit was on. I knew well the art. "I think you'll have to go to the Honor Society brunch on Saturday morning with me to even the score."

"You're right. But you're a stranger, and we all know you should never talk to strangers—or go out with them. So—" She grimaced.

"But am I?"

"Well, I didn't even know your name."

"Ethan McCarthy." I held out my hand.

She brushed it away. "I know that—now. Wait. Ethan McCarthy? Like the artist? I bet you get teased about that."

"Actually, he's my dad."

"THE Ethan McCarthy is your dad? The guy who does all those creepy, insanely beautiful paintings and doesn't sell any of them?"

"He lets one or two go now and then. We have to live."

"But you seem so—normal. I thought he was some kind of psycho recluse—" She looked as if her mind had just caught up with her words and informed her she'd been rude. "I mean—"

"Don't worry about it. He's my dad. I can pretty much confirm he's certifiable."

Rescued, Elizabeth crinkled her nose. "I know, right? My dad can be crazy, too." Silence hung between us. This was new to me. Without fail, once I had opened the flood gate, women flowed through. Elizabeth turned away in the direction of a little gray Mini

Cooper with white racing stripes. "This is mine." She dug around for keys in her school bag. "I'm Elizabeth."

"Elizabeth Dawson. See? We're not so much strangers."

"Yeah! 'Cause you've been cyberstalking me or something."

It was strange and exhilarating, this sensation of misstep, unhinged, one-upped. She was like a good book that hooked me and dragged me along from complication to complication.

"Or something. My dad met your mom on the plane from Boston to Dallas—on her way to look at a house." I leaned against the side of her car. "She made an impression. Dad told me to keep my eyes open for you."

"Are you from Massachusetts?"

"Yep. My dad got tired of the snow forests and decided to try life in the sun. God! Who knew Dallas could get this cold?" The air puffed from my lips. Ice streaked the parking lot. "So, does being from the same state counter the stranger danger?"

Elizabeth jangled her keys in my face. "Alright, we're not strangers, but I still can't go to the reception with you. I have plans."

I cocked an eyebrow skeptically.

"No, I do. I volunteered to drywall for Habitat for Humanity. You don't do rejection much, do you?"

"You know how to drywall?"

"That's sexist." She tapped my shoulder, misconstruing admiration for incredulity. "Your true colors are showing. Of course, I know how to drywall. I've been volunteering since high school."

My own secluded life mocked me in the face of her inherent social conscience. The only thing we ever did for someone else was lure them into the clutches of a murderous witch. The idea that the pursuit of happiness could mean raising the quality of life for others lit a spark in my dark world that I found oddly sexy. "I know," Elizabeth sighed, "my mom is a bleeding heart; my dad is a liberal. Makes me a huge bleeding-heart liberal."

"They sound nice." Authentic envy oozed from my voice. The ghosts of family stirred in my dusty memories. The urge to embrace Elizabeth, her family, her independence, and her will, consumed me and swallowed every other voice inside.

The lock beeped open. "It's genetic. I volunteer as a mentor too—and speak French. When I get done with school, I want to join Doctors Without Borders."

"Okay, I'll go with you instead. Will they let me?" After barely two minutes basking in her generosity, I would have accepted her invitation to a root canal.

"Can you drywall?" Elizabeth's brow arched skeptically.

"My dad's an artist; how hard can it be?"

"Text me your address. I'll pick you up at 8:00."

"P.M?"

"You wish." She slid into the driver's seat while I fished my phone from a pocket. Elizabeth typed in her number and handed it back. My numb fingers fumbled to text.

Her eyes popped open when her phone chimed and she read the address in the message. "You live in my complex? I've never seen you."

"Maybe you have; you just didn't notice."

"No, I'm pretty sure I'd notice you." Generally, compliments from women bounced off my jaded skin, but Elizabeth's seeped like heroin into my veins. A handful of her words floated me into an entirely new plane of existence. "Come on; I'll give you a ride."

For the first time, I understood my "father" and the demented existence that he had saddled upon us all. After ten minutes, I knew I'd risk everything to have this girl—even my soul.

Through a driving ice storm, warm and oblivious, I trudged back to campus to retrieve the BMW M3 convertible I'd abandoned in the parking lot when I accepted Elizabeth's ride.

Chapter 51
—Excerpts from the unpublished writings of Easton Ravenscroft

Paint smeared on her cheek and hair pulled back, Sara inspected the details of the petal. The stroke was a suggestion from Mr. McCarthy. He'd spent the better part of the class by her side, helping her perfect it. A flush snaked up her shoulders and into her neck at the memory. Shaking it off, she raised her arms above her head and flexed her hands to let the heat out.

She wished she could get some kind of opinion out of Jake. He excused himself abruptly from all things art. As much as she wanted to, she couldn't blame him. He'd been her first critic—not a role well suited to a husband.

The sun had shifted. Shrugging, she pulled open the shutters. The view of the golf course was one of the rare wooded sceneries available on the flat plains of the Dallas suburbs. Jake never skimped on quality. She had everything—except someone that loved her paintings as much as she did.

The doorknob scraped in its groove and Sara glanced at the clock. Her art classes had awakened such a profound obsession within her that she purposely drove her children to school and back to force herself to leave the house. School wasn't out for another twenty minutes. Rinsing her hands, she walked to the dining room and glimpsed the front half of Elizabeth's Mini Cooper at the curb.

This was one of the silver linings in the move. Well, the great deal on the house wasn't so bad either—and the time to rediscover her artistic side. But she loved that Elizabeth could come home whenever she wanted. It was perfect: all the fun of having a teenager and none of the endless independence tug-of-war. She momentarily indulged in a fantasy of renting Grace a little apartment. *Too soon. And then there was the new French boyfriend complication.*

Rounding the kitchen wall into the dim entry, Sara came face to face with a tall stranger silhouetted in the blinding sun of the open doorway. "Oh! Jesus!" The blood in her veins staged a riot and held her breath hostage. Jake and Elizabeth were constantly nagging her to lock the doors. She never did. And now she was dead.

It took a couple of erratic heartbeats before she recognized Elizabeth's laundry basket hanging from the guy's hand.

"Sorry! Didn't mean to startle you. Elizabeth left her keys in the trunk."

Sara exhaled, her hand rising to her heart. "So, she's here?" The shadow was rapidly taking on colors and detail as her eyes adjusted to the light. Elizabeth bounded up the steps, her blonde strands waving in a breeze of her own making. "Hi, kidlet! I wasn't expecting you." Sara hugged her daughter's stiff shoulders. "Are you staying for dinner?"

"Yep! I invited my friend. Remember? I told you about him on the phone." She flashed a teasing smile at the boy. Apparently, they'd been spending quite a lot of time together. "Is that okay?"

"Sure. You can always invite your friends." The young man had now fully materialized. Sara's head tilted. She knew him from somewhere.

"We go rock climbing on Thursdays, but Psych class got canceled today, so I thought we could drop in for a free dinner and laundry service. I wanted Ethan to meet you."

Elizabeth hauled her laundry down the hall, leaving Ethan to fend for himself in the kitchen with her mom. Moving strategically to the breakfast nook studio, Sara started cleaning up.

Ethan followed. "These are yours? You're an artist?"

"Yeah, well, that's a matter of definition. I'm getting back in touch with my artistic side. There was a little shop on the cape..."

The boy bent to gaze at the petal she had just finished. "This is perfect—I mean the stroke."

She'd been working on that stroke all morning. Laughing off the compliment, she pretended it hadn't gone right to her head. "I think I finally got it. I'm taking an adult ed. class at the university. The guest artist spent almost the whole hour trying to teach me. He was probably relieved when the class was over and I had to go home."

"I doubt that." The boyfriend flashed a smile that conjured up visions of Jake when they were dating. "Anyway, it paid off. You have this down cold."

"Are you an art student? I thought you met Elizabeth in psych class."

"Well, psychology fascinates me, but I've been around art my whole life—seems like forever. My dad—"

Elizabeth bounced back into the kitchen. "Ethan's dad's a famous artist. Maybe you can meet him, mom."

The thought made Sara a little sick. "Who's your dad?"

"Ethan McCarthy."

Her eyebrows flew up. "Ethan McCarthy? THE Ethan McCarthy?" She had to admit, the resemblance was uncanny. Pirates. She stopped to allow the coincidences to all catch up to each other. "He's the guest artist in my class."

"I thought I recognized that brushstroke." He winked.

Sara recognized the wink. "Small world. I sat next to him on a plane. Didn't make the connection between him and the artist Ethan McCarthy until the teacher introduced him in class. I guess you just don't imagine the guy sitting next to you is famous. How old are you?"

An odd smile flitted across his face. "Eighteen. Nineteen in a few months."

"Hmm. If he hadn't told me on the plane that he had a son in college, I wouldn't have guessed he was old enough. I thought he was in his thirties. He looks so young, except his eyes. Your father has an old soul, I think. You look a lot like him. Still, I never would have guessed."

"I get that all the time. He's actually in his late thirties." She squinted doubtfully. "Pushing forty. He and my mom got married pretty young."

"Your mom?"

"She died—when I was a baby."

"I'm so sorry!"

"So was he."

Chapter 52

The quick pulse, the smile that lingered around her lips on Thursday afternoons, Sara was a little ashamed of them. Yes, she had a reason for the little skip in her step. The scales had tipped—literally. She'd dropped 10 lbs. in less than a month. Diet and exercise—and an obsession.

The real coup was the new vision she had. Leana was right; her old series was too perky. She boxed it up and started fresh. Mr. McCarthy was inspiring and so positive about her new pieces. He nurtured in her a depth of shadow that she cultivated into an entirely new look.

Even Leana, who most definitely did not like her work, was compelled to muted admiration. "It would seem," she grimaced, "that the rather remarkable attention Mr. McCarthy has invested in coaching you has begun to pay small dividends."

Sara beamed.

Ethan glowered.

There was definitely something between him and Leana.

At home, Sara sat down at the computer. She still harbored the hope of landing a boutique to feature her new art. Unfortunately, the only email was an automated message from the middle school grading system. Danny's grades were abominable. He started on the honor roll and then crashed. Sara knew it was the video games…and the move. If the kid could grow up to install game systems, he'd do all right. She couldn't even turn on the DVD player anymore, but Danny had hooked up his games to the internet and played with his virtual friends; he even had Bluetooth. Too bad it was a nonprofit organization.

"It's not that I don't have friends, mom," he explained in exasperation when she summoned him to the desk. "I have lots of friends at school. Everyone likes me. It's just that I think they're boring and I don't want to hang out with them. And the ones that it might be fun to hang out with, they do drugs and crap, so I don't want to hang out with them either. Stop worrying about me."

"But you're brilliant. There's no excuse for these kinds of grades. You have to start turning in your homework." She stabbed a finger at the screen. "Look at this—F homework, F homework, F homework!"

Danny studied the screen. "I did all those. She just never asked us to turn them in."

Sara buried her head in her hands. Danny was the nicest kid on the planet. He looked like his whole world was crumbling if she frowned at him. "I don't want to ground you from your game and follow you to school to make you turn in your papers. You need to shut off the PS3 yourself, learn to handle your life, make decisions…set priorities. I'm sorry, but I believe in free will. I'm not going to hover."

"Mom, I don't do so well with free will. Someone needs to make me."

"I am not going to be that kind of mom. How do you expect to go to a decent university with these grades? You know what? You get straight As like you're supposed to, and your dad and I will buy you that Mustang you want when you're sixteen."

He patted her shoulder and trotted into his room to rifle through the sinkhole of his backpack for finished assignments.

Sara sorted through her inbox—an ad, a bill, and a note from Phil. She sighed and opened the email from Phil. He'd asked her to trade with him the week before. She'd felt like seventh grade all over again. Her own fear of rejection had been so palpable that the thought of rejecting someone else made her nauseated; in the spirit of reciprocity, she'd sent him a sketch she was working on. Sara wasn't expecting much. He was enormously self-centered and manic in class, completely losing interest when the discussion of his pieces ended. She suspected he had bi-polar disorder. She'd seen similar behavior in a few students.

The message had no attachment.

To: sdawson
Re: Critique
Hi Sara,

Sorry this took me a little longer than I had hoped. I love this sketch. I had to travel unexpectedly. Since I didn't have my computer I put my comments on the sketch. Do you mind sending me your address so I can put this in the post? I want you to have it before class on Thursday.

Thanks,

Phil

Danny shuffled back into the room with a handful of papers. "I think I can turn these in for a late grade."

In the middle of typing a polite response, Sara glanced at the papers.

Danny read over her shoulder. "Phil? Isn't that the crazy guy?"

She nodded, sifting through his pages. She recognized the names of missing assignments. "Okay. Please, don't forget to hand them in tomorrow." She typed her zip code and pushed the SEND button. One less thing.

"Did you just send your address to the crazy guy?"

Sara's mouth opened. She'd just sent her home address to a crazy guy. Danny shook his head and sighed. "Geez, mom, even I know not to do that. The strangers I play with online think I'm a fifty-year-old guy from Kentucky.

She shrugged it off. "He's weird. But he's harmless."

Chapter 53

—Excerpts from the journals of Ethan McCarthy, Jr.

The red handhold at the top of the climbing wall taunted me. Just an inch more. My fingertips grabbed it. Done! Elizabeth had scheduled our rock-climbing dates for Thursday afternoons. Ethan Sr. resurfaced on Thursday nights so that he could be in the art class with Sara. Technically, our bargain with Brann Sidhe only entitled the raven muse to Friday through Sunday, once a month. But "dad" was getting desperate. In the seconds after I emerged, his impatience and anxiety bathed my consciousness.

In jerks, I descended the advanced wall. The lever that released and held the belay rope was sticky. Elizabeth wrenched it sharply as I kicked off the wall and slid a bit recklessly. Milliseconds before my toe hit the ground, she snapped it shut and yanked me to a stop.

"Just one more time," she begged.

The time on my phone advised against another round. To make way for my older self, I'd disappear in less than one hour. I was supposed to have Elizabeth safely home by then. What was I going to do? Tell her "no"?

"My mom said I was a monkey." She rubbed chalk into her palms. Unhooking the ropes from my harness, I attached them to hers. "They bought me and Grace a swing set when I was four. The day after my dad put it together, I climbed up the slide, grabbed onto the main crossbar, and climbed to the other side, dangling ten feet in the air. A few months later, I was doing backflips out of the swing. Mom put me in my aunt's gymnastics class."

"That explains a few things."

Elizabeth was deceptively thin. She scaled the rock-climbing walls like Spider-Girl. Holding herself parallel to the ground, she scrambled across the underbelly of a rock face. She could hold her body weight a lot longer than I could, and I was no slouch.

Readjusting, I secured the lines and checked Elizabeth before she turned to the wall.

"My favorite game was 'dangerous.' I used to climb on the kitchen island counter and jump off to my dad." Her pink lips curve into a little smile while she talked. She chatted while she started up the wall. "My mom would say, 'No! That's dangerous.' After that, I always asked my dad to play 'dangerous' with me." A tricky combination of footings and an elusive handgrip stole her attention.

Bracing myself on the belay line, I fed her some slack, moving along the wall with her until she scrambled up to the peak. With a cheeky grin, she commanded, "Your turn."

The rope stuck as she kicked away from the wall. The lever resisted giving more slack. She slid a foot more and rappelled again. This time, I gave the WD-40 deficient lever a solid shove. *Too much!* Elizabeth plummeted like a baby chick out of the nest. We both heard the crack as her foot hit the floor and her ankle rolled. Her groan was already reverberating through the gym by the time I wrestled the lever back into the locked position. Lunging forward, I caught her as she lost her balance.

"Shit! Are you all right?" I knew she wasn't. The grit on her face would have given her away, even if the squeal hadn't. "I'm so sorry. The lever was sticking. I was trying to give you more slack, so it wouldn't be so jerky."

"I know. It's okay." She nodded her head like she understood, but her jaw clenched and her eyes tensed. "Let me see if I can walk." When her toe touched the floor, she strangled a little squeal.

"C'mon!" I unlatched the harness. She was too occupied being brave to help. "I'm getting you to the ER."

A small army of concerned employees—more concerned about legal issues than Elizabeth—waylaid us, but once I'd carried her out to my car and buckled her in, I ventured another look at her face. "This isn't going to impress your mom." Strapping myself into the driver's seat, I squealed out of the parking lot. "I took her daughter out and broke her; she's never going to let me near you again."

The old man is gonna kill me. That wasn't possible, but it was the thought that counted. I wasn't supposed to be falling in love with Elizabeth; I was supposed to be using her to get to Sara. That's how I'd bargained to get the extra hour that was going to make Ethan Sr. late for Sara's art class.

"I'm a big girl who likes 'dangerous.' My mom's used to stuff like this." Grimacing, she readjusted her ankle.

Hopefully, she was right. My phone reminded me that in a little over half an hour, I would take a step forward and cease to be myself. Disaster. I couldn't just drop Elizabeth off at the hospital and leave. What kind of guy would do that? "Which hospital?"

Elizabeth caught the nervous flick of my wrist. "I don't want you to miss your flight. This is my fault. I shouldn't have gone up for that last one. I'll call my mom and find out which hospital. She can come get me."

That would have been great, except for the fact that Sara was supposed to meet my older self at the coffee shop after class. It was all over the journals. My "dad" was sure this was his last chance. If Sara came to the hospital, she wouldn't show up for class, and the last chance would be history. I didn't put it past Ethan Sr. to tell Elizabeth his "son" had died in Boston and then never let me out again.

So ironic. To put us all on this tenacious path to eternal life, I'd ignored living and neglected love. Now that we all had unlimited life, I would risk it all to love, for just a short lifetime, this girl I barely knew, and yet felt in my bones.

Elizabeth finished breaking the news to her mother. "Don't worry about my flight," I whispered over the phone conversation, "I'll figure something out. I want to make sure you're okay before I leave. Which hospital?" It was the chivalrous thing to do—risk "the flight" to stay with her. I wasn't going to sabotage my chances with Elizabeth. My "dad" would just have to deal.

"First Presbyterian." Elizabeth wanted me to stay, even though she wouldn't say so. She accepted the gift. Whatever happened after was Ethan Sr.'s problem.

Chapter 54

—Excerpts from the unpublished writings of Easton Ravenscroft

Guilty pleasure. It wasn't the dark chocolate Lindt ball Sara snuck into her diet. Her painting was good, exceptional even, but her excitement to exhibit her new piece was all muddled up in the titillation of sensing she was the object of desire. She had no intention of fanning that spark, but she wanted to see the frank admiration in Ethan's eyes because he couldn't mask that his appreciation flowed beyond the art to the artist. It was selfish, like dipping her straw in his soda to siphon the foamy bubbles off the top.

Basking in the sunshine of a fresh project mimicked the thrill that buzzed her arm whenever Ethan brushed her hand to guide the strokes. He dropped his eyes abruptly when she looked his direction, lingered a few minutes extra, watching her work, and leaned closer over her shoulder. He was breathing her in like he hadn't had fresh air for a while. Sometimes, she suspected she might be going to class because of the irresistible appeal of being desired, but she never let herself believe it. Still, the look of unbridled longing she sometimes surprised when she caught him looking her direction compelled her to him.

Sara consciously refrained from encouraging him—not much, nothing more than politeness and a healthy appreciation for his professional attention. Although he was not much more than a stranger, the art between them forged an odd sense of inner connection. It wasn't fair for her to inflate her sagging sense of self-worth by fanning the air around a spark that had no hope of ever bursting into flame. *I'm going because it's improving my work.* She found the tinge of doubt unsettling—because of Jake.

Ethan was supposed to meet her at the campus Starbuck's after class—so he could pass her the names of a couple of agents who gravitated toward work like hers. He didn't feel comfortable singling her out in class with Leana there. Sara didn't drink coffee, the caffeine left her bouncing off the walls. But, she did like that frozen, strawberry and cream thing they did. Totally and completely a sin against her diet.

It felt a little weird, meeting with Ethan outside of class. But then, Jake went out with the women he worked with all the time. It didn't mean anything because Jake was hers and she was Jake's, totally and completely, joined by decades of running, scraping, falling, and climbing together.

After three months, she'd finally gotten the timing of a weekly class right and breezed in a few minutes early. Ethan wasn't there, but he often came in late. Unpacking her portfolio, she displayed her latest chef-d'oeuvre. Joan chatted and admired her work. Sara passed the name of a great book to Alice. Smiling politely, she listened to Phil's plans for the weekend until he dropped his chin into his hand and lamented loudly, "You're the most beautiful woman I know, and you're married."

Everyone averted their eyes from the disaster. Sara laughed it off. Leana started the class with a look at Phil's new piece. Ethan still hadn't shown up. Footsteps echoed in the hall. Sara's heart jumpstarted. The night janitor passed the open door.

It was just business, but she felt oddly stood up. At least, she could smile and pretend nothing had happened because nothing had happened. It was probably the silliest idea she'd ever entertained. In the end, she probably would have found some excuse not to go. She wasn't ready for an agent anyway.

She missed Ethan's comments, though. The rest of the class, and even Leana, certainly made up for them. That her hand would ever craft anything of the least interest to Leana seemed highly unlikely, and even less likely that the sight of it would overcome her for more than a minute. "This painting is a perfectly entwined balance of inspiration and execution. Share with us, won't you, Ms. Dawson, the inspiration for this most delightful piece of art." Blushing, Sara admitted it was from a dream that suffocated her thoughts until she gave it life on canvas. Leana's eyes narrowed and her fingers tugged at the purple stone on her chest.

Sara had simply woken up one morning and found the vision there, a remnant of her dreams. She threw on her sweat pants and stationed herself in the breakfast nook. As the kids wandered in with their groggy, feed-me faces, she pointed them toward the cereal cupboard. They rode the bus. Sara skipped breakfast, dropped leftovers in the microwave for lunch, forgot them, and painted all day until Annie called at 3:10.

In the middle of class, Sara's phone rang. Grimacing apologetically, she rushed over to her purse. Palming the phone, she slipped into the hallway.

"What's up, Elizabeth?"

"I think I broke my ankle."

"What? How?"

"Rock climbing with Ethan. I slipped."

"Where are you? I'll be right there."

"No, it's okay. He's driving me to the hospital. We just don't know which one to go to."

"Our insurance covers First Presbyterian. Do you want me to look up the address?"

"Nope, I can find it on my phone."

Leaving her daughter's care to a boy she barely knew didn't sit well with Sara. "I'll come pick you up. Class is almost over anyway."

"No. Don't worry about it. You don't have to come all the way out here. Ethan can take me home. I'll call you and tell you what they say. Maybe I just sprained it or something, but it hurts bad. I think I broke it."

She had just tucked the phone in her purse and made her excuses when it buzzed again. She glanced at the clock. Still no Ethan. "I think my daughter broke her ankle. Sorry." She stepped out to sympathetic nods.

The call wasn't Elizabeth. It was a text from Danny.

D: *We can't find dad's golf shoes.*

Sara sighed. *I must be completely delusional to think I could slip away and have coffee.* She couldn't even make it through a class without multiple calls from home.

She was a hack at texting, but since that seemed to be her children's main form of communication, she was adapting. She squinted at the letters and tapped back a message.

S: *Look in our closet on the shelf.*
D: *Dad already did.*

Sara rolled her eyes and picked out a response.

S: *He might have to look under the shirts. Look again.*

She had just joined the group around Stephanie's work when the phone buzzed again. "Sorry. Four kids."
This one was from Grace.

G: *Julien broke up with me.*

Unbelievable. Sara couldn't leave for two hours without the whole place falling apart. She pecked at the keys on her phone. One wrong button, and the whole message vanished. She started over.

S: *Why? Do you want to tell me what happened?*

It seemed better to just stay in the hallway until the phone traffic stopped. The phone buzzed. It wasn't from Grace. It was Danny.

D: *We found them. They were right where you said.*
S: *Have fun!*

The phone buzzed again as Sara hit the exclamation point. Elizabeth.

E: *I broke my tibia. It's a fracture. I'm supposed to go see an orthopedic surgeon tomorrow. Can you get me an appointment?*
S: *No problem. Do you need anything?*
E: *I'm going home as soon as the doctor comes back in with a prescription. Call me when you have the appointment set up.*
S: *Take care. Love you.*

Grace's response was two screens long describing some cell phone mix-up. Her battery died; Julien thought she was over at an old boyfriend's house. He'd announced the end of the relationship on Facebook. The whole drama lasted the drive home. By the time she walked back in the door, the happy couple was officially in a relationship again.

"This place would die without me." Sara slipped into her pajamas. Annie peeked in the door. She needed a long hug before she could find the courage to go back to her bed. She still had withdrawals from when Jake was traveling and she'd taken over his spot in the big California king.

It was good to be loved and needed. This "thing" with Ethan, whatever it was—or apparently wasn't—was like toying with drugs. She might as well stick a shot of heroin in her arm, get a short thrill, and then pay for it, over and over, until she lost everything she loved. That night, she dreamed she took a step out over a ledge before looking down to see the steep drop-off to nowhere.

Sara never went back to class. Instead, she emailed the group.

To: lbrann
Re: art class
Hi Ms. Brann,
Just wanted to let you know that my schedule has changed and I won't be able to attend the last few weeks of class. Thank you so much for your instruction. Your class has been very inspiring.
Best,
Sara Dawson

Chapter 55
—From the unfinished manuscript of Ethan McCarthy

Ethan Jr. was gone when they wheeled Elizabeth back into the exam room. She looked stunned when the door to her ER room swung open and she found that her boyfriend had aged at least twenty years while the doctor evaluated her X-rays. I introduced myself while the nurse arranged her on the patient bed.

"You must be Elizabeth. I'm Ethan's father."

"Oh, nice to meet you." Although Ethan Jr.'s memories showed me a confidant young woman, confronted with a stranger, Elizabeth retreated into a shy, little girl self. "Is Ethan still here?"

"No." Her face fell. "He wanted to stay. It was my fault. I made him go. He needed to catch that plane."

"I know. I told him he didn't have to stay; my mom could come." She began digging for her phone in the large silver bag at the foot of the bed.

"Please, don't bother her. I'm here already. I'll be happy to see you home."

"I'm not actually going home. I live in the same apartment complex as Ethan." Apparently, having her boyfriend's father take her home oozed all sorts of awkward. Having to lean on me, a stranger and an old guy, could only end in embarrassment. "It's okay. She won't mind. She worries."

"Technically, I'm not a stranger. Your mother knows me."

Elizabeth giggled and rolled her eyes. "Ethan said the same thing when he met me." She gently repositioned her foot on the bed. "Mom's told me about you. She loves your work and the new stuff you helped her come up with."

"She's a brilliant artist. All she needs is a bit of inspiration and she's off on her own."

"I guess you inspired her then."

"Makes life worth living, doesn't it?" I stared at her for just a second too long. "You know, you have your mother's smile."

"And my dad's lips."

The doctor came in with the prescription for pain meds. "The good news is, you haven't torn any of the ligaments, so it probably won't need a cast. We'll wrap it and give you a boot. But I do suggest you see an orthopedic surgeon."

By the time Elizabeth was wrapped up, she'd grown accustomed to me. My son and I had a lot in common. And she was infatuated with Ethan Jr.—when I resurfaced, his memories dripped with her affection. I wheeled her out to my son's BMW.

"Didn't Ethan go to the airport?"

Maneuvering her into the car, I hesitated for a fraction of a second. Hopefully, she got the impression we'd argued about it, not that I was lying.

"He took my car. He didn't have time to move all your climbing gear." I nodded toward the ropes and shoes in the back seat.

"It's not like I'll be doing much climbing before he gets back," Elizabeth muttered as I shut the door.

Chapter 56

—Excerpts from the unpublished writings of Easton Ravenscroft

Sara's husband had the uncanny ability to know when the detonator, buried deep in her complex, meticulously self-contained, bulletproof universe, was ticking down. On those rare, but strategic moments, he managed to slide in and defuse it at the 00:01 mark, just before she blew up in his face.

Friday evening, after she'd resolved to quit the art classes that had, over the space of a few months, dissipated the gloom of depression and loneliness hovering about her, Jake left work at 4:00. He surprised her as she stared into the open refrigerator wondering what and how much to make for dinner. Lately, she'd been giving Jake's dinner away to Julien.

"You're home!" Sara exclaimed, but then remembered that she was peeved to have been neglected for so long for the new job.

"Yeah, I needed to spend some time with my wife. They can live without me for the weekend. Shall we go out?"

"Where are we going?" Annie looked up from her Algebra textbook.

"*We*'re not going anywhere. I'm taking *your mother* out." He pulled a box from the freezer. "*You*'re having pizza, and—" he leaned around Sara and peered into the refrigerator. His left hand reached toward the carrot sticks, his right slid surreptitiously up her shirt. Gasping, she pushed it away, glaring at him with eyes that managed to be pleased, chastising, and seductive all at once. "—and carrots with dip."

He followed his wife around the kitchen as she pulled out cups and plates and piled the makeshift dinner on the counter. Under cover of their daughter's absorption in YouTube videos and Math homework, Jake took advantage of his wife having to reach for most of the shelves in the kitchen and made inappropriate passes while her hands were full. For the sake of dignity, she pushed him away, but her heart wasn't in it. While the art class had filled the voids of moving and loss of purpose, she'd struggled to fill the gaps between her and Jake. After over 20 years of marriage, they were so wound up in each other, that without him, she was missing pieces of herself.

While she fixed her face and hair, Jake did his best to convince Annie she was doing her problems all wrong, compelling her to prove she wasn't. She was giggling by the time Sara skipped down the stairs and dragged her husband away.

Jake pulled out of the driveway. "You look pretty. Is that a new shirt?"

"Yeah, well, I've been trying lots of different pick-me-up strategies."

"I have a couple you haven't tried yet." He wagged his eyebrows. Chuckling, she rolled hers. The glue that kept them together never turned toxic. Neither one of them lived to punish the other. The euphoria of the makeup drove them, not the passion of the breakup.

"How's the job?"

Jake shook his head, a smile of hilarity blossoming on his face. "Do you know Sheryl, my GL accountant?"

"Hmmm, GL. Wait, wait! General Ledger?"

"Smart cookie."

"Well, I do have a Master's degree." Bubbles of humor were starting to foam up between them. *Thank God!* The rifts were suffocating her.

"Sheryl is a piece of work. She rolls along for a while and then the wheels fall off. This time, it's butt fissures."

Sara's mouth pursed jovially.

Jake braked at the light and nodded in mutual comic astonishment.

"She told the office about this? I mean—TMI!"

"Well, I suggested she might want to try duct tape."

"Duct tape!" Sara's head fell back against the headrest and she indulged a throaty giggle—it had been a while.

"Yeah, fissures, duct tape. Keeping stuff all together, you know? I think she liked the idea. She thought it was funny."

"Good thing, otherwise you're gonna end up with a harassment suit."

"I know! Butt fissures, butt cheeks..." Reaching over the console, he took Sara's hand. "I love to hear you laugh. If you stop laughing, I'm lost."

Restaurants began appearing on the right. "How's the art going?" Jake swallowed hard. His glance approximated sympathetic interest but was warped by dread.

Sara recognized the gamble. He was offering an olive branch, but she might be allergic. This ground was littered with mines and had blown up in his face more than once, but it was also the path to her heart.

"The class was great. I'm not going anymore—too busy—but I met a few people who don't feel emotionally blackmailed by the prospect of critiquing my paintings. And then, I think maybe my style might have been a little dated. The class helped me catch up."

"I've always liked your edgier stuff. You should break away and experiment with it."

It was the wrong thing to say because it so blatantly implied that he didn't like what she'd been working on before. Of course, he had every right to not like what she did, and Sara knew it wasn't his genre—he was too much of a realist with an eye for the contemporary.

She absorbed the phantom dart with a ghostly wince. They were both trying—it had to be a mutual effort. He was mounting a major offensive and she wasn't going to sabotage him. Frankly, she wanted Jake back more than she wanted to be an artist, more than she wanted her life back. If the two of them were good, everything else fell into place.

"Yeah." She nodded optimistically. "I'm hoping to start a group like I had in Boston with some of the people I met in class."

Sara filled Jake in on the latest Grace and Julien drama. She lamented Danny's debilitating handicap that rendered him incapable of turning in his finished assignments. "Oh, did Annie show you her finger? She thinks it might be broken, but we're waiting until tomorrow to see. This will be her third break this year, including the broken nose at Halloween."

"I better put more in the medical savings account next year. I guess we didn't expect her to be the athletic type."

"Yeah, that's Grace. Annie wants a kitten now. We'll be overrun by animals soon. We should have just had another child for her to take care of."

Jake grimaced. His idea of a successful parent was one who raised the children so that they would leave and only come back for visits.

A block away from their new favorite Mexican place with the good salsa, the air welled up in her and Sara felt suddenly buoyant—like her best friend had moved back in.

"I love this, baby." She squeezed his hand. "Life is a happy place when you're with me. I just hate it when we're detached." For months, she'd felt as if she were swimming in murky water with one arm and one leg paralyzed. She'd finally found a sense of confidence in her art, a satisfaction in the act of creation, and a gut appreciation for her skills. Now, driving and chatting with her husband, she felt the plane of her existence tip. Her feet were on dry land again and her body was whole, rejuvenated by spring air.

"We're not detached. It's just the time. We've been apart for so long, but things are calming down at work. We can spend more time together."

"I'm okay with alone, with rejection, with drudgery. I just hate feeling like you don't even see me—or want to see me."

"You're all I want to see, Sara." He leaned over with a cheeky grin and tugged at her blouse a little so that the edge of her red bra and the small, round slopes of cleavage peeked out. "And I'd like to see a whole lot more of you tonight."

Sara cocked an eyebrow and slid out of the car. "Matching red lace." The thick honey in her voice oozed across the roof of the car. They walked to the restaurant holding hands.

It was early and only a few elderly couples occupied tables. "You know if I lose you, I lose everything." He leaned over and kissed her as she took a seat in the booth.

Enchiladas and root beer, movie, sneaking past the kids, it wasn't monumental, or even extraordinary, but it was them, together.

At home again, behind closed doors, Jake produced and dangled a boutique bag filled with lavender toiletries.

"Oh, I see where this is going."

Jake was an artist. Sara was his canvas; making love was his medium. When she lay cradled in the curve of his body, his Rodin hand cupping her breast and his slow, hot breath caressing her neck, their hearts beat in separate but entwined cadences. Sara basked in the undulating rhythm of their lives, twisting, turning together—living.

The customary knock on the door sent her scrambling for a bathrobe. It was tricky with teenagers; they went to bed so late.

"Good night, Mom. Good Night, Dad." It was Annie.

Saturday morning, Jake and Sara listened to the birds warbling in the trees that lined the trails meandering through the golf course. They stopped at the bridge to hold hands and gaze into the flowing waters of the creek. They hadn't been out running together for a while.

After breakfast, they took advantage of the early Texas spring. The nursery was swamped, but they managed to make off with several ivy plants and a few roses. Jake dug the holes for the roses, while Sara planted ivy at the base of the stone wall on the shady side of the house. Since Jake was convinced that manly men wore no gloves, when it was time to pull the roses out of their five-gallon pots, he swore and popped his finger in his mouth. "These are pretty prickly."

"I have gloves." She maneuvered around the pot until she had a firm hold on the exposed root ball. "Okay, I'll try to hold on to it and you pull it out from under me."

Silence. She glanced back at Jake to see what was holding him up.

His eyes twinkled. "That's pretty much the story of our lives."

They almost couldn't plant the roses for laughing. And she loved him because he didn't just see it; he said it. The bond between them was not a single entwining of two pieces of the same fabric into one. Their bond was the project. Every wall they had built together, every new onslaught of life that had pushed them to strengthen the ties between them to withstand it, the very forces that were ripping them apart, were melding them into one inseparable edifice. Her husband, her family—these were as much Sara's art as the people on canvas.

Sunday morning her eyes popped open and she wondered which run she should take. She squinted at the clock. Nearly seven; they were sleeping in. Jake felt her stir. His warm, heavy arms reached over and gathered her in. She fit perfectly like she was made to fill that curve. Maybe the run could wait.

"I love waking up to this beautiful woman in my bed." He laced her fingers into his. They indulged for a few more minutes. "Are you happy again?"

"Mmhmm."

"If you're happy, I'm happy."

"I know. I lost my footing, for a second."

"You know I'd do anything to make you happy."

He turned so her nose was looking up past his chin. The soft curls at the base of his hair always attracted her fingers. "No one can make you happy. You have to make yourself happy. But it's nice that you try." She reached for his lips and brushed them with hers.

Now that it was past, Sara could see the storm a little more clearly. She could see the damage it did to Jake when she was hunkered down against the driving winds. It wasn't anger she saw in his eyes when she was sad; it was fear. He didn't know what to do and didn't want to lose her.

Chapter 57

The dream choked her. Sweat soaked Sara's brow and nightshirt. Her heart raced as if she'd just run a 10K. Images billowed up and crashed into her consciousness like a tidal wave.

Friday morning. 4:00 a.m. Sara knew the signs. Her night was over. She threw off the stifling comforter, found her robe, and twisted her hair up in a comb. Early morning vigils had become a ritual. It was better to get the image on canvas than to toss around for two hours while it ripped and tore at the confines of her subconscious.

The subject that haunted her was a startlingly glamorous woman, not quite real. Tripping quietly over the wood floor to the kitchen tile, she dragged her sketch box out of the cupboard. Conveying the esoteric, ephemeral nature of the dream woman would be tricky. Sara's hands slid back and forth across the paper. Originally, she'd envisioned charcoal, but her fingers waded through the box and settled on a golden pen. She wanted to substantiate the creature before she endowed her with concrete form on canvas. The sense of floating that lingered in her mind eluded her fingers. She tossed several sheets to the floor.

Before her hand deciphered what her imagination was screaming, orange streams of light crept over the treetops outside the window and the familiar tune of Jake's iPhone alarm drifted through the family room to the nook.

A cloak—white as doves—furry, no, not furry—feathered—floating about the woman.

Alarm clocks buzzed upstairs. 6:30. She was running out of time. Her pencil flew frantically across the page in tiny strokes, fashioning downy plumes in perpetual flight. The clap of Jake's dress shoes announced him. He slid in behind her and kissed her neck.

"Can't sleep?" For the first couple of months after the move, he'd only seen her in bed, just rousing herself as he left and dozing off when he came home. Since she'd started painting again, Jake rarely saw her asleep.

Reaching her arms around his neck, she exhausted the remnants of the morning's passion on his lips.

"Must be something erotic you're working on." He leaned over her shoulder and nodded appreciatively at the creature taking life from her hand. "Should I be disturbed that a woman excites this much passion in you?"

Sara giggled. "I dreamt her up last night. It's not the subject that makes the passion; it's the thrill of bringing it to life." She kissed him again, girlishly.

"Whatever lights your fire." He tossed her a cheeky grin and grabbed a handful of almonds from the open bag on the kitchen island. "I just hope some strange guy doesn't show up and get to you before I do when you're all lit up."

"Yeah, right. I barely leave the house. Anyway," she stood up and imprinted her lips on his, softly, with the familiarity of 23 years, "you're the only one who lights that fire."

"Then you should take a nap today and wait up for me. I'll see if I can slip away a little early." He winked and tossed a couple of almonds in his mouth on his way out.

Sara sat down to her drawing and inhaled life the way it was meant to be. Tilting her head, she contemplated the creature she'd given birth to. Reaching for the box of crayons, she pulled out a fiery red one. In broad strokes, her fist engulfed the woman in flames.

The still and quiet upstairs distracted her. The alarms had been shut off. She jumped up and plugged her new i-Phone into the speaker system. The billowing tones of Evanescence *Bring Me to Life* emanated through the house with the push of a button. Pancakes on the griddle greeted the morning zombies who appeared on the staircase.

Chapter 58

The door swung open. Sara looked up from the canvas she was plastering. 2:00 p.m. The kids didn't get home until 3:00. Blinded by the sunlight streaming in through the kitchen windows, she squinted into the relative darkness of the two-story entry. Elizabeth's voice echoed through the house. "Mom, you didn't lock the door again!"

Sara rinsed her hands in the sink and walked toward her daughter drying them. "Is that you, kidlet? How are you?" Elizabeth, her ankle bound up in a boot, stood in the open doorway, leaning on crutches. "Does your leg hurt?" She hugged her little girl, who wasn't so little anymore.

"No, it's okay." She hobbled onto the rug. "But I have laundry in the car."

"I'll grab it."

"Don't worry about it. Mr. McCarthy is bringing it in."

"Mr. McCarthy? He's here?" Sara peeked around her daughter to see the famous artist lifting a rather full laundry bag out of the back of Elizabeth's Mini-Cooper.

"Well, yeah. I can't handle the clutch. The doctor said it would be a couple of weeks. Can I trade cars with you? The Toyota's automatic."

"Of course." Sara looked for words and reactions but couldn't seem to find any there in the entry. The sight of Mr. McCarthy hauling her daughter's laundry up the stairs disturbed her on so many levels. Her children had dragged her into more sticky situations than she cared to remember, but this was a muddy, quagmire of a sinkhole. "I could have driven down. Where's Ethan? I mean, the younger one? Couldn't he drive you up? How will Mr. McCarthy get home?"

"That's the thing. Apparently, his dad has some meeting up here. They were going to send a car anyway."

"Who?"

"I don't know, the museum or some art shop. Anyway, Ethan had another interview. He won't be back until Monday. I decided to come home for the weekend to camp out on the couch with my foot up while you do my laundry." She favored Sara with the cheeky grin she'd inherited from her father. She'd also gotten his brazen decisiveness.

Ethan was halfway up the front steps and Sara began to flutter like a bird in a cage.

"What's wrong with you, Mom?"

"Nothing, uh—" She sighed and sifted her fingers through her bangs. "I just haven't showered today. You should have called me, sweetie. You didn't need to bother Mr. McCarthy. Why would you call him instead of me?"

"I didn't bother him. He came to the hospital to send Ethan to the airport and then drove me home."

"Mr. McCarthy took you home? He was at the hospital last Thursday night?"

"I just said that, Mom."

"Oh." Sara's mind was running on a two-second delay, making the connection with Ethan missing art class because he was driving her daughter home from the hospital. "Oh!"

"I mentioned I didn't think I could drive my car and I would have to switch with you and he volunteered. I tried to tell him 'no'. But he insisted. I didn't have time to call. I had three tests this week."

Sara stuttered, but Mr. McCarthy was in earshot now.

Elizabeth got indignant. She had a tone that made the younger siblings fall in line, not to mention her parents. "Mom! Chill! It's no big deal. I like Ethan—a lot. Don't be weird about this."

Sara's mouth opened, but no sounds came out. Mr. McCarthy's shoe creaked on the threshold. The consternation vanished, the well-practiced, gracious mother smile appeared. "Mr. McCarthy, we so appreciate your help." *We* included who? Jake? "I'm afraid Elizabeth's an incorrigible dare-devil. It was a concussion last month."

He shook the hand she held out in gratitude. Shiver. *Good grief! Could this be any more awkward?*

"It's nice to see you outside of class. Please call me Ethan."

"Then we'll all be confused when we see you and your son together. We can barely tell you apart anyway." Her mouth was leaking like a broken valve.

"That's not a high-frequency issue. Ethan's a big boy now. He has a life of his own."

To Sara's great relief, Elizabeth stepped into the conversation. "Let's have them up for dinner next Sunday, Mom. Dad can make vegetarian chili." She turned to Ethan and didn't see her mother's mouth drop open. "Everybody loves my dad's chili."

Apparently, this could get a little more awkward.

Mr. McCarthy moved to ease Sara's obvious discomfiture. "That's very kind of you, Elizabeth. I'm afraid I have prior engagements, but I'm sure my son would be more than happy to come and eat you out of house and home. I'd say I'll have to content myself with seeing you on Thursday night, Sara, but I hear you won't be joining us anymore."

And even more awkward still. Elizabeth waited open-mouthed for an explanation. Sara had gushed on more than one occasion about how much she loved her class and how her work was getting so much better because of it.

"Well," she chuckled nervously, "you know how it is with kids. In a week, it'll be May…the monster mommy month…choir concerts, school plays, sports banquets…and all on Thursday." She sniffed and gasped a bit. *Dear God, please don't let him mention coffee last Thursday.* "Whoever picked May for Mother's Day had to be a Father." *Nice save. No, it wasn't.*

"I'm very sorry. We'll miss you…your comments are always so insightful."

Gratified pleasure buzzed Sara's fingertips at the overt sincerity. The undertones were escaping Elizabeth. Her face was plastered with that familiar look of indulgent disdain that she'd worn ever since she turned seventeen and decided her mother was a benevolent mad woman.

Sara turned back to their guest. "Really, Mr. McCarthy—Ethan, you didn't need to put yourself out to come all this way. I would have picked Elizabeth up. My schedule's wide open. I'm not working."

"It was no trouble. One of the art dealers in town is a friend. We have some business. My son would never forgive me if I didn't do this for him." He gestured at the table cluttered with Sara's morning project. "What do you mean you're not working? Of course, you are."

A shiver rippled down Sara's spine at the acknowledgment of her art as her work. "That? Well, yeah. I, uh—" Elizabeth abandoned her mother to entertain Mr. McCarthy and hopped on one foot up the stairs to her room. Sara's icy glance bounced off her unsuspecting back. "I have trouble sleeping sometimes. I had this dream—the loveliest—" for a few seconds the reality in front of her faded and her mind receded into the realm of vision.

"A dream?" Suddenly Ethan was all business. He strode to the table. "I guess if you're not coming to class, I'll have to make house calls to check up on your work." He smiled back at her.

Slay me, now. Could he be any more gorgeous? Could this be any more wrong? Of course, it was wrong. If Jake came home right that minute, she'd stutter and stammer as if something were going on, when nothing was going on. She'd make darn sure she mentioned this little visit to her husband after dinner.

"No!" she objected, a little too strenuously, and then laughed politely. "You don't have to do that." She reached for the paper that his paint-dyed, calloused fingers were already holding. "I'll muddle along on my own. I think Stephanie and Joan may want to put a group together."

"Sounds great. Send me an email. I'll join. I could use some fresh perspectives on my work." Sara stifled a giggle at the absurdity of amateurs like her and her classmates offering Ethan McCarthy critiques on his work. He looked down at her sketches. His face turned to stone. Sobered, she hastened to grab the paper, but he turned away so that she spoke to his back.

"That's only scratch paper. I had to get the basic idea out." She bit her fingernails and then slipped around him to the table and lifted the drying, plastered canvas. "I thought this would be the perfect medium…give it a taste of antiquity."

In the silence, she read, *if you can't say anything nice—*
No confidence.

Ethan turned abruptly, his palm descending on her wrist. She winced and bit the inside of her lip. "You know I love your work, Sara." She looked away. The words on his tongue were not the words in his eyes. "This is not you. Don't pursue this piece."

Her brow wrinkled. There was no word for the emotion that slithered about her heart and squeezed until vinegar ran into her veins and erupted in her fingertips. He was wrong! Sara knew this was the piece that would open the door to a whole other world. She could feel it in the hot core of her gut.

A phone blared in Ethan's pocket and brought attention to the low rumble of an engine running outside on the curb. "I have to go." Ethan turned his body toward the door but his eyes held their ground in hers, the sketch suspended between them.

Sara didn't trust herself to respond. She stared out the windows, her fingertips nervously rubbing the hollow of her neck.

"Don't pursue this, Sara." He let the sketch flutter back onto the blank pad. "Don't."

Chapter 59
—From the unfinished manuscript of Ethan McCarthy

April in Dallas was a lion on the prowl. It pounced suddenly on the newborn spring, brandishing lightning and churning clouds. Rain pelted the windows of my bedroom. Brann Sidhe liked to lie in my bed in front of a roaring fire. I'd been particularly attentive to my mistress this evening. When she was most human, she was most vulnerable. The painting in front of me could not fail to satisfy even her insatiable appetite. The image exuded the angry passion that had stifled me since I'd laid eyes on Sara's new sketch. Wiping the sweat from my brow, I tossed the brush into a small can of fluid and strode to the bed, gloating at the ecstasy on the muse's face.

Even more stunning in the afterglow of her feasting, Brann smiled seductively, victoriously. My organs cringed. She was completely irresistible—water in the drought. After a century and a half deprived of Elizabeth, my unnatural life was a desert. The siren's lips sang to mine. Stooping, I found them and drew her to my chest. Abandoning herself to the concrete, she materialized and bathed in the wash of human emotions.

"You see how you love me, Ethan?"

"I could never love you. You are a murderous witch." My teeth clamped upon the soft whiteness of her ear lobe.

Her laughter, laughter that had engendered countless symphonies, rang low. She preferred a reluctant lover. My hands strangled her wrists, pinning them to her sides as I straddled her. Her body curled into mine, inviting.

"Renounce your Sara, love," she whispered, breathless. My eyes narrowed. The muse, braced on her wrists, drew herself up to my lips. "Renounce her and be mine. Beside your nectar, all others are naught but sour dross. Renounce her and we will end this game. I will forfeit all claim to your souls."

The offer gave me pause and I relinquished my grip. "Be mine, Ethan. Forever—or nearly so." She caressed my cheek with her nail. I did believe, that in her own foul and twisted way, the muse loved me.

"Give up Sara to save our souls? Serve you for countless centuries until you have used me up slowly, or until I murder myself to be rid of the visions in my head?"

"I used the others wastefully, I know." The contrition that marred her face was almost believable. "I find temperance so difficult when the fruit seems so dry and bitter. I fear I wring it in exasperation. But your nectar is so delectable. I would use you most delicately, savor every drop." Gently brushing my lower lip with the tip of her tongue, she inhaled the flavor.

"Clever deceiver. You tempt me to sell myself for what may be mine at no price. The game is not yet up. When Sara is mine, all the pieces of our souls will be free anyway."

Again, her laughter danced in the room. "I am no deceiver, Ethan. It is my gilded dove of a sister that delights in deception. She prefers the flavor of the innocent victim led blindly astray, whereas I find a guilt-ridden conspirator far more palatable."

The mention of Cailen Sidhe rekindled my anger and resolve.

"It is simply a gamble that I offer. Were the game up, I would have no cause to be so generous." Her face stiffened. "You will find, come the end of our little game's season, the leaves of my generosity will have withered." The stubble on my chin prickled against the lily whiteness of her hands until the conjured warmth of her icy flesh disgusted me. "Come, my sweet, the odds are strongly in my favor, and yet I offer you such munificent terms. You know 'young Ethan' no longer seeks Sara; he has veered from the target and set his sights on the daughter. I know him—stubborn, unacquainted with loss. He cares nothing for your suffering, but I can transform it into exquisite beauty." Brann turned my face back to hers.

The foolish love of the boy lingered in my memories. His unwavering focus on a goal had won us the secret of life unlimited, had surmounted all obstacles, ignoring all consequences. And now the goal on which it had fixed itself would enslave us across universes. Ethan Jr. would sell our souls for a season with his Elizabeth. And who was I to condemn him?

The muse read my thoughts and reveled in their tragic irony. "Sara has already rejected you so many times. Admit your loss; be my prize and I will be yours. The reality of your dream has not lived up to the inspiration of it."

At the mention of dreams, my jaw locked. Wresting her hands from around my face, I pushed the nearly human creature flat on the bed, pinning her slender wrists to the pillow with one hand. "No matter what you think me, I am no fool. You would not be so generous if you did not fear to lose your prize."

Perhaps she did not know that I had witnessed the handiwork of her sister upon the table in Sara's kitchen. She had no cause to fear me because of my bond to Elizabeth, but she should have feared the patient and meticulous revenge of her sister. Cailen was bound, sooner or later, to wrest back the meat still upon the bones of her pilfered prey.

My free hand found Brann's neck, warm and substantial. "Why does your sister haunt Sara's dreams?" The muse wrenched beneath me. I tightened my fist. "Do you think I might murder this human form before you have time to melt away from me? I have a lovely iron dagger." She knew of the dagger. To conceal the bullet, I made no secret of it. The Leanan Sidhe do not fear guns with their lead bullets that pierce their shadowy forms but leave no scar.

"You would not murder me. I would rise again." My fingers strangled her words. The iron of my ring streaked red the gleaming white canvas of her neck. She winced.

"But you would have no recollection of me or our bargain. Do you imagine I have not done my homework, foul mistress? I would be free of you, soul and flesh." I'd thought about it, imagined the scene, sketched it. But, after a century, she was under my skin— God help me—in my very blood; I was infected with her. To kill her, I would have to kill the parts of me where she flourished. And then, I would become her—a creature who murders to live.

"You cannot kill me. I love you." She believed I would indeed murder her to escape our bargain. So why did I hesitate? Had I grown so fond of the tyrannical fiend that held me hostage with my love? Had my love diminished in her grasp? No. What I had failed to learn, stayed my hand. At the demise of the demon, would the flesh of those that her magic sustained also expire? Would I murder Sara—and Jake—to free myself from the fingers that bound me?

Having once cut Elizabeth's life short, I would not risk it again. "You know nothing of love." My weight pressed on her chest. "You are a virus that loves only to feed and you kill what you cherish. Tell me what you know, lovely monster. What does Cailen Sidhe want with Sara?" I squeezed the downy soft skin and felt the bones. The sizzle of Brann's flesh released the aroma of mulled wine.

Her fear became anger. "My sister has no stake in our game. I have not conspired with her since I bargained for one night of your love to recompense her loss with the child you begat. We are even."

"Ha! You suppose your sister satisfied?" I relinquished the hold on her breath, knowing the Sidhe were bound to speak the truth. Their only deception was the truth they hid. Perhaps Cailen Sidhe had laid her snares so surreptitiously that even her sister ignored the presence of a rival predator upon her territory.

Pushing away from bed and mistress, I strode to a second veiled canvas by the fire and tore away the sheet that hid it. I would read the unspoken truth in Brann's reaction to this masterpiece.

The sculpted figure of the almost woman I had scorned rose from the blankets. She stood naked, the reflection of the flames toasting her translucent skin. The angry scar of iron burned against her lily-white throat. A mist of down encircled her ankles, and a robe of feathers rose and fluttered about her in blackened hues of red and orange, stolen from the hearth. Brann advanced cautiously, having not yet shed all of the humanity she had summoned to better enjoy me. She scrutinized the painting.

Cailen's golden eyes stared back at her from the canvas, mocking, even as the flames rose and singed the downy white edges of her feathered dress, withering her willowy limbs.

"This is the second time you have burned a portrait of my sister." Brann, galled by the painting of her rival, rendered so exquisitely by the hand of her lover, grimaced.

"This is the second time your sister has planted the seed of her likeness in the imagination of my wife." I nodded at the painting that could have been the fulfillment of the sketch I'd found on Sara's kitchen table. "Only this time, it is I, not Elizabeth, who has painted it."

Chapter 60
—Excerpts from the journals of Ethan McCarthy, Jr.

"Hi, mom!" Elizabeth chirped into her phone on speaker. "Hey, kidlet, what time will you and Ethan be here? Dad made a huge pot of vegetarian chili."

"Well, that's the thing. Ethan got all confused. He thought his dad told him to invite *me* to dinner at *his* house. He already made all this vegetarian stuff, so I'm going over there."

"What are we going to do with all this chili?"

"Save it for me!" Elizabeth glanced slyly at my profile as I drove. She was dying to see where I lived, not my apartment, which was pretty standard, but the old Victorian mansion where my "father" lived. "And, mom?"

"What?"

"Lock the doors!" She smiled broadly at me from the passenger side. We could have walked to my house if it weren't for her ankle. Unbeknownst to all but a very select group of art dealers, the famously reclusive artist Ethan McCarthy lived not far from UT Dallas.

"So, did you cook, or did your dad?"

"My dad's out of town. You're stuck with what I could rustle up."

"Yuck! You do know what a vegetarian is, right? No meat. That includes chicken and fish, not just beef and pork. Nothing that lived and breathed at some point."

"I get the general idea." The very long driveway cut through a veritable forest of trees.

"I guess your dad likes his privacy. Is he keeping other people out, or you in?"

"I'm basically unsupervised. He likes to avoid publicity."

"Does that mean I can't take pictures on my cell phone?" Elizabeth waggled her iPhone out the window.

"Keep your arms and legs in the vehicle and no flash photography."

The trees cleared and a house emerged. The wrought-iron gate creaked slightly as it rolled open beneath the security cameras.

Elizabeth clapped and giggled. When she laughed, my blood bubbled. "You think my house is funny?"

"No, but I definitely don't want to be taking any showers in there. You don't have your dead mother propped up in a chair by that little attic window, do you?"

Winking her direction, I parked the car in front of the porch and jogged around to open her door. "No such luck." I handed her the crutches. "But there is a very large cat and she has sharp teeth and long claws."

For centuries, Ethan Sr. had spent months in my body to maintain his youth. During those stolen days, I pursued all the frivolities of life that I had denied myself in my natural time while I pursued the secrets of eternal life. The beautiful women of all shapes and sizes, the fast cars, the clothes, nothing had ground me to a halt and made me wish for reality as others lived it like the fresh, effervescence of Elizabeth. Her pink lips breathed new life into mine and made my heart light again. Sometimes I feared she might smell the debauchery on me. Elizabeth hopped on her crutches up the steps to the porch. Her agility, despite her injury, astounded me. Her resiliency and perpetual energy turned me into a four-year-old in determined pursuit of a bouncing white butterfly, almost, but never quite able to snatch it from the sky and hold it in my hands. She stopped on the threshold of the open double doors. A mischievous smile blossomed on her face as her eyes adjusted from the bright sun to the dim two-story entry.

A step ahead of her, I led her past the grand staircase and down the hallway. Elizabeth *ooh*ed and *ahh*ed at the carved cherry-wood moldings, the leaf-patterned carpets, the stately wood and marble floors, and the furniture she said her mother loved to look at in catalogs but never bought because her children would just destroy it. She made me stop at every painting while she leaned on her crutches and let the wave of emotion they conjured wash over her. Dark lines, sharp angles, heavy-handed brush strokes, stark colors and contrasts of shadow—life in its most gripping tragedy. My chest swelled when she stopped to marvel at one of the paintings

Brann Sidhe had wheedled from *my* fist. I tended more toward abstract and the paint depicted a plurality of the soul cloaked in all its misery and the lassitude of perpetual existence.

"Your dad is amazing. He didn't seem like such a depressing guy at the hospital. How does he come up with this stuff?" She stopped in front of a particularly horrible rendition of a rape. Elizabeth had described similar paintings from the Louvre that she'd seen on her senior trip to Paris with her mother, but they were classical and mythical. This was set in war-torn Africa. "Look at this!" Elizabeth covered her mouth in some bizarre marriage of awe and revulsion. "It's horrible and pathetic. You want to cry for these people." Her eyes scrunched as she reached a finger to, almost but not quite, touch the face of the miserable woman. "But it's so compelling." She stepped away from the agony in front of her face and took in the whole of the composition. "It's breathtaking, but I think I'd kill myself if all this trauma and horror were spinning in my head."

My voice was barely audible. "Some artists do. Painters, poets, musicians—they die young. Must be the price."

"Misunderstood genius? Is that why your dad doesn't get out much? You can't be misunderstood if no one knows you."

"Maybe so." I exhaled loudly. "Well, enough of the creepy artwork. I'm starving." Shuffling her off to the dining room, I arranged her in a high back chair.

"This is lovely! I can't believe we've been dating almost every night for over three months and you haven't ever brought me here."

"Actually, three months and 6 days. We met after class on the last Friday in January."

"Look who's keeping track." Elizabeth rewarded me with six small kisses, "one for each day," before detangling herself from my arms. They latched around her the moment she was within reach. "I saw a dining room just like this when we visited the mansions in Newport, Rhode Island. Have you been? In Massachusetts, my mom always took anyone that visited us to see the mansions. So cool!"

"Glad you like it." I leaned an elbow on the table beside her so that our noses nearly met. "But I hope you don't just like me for my fast car and my big mansion."

"Of course not! I like you for your famous dad, too." Her arms encircled my neck as she melted her pink lips into mine and then stole them away again before I'd had my fill. "And you have killer kissing lips. I like those, too."

"For that, I will feed you."

"Smells yummy! What did you make?"

"Vegetarian Lasagna. I watched the recipe this morning on YouTube."

"Yikes! Will I like it?"

"Boo didn't. But she's not vegetarian, so I think she's an unreliable critic."

"Boo?"

"My cat."

Pronouncing her name produced the creature in question.

Elizabeth squealed. "I love cats. She's beautiful. Here, kitty." She put her fingers out for the cat to sniff. Recognizing a minion, Boo jumped into her lap. "She's so soft; I love all the colors—like spice and smoke mixed together." Elizabeth petted the cat, who curled up and purred in her lap. "She's so friendly. How long have you had her?"

"As long as I can remember." The butler's door swung shut behind me.

Ignoring my plate, I watched Elizabeth savor my vegetarian creation until she looked up and caught me staring, and then I dove in like I was famished. The sly turn of her eye and the cheeky grin told me she knew I'd rather be having her than food. I was strolling along the side of the road, waiting for her to roll down the window and wave me in.

By the time she finished her crème brûlée, Elizabeth's face burned with pleasure. She wanted the house, the life, and the boy—I was part of the package.

"I'm thinking of doing a Psych internship in Romania next winter." A chill rippled through the warmth in the room. She was testing the water and was, obviously, pleased to see my face fall at the mention of her going away. I knew how Elizabeth thought. She didn't want to slip into *my* life; she wanted to wrap me up and add me to *her* backpack. She had her course across the universe neatly mapped out and was looking for another road warrior to share the ride.

"Romania? How long will you be gone?" I made a brave pretense at unconcerned.

Playing with her food, she assumed a tone of utter blasé. "Only a semester. UT Dallas has some ties to a mental hospital for children with neurological disorders and an orphanage. My mom thinks it's a great idea."

"She would."

"What's that supposed to mean?" Elizabeth feigned offense, but she clearly enjoyed inspiring tortured love. "My mom said doing Study Abroad in Paris was one of the most educational and fun experiences of her life. She's all for it." A wicked smile crept around the corners of her mouth. "She says it saved her from marrying the wrong guy." My face twitched. "She met my dad there, you know."

"Yeah, I think I knew that." My face betrayed me and I couldn't hide my disappointment. I was so obviously depressed that Elizabeth took pity on me.

"You should come with me!"

"You want me to come?"

"Of course! You're a psych major. Think how fun it would be." She hopped out of her chair and hobbled to the back of mine, draping her arms over my shoulders so that she was whispering in my ear. "You and me in Romania. And we get college credits for it. I thought I'd have to pay part of it, but my mom told me they've been saving up all the extra money dad got when we moved here so that they could fund 'educational opportunities' like this. Come with me!" She leaned around my neck and kissed me so that I'd know exactly what I'd be missing if I didn't go.

Not getting enough of her from that angle, I was out of the chair with my arms wrapped all around her before she came up for air. "Do you think your dad will let you?"

My gaze shifted. That wasn't a question I wanted to look in the eye. "That is the catch, isn't it?"

"You could talk him into it. Just explain how much of an advantage the experience will be when you finally have to get a job."

"I think my getting a job is not exactly his first priority." Elizabeth's face inspired my resolve. "I don't see how he can stop me, though. Who knows? Maybe he'll buy a house there."

"He could do that?"

I smirked at the paintings on the wall. "He can have anything he wants—" The sentence hung unfinished on the air. What I was saying wasn't quite true. "—almost." The last word was just barely audible. If she hadn't been leaning on my chest, she wouldn't have heard it.

Before carrying dishes back into the kitchen, I recited directions to the nearest bathroom. Boo trotted along in front of her new crony. Glasses clanged and silverware chimed. By the time I'd cleared, rinsed, and tucked all the dishes into the dishwasher, I wondered if Elizabeth had taken a wrong turn in the winding hallways or if one of the slightly sticky, century-old doors had locked her in.

As I approached the back of the house, listening for sounds of distress or hopping, her voice, almost as if it were amplified, floated into the hall from the room outside Ethan Sr.'s studio. I jogged that direction.

"Hey, Boo. Is that a door out? I thought it was a bedroom. Here, kitty. I'll look for you." After a couple of hops on padded carpet, she corrected herself. "Well, it's not outside. How do I know you're allowed in here?"

I rounded the corner. The dull light of the sitting room beyond the studio glowed at the back of the long hallway. In my mind, I saw what Elizabeth would see if she stepped into the room where my "father" worked slavishly.

It needed electricity in the evening. For most of the day, the wall of windows, that overlooked a small garden, flooded the space with light. The clutter of easels and a large table covered with paints, pigments, linseed oil, a glass muller, bottles of turpentine, as well as the sharp odor of chemicals would tell her this was Mr. McCarthy's private studio. The walls dripped with the crowning jewels of our talent.

She would stare open-mouthed at the wealth of art before her. All around her the walls would proclaim the unknown soul of the artist the world thought it knew so well. There, she would find no tragedy, no pain, no horror, or suffering. There, love hovered above the beholder, unbridled, deep, gentle, passionate, and sad. Soft fluid lines, rounded cheeks, pastels, and fading brushstrokes. She would absorb the warmth plastered all over the room and imagine herself spying upon the secret life of God. She would look from one serene face to the other of the women who lived in this world of color and oil—women stretching back through decades.

And then—*oh, God!* I broke into a run—and then her eyes would narrow, the blood retreat from her core and invade her extremities. She wouldn't be sure whether to run or be sick. She would step closer to the painting nearest her—a husband of the last century locked in battle with the Grim Reaper come to collect his wife and newborn child. Her fingers would reach out and touch the tragic lines of the woman—

My footsteps crossing the threshold made her jump away from the canvas. "Elizabeth? Are you in here?" A lilt of anxious irritation tainted the words.

She turned to face me, tottering as if the ground beneath her was no longer stable. "I got lost." She sounded small, unable to hide the fear hovering about the edge of her voice.

The paintings revealed too much. I wiped my hand over my chin. "Look, this isn't—"

She pointed at the painting. "This is my mother. These are ALL my mother!" It was all she could do to keep her finger from shaking uncontrollably. It was hard to guess what she was feeling. Something between fury and fear.

My hand open before me as if she held a loaded gun she'd found in a secret drawer, I stepped toward her. "Elizabeth, don't—"

"What the fucking hell is going on here? Is he a stalker? Is that why my mom stopped going to class?" She stopped for a breath. "You knew! You knew and you let him drive me home from the hospital?" The worst of all the possibilities played themselves out in her imagination. "Is that why you—" She couldn't finish. She rushed by me, dragging her broken ankle mercilessly. "He knows where we live!" As much spit spewed from her mouth as sound. I grabbed desperately at her arm. She wrenched me off with a withering stare. "Don't touch me." Fear steered her to the door. She gathered her crutches and pulled it open.

"Elizabeth! Stop! Let me drive you home. You have a broken ankle."

"I'm not getting into a car with you." She practically vaulted herself down the stairs, stopped short, and turned back. Hope blossomed on my face. I knew she loved me. She couldn't just break off what we'd started without a look back. Of course, she would give me a chance to explain.

"Open the gate, or I'll have to climb it with a broken ankle."

"Don't, please. I can—"

"Just let me go!" She swiped viciously at tears welling in her eyes and fished the cell phone out of her pocket. "I'll call the police."

With a deep sigh, I turned back and pushed the button to the gate. Elizabeth didn't look back, not even after it snapped closed behind her. Outside, she stopped and tapped the screen of her phone frantically. She couldn't walk and talk at the same time.

Growling, she shook the phone as if no one were answering. She dialed again. Her head jerked when someone finally picked up. Elizabeth practically dived into the mouthpiece. "Mom?" I could hear her on the intercom.

"No. I'm still at Ethan's. We—we're not together anymore." The words stung. She tried to sound stoic but her voice cracked on the "anymore."

Her mother's response was unintelligible, but it exacerbated Elizabeth.

"I don't want to talk about it right now." She swiped at the wet streaks on her cheeks. The sound of her mother's voice got the water running, despite her apparent determination to stay dry. "I'm tired and I want to go home and sleep. I just called to tell you not to go to class this week."

This was going to be worse than I thought. Of course, Elizabeth would tell her mother the whole story.

"I have to go to class tomorrow morning, but I'll come up and tell you about it later."

Pause.

"Yes, I'm sure. Don't come up here. And, Mom," she glanced directly at the camera, "don't forget to lock the doors! I'm serious." She tucked the phone back in her pocket and hobbled into the trees.

Chapter 61

The trace of Elizabeth's lips lingered on her crystal goblet the next morning. Picking the glass off the kitchen counter, I tasted her lips on mine and knew I would never taste them again. Roaring, I hurled the crystal at the wall. It shattered and fell to the floor in dozens of fragments.

It was intolerable that the obsessions of an old man I barely knew, and yet shaped with every breath I took, should so overshadow this freakish, disjointed life I lived. I didn't belong here. My time should have come and gone and been buried in the man that I would become. But I was here, living, sporadically and anachronistically, but frequently, and long enough to have become an entity, a self. I had a life, a life separate from the desperate designs of the man who created me and whom I had, in turn, created. It was unnatural that something so intrinsically entwined should be so separate. I longed for wholeness and continuity. I longed for love, enduring and constant. I longed for Elizabeth. That very longing connected me so seamlessly to the man from whom I felt rent.

In a few hours, I would step out of myself. The elder Ethan would know that all was lost. I shouldn't have invited Elizabeth to the house. But it was the only way I could think of to loosen her resolve, end the gnawing craving, and finally have her. But it was the resolve that I loved. Elizabeth was solid, whole, and constant. I should have been happy with the gift the old man's contrivances had let fall at my feet. But I tried to grasp it all like I had tried to grasp at the life I watched slip from my brother and parents so many lifetimes ago. What I grasped at voraciously, I distorted and tore until it slipped in shreds from my fingers.

Sinking into a chair in the breakfast nook, I buried my face in my hands. The heavy morning sun streamed through the windows and transformed the kitchen into a cathedral of light. Upon the beams, tiny specs of dust sparkled and danced. Shooing away the glittering particles only invigorated their floating revelry.

Perhaps it was simply my lot—the disease of my age—to live, forever reaching and unsatisfied. Perhaps contentment belonged to an older piece of myself. I half hoped that the old man would be so angry that he would banish me forever, and yet, I languished for Elizabeth. I would have gladly thrown over the old man's game—if it weren't for the question of souls. Tampering with life had brought something less than the paradise of eternal youth I had imagined. I did not dare tamper with souls.

Sailing on the cascading light, a mist of gold, like sparkling sun gems, intermingled itself in the dance of the floating specks. The mist congealed into sparkling dust. The dust took fire until its particles burned as floating white diamonds.

As I sulked, fist supporting my chin, the white gems cooled and melted in a spiraling fury into miniature plumes. The storm of down subsided into a waltz of snow-white feathers that spun themselves into a dress. An obscenely fair woman appeared within the dress that fluttered and settled itself about the soft curves of her silhouette. Her skin shimmered in golden highlights resonating from the tresses that enveloped her shoulders.

This was no stranger. She had often strolled through my dreams, coaxing and cajoling, but I had shooed her away at dawn. She returned, again and again, perfumed with visions of loveliness that made my breath catch as I slept. My parents' fate, the skeletons that lingered in her icy flesh, immunized me against her charms.

"Ah!" The apparition savored the air of the spring garden in bloom. "The tantalizing prick of human senses."

"Cailen Sidhe. Why do you insist on showing up where you're not wanted?"

The dove muse laughed and the sound of church bells echoed through the kitchen. "Why do you assume I am not wanted? I am always wanted—eventually." Her lips curved, pink versions of Brann Sidhe's.

"You are a hypnotically gorgeous, life-sucking parasite. You're never wanted."

"Ethan, my sweet, must you be so ungenerous? Even monsters have their virtues, and virtue is always wanted." She leaned seductively close to my lips. "My virtue is patience."

"There's nothing to wait for here." My fist dropped from my chin, smacking the table. "Your sister has already laid claim to the spoils. She stepped in at the last minute and stole your prey out from under your nose."

"Did she?" Cailen backed away and then turned to admire the flowers outside the window. "What can be stolen, can also be redeemed."

"That's not going to happen. I've pretty much just blown our last chance with Sara—my only chance with *my* Elizabeth. In less than three years, my soul and hers will belong to your sister. Bad enough that we have to be her playthings in life, but after that? You know as well as I that our bargain extends through universes." Avoiding the face of the beauty in front of me, I spoke mostly to the wall of paintings. "What is that like, to have your soul enslaved by a monster? My last hope was that, at least, in the end, our soul would be free, not led about on the whims and imaginations of another imperfect being."

"Imperfect?" She cocked a single eyebrow, a rearrangement of her features that caught my breath. "Is that what you fear? The fate of the souls?"

"I've gorged myself on this life. I would puke it out if it weren't for your sister and her damn game that'll leave our soul on the table."

She brushed my cheek with the palm of her hand, shivered at the touch, but then collected her senses. "Poor boy." The coo of doves swirled about the room. The authenticity of her look of pity amazed me. "You see? My patience has served me well. I am wanted here. Just as I was wanted once before." Lightly she fondled the coin nestled at my throat.

I recoiled from her touch, from the memory of the grasping greed that led my older self to sacrifice two years of Elizabeth's life in exchange for the coin. Had I not hungered so for life, our soul might still be in our grasp, Elizabeth might have lived out her normal span. "You have the solution to my problems?" I crossed my arms.

She circled behind me, draping her arm across my chest to whisper in my ear. "Solution? There is never only one solution to the puzzle. The trick is to choose what best suits your needs."

"Our needs, or yours?"

She chuckled in tinkling chimes but raised herself and paced about, tapping one golden nail lightly against her chin. The plumes of her dress floated about the kitchen and brushed the broken crystals that crackled beneath her feet. She glanced down at them and then turned a curious eye on me.

"I'm not quite certain why you have never spoken to Sara, explained this affair of souls, the debt she owes to you for her life renewed? It would be so much simpler with her cooperation."

I fixed a stare of contempt on the muse. "I can't. You know as well as I do that was part of the bargain. He swore not to speak of it; the words freeze on his tongue."

"On *his* tongue, yes. But on *your* tongue?" I stuttered. "By your silence, I must infer that you have never even tried to speak. I am all astonishment. Are you so enslaved by the boundaries of your 'father's' reality that you have never tested your own?"

Never imagining that the chains that clung to my "father" did not also link to my own feet, I had walked blindly in his shackled footsteps. I'd read the oath, written in his hand. "But the oath he made bound us all."

Cailen's laughter suggested the jingle of the court jester. "Yes. The oath *he* made." Crossing the room to my side, she ripped the sleeve from my shirt, baring the smooth, clear skin of my right shoulder. "Where is *your* mark? *You* have none. *You* made no oath."

"I am not bound?" The evidence was clear, but the practice of long years made it incomprehensible.

"My sister tampered with what she does not understand. She has the power of death to wield, but I have the power of life. She does not understand its intricacies. For you, the man who made that bargain does not yet even exist. You are not bound by his choice."

"But Brann Sidhe said—She can't lie."

"We are both bound by truth. But neither one of us tells all. It would not suit the devotion of our adorers to know all the truth. We choose what leads them to best serve our purpose. It is always the hidden truths that shackle them in a prison of their own making."

In silence, I bent my consciousness to see reality from a new perspective. I had been a prisoner in an imaginary cell. The years—the decades! Wasted! My head shook in my palm as I saw, without seeing, the intricate lines of the wood grain in the table. "Perhaps I am free of his oath," I agreed slowly, ruminating, "but the soul binds our fractured skins. Even if I am not bound by his oath, I am bound to save our soul—and Sara's. He had no right to bargain with hers."

"There, you are wrong." She stooped to look me in the eye and smiled frivolously. "You do have the most beautiful eyes," she touched the corner of one with a long, gilded nail, "shades of an angry sea." My flinch dampened her reverie. She straightened herself and returned to the subject at hand. "Their souls were bound in the oath—the marriage made one soul of two. Neither one can lose their soul without losing the other's."

I sat back in the chair. It was such an archaic idea. Marriages had come and gone around me for a century with no thought to the impact of the binding and sheering of souls. I thought of Sara and Jake. Once a guest in their family, I had felt the strength of the ties that bound them—invisible beneath the surface but running through every pore and crack of the mortar that had built their life together. It was one of the things I loved about Elizabeth. She was part of that—a branch of the vine that connected her parents. I wanted the vine. "What are you suggesting?"

Cailen Sidhe circled me, trailing fingers in my hair, building anticipation. Her hidden smile revealed itself in the flowering of the air. This time, I tolerated her touch. She stooped over my shoulder and whispered, "I could give you control of your life again. You could grow old and disappear within yourself, like other men." She slid around to face me, never loosening the embrace of her arms around my neck. "You can trade eternal life and have love for yourself—for a small price." She graced me with her angelically bewitching smile.

My eyes shifted. She was moving too quickly. Shoving back my chair, I disentangled her arms. My shoulders swayed skeptical in the face of her haggling. "Let me get this straight. You can glue us back together? I could start over right now, with me?"

She nodded.

"I'd just live a normal, regular life—get old and die like everyone else?"

The golden curls fell forward as she agreed. Tiny bells jingled in the wind when she waved them back with a small shake of her head. Her eyebrow rose. She sensed I was open to the idea—not just open; I was standing on the corner yelling and waving it in. There was no telling what she was hiding. But wouldn't it be worth it? Whatever the cost? The implications of the possibilities I was piecing together began accumulating in my mind. I turned away from the muse.

"Great! I'm whole again, not some fractured piece of a freak, but I'm still going to have to talk Sara Dawson, the mother of the girl I'm *in love with*—" I turned to emphasize those words to the dove muse. "I'm going to have to figure out a way to talk her into leaving her husband and her family and marrying me. And then have a baby together!" I snorted. "Killer plan, lady! I can just see that happening."

"Surely not!" The muse giggled like a child watching a wind-up dog bump tenaciously into the wall. "Ethan, my dearest boy, did you not just indicate a certain attachment to the daughter? What would possess you to pursue the mother?"

"Oh, nothing. Only our souls! That was the deal. We marry Sara and have a baby with her before she's fifty or we both lose our soul." The whole thing was ridiculously impossible. "Can she even have a baby still?"

Cailen shook her head in pitiful silence and spoke very softly. "When will you learn to think for yourself, boy?" Raising her arms, she bent them in a lovely right angle. A book appeared in the flat of her palms.

I recognized it from long acquaintance. It was the elder Ethan's journal, the Bible of our fractured lives. A gentle breeze carried it to the page she sought. "…'mix my blood with Sara's in marriage before she turns fifty.' Your father has settled for such a narrow interpretation—or perhaps it best suits his interests to imagine this his task."

"And you have a more liberal interpretation?"

"Did I not tell you that my sister was meddling in powers that were not hers? She has failed to be quite precise. The elder Ethan's interpretation of the oath is quite true. But there are others that Brann Sidhe did not see fit to mention." Stretching her nails, she admired the way they glimmered in the sunbeams streaming through the blinds.

I was being sucked in. I wondered if this was how it had begun for my parents nearly two centuries ago. But the power to reach beyond the confines of my present constricted existence, the image of something broader, was so tempting. "Such as?"

The muse caressed the feathers of her fluttering robe. With a delicately carved pinkie finger, she brushed a few wayward golden tresses from her serenely seductive face. "For one, you could simply marry the daughter and have a child. Your blood would be mixed with Sara's blood in marriage."

My face lit up and then darkened. "What are you not telling me?"

When Cailen Sidhe smiled, a wave of unbridled pleasure rippled through the kitchen. "I have taught you too well. Yes, it is beyond fortunate that the young lady has grown fond of you since her blood is also her mother's. But time is of the essence. If I sell you the secret of restoring your splintered being into one whole and finite entity, you will reach the age at which you contracted this bargain at the same time that Sara reaches her fiftieth year. That is why now is the only moment at which this option will be open to you. I am powerless to undo the terms of my sister's bargain, but I can manipulate them. As long as my spells do not interfere with the terms of hers, I can give you what you desire."

Hope bubbled all about me, making me almost giddy. Cailen Sidhe was truly a master of seduction. I bridled the bolting excitement. "Of course, there's a price to be paid for this generosity."

"Of course. I must live as I can. But shall we not both benefit equally?" She stepped very close and looked me in the eye, without touching me. "Do you understand that if you have not fulfilled the conditions in the three years that you have left, you will still forfeit the myriad pieces of your soul to my sister?"

"You know I've lost her, don't you?"

"I saw her leave."

"Is that why you're here? Have you swooped like a vulture onto a dying beast? Do you know this is a losing battle, the way you knew Elizabeth would die and my 'father' would be facing forever alone?"

I expected her to bristle, but her eyes softened and she spoke as if I were five. "I told you, my sister understands only the ultimate power of death; she has no appreciation for the subtleties of life and its fleeting, but exquisite joys. I am not greedy, Ethan. I bask in life, it gives me my power and sustenance." She licked the tip of a lily-white finger and trailed it down my exposed chest. She watched my eyes as the tip of her finger met the tip of her tongue and she shivered. "I wish to taste all of its delicacies, but I would not have them used up. Surely, with her mother's help, you can win her back. The offending elder Ethan will have ceased to exist. His early exit from the game will release the chains of the bargain that entangle Sara. Her soul will be safe."

My eyes narrowed. "And when I reach the age at which I made this bargain, what then? If my soul again falls into play? What about Sara's?"

"You do not have the marriage ties that bind your soul to hers. Even when you reach the age of your vow, Sara will still be free of him, since he no longer exists."

I relaxed a bit. Where my alter-egos had failed time and again with the mother, I felt with my whole being I could succeed with the daughter—if I got another chance, if I could just explain.

Curiosity tempted me to believe our childhood tragedies had tainted our memories and prejudiced us against this creature. My fingers reached out of their own accord and sampled the flowing gold that called to them. "How much? What is your price?"

Her hand closed around my wrist. "Two years."

The allure of freeing Sara's soul from the bargain of my older self was too attractive to dismiss. I felt I owed this to her, to the Elizabeth that I had never loved and to the Elizabeth I now loved. "For two of the three years I have left to win her, I'll be chained to you? Will you also cut off my hands and disfigure my face?"

Her smile was a ray of lightning sun cutting through the grey-cast clouds of a summer storm. The muse brought my hand to her lips. I felt the electric magnetism of her touch swell my chest. "I would never harm these hands. These are the hands that will feed me—and I will feed them such delicacies as no others have ever tasted."

The gold of her eyes swallowed me. I dragged my gaze away.

"It is the soul that makes you hesitate to embrace this bargain?"

"The soul belongs to all of us; it ripples beyond us to universes in infinite copies." I looked back at the face of the risk I was willing to take. "The gamble I'm making is for all of us. I hate that the oath he made has constrained my existence. Alchemy 101—life without love is soulless. What, then, is eternity without a soul? Before anything, I have to consider the soul."

"Don't you see, my love? I would want you to succeed. I would do all in my power to assure that you had satisfied the terms of your bargain with Brann Sidhe before you reached the age at which your bargain was struck and your soul would again be forfeit to her for losing."

If I had looked away for a second, I might have missed the tiny curl at the corner of her mouth or the faint puffing up of victory that flashed across her face. She was so sure of herself. I hesitated to place a foot in the trap.

"There is another solution—" she paused, letting the idea find a soft spot cushioned in my fears, "—a way paved with much less uncertainty, a way which guarantees the salvation of the soul, a way which frees you completely from the tyranny of Brann Sidhe."

I waited, breath suspended. So why didn't she mention it first?

"If Sara were to die before her fifty years," I recoiled from the touch of the glittering snow-white creature, "the entire game would be forfeit, all wagers void."

Chapter 62

—Excerpts from the unpublished writings of Easton Ravenscroft

(O)utside the middle school where Sara had just deposited Annie and Danny, Sara's phone buzzed with a text:

D: *Can you bring my flash drive? I forgot it and my English project is due after lunch.*

Sara sighed—at least he was turning something in.

S: *Going to gym. Bring it when I'm done.*

The no-carb diet and running were working. She was seeing numbers on the scale she hadn't seen for almost a decade. Since she and Jake were both in training, even when she was in the gym alone, it felt like they were working on something together—a common goal. Her painting obsession wasn't hurting. Sometimes she forgot to eat until the kids got home.

After her workout, she hunted down the USB drive that was still on the floor where Danny dropped it. The dog followed her out to the car and jumped in. "Why not, Flash? Everyone else is getting a free ride today." She rolled down the window just an inch to make it more interesting for him.

Danny's science class was outside working on a project. She left the drive in the office and texted him back:

S: *I have to leave. Flash in office.*

She was in the car by the time he responded.

D: *The dog?*

How could such a bright kid be so clueless?

S: *Why would I leave the dog in the office? The flash DRIVE.*

It was 10:30 already. Sara was hoping to finish the portrait—despite what Mr. McCarthy had said about it not being her thing. Comments and critiques were all very helpful, but sometimes, she had to trust her gut. This painting was a cut above anything she'd ever done. Only the flames blocked her. She'd seen them in the dream, but she couldn't quite see how they fit into the overall composition.

She needed a shower. The stream of water would open the flow of imagination. In a couple of hours, the kids would be home and her life would be swallowed up in theirs.

Flash's paws clicked at her heels, through the family room, and into the bedroom. He liked to camp on the bath rug until she was done and then sneak into the shower and lap up the water. She reached down and scratched his ears before stripping off her running shorts and bra. Dumping them in the laundry basket, she lamented again the one failing of the master suite. No doors to the bathroom.

The bedroom had a nice set of double doors. But the bathroom was only an open arch away. Of course, there was a door for the commode, but Sara preferred a bit of privacy in the shower.

A car engine rumbled up to the curb just beyond the master closet window. She stuck her hand under the spray. The water trickled onto her palm, warming slowly. Flash pricked up his ears.

"Grace? Is that you? I'm in the shower."

No answer.

Stepping into the steamy water, Sara thought she heard someone rifling through paraphernalia on the kitchen table.

Must have been a drive-by pick up. Forgotten homework? She could have at least yelled "hi."

Flash disappeared to investigate. The dog was more of a greeter than a guard. The closed door stopped him or he'd have viciously licked to death whoever was there. The shih tzu reappeared, dancing about like a four-year-old that had to pee. "Hey, Flash," she swiped the steamy glass, "who's out there, puppy? Is Liz home?"

Heavy footsteps approached the door—too heavy for thin little Elizabeth. Sara poured shampoo into her hand and lathered up her hair. "Jake, is that you? What are you doing home so early?" *I might as well just give up for today. I'm never going to get to the painting. It's just not in the cosmic plan.*

She leaned back, water and shampoo dripped down her face. Closing her eyes, she shook her head. The fat slap of rubber soles on marble tile opened her eyes too soon. She blinked at the sting and then jumped back from the foggy glass, emitting something between a gasp and a squeal.

No matter how many times he did it, Sara would never get used to the sudden appearance of her husband's silhouette outside the doors. "God, Jake! You are seriously going to give me a heart attack." She rinsed the stinging film of soap from her eyes, grinning just a bit. Pushing back her hair, she turned a smiling face to the welcome appearance of her husband in the middle of the day.

It took a fraction of a second suspended in a void of thought and breath before her scream ripped through the bathroom. Sara covered her naked breasts with her arms because they seemed to be the focus of the eyes outside the glass. It took another fraction of a second to recognize the soggy skin and greasy grey locks of the stranger and explode in anger.

"Phil? What the hell are YOU doing here? Get out!" Her whole body shook and tensed with the sudden rush of adrenaline. She twisted the water off, shoving the door against the intruder. His corpulent belly absorbed the blow. He huffed while she groped for a bathrobe. "Are you crazy? Get out of my house!" She jerked the robe around herself; her hair dripped in her face and soaked her shoulders. Anger flushed her cheeks, visions of another man in the Metro assaulted her brain. "Get out!" Her fist slammed into his flabby chest.

"No! You have to come with me." He snatched her wrist as she shoved by and twisted her around to face him. "You weren't in class again last night. So, I had to come here. SHE told me I had to come."

His touch curdled her stomach with a bitter brew of loathing and fury. Gut tensed as if a snake had curled around her wrist, she twisted against his grip and backed toward the bedroom door. *Oh my God! This doesn't happen—not to me.* And yet, it was happening. Phil was fat and out of shape, but twice her size. "I don't care! Get off me!" She pounded at his arm.

He tugged her back. "No! The angel told me you were mine."

If it hadn't been clear weeks earlier, it was now painfully apparent that Phil was totally delusional. Sara's wet feet slipped across the wood as he dragged her out of the bedroom. "Help! Someone help!" She knew there was no one there. "Get off of me, you creepy son of a bitch!" He tugged on her arm, and she leaned back with her whole body, twisting, writhing, and pounding against his pudding limbs.

"It's a sign, Sara. You saw her too." He slammed the door on the dog, who whined and then yapped a tiny objection. Sara pummeled Phil's back as he hauled her, screaming, through the family room. On the way to the kitchen, they passed the entry and the front door, slightly ajar. Sara yanked hard at her wrist and bolted. Phil, unsuspecting, completely absorbed in his delusion, jerked forward, teetered, but did not let go.

"Damn it! You crazy bastard! Let me go!" She kicked and thrashed. The ghostly whines and intermittent yapping of the dog punctuated her insistence.

Sara regretted the accusation that Phil was mad the minute it escaped her lips. Before her eyes, reality burrowed beneath his pasty skin and glazed his angry stare. His doughy palm struck her cheek like a brick, jilting her head sideways. The throbbing that coursed hot across her face was enough to jolt her back into a state of reasonable conciliation. She breathed through the fear pulsing in her fingers and gripping her chest. Phil was too strong for her, but she knew his character was weak, vulnerable, and very needy. Her best defense, her only hope for taming the rabid dog loose in her kitchen, was to offer it the soft petting hand it craved, take it off its wary guard, divert it, and then bolt.

Her resolve stiffened with her stance and squelched her heaving chest. "I'm so sorry, Phil." She adjusted the tumbling folds of her bathrobe. "It's—it's just that you startled me. No one told me you were coming to work with me. I just wasn't ready."

His eyes narrowed, but she could read the hunger there. He wanted desperately for her to dance with him in his fantasy.

He lowered his eyes. "I shouldn't have hit you, but you have to see it. You have to understand." Passion foamed on his tongue and sprayed spittle into her face as he raved. He dragged her to the table where her chef-d'oeuvre waited impatiently for the final touch of flames. Phil jabbed an accusing finger at the canvas. "You see! When I saw her there on the table, I knew it was real. It's a sign from God, Sara. The angel said you have to be with me. It's what God wants."

Sara's eyes searched the kitchen for a weapon. The old-fashioned ring of a dial telephone rippled out of her cell on the kitchen desk. She found it vastly annoying that whoever was on the other end was so oblivious to the violence of the scene they were interrupting. "Phil," she whispered gently, patting the wrist enslaving her, "you know I can't do that, Phil. I have a husband; I have four children. I belong with them. God wants me with them."

"No!" He yanked her arm and dragged her to the painting. "The angel said you were mine, and you have to come with me." Blobs of angry tears pooled and then plummeted down the pudding cheeks when he blinked.

Sara was hopelessly out of her league. Her lips and breath made valiant efforts to form words that would not come.

Phil blubbered on. "You have to come with me, Sara. You have too."

She shook her head, more out of not knowing what to do than refusing.

Grabbing her waist, he jerked her whole body into his and planted his lips on her, like a worm sandwich. Sara gagged and screamed. The stench of old meat invaded her mouth. Her body clenched and revolted against the oppression that stifled her. Grimacing and retching, she pounded his chest until he pulled away.

In the scuffle, her bathrobe flapped open, exposing her breasts. Phil drove his hands through the folds. His arms slithered around her bare torso, cold and leathery as snakes. "Oh, God. Get off of me. What the hell!" She beat against his face, writhing out of his grasp. He was just too big. With the narrow gap she'd opened, she jammed her elbow into his gut.

He huffed and doubled over. Sara scrambled toward the door, yelling for help, but he caught the trailing tie on her robe and yanked. Stumbling, she banged her palms and knee on the hard tile.

His face blocked into icy stone. "You have to come with me or I have to kill you," he wheezed. Reaching into his back pocket, he produced a large knife. "You can't be with anyone but me. It hurts!" He thumped the fist that held the knife against his chest. A fresh batch of weeping shook the flab as he gathered her up from the floor. "It hurts to know you're out there and you're not mine."

She shoved away his attempts to pull her up and scrambled to her feet. "Get away from me! Help! Please, someone!" Adrenaline invaded her veins, hijacking her heart; her breathing quickened— everything happened that was supposed to in a situation like this, and none of it made any difference. With tiny steps, she backed away from the knife. His grip on her arm held her. The knife changed everything. Her blood chilled and she stiffened. Her only goal was to placate the wild beast panting in front of her face. "Okay, Phil. Let's stay calm here. Let's talk about this."

"I don't want to talk about it." Phil's anger flared again. "You come with me or I have to kill you. That's what the angel said. Didn't you listen?"

"Yes! Yes, I understand." She patted his shoulder.

His face relaxed.

"I saw her. But, Phil, she was burning in my dream. She's not a real angel."

The insanity contorted into perplexity. She had entered into his delusion but through the wrong door. "Flames?"

"Yes, flames. Like in hell. She's no angel. She's an imposter deceiving you."

"Flames?" He shuffled through the sketches, looking for a way to turn the story back into his own. His grasp on her wrist tightened. Tears stung her eyes. "But you didn't paint any flames." He shook her wrist accusingly. "You're the deceiver!"

The front door creaked. Phil looked up. Sara twisted her arm, yanking and straining. "Help!" A fraction of a second later, a chilling fear for her children gripped her. *Who else would be popping in?* "Get out! Quick! Call 911!" Hopeless! None of her children had ever done anything she'd asked, obediently, the moment she asked it. The little dog whined as Sara broke away, sliding a chair between her and Phil as she ran.

Furious, he shoved the chair, lunging at Sara and dragging her around it as it tipped. She stumbled into his heaping mound of flesh. In a desperate reflex, she jabbed her knee up to defend against his massive person, but her bulky bathrobe caught on the wooden post of the seat back as the chair toppled over and she missed the mark, ramming instead his thigh.

Phil slapped her again, all two hundred pounds of blubbering anger reverberating through the side of her head. Staggering sideways, her bare feet slipped in the puddle that had accumulated from her dripping hair. She fell backward, striking her head on the corner of the table. Phil, shocked by the unexpected violence of his action, relinquished her wrist as she crumpled into a heap on the floor.

Sara's head throbbed and her vision warped. The barest hint of purple flashed around the corner. "Jake?" Sara was not sure the words actually exited her lips.

Black. Blank. Light. Voices. Blood at the corner of her eye. "Jake?" She turned her head to the voices spinning and towering above her throbbing head. *A woman. Tall. Raven hair. Purple dress. Black boots.*

The warbling that passed between the two undulating figures faded into words. *Ms. Brann?*

"I can't possibly let you put an end to my little game, can I, Philip?" The voice was familiar but too thick.

"I don't have to do what you say anymore. I'm hers now. The angel told me. If Sara won't come with me, she said I should kill her and her soul would be free. Then, she'd be mine and I'd be free of you." Phil's voice quivered in the fog clogging Sara's brain.

Ms. Brann walked to the table and stood where Philip had tossed the painting. Sara tried to raise her throbbing head.

"Well, isn't this nice." She turned back to Philip. "I see you have met my sister. But I am afraid, dear Philip, that you have been deceived." Philip stood mesmerized, the knife clasped in his fist. Sara could only see the profiles, distant and faded, badly focused.

Brann placed the flat of her palm on Phil's breast. Sara's muddled brain tugged at her hand, willing it to rise, to warn the woman about the knife, but she couldn't get a response from the limb.

"You will always be mine, Philip—"

In the haze of fading lucidity, Sara shivered at the lovely half-smile that stole across the woman's lips.

"—until I have no more use for you." Ms. Brann sighed. "Sadly, it seems my sister is using you, Philip, to spoil my game. You see, if Sara dies before she reaches her fiftieth year, my game is forfeit. I'm afraid we can't have that, can we, Philip?"

Frankly hypnotized, the man shook his head in slow motion, wholly in agreement.

In her daze, Sara marveled and relaxed at the adeptness with which her art instructor handled the insanity of her student. The woman placed her other hand on Philip's shoulder and anchored his chest against the pressure of her palm. Sara watched, retreating into the folds of haze enveloping her, registering the return of consciousness and rejecting it again in the face of the illusory scene before her.

Ms. Brann inhaled deeply, the way Sara's children did when they came home from school and smelled cookies baking in the oven.

Philip's face illuminated at the pressure of her hand. He grew euphoric. "Oh, God, more! More!" His body arched toward her touch and climaxed. Brann pushed deeper, a look of utter satiation on her flawless features.

And then, Phil fell silent, suddenly, finally. His body froze in ecstasy and then crumpled. The deranged artist rapped his head on the side of the table before collapsing with a loud "thud" into a lifeless heap on the floor beneath Sara's nose.

She gave up the struggle against the throb and fog. Closing her eyes, she faded away to the melodious notes of Leana Brann calling 911, reporting a heart attack, and requesting an ambulance for an unconscious woman.

Chapter 63

Jake strolled into Sara's ER room smiling sympathetically. "I told you not to be nice to the crazy ones." A thick bandage covered the wicked gash pounding her brain. The lines on her husband's face betrayed the concern behind his ironic smile. "Throw 'em a life-line, yeah, but don't jump in with a drowning guy who's going to suck you under." He leaned over and hugged her. For the first time, Sara felt unguarded. Tears welled up and dribbled down her face. "You okay?"

Nodding, she wiped her eyes. "How'd you find out?" Jake's presence lent a concrete solidity to the world around her that had, for the last several hours, seemed so viscous.

"Your art teacher." He slid the extra chair from its station by the utility counter to her bed and took her hands in his. "I'm your emergency contact."

"What was she doing there? I mean I'm glad and all..." Splotchy memories, quickly fading, left Sara uneasy about her art teacher showing up.

"Apparently, she's been aware of Phil's 'mental issues' for a while. He made some weird comments in class and then she got a very disturbing phone call and he mentioned you. Seems he was taking some medication for a weak heart."

Unsatisfied with the distance imposed by the chair, Jake shifted onto the bed, resting his feet on the seat. The slope of the mattress tipped Sara toward him. In her half-conscious state, she had imagined that Ms. Brann had somehow inflicted the heart attack. Of course, that was absurd. Leana was probably trying to support him when he began to collapse. The doctor told Sara memory loss was a common side effect of head trauma.

"I guess the sight of you naked was more than he could take." Jake cracked a cheeky grin. "It always is for me."

Sara slapped his shoulder. "Nearly gives me a heart attack every time. But there won't be any more times! From now on, you announce yourself loudly and clearly before you stalk me in my bathroom."

"How about you just lock the doors?"

"What doors?" she scoffed and then choked as Ethan McCarthy walked through the doorway.

"I'm glad to see you're not totally traumatized." The celebrated artist looked from Sara to her husband. Jake and Ethan had never met before—never even seen each other. Jake had bristled slightly when Sara first prattled about the famous artist that encouraged her work. Why wouldn't he? It was a void in her life he couldn't fill and another man was filling it. So, she stopped talking about it— except to Elizabeth.

"Mr. McCarthy!" Sara stole a glance at her husband. Jake assumed a calm placidity that told her he was anything but. The tightness about his eyes and lips gave him away.

"Jake, this is the *famous* artist Elizabeth and I have been telling you about." Sara was trying to ease the tension with a little ironic flattery. "He's a friend of my art teacher and gives us amateurs a few pointers." The tremor in her voice gave away her flippancy. She was ruffled. She rummaged around for innocuous introductions. "Ethan's dad." She hadn't mentioned the breakup to Jake.

Jake acknowledged the neutrality of the last title with a nod. "Good kid. Seems to know what he's doing. Mature." He offered a hand. Ethan took it.

"Thanks. He's lucky to have met your daughter. Lovely young lady."

Sara stepped in on more solid ground. "Remember, Jake? Mr. McCarthy was nice enough to drive Elizabeth up to change cars with me when Ethan was gone." They all shook heads, pleased with the exchange of civilities. Sara looked around the room. Jake looked at her. Ethan looked at Jake.

Ethan finally explained his presence. "I heard about Phil from Leana."

"That's Ms. Brann," Sara clarified for her husband.

"Glad she showed up." Jake deflected the awkwardness in the room and came to Sara's rescue. "Apparently, the guy has had psychotic episodes before?"

"Leana did mention something about medications. She also told me you were here." Ethan nodded at Sara. "I guess, other than that bandage, you're all right."

"I'll be locking my doors in the future. I don't remember a whole lot. I remember being scared stupid by the sight of him standing there—"

Sara shivered as the image stirred up the adrenaline again. Her hand slid to the warm comfort of Jake's thigh. His arm pulled her shoulders into the safety of his chest. "But I do remember the knife. It was huge." She tangled her fingers into Jake's and then pressed their hands tightly together. His hands in his pockets, Ethan seemed to be brooding over the silent intimacy passing between Sara and her husband. "It was that painting I was working on that set him off. You were right, I guess. I shouldn't have kept going with it. It wasn't me. When he saw the painting, he was sure it was a sign. Evidently, the angel I painted told him to kill me."

"In his dream?" Ethan's stark reaction astonished Sara. It was only a dream, but the response on his face bore the weight of reality.

"Yeah, how'd you know?" She tilted her head. Somewhere in her still muddled mind, she imagined that Ethan might clarify some of her undefined suspicions and fears.

"Phil has quite a few dreams. It's a phenomenon of art. The muses wander about dreams, knocking, hoping an artist will answer."

"The weird thing I do remember is," snippets wandered her brain, but she drew too many blanks, "when Leana showed up, she said something about him not spoiling her game. That if he killed me, the game would be forfeit." Sara saw the look that passed over Jake's face as the absurdity of what she'd just suggested materialized into solid words. But Ethan's eyes narrowed. Fury boiled up and rippled the edges of his signature smooth countenance.

Sara wondered if Ethan and the dead man had been friends. She'd always thought there was something freaky going on between the doughy artist, the teacher, and the celebrity recluse.

Her husband's crinkled brow told her he was suddenly convinced the concussion might have been more serious than she thought. "I was probably delusional by then. I hit my head pretty hard." She folded her hands in her lap. "I'm sorry about Phil, though."

Jake rolled his eyes. "Better him than you."

Ethan looked visibly upset and seemed to be straining to leave against some invisible chord that held him in the room. "Mr. McCarthy, uh, Ethan, if you wouldn't mind, I don't think we'll mention this to the kids. I mean, I may have mentioned that Phil was a little, uh, unstable…but it happened while they were in school. I can't think of any way it would be helpful for them to know someone invaded our home." Sara nudged Jake for some accord and smiled. "Can you imagine what Annie would do? We'd never be able to sleep alone again."

"Of course. You have to do what's best for your children." Ethan said his good-byes and ducked out of the hospital room as if hot coals smoldered in the soles of his shoes.

"That wasn't very nice, Jake. Phil is dead. What if he and Ethan were friends?"

"I don't care if it wasn't nice. *He* wasn't nice, Sara. He tried to kill my wife. The son of a bitch walked into my house and stood there watching you shower like some damn, sick, twisted pervert. Let's not feel sorry for him." He leaned over and wrapped his arms around her, squeezing her so tightly that she could barely breathe. His silence screamed his anger that he wasn't there to keep her safe. "God, Sara, if anything ever happened to you, there wouldn't be any point left to living. You're so damn strong, and independent, and smart, I forget how small you are."

They checked out of the hospital. Ten minutes after they got home, Jake had Sara installed comfortably with a blanket in front of the fire. He was in the master bedroom measuring the bathroom archway for doors. Every time she closed her eyes, Phil's pasty, tear-stained face haunted her.

While her husband ran to Home Depot to scout for doors with locks, Sara scooped up the sketches and the painting she'd been working on and dropped them in the fire. She watched as the edges of the paper blackened and then curled. The flames devoured them and then licked the borders of the painting. A minute later the image of the dove woman clouded over and shriveled away amongst the vivid orange flames.

"I guess that's how they fit in."

Chapter 64
—From the unfinished manuscript of Ethan McCarthy

Writhing figures howled silently from the walls in the dim hallway. Seething, I raged against the treachery and petty rivalry that had nearly ended Sara's life. "God damn you, murderess, lying witch! Where are you?" Stopping at one of Brann's favorite paintings, a child weeping over a dead bird, the cat still crouched low, murder in its eyes, I ripped the priceless specimen from its perch and hurled it to the floor.

At the end of the corridor, I threw open the door. The sun had abandoned the private studio. Brann Sidhe lounged in a purple armchair that faced the windows. The rather stiff straightness of her back betrayed her air of serenity. The glimpse of her sent me, not straight at her throat, because I knew better, but to the large, antique sideboard scattered with various objects of unknown value. Laying my hands on an inlaid box about an inch wide and eight inches long, I flipped it open, exposing the iron dagger it cradled.

In a hidden compartment of the table, lay the small pistol with only one iron bullet. But I was better with knives. Blade or bullet, this game would end today. I hesitated only because I still could not be certain that the muse's death would not trigger Sara's. Yes, she only lived because I had purchased this second chance for Elizabeth, but I had purchased this second chance because it was I who allowed Elizabeth to squander her first for the sake of the coin of youth.

Watching Sara cling to Jake, the man who had, so many times and existences, stolen Elizabeth from me, I knew I had lost again.

The hilt of the knife in my fist, I turned in the direction of the raven-clad beauty in the chair. Perhaps I would wring from her the promise to release Elizabeth's soul in exchange for staying my hand. I was not naïve. I had not forgotten that the Leanan Sidhe do not die. They are immortal beings and can only be forced to start over, but all slates would be razed and memories lost. If death punctuated this existence prematurely, the reset would at least free our souls and end my slavery.

Brann did not flinch, but the space around her darkened as if the clouds had obscured the sun—but there was no sun, and there were no clouds. "Do you believe I would tarry here long enough for you to carry out your murderous designs?" Not the slightest nod nor tilt of her head acknowledged the impending doom clutched in my hand. "You haven't even given me the pleasure of seducing me into enough human flesh to try your hand."

"Cailen Sidhe sent Phil to kill Sara. What are you and your sister playing at?"

"I see. Did you come here seeking a bloody battle? Perhaps you were hoping for thunder and lightning?" The room darkened to pitch, and then flared in an electric flash that illuminated the razor-toothed demon with blood-shot eyes that hid behind the face of glamour. Instinctively, I recoiled from the beast. She flew from her chair and grasped my fist, careful not to touch the iron. Her symphonic beauty cackled in discord with the gripping power so much more in harmony with the demon she hid within.

Against her supernatural strength, I wrenched. Slowly, she turned my hand upon my own breast. The tip of the dagger pierced the skin of my throat. I stiffened against the prick then submitted. The game would end with the event of my demise—all wagers null and void. I was ready. Had I not struggled boldly? Had I not maintained the course in the face of driving guilt, on the brink of insanity? To no avail. Brann had won this bargain so many years before. Even then, she understood Elizabeth—Sara—so much better than I ever did. The game was up. All that was left for me was to salvage the souls before they, too, were lost. If I lost the lives in the process, they wouldn't be our last.

"Is that what you desire? An end to the game? You would give up the life you sought with such vigor and tenacity? For what? The souls? Trifles and playthings. If you murder yourself, what would stay my hand from taking back the happy life I gifted Elizabeth?"

Her grasp dissolved and she disappeared in a small cloud of ash. The dagger clattered to the floor and the muse reappeared in her chair as if nothing had passed between us. But, in chastising me, she had tipped her hand. Elizabeth's stolen life thread was not dependent on Brann's magic. "You saw the love, didn't you? Looked it in the face, felt it sticky upon the air between your Sara and her Jake."

"She'll never leave him. I'm not sure anymore I want her to. The severing would kill them both. I'd be no better than you— murdering to feed myself." My face convulsed in anguish under the weight of the admission spoken and therefore so much more binding. Sweeping the sideboard clean, I scattered the items about the room in a clatter of glass and metal. "I'd rather die." I lunged for the knife. Death before its due would secure the free travel of our souls from one plane to another.

My joints locked. Thin air chained my fingers. My body froze. Brann's lips curled like the blossoming of a lily. "I offered you an end to the game once, my dear Ethan. Perhaps you will not spurn my generosity now. So many before you have clamored at my feet and been rejected. But you, I would make my consort. I would give you power, not just life."

The muscles of my face twitched, fighting the strain of her hold, willing myself to reject this new ploy. She was willing to give up the souls. Squeezing my eyes shut, I willed her out of my skull. But she would not leave. She could sense me relenting. Such a clean solution. Elizabeth lives, I live, our souls are free. And at what cost? The simple price of giving my nearly everlasting youth in this life over to the leanan sidhe to use as she pleased. Was it so abhorrent, this life of the gifted artist? As much as I scorned my mistress, I could not help myself. I loved the exquisite depth of imagination at my fingertips. But the servitude. No! I could not do it, not for an infinity of years. But, could I to free my soul—and Elizabeth's?

The ice in my limbs melted; the chains fell. I opened my eyes. My hand still stretched toward the dagger. Oh, God! It was infinite this web of deceit and lies so dexterously woven with glittering strands of desire, love, and tragedy.

While I pondered the weight of freeing both our souls by relinquishing this lost cause and giving myself up to unknown years of torturous servitude, a tiny prism of ice lit upon the floor by the hot gray metal but did not melt. Another joined it, and then another. Soon, a small drift had formed. The ice turned to down and swirled up in a vortex of rioting feathers to clothe the snow and gold creature that breathed herself into it.

The familiar touch of her fingers, like a swarm of nectar-buzzed butterflies, flitted across my drooping wrist. Fury churned up bile at the ephemeral touch of the vision that had murdered every soul whom I had ever held dear. Behind the apparition, Brann Sidhe rose from her chair. I did not know which of the sisters to abhor most.

The silky strands of Cailen's words bound my hand before it could touch the iron blade. "And what about the boy? Will you kill him, too?" I would have plunged the dagger into the heart of this angel of murder, but I knew she was still too ethereal.

It was only the rivalry between the two that stayed my hand at the moment. "You murdered my parents and my wife, and then you sent that mad man to murder her again. How dare you foul the air of my home!"

Her eyes met mine, grace for rancor. "I did not murder anyone. I sold them what they desired more than life. It's what humans do, my dear boy, they sell a bit of themselves for what they want. Isn't that what *you* did?"

My knees buckled and the weight of my body, laden with guilt, thudded against the bare wooden floor. "I never bargained for this misery. Neither did they."

"And I never bargained for their happiness—or yours. Misery is the traveling companion of desire." Her lily-white hand caressed the air as she smiled serenely at the state of things that so suited her monstrous appetites.

I would not let her sweep away the centuries of suffering and blame that I had lain at her doorstep. "You lying bitch! You deceived them. None of them knew that your small price would cost them their lives."

"Ah, but there are so many pieces to the truth, aren't there, sister?" The serene demeanor of Brann Sidhe's face cracked, and for a brief second, the beast within snarled. "You, too, were deceived, dear Ethan." Cailen Sidhe knelt to peer into the recesses where the pieces of my life huddled. "It's there, in your memory, in the mind of the boy. He knows of the deceit. Find it! Find it and know that if you kill yourself to end her game, you kill him and the chance he has to live free of Brann Sidhe, the chance he has to save the souls and live whole." She paused, waiting in her diabolically infinite patience until I looked her in the eye. "The chance to have love." She stepped away from the iron dagger.

My hand wavered, and reached, and then wavered again.

Neither muse moved until I should make the choice. Neither one would allow my death. Both desired greedily to suckle at my life.

Brann Sidhe stepped forward. "Have you no shame, Ethan. Would you feed the whore that assassinated your parents, your wife, and your child?"

Cailen Sidhe spoke with the face of mercy. "Poor young Ethan, he has lived for year upon year, his entire existence strangled in the creeping vines of your past and the tendrils of the future. Will you not cut him free and allow him to bask in his present? Must he know nothing but the shadow of your sorrow and oath? Will you not free him from your bonds and let him struggle as he will?"

"Struggle as he will, but in your service?" Brann Sidhe would never set me free. Even faced with losing me to the fierce rivalry of her sister, she was not willing to relinquish my immortal service in this life. The question was: should I risk our soul to give the boy a chance at love or take us all irrevocably with me, our loveless soul shattered but unfettered? "You would have me trade my master for his?"

Cailen Sidhe stepped farther away from the lethal iron of the knife. "There is always a master, but there is not always a chance at love."

The old house creaked on its foundation, rocking the pregnant silence. The clock on the mantel, always anxious, ticked out its inexorable trudge toward the future. My shoulders drooped beneath the bulk of a century of chains, lifetimes of frustration and rejection, and the new bloody stripes of deception. I saw my youth: indomitable, tenacious, charming—in love and whole. Could I deny that boy his chance at the one thing that gave existence meaning? My shoulders sagged under the burden of such a choice.

Leaning my weight onto one hand, with the other I picked up the dagger. Both muses tensed, the air around them turned crisp. Would the boy's path bring him again to this very spot where I bowed, defeated, worn, and hollow? It might. I had placed one foot upon the flagstones already. But he might not. Bringing myself to my full height, I settled my stare on Brann. "You may yet win the war you wage for my soul, but for now," tossing the dagger onto the sideboard, I nodded toward Cailen Sidhe, "your sister has won the battle. Let the boy take his chance with our soul. I will forfeit my eternal youth to be whole again, to be free of you, and to free Sara's soul."

Victorious, Cailen inhaled my aroma. The downy white plumes of her dress fluttered in the breezeless room.

Brann's dark eyes compelled mine to hers. "You talk of war, Ethan, as if we were human. Do you expect cannonballs of lightning cast in anger? Are you waiting for feathers to fly, for scratching and clawing, and the baring of fangs?" The raven feathers about her bristled. She vanished, only to reappear in my face, her hand poised on the sideboard. She dismissed the image of violence with a wave of her hand. My shoulders relaxed and she leaned close enough to whisper in my ear. "I would fight this battle in your dreams. The blood of it would mingle with the subconscious streams of your youth, and the carnage would lie rotting in your imagination." Sneering, she glared at Cailen. "But I will not give my sister the satisfaction!" Grabbing the dagger, she screamed as it burned her palm. With the force of the demon within, she drove it into my chest.

The point pierced the space between my ribs. I groaned and cried out, clutching the handle. Cailen Sidhe screeched, shedding her dove-like calm. The searing cut brought me to my knees before the muse relinquished the blade in disgust. "If you will not have me, you will have no one in this life. Die! You are mine!" She stabbed a purple nail at her chest. "You will always and everywhere be mine."

My lungs collapsed around the wound. I couldn't gather air enough to groan. Nothing but gurgling and gasping escaped my lips. The room erupted in darkness. Electric bolts flashed as Cailen Sidhe grew claws and fangs and attacked her sister. The sheer force of self-preservation—not of this self that was done for, but of the others that Brann might pursue in the Barrow—drove me to gather what strength I could muster to fumble for the latch beneath the table. Only my arm anchored me from slipping to the floor.

My fingers stumbled across the wooden notch. The drawer popped open.

"Treacherous fiend! You stole him. He was mine, bought and paid for." Cailen's claw scraped across Brann's lily chest, opening up a purple gash of blood.

Brann recoiled, stung, but not subdued. The feathers in her gown melted into buzzing, black wasps. She flung the swarm at Cailen's face. The dove muse squealed against every sting, thrashing her arms to slap at the tiny predators.

Brann, her torso bare, purple blood oozing across the decaying grey of wart-ridden scales, smirked at her sister's suffering.

My numb fingers fumbled for the pistol in the drawer. Strength failed me, and my knees buckled. Choking, my lungs burning and throbbing as if I'd been struck by a club, I gripped the edge of the sideboard and crawled back up. Blackness encroached on the limits of my vision. My life ticked away in drops of blood.

Having distracted her sister, Brann stepped toward me to finish the work she had done, or perhaps to gloat. Who knew what curse the death muse hoped to fling at my dying corpse?

Seeing my peril, Cailen—desperate to salvage her prize—abandoned her fight against the wasps, whipped her arm out toward her sister, and launched a furious horde of doves that ripped and pecked at the exposed blood on her skin.

Brann screeched and flung herself at her sister. The two of them, engulfed in swarms of flying predators, crashed together. The force of Brann's charge bowled over the fairer sister. Where my human flesh would have run right through her ephemeral mass, the clash of two like masses produced a crash that rocked the windows. The swarm of doves sank to the floor as the force of impact stilled Cailen's form. Brann recalled her wasps and straddled her sister.

Forehead sweating, I touched the cold steel of the pistol. Gasping for air, I had not the strength to grasp it and sank again, my hand slipping out of the drawer. So little of me still floated in this world. The faint voices under the Barrow called to me.

"Would you like to know how to murder a leanan sidhe, dear Ethan? It's quite logical, really. You simply remove her tongue." Turning, Brann held up one purple, razor-sharp nail. "Without her tongue, she cannot whisper her visions; she cannot lick at the drops of life that sustain her—" Leaning over, Brann grasped Cailen's mouth, top and bottom, and pulled. "—and so, she dies." The force of her jaws parting awoke the muse. Gagging, she thrashed beneath her sister's legs.

Finished, my only thought was to deprive Brann Sidhe of her power and prevent her from hunting me down again. I could not risk her using the diamonds to wreak vengeance on Sara and Jake. Brann had ruled this misery we called life and now she must end, for I would not serve her in another.

My sight blackened at the edges. My head floated in worlds beyond. I had only seconds left. Heaving myself above the board, gasping, I grasped the pistol, flopped my arm onto the steadying boards of the table, and pulled the trigger. The crack of the shot cut short Cailen's squeals and consumed the last of my energy. Air forsook me, black engulfed me. I did not know where the bullet fell.

Chapter 65

I found myself in the Barrow, formless and tossed about by the winds that rattled the roots. The voices all around me cried and moaned, "What's next? Where shall I go? Help me! I'm lost." I was not lost. The dagger in Brann's hand had ended our game. I was moving on to another existence, another chance with Elizabeth—whatever clay her soul might wear when we met—and we would meet. The boy within reviled me. He had a chance with Cailen Sidhe, a chance at love. And now there was nothing and we would be forever fractured and divided. The wind whipped from tuber to tuber, rejecting us in portals that would lead to planes of existence we'd already lived, tossing us on in our search for somewhere new. We swirled and groaned in the vortex until one root caught and sucked us toward the gravity of a universe unknown. The lips spread wide. We felt the chill of the vacuum and then heard the voices whispering from beyond.

A sudden jolt revived in us a sense of chest. Gravity grabbed at our feet and pulled us back from whence we had come. The dirt of the Barrow melted around us, the wind whipped us up, and up, and up. Light pierced my eyes. The force at my chest seared my very heart. I was again in my corpse where the living lungs pleaded for air. Sating them struck a blow so intense that I sprang up gasping. The empty wound in my chest bled soggy crimson onto my white shirt. My lungs still collapsing, I opened my mouth to scream in agony, but the air would not come.

Cailen Sidhe knelt by my side, a palm covering my face. The iron dagger had branded the shape of its handle into it. The other hand pressed against my heart. Pushing my back against the floor, she squeezed a cut in the center of her palm. Molten gold trickled from the laceration. Three drops dripped luxuriously into the seeping hole in my chest. Heaven trickled through my capillaries and veins. The wound mended itself. Air filled my lungs again and embraced my brain. Visions of unspeakable beauty shrouded in white butterflies and fields of golden wheat embraced my imagination.

Choking on the affluence of oxygen, I sat up, bewildered. On the floor beside me, a thousand black feathers fluttered listlessly. In the midst of them lay an iron bullet and an aqua egg, dappled brown.

"My life for yours." A lock of Cailen's hair had tumbled out of place. Her countenance had dimmed ever so slightly. "A fair trade."

"And Brann Sidhe?" I coughed.

Cailen's laugh rippled sunshine through the shadows in the room. A gentle breeze emanated from her skirts and scattered the raven feathers.

"She's finished?"

"Hardly." The egg barely filled her palm and disappeared into the folds of her gown. "But from this new beginning, she will require more than a century to find again all that she was. You will not see her in this life. She'll remember nothing of you until she sheds the form of the raven and begins to dabble in humanity."

I lay back on my elbows and sighed deeply, the weight of a century fell from my shoulders. "But the bargain? What now?"

"The bargain is gone." She ripped the sleeve from my arm. Indeed, the tattoo had disappeared with its creator.

Fear gripped me. "But Sara and Jake? Brann's magic gave them life. Are they—did her death—?"

Cailen sniffed. "I told young Ethan that Brann's realm is death. She meddled in my realm. Your Sara is safe."

I stood slowly, not quite convinced that the mortal stab of a blade could heal with no price. "And now what? I'm free?"

Tenderly, Cailen placed a hand on my elbow and helped me to my feet. "Do you not mean 'we,' my pet?"

Cailen Sidhe, most certainly, did not restore my life out of the goodness of her cold, golden heart. "I did not ask you to bring us back. I would have gone willingly into the Barrow and the next existence."

"No, you did not ask. But he did, young Ethan. He cried out, didn't he? Is that what you want, Ethan. Do you wish to continue in this fractured, never-ending existence of loss?"

The answer was so simple. I did not. I was willing to die to mend my soul and move on. The muse read those thoughts.

"But you can never move on. Don't you understand? You will be forever fractured, aware of all you have been, all the pieces disjointed." She leaned close and the stark smell of sandalwood encircled us. "You will be mad, wherever your soul roams. The voices will haunt you."

My face blanched.

The muse smiled and tiny bits of light sparkled about her visage. "Unless I heal you."

"And that would cost—?"

She dismissed the price with a wave of her hand. "A trifle." Her eyes narrowed and her face tensed. "Two years."

Yes, I should have run. But they would have run with me. All the voices of past lives that clamored in my head, moaning their losses. The youths within. They dug in their heels. And the one I called Ethan Jr., oh, he railed against the very thought of fleeing the chance he had at love. He wanted out. He wanted the life he'd been denied because of his obsession with life. I could not run from the voices.

Closing my eyes, I bent my head to inevitability. "Yes. Two years. Heal me."

The muse clapped like a five-year-old with her first pony. And then her shoulders and brow twitched. "But the love. I've given three drops of my blood so that he can have love. I must have a game for the love."

My fists clenched. "I will not bargain with the souls. I know too well the cost is not what it seems."

"Ethan, you pain me. I am not my sister. I do not guzzle dry my prize in gluttony. I wish only a small reward. Shall we have three years more if the girl will not marry him in two? It seems a small game and a paltry price for love, but I am willing to be reasonable."

What was the worst? Five years of service to this white witch? After the tortured slavery in the bitter elegance of Brann Sidhe's misery, perhaps service to this dove-feathered fairy would prove almost pleasant. "Done."

"Then let us proceed without delay. You, my dear Ethan, are a bit too calloused for my taste. I crave the fresh naïveté of your 18-year-old self. We shall endeavor to recreate you in a lighter fashion."

Shivering at the touch of her finger on my neck, Cailen unfastened the gold coin. With never a glance back at our new master, I strode out of the room toward the kitchen. She followed. She would always follow, like a puppy hoping for scraps. But when would the puppy grow fangs and claws and turn on its master? Young Ethan did not know her as I did, and the boy would not have my mature memories to guide him like whispers in the wind of his subconscious. Would the dormant voices of the shattered pieces of lives-lived bubble up through his subconscious and warn him? I could only hope and fear that they might.

Standing at the cupboard, I made my weekly youth tonic, dropping the coin into the cup.

I did not inquire; Cailen Sidhe needed no bidding to speak.

She reached for a small sauce bowl and set it beside me. "He will need only a spoonful of your blood—and the coin—nothing else. The mixture of the new blood with the old will fasten the spell."

My face blank, void of fear, void of loss, I reached for a knife and slit open my thumb, barely wincing at the numbness. My old blood dripped into the white bowl.

I needed to think of nothing, make no plans. All my affairs were a well-played game. From time to time, I disappeared, leaving my estate to an entity of my youth, so that the records would be right. The papers were all drawn up. The ravenous muse at my side would see to all the details.

"How will he know that you have agreed?" She watched, fascinated as the blood dripped. "He wasn't sure of himself."

"And you find that surprising? We are none of us sure of ourselves. We are not fools, although we are sometimes foolish."

Wrapping a towel about my thumb, I squeezed it tightly, strangling the flow of blood. "He has always been aware of my last desire before the transformation, but here, let me make it plain for him." Reaching across Cailen to the shelf, I brushed the whole array of herbs, minerals, and metals, with one sweeping blow, to the floor. Glass and pottery hopped, crashed, and skidded, littering the wood beneath our feet with the makings of my perpetual youth. Crushing it beneath my steps, I refastened the coin about my neck.

"Are you satisfied he will understand my desire?" The tonic disappeared down my throat in one large gulp. An angelic smile curved Cailen's lips as the ground quaked slightly and the air around me shook. I stepped forward and surrendered my future to my youth.

Chapter 66

—Excerpts from the unpublished writings of Ethan McCarthy, Jr.

Doorbell chimes, deeper and more resonant than the clock, rang in the entry. Wiping her hands, Sara stepped back to assess her progress. It was harder without a group. Her kids didn't quite care enough to offer any real suggestions and her husband always made the same comment. "I like your new stuff." A few of the women from class had set a date to meet in the library in Plano. It was a bit of a drive, but she needed the critiques.

Sara brushed the moisture from her brow and the towel caught a little on the rippling edges of her bandage. That could come off today.

Her flip-flops slapped at the kitchen tile and then faded to a light thud on the entry rug. The lock still stuck a bit, but after two weeks of her new morning lock-up routine, she was getting the hang of it.

It was Thursday, and she was expecting Elizabeth to come after her finals and spill the whole drama of why she and Ethan were no longer dating. Sara had tried to call a few times but realized Elizabeth was busy studying and resigned herself to patience. Opening the door, she found herself face to face with the story himself. Ethan Jr. stood on the front porch, half his torso obscured by a rather large, antique strongbox.

"Ethan!"

"Hi, Mrs. Dawson. Can I come in?"

"Of course, you can. You know I'm not expecting Elizabeth until later. I thought maybe she'd taken her finals early." Rambling provided camouflage for her vague distress.

"Actually, I was hoping I could talk to *you*."

Sara's eyes rounded, her mouth opened. Unsure how to proceed, she nodded graciously and ushered him in.

At the kitchen table, Ethan deposited the box and then occupied the chair next to hers. "Can I get you something to drink?"

Politeness smoothed the awkwardness of chatting with the jilted boyfriend.

"No, thanks. I'm good." He cut right to the chase. "I wanted to talk to you before Elizabeth got home. Did she tell you what happened?"

Squirming in her chair, Sara grimaced. "Well, a bit. She said you weren't dating anymore." She noted with motherly satisfaction the despair in his face because every mother who is loved wants her daughter to be loved.

"Did she tell you why?"

"No. She said she'd explain when she got home, but then she told me not to go to my class and to lock the doors—but she always says that, so I'm a bit confused."

"She is, too. That's why I came. I wanted you to hear the story from me." He put his hand on the box in front of him. Then he leaned forward, closer to Sara, like he was going to whisper. She recoiled reflexively. The trauma of Phil's assault still lingered. "I'm going to tell you something that sounds a little bizarre. I would have said something earlier, but I didn't know I could."

If she was confused before, Sara was mystified now. Always the picture of diplomacy, she found refuge in her teacher face. Ethan was no longer the son of a misguided crush or her daughter's ex, he was simply a student explaining why he was failing her class.

The sheer creativity of his story would have earned a passing grade. It started, like most, with a description of a tragedy at home.

"I need to tell you about my dad's wife—my mom—and how she died." The truly pathetic tragedy of death in childbirth quickly disintegrated into some kind of wild fairy story about an alchemist discovering fountains of youth, muses with vampire tendencies, an oath of silence and servitude, a soul conjured from paintings and stored in a diamond, and dreams that inspired breathtaking works of art—that part was less fantastical. She felt reality and delusion coalescing in her mind.

Teeth gnawing at the inside of her lip, Sara squinted to repel any signs of incredulity while not letting herself slip into the murky waters. She sat rigid, nodding sympathetically, her body shifting away from the storyteller. She'd done her quota of crazies for the year. Maybe one too many—this one was starting to sound logical.

In the nervous gesticulating of his hands and the elevated tone of his voice, Sara could see Ethan was desperate. The thin mask of sympathy kept slipping off her face. Finally, the boy pulled a gold coin from inside his collar. "I know I sound as crazy as Phil. Phil's what happens when the Leanan Sidhe get their teeth in someone. But I brought you this so you could believe me." He held out the gold coin. Sara nodded but flinched away from the talisman's proximity. A pleasant smile curled her lips, but her eyes screamed, "Lunatic! Keep away from my daughter!"

"I know you're wondering what this has to do with you or Elizabeth."

No, I'm wondering when I became a magnet for the depraved. "Well—" Sara couldn't think of anything appropriate to say.

"You're her." He said it unflinching, totally serious.

"Who?" Her brow wrinkled and then lifted in dawning realization. "Oh, my God. You think I'm your dad's dead wife?" *Think, Sara, think. What the hell do you do here?* There were no stray knives out on the counters. Her gaze fell on the box. *Oh, God! He's probably got one in there, or worse.*

"You're her soul brought back again. The life you're living is the life he bargained for."

Desperately calm, Sara put her hand over Ethan's. He smiled, encouraged. *All I have to do is get us through this moment without any damage to either of us. Then he'll go home like all my other students and his parents will deal with the rest of his life.* "Ethan, I think you're upset about the breakup. Let me call your dad. Maybe we can all—"

His face wrenched and he shoved back his chair with a screech against the tile floor. "No! You can't call my dad."

Sara downshifted into calming mode. Her hands in front of her, she pressed at the tense air. "It's okay. We don't have to call him. I just thought—"

"You can't call him because he doesn't exist anymore. I'm him!"

"Okay." She slid her chair back slowly to face him, staying seated—less intimidating. Definitely, some serious father-son issues going on here. Maybe the tortured look on Mr. McCarthy's face when she first met him wasn't the loss of his wife; it was the day to day endurance of a lunatic teenage son. "So, you don't want your dad involved."

"You don't get it. I'm him. We are all him. That's how he's been doing this for decades, over a century. He jumps into younger versions of himself. He would never have gotten any older, hopping around between us, if it weren't for Brann Sidhe...Ms. Brann. I am the younger version of the man that cut the deal with her."

Sara dared to stand slowly, placating him. "So, I'm your wife that died a century and a half ago." Her attempts at understanding only exacerbated him.

"No!" He rubbed his temples with his fingers. "I'm messing this all up. I never made the deal. I didn't even know you. He met you a couple of years later than me. That's why I can talk about it—I didn't know that before, or I would have explained because I don't love you; I love Elizabeth."

At the mention of her daughter, Sara's maternal instinct blanketed her face in chilling determination. "Ethan, I don't know what you're dealing with here. I'm sure you and your dad have some serious issues to work out, but I don't think Elizabeth should be involved with you while you deal with it. I'm starting to think that's why she broke up with you and told me not to go to class."

Ethan groaned. "Stop saying that. There is no dad. We were all him, all the stuffing pulled out in pieces, each pretending it was a little doll, alive, but only a puppet. But Cailen put us back together and now it's just me, but I'm whole. I only have two years, Sara. You've got to help me or I'll have to serve another three."

Sara tensed to run.

They stood in silence, him pleading, her praying. Then he looked away, despairing, until his eyes fell on the box. He jumped for it. Sara's heart ticked up a beat and she pulled the chair firmly between them. He saw the move and the surge of terror. "I'm not going to hurt you, Sara. Cailen Sidhe said it would be easier if I did." She recognized that name again—the one Phil kept repeating. That was the name he called the angel she'd drawn. Her arms stiffened on the chair as she wondered why the angels were out to destroy her. She considered herself an above-average nice person.

Ethan rambled on. "You've read *Macbeth* and *Crime and Punishment,* right? I learned by the tragedy method that when you take the easy way to what you're grasping, it slips away from you in the end. I don't want to lose Elizabeth." He opened the box. Sara moved to flee. "No, don't run from me." It was the desperation of a child that kept her—and the strong grasp of a youthful fist. "Look! Look at these and you'll understand."

She swallowed hard as he reached into the box. She expected metal—a gun? Her captive breath escaped when he tossed an old photo onto the table in front of her. She recognized her face and Elliot's immediately. Homecoming—from high school. Elliot kept a whole scrapbook of their romance. "Where did you get this?" Her curiosity slightly dampened the fear.

"It's mine. Look at it, Sara. Look at me." She inspected the boy in the photo and the young man in front of her. The resemblance was too close to be a coincidence, even too close to be family. Her insides quivered. "If that's me, and it is," he reasoned unreasonably, "I'm not old enough to be him now. I should be your age, nearly a year older than you." He dumped the box on the table. Letters, photographs, ticket stubs, programs floated across the table.

"Easton!" Sara exclaimed under her breath. She picked up the photo of the fiancé she'd jilted to go to Paris. "That's Joe's sweater—the one I stole from Margaret. I loved that sweater. And I remember this day so well—Red Pine trail. It was my birthday." Easton was an exact match, but older, than the boy standing in front of her and the boy in the Homecoming photo. She didn't wonder if this was some sort of Photoshop conspiracy. She had copies of most of these photos stuffed in plastic boxes waiting to make their way into scrapbooks. From a corner of the box, she pulled out the ring she knew so well because it had adorned her hand for months before she fled to Paris. Wriggling her finger from Jake's wedding ring, she tried the band. It still fit.

Fact and impossibility clashed in her brain. "How could they be the same person? Elliot was a year older than I was. Easton was twenty-three when I was nineteen." She pulled out a class photo of the art teacher, Elliot, with whom she had collaborated in Boston. "The art teacher, too?" In her head, she did the math. But the numbers wouldn't add up. "He was much younger than I. These are not the same person. What's going on here?" Too much dissonance, too much adrenaline, too much evidence of the impossible. Sara's stomach lurched, her head rattled. Pulling the chair behind her, she sank into it. "This is not possible."

"It is possible." Ethan yanked the coin out of his shirt and shook it at her. "That's what I've been trying to show you. The Ethan you know has been around for almost a century and a half trying to win your love again." He reached for her left hand. "This diamond you wear, that came from a 'distant relative,' it was your wedding band. It held your soul for one hundred years and then brought you back. The elixir brewed from this coin allowed him to transform into us younger versions so that he would never grow old. Except he did. Because he sold Brann Sidhe his immortality in exchange for your second chance at life."

The truth was there in the photos. Sara couldn't imagine it before because the puzzle pieces couldn't fit together linearly. She'd never tried to link them in a timeless plane. Her fingers walked through the photos and mementos; her mind strolled through the memories of a girl always loved, always connected, and yet, somehow looking for something beyond. She didn't know how to feel. Had she been stalked her whole life? Or had she been left free to choose? Everywhere, this same boy had made her feel loved and then given her the freedom to fly. "It was all so lovely," she admitted. Her eyes dropped back to the photos, the moments captured. "I loved them all, in their own time."

"They all loved you. I'm the anomaly. The old man is only a premonition to me." Ethan paused, disconcerted. "I never fell in love with you—her, Elizabeth, the woman that died. That happened later—to the man I became. In my time, I was too focused on my ambition to even think about love. I only wanted to defeat death."

The whole story, from a spectator seat, made Sara's skin crawl. It would have been so much easier to stomach from the mouth of a man her own age. But from the lips of this boy, her daughter's boyfriend, it grated like nails on a chalkboard.

"But I fell in love with Elizabeth—your daughter. Probably for the same reason the older version of me fell in love with you. But the two of you are different. There's something about Elizabeth—" Ethan grinned, "—you, but—"

"—unfettered. Yes, there is something about Elizabeth." There was something about his cheeky grin. She'd seen it over and over. It was almost on the strength of that one curl of the lips that she felt the whole soupy story begin to solidify. "She has something of her father in her."

The mention of Jake brought a squint to Ethan's eyes. His stare fixed on her face before he decided to proceed. "Your husband Jake, Jackson, he's part of the story, but not part of this moment. That can wait." Fending off the silence that settled between them, Ethan fished up from the bottom of the box a very old photograph and handed it to Sara.

Her hand trembled a bit as she took it. The greenish oval matting was faded, the corners a bit worn, but overall, the image was very well-preserved. She'd seen family photos from the late 1800s. Her mother was something of a collector.

This particular photo of a couple had been taken against a white background. The newlyweds were dressed all in white so that the dark lines of their faces floated out of the picture. Sara's breath caught. The face of the bride smiling wistfully in the photo was her own. From above the wreath of white flowers that crowned her head, Ethan's face, a bit older and tilted toward his new bride, confronted her with the truth. On the woman's hand, glinted the antique ring on Sara's finger.

Speechless, she looked up at Ethan Jr. She knew it was real. His story, his fantastical confessions, they all rang true, as if a tiny choir made from voices hidden in every cell of her body proclaimed them.

"Brann Sidhe knew what she was doing when she made him promise not to tell me, I can feel it—down in my bones—but I would never have guessed." She looked at the picture again. A sadness of loss washed over her. "I would have married Easton if he'd told me—never gone to Paris."

"I don't know his thoughts and what moved him, Sara. Maybe he knew the younger ones could speak but didn't want us to. It was Easton who loved and lost you. He made his bargain with Brann Sidhe. He could not speak. The soul she breathed back into you was linked to him when you got married. Maybe, in the end, he didn't want you to love him out of obligation or pity. But, I think he wanted you to choose him—the way I want Elizabeth to choose me."

Sara agreed quietly. "It must have been unbearable. All those years—waiting, hoping, losing."

"Don't go there, Sara. It's dead now. All we have left is the present. You're happy, and I have a chance to be happy."

She nodded and bit her lip.

Ethan motioned toward the door. "Now that you don't think I'm totally insane, will you come to my car? I have to show you why Elizabeth broke up with me."

Still a little leery of him, but beginning to embrace his tangled reality, Sara shrugged. If he was insane, they were better off outside where people could see what was going on. She kept a safe distance as they descended the front steps. Warm winds stirred the air outside, ushering in a new spring and the promise of a warm summer. He turned the key in the trunk of his car and opened it. Sara remained on the sidewalk.

Any museum curator would have gasped at the value of his cargo and his total lack of respect for it. Several paintings lay stuffed inside, one on top of the other, without any padding between. Sara gazed at the one on top and saw her face gazing back. Inching forward, she lifted the frame to peek at the next. On every canvas, she saw her face, her body, locked in the embraces of a man that wore Ethan's face.

"These are stunning. He did them?"

Ethan nodded. He pulled out a particularly erotic rendition and handed it to her with a shrug. "You were in his dreams. All the time."

"Yeah, that's a little creepy." She studied the painting feeling as if someone had a big spoon dipped inside her guts and was stirring. "Let's not tell my husband about that. Ever."

They both nodded.

"They're so not Ethan McCarthy's style," she mused. "They're romantic and euphoric."

"That IS his—our—style when we paint without the leanan sidhe. The style Brann Sidhe brings up out of his gory depths is the one he's shown the world. This one he kept for you."

Covering her mouth with one hand, she touched the reality of such fantasy with the other. "It's true then? This whole life I'm living, this second chance, he gave it to me?"

"Yes. He gambled your souls on a love that was cut down and rooted up by an early death. You made your own bargain with Cailen Sidhe—he got this out of the deal." He pulled out the coin again.

Another reference to the angel of her dreams. It was hard not to believe him when she herself had seen and painted the muse. Even harder that she knew that what she had assumed were figments of her trauma were the truth. Phil knew about the leanan sidhe. Sara saw Leana's power. There was just too much evidence to deny. No wonder Ethan—the older one—had warned her not to finish that painting. He'd spent a century in the service of his bargain with a leanan sidhe and lost his wife—her—to a bargain of only two years.

Sara twisted the gold band on her finger. "I was meant for Jake. I never see the kind of love we have. It's rare. It grows—through everything." She stopped, touched the paintings again. Her eyes wandered to the house and the ivy she and Jake had planted that was winding itself up the stone. "I'm so sorry I let him, you, down. But, I love Jake. I love this life we've built together. I wouldn't trade it for anything—not even more of it." She shook her head.

Sara wasn't religious, but she felt the spiritual bond between Jake, her, and everything else they'd built. The love had grown strong in the building. To her, God was a sense of connection—love. "I truly love this life I have. If I do owe this second chance to you—or to him—thank you." She paused, looking down, and then met the younger man's eyes. "Ethan—the older one, I mean—had no right to bargain with my soul. Now that I have Jake, I can't choose between love and my soul—they're the same."

Ethan shook his head, breathing in deeply, looking like he'd just won a battle. He exhaled, ready to jump back into the fray, with one notch already on his sword. He leaned over the trunk and looked her in the eye. "That's just it. That's why I'm here. The souls are free now. I'm whole again, but I need your help."

Chapter 67

"You have to tell Elizabeth."

Ethan nodded solemnly. "I promise you, I'll tell Elizabeth. She's the first to admit that free will doesn't truly exist, but I want her to make a choice. I don't want her to pity me. I want her to be with me because she loves me. Otherwise, it won't be real."

Sara and Ethan sat in the kitchen, passing photos and letters between them.

"It's so obvious—" she stood up, shaking the mess out of her head, and went to make food, drowning the fantastical in the mundane "—now that I see all the pictures together. But it was all so jumbled and illogical. I just thought I was pathetically predictable when it came to boys."

"Actually, you're anything but predictable," Ethan muttered.

Sara chopped onions and stirred them into egg salad. "Don't blackmail Elizabeth. I'm only doing this because I've never seen her so smitten." The green onions stung her eyes. Tears welled up. If she knew anything, she knew that love, so abstract, so elusive, was the only concrete reality of the soul. Without it, life was a meaningless ramble of words and emotions. "If she walks away, you let her go." She punctuated her demand with the point of the knife.

Handing Ethan a sandwich triangle, she sat down by him and picked one up for herself. "I'll help smooth over this mess—" she gestured toward the pictures, "—but I don't want to influence this. Ethan gave me the choice—even if I didn't choose him." Ethan Jr. had a tiny smear of egg at the corner of his mouth. Sara passed him a napkin.

Mr. McCarthy was gone. The ever-hovering presence of that man didn't exist in this younger version sitting at her table. She might as well have been chatting with Danny. "I'm sorry. And I'm grateful for your gesture. I just hope you haven't started down the same rutted path you traveled before. This life, the love I have with Jake, it's priceless—and I know that your older self paid dearly for it. But I can't force the burden of that on my daughter. Let her choose. If she chooses you, so much the better. If she doesn't—"

"You have my word." Sara believed him because he had told her the story of the tangled roots of existence under the hill. He knew that somewhere, under another set of stars and rotations of planets, he might have a second chance.

A car engine slowed and stopped out front. It was sure to be Elizabeth. Ethan stiffened, looking hunted like he might bolt for the closet.

"I'll handle this." The bell rang and someone pounded on the door. The lock stuck tight but, after Sara fumbled with it, consented to open.

"You locked me out!" Her disgruntled daughter stood on the porch.

"You told me to lock the doors." Sara hugged her boney shoulders.

"What happened to your head?" she demanded, indignant that her mother should have let something happen to herself.

Here we go. "I slipped on the wet kitchen floor—hit my head on the table." All true. No need to mention that I came into the kitchen with sopping hair because a lunatic dragged me from the shower.

Elizabeth put her hand out to touch the bandage gently. "Are you okay? Does it hurt?"

"I'm fine. Thanks, kidlet. Come in. I'll get the laundry." Elizabeth was home for a few weeks until the next term began. She hobbled into the entry and arranged her crutch and bag. Sara was coming in with a stuffed-full laundry basket when Elizabeth spotted Ethan sitting at the kitchen table.

"Hi! I didn't expect you to be here!" she exclaimed in a perfect imitation of her mother's *I'm freaked out but too polite to show it* voice. Her eyes shot bullets at Sara.

Ethan reached for the basket in Sara's arms. "Hi, I, uh, I'm, uh— I wanted—Can I get that?"

"No, I've got it. Let's put your stuff upstairs, Liz. He won't disappear while we're gone." Sara smiled and glared at Ethan as if to say, "I've got this, too. Be cool!"

Over the top of the laundry basket, she caught the corner of several expressive looks Elizabeth cast back at Ethan.

"Mom!" She turned on Sara as soon as she'd shut the door. Elizabeth's hand flew to her hips. Sometimes Sara felt like she was three around her oldest daughter. "I told you not to see that artist anymore."

"Ethan? You told me not to go to class. You just said you weren't dating him anymore."

Elizabeth rolled her eyes and exhaled in exasperation. Her shoulders stiffened. "Mom—"

"Just listen, first. There's been an accident."

Elizabeth's face changed immediately.

"Ethan's father died in a car accident abroad." Sara improvised, twisting her face into something that resembled sorrow at an unexpected tragedy. It wasn't a lie—well, the car accident part was—but the boy's "father" was gone and was never coming back. According to the official paperwork, the elder Ethan was dead. "He told me about dinner. I need to explain. It wasn't what you think."

Elizabeth's eyes narrowed, but in her face, there was a willingness—no, an ardent wish—to believe. "I didn't recognize him because he goes by a different name, but I dated Ethan's father when I was younger, for quite a long time." Her daughter's eyebrows went up. "Ethan brought over the photos. You can see them. We dated off and on for several years, in high school and college, before I met your dad."

"Mom, you didn't see what I saw."

"Yes, I did. Ethan brought some of the paintings, too. Listen. You know how when I'm painting, even though I'm not painting you, or Danny, or your dad, I use your faces? It makes the people I paint more alive because I'm so familiar with the lines of every expression. Well, it was the same thing for Mr. McCarthy when he was first painting. He just used a face he knew…very well."

Elizabeth's frown and stance relaxed. "Oh, well, it looked like he was stalking you or something."

"Actually, we were engaged once, but I broke it off to go to Paris…where I fell in love with your dad." It was better to mix as many actual truths as possible into the story. The chances of it falling apart on closer scrutiny were slimmer. But Elizabeth wasn't likely to scrutinize. Sara could see her thoughts racing. Her daughter wanted to be convinced. The two children exuded a nearly tangible connection. It seemed such a travesty that the missteps of their parents should dam the route for them. "He's gotta be pretty lonely right now. I don't think it's sunk in yet. He brought the paintings because his father wanted me to have them, but I'm not sure your dad would like that."

Elizabeth's eyebrows shot up and her lips curled in her father's smile. "Pretty sure he doesn't want them."

"Anyway, I know you broke up, but now that you understand, we should probably do what we can to be there for Ethan."

"When's the funeral?"

"It's not. You know how Mr. McCarthy hated crowds and people? Ethan wants to respect his dad's memory, so he's keeping it quiet." *Sounds logical.* "He's flying out tomorrow." Sara looked her daughter over carefully. "Are you okay with him being here…"

"Well, yeah, now that I know he's not a crazy stalker, like his dad, or a suicidal art student like that Phil guy. Geez mom, you sure attract the psychos."

"—'cause I invited him to stay for dinner. I don't think he should be alone."

Elizabeth dropped her eyes and grinned sheepishly, more like a thirteen-year-old. "Good, 'cause I've kind of missed him. He's so cute, and he treats me like a princess, but he's smart, too."

"I know. You've always wanted to be a princess—an Amazon princess. There are egg salad sandwiches on the table. Did you have lunch?"

"No, I'll be down in a second."

"Don't trip!"

Sara skipped down the stairs.

"Well, that went better than I expected." Her eyebrows arched as she sat back down to take a bite. Her children weren't the only manipulative masters in the house. "Your father was killed in a car accident in Europe. It's not real to you yet, 'cause you haven't seen him. You brought the paintings because he left them to me, but Elizabeth's dad probably doesn't want them. I dated your dad for several years in high school and college and was engaged to him but broke it off to go to Paris. You're flying out tomorrow." Sara patted his back. "It's up to you now, sport."

Ethan nodded and took a deep breath like he was waiting for the starting gunshot of a marathon. "What if I can't—I mean what if she doesn't—?"

Sara leaned forward, looking deeply into the expanse of his green eyes, looking for someone who might still be lingering there. "If she doesn't, she doesn't—and you're in for three more years."

Ethan nodded.

Elizabeth tripped down the stairs. She'd done her hair and make-up. Her big blue eyes looked sympathetically at Ethan. He jumped up and helped her to the bottom step. "I'm so sorry." She was. A tinge of guilt skittered across Sara's face, but then the radiance on Ethan's smoothed it over. The boy did his best to look forlorn.

Elizabeth loved him. She wanted everything to be smoothed over. "I'm sorry about the other night; I didn't know about your dad and my mom. It looked—"

"—strange," Ethan finished.

"Let's start over, okay?" She reached up on her toes, entwined her arms around his neck, and gave him her pink lips. Sara stepped out quietly to give them some space—and called Jake.

My dearest Elizabeth,

Did she marry him? Does it matter? That existence has long dissipated into the pinprick stars of portals that twinkle in the dark under the hill. That was not my reason for committing to words this tragedy that is forever engraved on the fiber of my being. Or perhaps, it is not tragedy but only a prelude to love. The cycles turn eternally, one engendering the other.

You are out there somewhere in this here and now, searching as I search—Elizabeth, Sara, Suzanne—whatever name you wear. Remember me. Put aside this account of things that have been and are no longer. Find me—before THEY do.

Forever,
Ethan

FIN

Acknowledgements:

Thanks to my astute readers, especially Natalie, Janie, Libby, Rebecca, Esther and Curt for their comments. Many thanks to the several generations of friends in diverse places that helped nurture this story along: Chris and Elena ages ago, Norm, Janet, John, Anna and Pat, more recently. Thanks to my father for opening the portal to the mysterious world of the English language and to my mother for teaching me the ways of humanity.

About the Author:

Rachel DeFriez lives in the Salt Lake metro area where she teaches high school French and creative writing and advises the literary magazine. She lives with her husband, Golden Retriever, and Maine Coon. Her four children all found best friends to join their team and moved out to pursue careers in the extreme sport of life.